MW00826852

JAYMIN EVE

SHADOW BEAST
SHIFTERS
COMPELLED

Embrace your kinks.
Who knows what you might discover.

JAYMIN'S NERD HERD

The best way to stay up to date with the Shadow Beast Shifters world, and all new releases, is to join my Facebook group:
www.facebook.com/groups/jayminevenerdherd

Chapter One

The incessant shrieking of my alarm grated against my sensitive hearing, and in my half-awake state, I swiped at my phone, determined to throw it through the window. All I ended up hitting was my wicker side table, since my more coherent side had known to leave the phone out of reach last night.

I'd learned the hard way *not* to keep anything breakable close by in the morning—I didn't have the funds to keep replacing items that annoyed me.

It was my own fault, really, using an alarm that shrieked like a banshee, but I was a fucking terrible morning person. If not for the screech, I'd sleep half the day away.

Groaning, I dragged myself out of my twin bed, blurry vision clearing in seconds with the help of my wolf. She might be weaker these days, but what remained of her strength still fueled my own.

Kicking clothes out of the way as I went to the bathroom, I chuckled at how lazy I was getting. No one ever visited me, so I saw no reason not to use my floor as a horizontal wardrobe. Had to be some benefits to the reclusive life.

In the bathroom, I pushed open the tiny window to allow some airflow and tried not to think about the fact that, once again, I'd spent my Saturday night at home living my best damn life with popcorn and *Teen Wolf*. Was it a touch ridiculous that a shifter enjoyed watching *shifter shows*, especially when they got so many of the details wrong? Maybe, but it was my secret indulgence.

Unlike dating, which was now a proven recipe for disaster.

I'd had exactly five dates in the past year, and each of them bored me to the point that, on my last date, I almost smashed my face into the main course when I fell asleep and my head slipped off my hand. In my defense, that Tucson pack shifter had droned on about horticulture for thirty-seven minutes. Thirty-seven of the longest fucking minutes of my life.

Before that was a female shifter from New York. Apparently, during the time Torma had been suppressing us and keeping our pack under lock and key, other packs had been discovering social media. She cared more about her likes on a post than she did about getting to know me, and I'd had to bail early.

Suffice it to say, there would be no second date with either.

I've always said I fall in love with hearts not parts, and that stood true, but so far I hadn't found the one with the heart I was searching for.

Checking the time before I jumped into the shower, I noted that I had to be at the shop in twenty minutes, and since I now lived in my best friend Mera Callahan's crappy, former apartment across Torma, I needed to haul ass.

I had very few things left in this world that were mine, but my shop was one, and I took my role as a businesswoman seriously. Not that I was cashed up or anything. Torma pack wasn't into literature; another reason I should have left years ago.

The pack was free now, but it still felt empty. With Mera—and my parents—gone, there was nothing here for me any longer. The shop had been a fantastic distraction and I still loved it, but I could open a business in any shifter pack. Try somewhere else. Something new.

If I lived for a few hundred more years, I really didn't want to waste them in this shithole. Torma had once been considered the strongest pack in America, and I'd been happy here with Mera. That life was over the moment my bestie was rejected by the alpha, terrorized by this fucking pack, and then kidnapped by a scary-ass shifter god... who, luckily, turned out to be her true mate. My wolfie-sister was now living *her* best life, which didn't include Teen Wolf, and I missed her more than I'd ever thought possible.

She'd cleaned up Torma before she left, but it didn't matter. I had nothing here without her, hence my need to start a new adventure. Hell, maybe there was a growly, sexy, change-his-or-her-size shifter waiting out there for me too. Couldn't be worse than the horticulturist.

After ten minutes under the hottest stream I could get from my rusted showerhead, I finally felt somewhat awake. Throwing on underwear, black skinny jeans, a red flannel shirt with the sleeves rolled up, and a pair of black flats, I was ready to get to work. There was no need for makeup since I had no one to impress, and a quick brush was all it took to have my long, dark hair smooth and shiny—a gift of the few generations removed Japanese heritage on my mom's side.

My parents were exiled when Mera excised the cancer from Torma, and I barely even noticed they were gone.

As former enforcers, they'd always been more concerned with pack business than with their daughter, so it was no huge loss that they were out of Torma, living a finite human existence.

On the street, I found it was still quiet, allowing me to hurry along without interruption. Soon the pack's school bell would chime, and with it, all the late students would rush across town. I'd be in my shop before that of course, and it was the best fucking feeling to be done with school.

My shop appeared on the horizon, nestled in the main street of businesses here in Torma. It had a stunning red brick front with a forest-green awning. I'd picked that out as my first step in revamping the space, and I still loved the way the green contrasted to the brick.

After unlocking the door, I stepped into a dark and cool space, but as the spring days heated up, I'd have to get all the fans running to keep the small area from turning into an oven. Hitting the lights near the front, I took a second to appreciate each flickering beam highlighting a shelf below, filled to the brim with all genres of stories.

Like Mera, I preferred my books heavy on romance and fantasy and absolutely filled with angst and drama. But in my store I included a few other genres in the hope that no matter who walked through the door, there would be something in here to tickle their fancy. I mean, who was I to tell a shifter that they were probably a serial killer because they enjoyed biographies. Or classics.

Just as I was storing my keys and phone in the drawer, the door dinged, and I looked up to see my neighbor, Ethel. She was an ancient shifter who looked a million years old but was probably only two hundred and fifty. She ran the craft supply store a few doors down.

"Sim," she called, hobbling over, stretching out her back as she walked. "Slept funny again last night. Can you help an old wolf out?"

Annddd there you had it, the full extent of my current social interactions. "Sure," I said with a sigh. "Happy to help."

We'd done this many times now, and as I twisted her arm to the side and pulled gently, I heard a few pops as everything went somewhat back into place. Ancient shifters stopped healing as efficiently as when they were younger, but she still made it to work every single day. Lady had some strong vagina energy, which was much more impressive than big dick energy. Or so I'd heard.

Not a lot of dicks around, big or not, to test that theory.

Ethel left soon after, and it was just me, my store... and a new box of books waiting to be sorted and priced. As I tore open the tape, no lie, I breathed in the scent the same way others might breathe in food.

I was straight up crack-addicted to this shit, and no matter where my path took me, I would never not have a large collection of books around me.

Lifting the first paperback free, the cover caught my eye with its broad-shouldered and tattooed male, fire swirling around him as he raged. This series was one of my favorites, and not just because the male main character reminded me of Mera's beast. There was a forbidden-love element that kept me hooked for the entire four books in the series.

One of those stories you fell into, forgetting you were even reading.

Possibly an even rarer find than a magical soulmate who created solar systems.

When I placed the book on the desk to grab the next, I felt a flicker of energy from within the drawer below. A familiar flicker linked to a piece of parchment I hadn't looked at in days.

Mera!

Ripping the drawer open, I shifted the top layers of my crap to find the paper I needed. The parchment had an ancient feel to it, made from a material not found on Earth, and as more energy shot up from it, writing appeared in quick, jagged script.

Simone. Mera is in labor.

The moment I read that sentence, it disappeared, part of the safety in these hidden messages. Another jolt of energy followed. *Inky is on its way. Do not delay.*

The parchment fell from my hands as I bounced on the spot, having had no idea that today would be The. Fucking. Day. The day that my best friend had her baby and I got a little adventure out of this town. Grabbing up my phone, I shot a text to Sam, my friend in another shifter town, letting her know Mera was in labor and I'd be MIA for some time.

All I got in return was a smiling emoji and a thumbs up.

Fuck me. Thumbs up should be banned as a response tool.

At least it seemed Sam was alive, even if she would only talk to me on the phone for five minutes a week. Clearly, she was in the middle of some shit over in her pack, and as much as I wanted to swoop in and save her ass, she was an adult shifter who needed to handle her business alone. I respected that.

Lucky for her, Mera had been busy growing a baby and saving the worlds, otherwise she'd have dragged Sam out by her hair. Probably after this baby arrived, she'd still do that.

With no one else to tell in my sad life, I quickly hurried to turn the lights off again and flick the sign on my door to closed. Nerves rolled in my stomach at the thought of being back in the Library of Knowledge. Back in the Solaris System gateways. Back near... him.

Funnily enough, my boring life hadn't always been this way, but in a concerted effort to keep the past in the past, I now spent my time dating horticulturists and social media experts. And I absolutely did not date master vampires.

Safer for everyone.

Chapter Two

I nky showed up a few minutes after I'd shut everything down inside and stored my phone in the drawer, since I wouldn't need it where I was going. My guide to Mera was a black cloud of power originating in another world—the Shadow Realm—and was bonded to the Shadow Beast himself. The first few times I'd met it, it had scared the ever living fuck out of me. I was used to it now, though.

Mostly.

Since most shifters were not as cool as me around clouds of power, I ushered it inside so it could open a doorway to the magical library in privacy. I didn't hesitate to step through once the swirling portal appeared, and then I was sprinting along the hallway toward the library.

Labor was not an act I was familiar with, but I had watched enough shows to know it was fast for some and slow for others. Mera never did shit half-assed, and I did not want to miss holding her hand when she birthed her child. Neither of us had ever thought we'd be moms, so it hadn't been a childhood dream for us. But now that it was happening, I couldn't imagine another path for her. This was fate. Destiny. Whatever bullshit you wanted to call it.

Kismet and serendipity had come together the day Mera called the Shadow Beast.

"Will I make it in time?" I huffed to Inky as I ran along the hall.

It bobbed up and down before vibrating and shooting sparks of lightning around, and I took that as a most decisive yes.

My flats slapped against the ground as I ran. More appropriate footwear would have been useful, but there'd been no time to change. If I ended up staying for a while, there were always spares in Mera's magical wardrobe, aka the beast's way of dressing his mate in the sexy-ass outfits he liked to see her in.

Again, I would never be jealous of my best friend, but she did get a mate, a library, and a fucking magical wardrobe. Least she could do was share some of her goodies.

Not the mate, he terrified me, but the clothing I'd take.

When we reached the next swirling portal, I stepped right through into the Library of Knowledge, which was both a room containing information from all the worlds connected in the Solaris System and Mera's home. It acted as a hub, allowing beings to walk between multiple worlds using the doorways that lined its white, window-filled walls.

Stepping into a place so beautiful, with its massively high ceilings containing hand-carved depictions of gods and images of battle up high, always took my breath away and had my heart pounding.

Today, though, I had one focus.

I didn't bother to glance at the supernaturals who littered the aisles and shelves, each of them from one of the ten worlds. Without even looking, I already knew some would be very alien in appearance, while others more humanlike. This was a neutral zone for all of the worlds to gather and learn, and if any tried to disturb that, they'd have one pissed off Shadow Beast up their asses.

No one wanted that... except maybe Mera, but that was an *entirely* different scenario.

Picking up the pace, we made it to the farthest end of the library, where one final door existed. Shadow's private domain.

I'd never been into this space—the beast was very territorial with everyone except Mera—but when the door opened of its own accord and Inky zoomed through, I figured I'd follow.

There was no resistance, and on the other side I barely managed not to gasp at what lay beyond. "That bitch has two libraries?" I cried. "We really need to have a long conversation about sharing."

Inky couldn't reply, but I liked to think that it agreed with me, as it grew larger and started to spark. It was either that or it wanted me to hurry up, and with that in mind, I managed to ignore the long expanse of heavy, dark wood shelves, gorgeous chandeliers, and the scent of books as I followed Inky deeper into the beast's lair.

We ended up at a door, a nondescript wooden door that opened before I'd touched it, and words spilled out. *"You fucking did this to me, you stupid, oversized beast. Of course, you would create a giant baby trying to annihilate my vagina."*

Some of my panic faded. That was Mera, my best friend for life, and she appeared to be doing just fine. I hadn't missed the birth yet. We'd only reached the cursing-your-mate-for-knocking-you-up stage.

This was going to be fun.

With a smile on my face, I was about to step through the door, when I felt a strong wash of power. It tickled across my shifter senses, stirring my wolf deep inside. She surged to the front, but I was too controlled to let her out when I wasn't ready. My wolf and I had been at odds ever since Valdor, which was an issue we'd have to deal with sooner or later.

My vote would be later.

My time in the vampire world had been not without dramas, and lots of shit had gone down. Shit I didn't talk about—mostly because I couldn't. But ever since then, I'd been struggling with my energy and senses. Sometimes they were strong, and other times I felt as weak as I imagined a human did.

On the rarest of occasions, there was a swirling of energy deep in my center that I didn't recognize, and it scared me the most.

It was this foreign energy that sprang to life when we felt him: Lucien, master fucking vampire and thorn in my damn side.

He was right behind me.

Move, Simone.

Despite my inner voice pushing for avoidance, a part of me was curious at how it'd feel to see him after all this time. Would he still stir my body in a way I had no experience with and yet craved desperately? Would he send fire through my veins and anger into my heart? Would I hate him, while at the same time longing for what could never be?

There was only one way to find out.

"B," he said softly. "I've been waiting for you. I need to tell you something."

My throat hurt at the nickname, and not only because this pointy-fanged fucker liked to call me by my blood type—the cunt—but because I had missed hearing that smooth, sexy rasp of his voice.

Knowing it would hurt less if I just ripped the Band-Aid off, I turned and faced him. "Can I help you, Lester?"

The master vampire was still the most beautiful man I'd ever seen. Towering over me, huge, blond, and muscular, he had piercing green eyes that cut through the bullshit and saw into your soul. Eyes that contrasted so brilliantly to his golden, sun-kissed skin. He was sex on legs, and I barely managed to conceal my expression at the jolt I felt in seeing him again.

Apparently, despite all the growing up and changing I'd done in the time since I saw him last, part of me had just never let him go.

His lips twitched, even if a darker emotion burned in the green depths of his irises. "Lester? I don't think so, sweetheart. You remember my name."

Faking boredom, I stared at my nails. "Sorry, Linc, but I'm super busy right now. My best friend is about to have a baby, and I kind of don't want to miss it. Was there something you needed to tell me?"

At this, Lucien sobered. Yeah, the bastard was right—I'd never forget his name. My dreams wouldn't let me.

"I've been waiting for the birth, knowing you would be here," he started. "I've put this off as long as I could, but the masters have spoken. You have to return to Valdor."

My body went cold. Lucien had taken me to his vampire world a year or so ago when the library had been compromised. In Valdor, I'd learned that I was nothing more than a walking blood bag to those fuckers. Shit had gone down, and I'd broken a rule or two, but...

"I thought it was all sorted. You promised me..."

The perfectly smooth skin around his eyes pulled tighter. "I've been protecting you, just as I promised. But this went above my head to the full council of tier one masters. If you don't return, they will send others to bring you back."

Lucien was a tier one master, too, which meant he was one of the ten that governed the various vampire enclaves. I'd had brief dealings with some of the others my last time there and hoped never to again.

Before I could shout out my fear and frustration, a second power joined us: Len, the fae. "You're here too?" I blurted, taking in the silver-clad immortal. He was one of Shadow's and Lucien's best friend slash brothers, so of course he would be here for the birth of this baby. My brain was working a little slower after the summons to Valdor.

He nodded. "Yes, we're all waiting for the child to be born, but once it's safe, we will accompany you and Lucien to Valdor. Vampire politics be damned, nothing will happen to Mera's best fri–"

He didn't get to finish his sentence as said best friend screamed, the sound echoing through the partially open door. Moving on instinct, I was inside the bedroom taking a step toward Mera when Lucien's power wrapped around me, rendering me motionless.

My rage built again. I'd told him to never use his powers on me, but as usual, he did not freaking listen. "You broke the rules, B," he said, reminding me of the worst day of my life, "and now you must answer the council's questions about that day."

With that final statement, he released me and walked away, letting the door close between us. My body trembled as I fought to keep strength in my legs.

Lucien was right. I did break the rules and he'd saved me. Protected me.

Looked like he was finally done.

Mera shouted again, swearing as she sobbed, and I pushed my worries away. Today I would be by my best friend's side as she brought a god-baby into the world, and tomorrow...

Tomorrow I would return to the land that had almost stolen everything from me.

Including my heart... and my life.

Chapter Three

T rying my best to clear my mind, I focused only on Mera as I hurried into the bedroom. It was a massive room, dominated by one of those California king beds that look like two beds joined together. There were more people inside than I expected, but Mera had never really been shy, so there was no reason to expect she wouldn't have a three-ring circus staring at her vagina as she pushed a damn baby from it.

Needing this distraction from Lucien and vampire drama, I fully immersed myself in the scenery around me. Despite a complete lack of windows, the room felt cool and fresh, as if a nice sea breeze was drifting in—no doubt one of the powerful beings in here was responsible for that. I was grateful for how bright and open the room was too.

"Sim!" Mera cried out, reaching a hand to me as I hurried toward her. She was laid out on a blue duvet, towels under the white flowing dress she wore. Her legs were bent up and I assumed she was naked under the wispy dress, but I couldn't see anything at the moment. On her right was Angel, wings away and dressed in a simple, black shift-dress, and on her left was Shadow in his usual black-and-scary attire.

Near the end of the bed hovering close to Mera's raised legs was Gaster.

Now, normally, I'd be wondering why the goblin, whose job was to run the Library of Knowledge, was in the birthing room, but I'd learned a lot about him from Mera and Lucien. He was ancient and powerful, particularly gifted in healing arts, and no doubt a solid choice as a doula to help get this god-baby safely out of its goddess momma.

It was surreal to know that we'd soon meet the child.

Just had to get Mera through the next *however freaking long it took* first.

"Damn, girl," I said as I moved closer to where Angel sat, knowing better than to push in on Shadow's side.

Angel was Mera's other bestie, an absolutely stunning warrior from the Honor Meadows world who was also super pregnant, her baby belly obvious on her tall, lithe frame.

I'd been nervous around the powerful angel-like being the first few times I'd met her. But just like with Inky, I'd found her loyalty to Mera comforting, and now we were solid.

"Thank you," I murmured when she moved over to give me room to sit beside the sweating, panting, pregnant lady. Leaning over, I pressed a kiss to Mera's cheek. "You're having a freaking baby," I said with a chuckle as I pulled away.

Mera cried and laughed at the same time, and I reached out and pushed back some of the mess of red curls from her face. Mera was stunningly beautiful, no matter the circumstances, but today she looked tired. Dark circles ringed her hazel eyes, and her tanned skin was pasty. As a goddess who healed almost instantly, it concerned me that she was struggling so much with birth, but we'd been warned that this god baby was going to be one of a kind. A special being who would need a massive surge of power to arrive unscathed into the world.

Mera had dismissed my worries, always confident that she was strong enough. And no doubt she was. I'd seen her weather plenty of massive storms in her life, but that didn't mean I wasn't worried.

My only reassurance was the calm on Shadow's face. Perched beside his true mate, he held her hand, allowing her to squeeze the ever-loving fuck out of his palm. Despite the swirling fire in his eyes, the rest of him was the normal-looking Shadow Beast. *Normal* being seven feet tall, dark hair lightly tousled, bronze skin, and a face carved like a damn angel. He was the dark god to Lucien's blond beauty, but only a fool wouldn't see them for the predators they were. Predators wearing a façade of civility, but if you searched deep enough into their eyes, you'd find their primal, animalistic natures.

Right now, Shadow was keeping himself contained, and that allowed me to breathe deeply. If Mera was in true danger, the façade would vanish and we'd all be fucked.

Gaster pushed forward, moving some of the material so he could place his hands on her bare thighs. Mera lifted herself using her elbows and stared down her body at the goblin. "How's it going?" she huffed, clearly ready for this baby to arrive.

He didn't smile as he might normally, the furrowed lines of his face deepening as he nodded. "There's no true precedent for a child like this, but from what I can infer, the child is healthy and so are you. It will come when it's ready."

"Just stubborn, like her parents," Angel said with a laugh, and I turned to see her cross her arms over her chest, resting them on the large but perky belly she was sporting.

"You keep saying *her*," Mera groaned, her body tensing as she reached for her stomach. "How do you know it's a girl?"

"I just feel it, the same way I feel that Reece and I will have a boy."

Mera's face softened briefly, but that disappeared the moment she arched forward, her body shaking as she cried out. She gripped Shadow with one hand and her stomach with the other. "Contraction," she gasped, trying to breath but seeming to mostly be sobbing. "I've died and it hurt less than this."

A rumble escaped the giant beast, and some of my calm from before fled at the tendrils of darkness that were sliding across his skin. His use of the shadows reminded me of Inky and Midnight—Mera's bonded cloud from the Shadow Realm—and I looked around to find they were high up near the ceiling, staying out of the way but still there for their bonded ones.

Mera's contraction lasted about a minute, but it must have felt like a year for her, as she finally collapsed on the bed, breathing rapidly, her skin even more sweaty and flushed than before. Angel, moving in beside me, reached out and placed her hand on Mera's shoulder, and it felt like she was sharing energy.

A creosote scent hit me as Angel leaned over, and if I'd closed my eyes, I could have imagined I was in the deserts. That had to be a part of her true mate bond to Reece, the desert deity. Before their mating, Angel had smelled like the strike of a lightning about to hit earth—an electrical storm of great power, as ancient as the worlds.

That was still there, but now there was an entirely new desert element.

Her baby with Reece was going to be strong, just like Mera's.

Two powerful babies.

I really hoped I got to see the way they turned their parents' lives upside down.

Chapter Four

When the next contraction finally broke, Mera declared that she needed to get up and walk around. Gaster assured her walking was a great idea, since she wasn't fully dilated yet, and the baby still hadn't made up its mind about the right time to move from Mera's comfortable womb into this shit show of a world.

Shadow followed her, hovering like a worried mother hen, and Angel left to update the men who were all waiting outside. "Reece is freaking out," she said with a chuckle, hands on her hips as she stretched out her back and walked to the door. "I'm sure the others are as well. I better give them an update before they bust in here."

When she was gone, I got to my feet as well. "Can she hear his thoughts?" I asked, still trying to wrap my own mind around these Solaris System true mate couples.

"It's mostly sensing emotions, among other things," Shadow rumbled, and as usual, I got nothing else out of the broody male.

While he was escorting his hobbling mate back and forth across the room, Gaster got to work changing the sweat-ridden bedding and placing new towels down. When he left the room, arms full of sheets, it was just Mera, Shadow, and me.

Feeling somewhat useless, I just kind of bopped on the spot, my mind fracturing under the pressure of *not* thinking about the vampire and fate that waited outside this room. That bastard could have delayed telling me until after the birth, giving me this one last day to just focus on Mera and not my own impending doom.

I'd really liked living in blissful ignorance.

"What's up, Sim," Mera said as she marched closer to me, her body seeming to move more freely now that she'd warmed up. "I've seen that look many times before, and I know it means some dark thoughts are swirling in that pretty head of yours."

She didn't stop her *get the hell out of me* walk, but she also didn't remove her shrewd gaze from my face, even as she moved toward the back of the room. Shadow shook his head, one hand out to catch her if she tripped since she wasn't watching where she was going at all.

"I'm fine," I said quickly, knowing if I said nothing, she'd just work herself up worse. "Worried about you more than anything."

The look Mera shot me would have knocked a lesser being to their knees. It was filled with derision and disbelief and a definite side of *you have to be fucking kidding me.* "I'm going to forgive your lies," she huffed out before pausing, both hands landing on her stomach as she breathed in and out for another beat, "because this is a stressful situation and I know you're just trying to stop me from freaking out about whatever is happening to you. But"—another pause, her face screwing up as additional rumbles left Shadow—"I promise you, bestie, if you don't tell me right this very second, I will not be held accountable for my next actions."

A whiff of smoky air hit me as Shadow chuckled. It wasn't a particularly amused sound, since he was likely still worried about his mate's current discomfort, but he always enjoyed her fire. No matter the circumstances.

"It's just a little issue with that stupid vampire out there," I finally muttered. Mera would not let this go, and she needed to be focused on the childbirth she was currently going through.

Shadow chuckled again, the sound mingled with a low, deep growl. Mera's forehead creased further as she stumbled toward me. "Lucien?" she said in a huff. "What the hell has he done now? Or at all, considering you've never really told me anything from your time in Valdor."

One thing she hated was being kept in the dark, especially when it involved her friends. Mera was a lot of things, and insanely loyal was high on that list. If she didn't know what our problems were, she couldn't help us solve them, and that didn't sit right with her.

"Compelled, remember," I said quickly. Images and words formed in my head as I said it. Most of them were of Crimson City—an unofficial name that had turned official at some point, since that's what Lucien's home city was called now. The place I'd spent weeks getting to know as I fell for the vampire, only to learn that he didn't even remotely feel the same.

I opened my mouth to attempt to tell her the smallest detail, but my tongue was still. My lips unmoving. My words frozen in my mind, never to be spoken out loud. Unless I could link my damn mind to Mera's, nothing that had happened in Valdor would ever be revealed.

Mera was close to me now, her ashy scent stronger than usual as the flaming phoenix in her core skirted just below the surface of her skin. "There has to be a way to break this compulsion," she snapped before jerking her head to the side to find Shadow's gaze. "Mate, you'd better find a damn way to break the compulsi—"

Before she could get her entire sentence out, the door to the bedroom burst open, slamming hard against the wall. There was no way Angel or Gaster would enter like that, so I was already on high alert, shifting my position in front of Mera.

If I'd have had a second to think it over, I would have known there was no true danger. This was Shadow's dominion, and no one could take him by surprise here, but instinct was a powerful shifter trait.

A growl spilled from my lips when Lucien raced into sight, and as he did, I felt a rush of heat from beside me. Turning, I was surprised to see it was Shadow who was stoking the fires of his power, darkness creeping from his pores as the literal shadows he was named after obeyed his command.

"You felt them," Lucien snarled, his fangs visible as his body grew larger. Master vampires had this ability to hulk out when enraged.

"What are they doing here?" Shadow rumbled, his words barely comprehendible through his anger.

"It's complicated," Lucien said quickly, "but if we don't address them, they'll use the bounty status to break rule four."

At this point I was confused, as was Mera who added her own impressive growl to the mix. "You two better stop talking in fucking code," she shouted, "and tell me what the hell is happening in my library. I feel the disturbance through my bond to Shadow, but the bastard is blocking out most everything else to keep me calm." She started waving her hands around, clipping my shoulder. "Do I look goddamn calm to you all?"

She looked like a beautiful, fiery, slightly unhinged shifter-goddess, but there was not one ounce of calm in her wide eyes or her slightly curved hands, which she waved like talons. We all knew it, and only Shadow was brave enough to step forward and wrap his arms around his pregnant mate.

His fire raged higher when it met hers, and I swallowed down my envy at the damn perfection of their relationship. Even at their worst, they still made each other better. Enhanced each other. Or some soul-mate crap like that.

Lucien met my gaze as if he'd heard that thought, and as always, the memories of my last night in Valdor filled my head. My almost death, his mouth on my skin, his blood... My wolf slipped free, teeth sharpening as I snarled in his direction. He didn't get to meet my gaze like that, with vampire energy riding along his skin, its golden glow increasing.

This was just beyond unfair, and I still had no idea why he'd burst into the room.

"What happened?" I finally asked, unable to hold my tongue any longer. "Is this something to do with the masters' request that I return to Valdor?"

I might not be a magical goddess, but I also wasn't an idiot. Lucien wouldn't have entered this room unless he had a good reason —something serious. He'd asked Shadow if he felt *them*, which made me think the vamps were already here. In the library.

"Tier two masters from Valdor," Shadow rumbled, his head tilted back like he was listening to a conversation the rest of us couldn't hear. "They're entering my library with violent intent. They're asking permission to take Simone."

His focus returned to us. "They don't need permission for a legit bounty, though, and they know it."

That was all I needed to hear. "I'm the bounty?" I got out, a slight shake to my voice. "I have to return to Valdor to answer questions about wha—" The words died on my tongue. Ah, this fucking compulsion was such bullshit. "Bastards couldn't even let me be here for my best friend while she has a damn baby."

Mera exploded, energy and fire swirling around us. Her scream rang out through the room, and I attempted to rush forward to see if she was okay. Her flames licked across my skin, and I felt strands of my long hair catch on fire just as strong hands yanked me backwards.

I landed against a firm chest, the scent of cherry-and-oak red wine engulfing me. I'd called Lucien "Crimson" as a nickname when I was in Valdor because not only was he the master of Crimson House, his scent also reminded me of my favorite red wine from back home. I'd drank it long before I knew vampires were real, and it was called... Crimson Heart. Crimson Heart with a cherry and oak flavor, which was a weird coincidence I didn't really want to think about.

I hadn't used his nickname for a long time, though.

"Stop," I snapped, pushing myself away before I could get comfortable against the master vampire. "Just stop. I don't need you to take care of me any longer. Look how fucking well it turned out last time."

I was being unfair. What had happened was not his fault, outside of the fact that bringing me to Valdor had been a huge mistake. But the rest was on me. I'd chosen my own fate, and now I had to answer for it.

"I'm not taking care of you," Lucien snapped back, and it was surprising to see him lose his cool so quickly. Mr. Suave was nowhere to be seen—he was almost animalistic. "I'm taking care of my responsibilities. I brought you into my world... into Valdor. I didn't watch you closely enough. It was my frien—" He cut himself off, but even in her rage, Mera didn't miss that little slip.

Her screams and fire died off, and with a Shadow Beast wrapped around one side of her, she managed to storm toward Lucien. "Your friend did what?" she raged. "What did they do to Simone that she can't even speak about it with her family?"

The energy in this room was building, and I wasn't at all surprised to notice Angel and Gaster, along with Reece, Len, and Galleli in the back of the room near the doorway. Mera's baby-induced fury had even brought Inky and Midnight down from the ceiling.

All of them knew better than to step closer though.

Lucien straightened, still far too close to me. His hands remained in front of him as if he was prepared to pull me out of the way if Mera lost it again. "Simone trusted someone because I trusted him," he said, and I was nearly shocked out of my fear and anger by that somewhat honest reply. "He led her down a path that almost took her life."

I opened my mouth to add that Lucien had avenged me and killed his friend, but of course, I couldn't say anything about it.

"The tier one masters," he continued, "were the ones who compelled her silence. There's no breaking it."

"You're one of those damn masters," Mera said, more of her fire dying now that she was finally getting answers. "And you can clearly speak about it."

"It puts her in danger," he snapped back, not concerned even when Shadow shot him a dark look. The beast did not like anyone yelling at his mate, and the last thing we needed was for him to lose his shit too. This room would be nothing more than toothpicks if that happened.

Mera examined the vampire for many long minutes, and whatever she saw in him, it calmed her even more. Or maybe she remembered she was having a baby as another contraction sent her hunching forward, hands on her stomach.

Shadow held onto her, helping her breathe through it, and it seemed for the moment, vampire masters and bounty hunters were the last thing on anyone's mind.

Chapter Five

By the time Shadow had swept Mera into his arms so he could place her back on the bed, Gaster was front and center, ready to deliver the baby, and Angel had shooed everyone from the room except Lucien.

With reluctance, I shuffled closer to him, and pitching my voice as low as I could—which was probably still not low enough for the advanced hearing in the room—I asked him, "Is it best if I leave? Am I putting everyone in danger? How powerful are these tier two masters?"

His scent grew stronger, and I could feel his energy simmering. He was no calmer than I was, even if his outward appearance was expressionless. "No danger to anyone except you," he replied tersely. "They know better than to attack in Shadow's territory. But they also know the laws, and our hands are tied as long as you're considered a fugitive and a summons is being requested."

In my head I was picturing a damn wanted poster plastered across the world with my face on it. Fugitive...

"Wait, how much are they offering for my capture?" Was it stupid that I hoped it was super high because they all feared me so much—

"Nothing." Ugh, the asshole could have at least pretended I was worth the big bucks. "The masters told me you're being called in to answer some questions about what happened when you touched the stone. I have no idea why they've waited so long, but I was assured that you won't be harmed as long as you arrive within the next few sun arcs."

Valdor had one red sun, which gave off about the heat of a California spring. It never disappeared from the sky, the red light eternally there. It did move back and forth, though, so they traced the movement of time via this arc.

A shudder traversed my spine at the thought of being back there, and my wolf whimpered from where she existed now, compressed under foreign energy.

Energy I was starting to understand, since it'd felt stronger and more reactive since I'd been near Lucien, telling me, it was definitely vampire related.

"Could the energy from the stone be the reason my wolf is subdued?" I asked him. No one else must have been able to hear, or the compulsion would have stopped me.

Lucien's hand wrapped around my right biceps, encasing it completely as he pulled me into him. "Your wolf is subdued?" he asked.

I nodded, swallowing roughly as I said, "I barely recognize her. At times I have heightened senses, and then other times, it's as if she's asleep. It's almost like—" I cut myself off, unable to finish that crazy thought.

"Like what?" he bit out, those green eyes nearly drowning me in their striking intensity. Lucien's ability to focus so completely on me that it was as if the rest of the world didn't exist was part of the reason I'd fallen so hard for him in Valdor.

He blurred the world around us, and I'd never had anyone create feelings of *calm* and *home* inside me like he could. At least when he wasn't driving my hormones crazy, turning me into a mess of neediness.

He'd rightly rejected me, of course—vampires never dated outside their race. And I'd acted like a fucking moron, almost getting myself killed in the process. I'd learned a lot from my time in Valdor, and I'd grown up.

I just didn't want to go back there and fall into old bad habits.

"B," he pressed, and I shook my head.

"One: stop calling me by my damn blood type, asshole," I whispered tersely. "And two: I think the stone shared some of its energy or something with me because there's this foreign power swirling inside me now."

His grip on my arm tightened; he wasn't hurting me, but I could feel the strength in that touch. Lucien was more powerful than any alpha shifter I'd ever known. "You should have told me long before now," he rumbled, and fuck if my traitorous body didn't react in the complete opposite way it should have.

The emotion and need he stirred inside me was what had gotten me into trouble in the first place.

Jerking myself out of his grip, or at least attempting to until he released me, I fought the urge to rub at my arm. At the brand his energy had left across my skin.

Before I got a chance to say another word, Mera's scream ripped through the room.

It wasn't that I'd forgotten my best friend was having a baby, but it had been a background thought as I dealt with the more pressing issue of Lucien and the vamps. That scream, though, was filled with a sort of terror and pain that had every part of me freaking out.

"Can you give me until Mera's baby is born?" I said in rush. "I can't miss this, and I know I already owe you from last time, but just add it to the goddamn tally."

Lucien looked like he wanted to say no, but thankfully, he didn't. "I will run interference. Go to Mera."

Spinning on the spot, I raced across the room. Even though I hadn't been far away, it felt like a lifetime before I reached her side. She was in the same position as before, her head now cradled in Shadow's lap. The massive beast held her like she was the most precious thing in the world, and I could feel power pouring from him as he shared it with her.

Gaster was at the end of the bed between Mera's legs, both of which were bent at the knee. Pillows elevated her lower back. Angel was on her right side, holding her hand, and I slid across the bed to her left. Mera, her face streaked in tears, cried out and reached for my hand. My chest was tight as I fought through the panic.

Women died in childbirth, a truth through every part of history. But there could be no way that was a risk for Mera, right? She was immortal. Practically indestructible.

Could this child be her one weakness?

Her grip tightened on mine. She was so much stronger than me now that it legitimately crushed my bones, but I bore it without complaint.

I'd die for Mera and her child, so a few broken bones were hardly anything to worry about. "Is everything okay with the masters?" she huffed out, still more worried about me than herself.

"Everything is fine," I told her firmly. "You have nothing to worry about; Lucien and I have it handled."

A quick glance told me the vampire was gone, and I refused to examine why that had me feeling as empty as the space he'd previously occupied. At least he was keeping his word and running interference.

Another contraction hit Mera, and she was screaming once more, her grip cracking a few more bones, which, thankfully, my shifter energy would heal in a few minutes.

"The contractions are coming faster," Angel said tersely. "Is the baby close?"

Gaster didn't look up, his entire focus on whatever magic he was weaving. "Yes. But it's fighting the release. It's very possessive of Mera, wanting to claim her energy as its own."

Mera laughed through her pain, shaking her head. "Sounds like someone else I know." Her pinched and drawn features relaxed as Shadow brushed her sweaty hair back from her face, and she tilted her head to meet his gaze. He didn't smile as his beast flickered across his normal form like he was barely holding onto himself.

"It will be okay, mate," Mera told him softly. "Our baby is almost here. They'll let go when the time is right."

"Sunshine," he bit out, the word strangled. "I need you to survive. The worlds need you to survive; do you understand?"

"We will both survive," she said without hesitation. The brightness of her personality and power shone through, fighting against her pain. A sense of calm came over her as the last of the tension left her features. "I can feel it."

Angel tilted her head back, her hand still wrapped around Mera's. "Peace," she whispered, serenity caressing her face too. "You're both finding it. The new path is clearer."

And just like that, everyone, including Gaster and Shadow, relaxed. I had no idea what peace they'd all found, but I was taking this as a positive that Mera and her baby were going to be okay. The battle to release this child into the world was over, and now they were on the path to freedom.

This time when the contraction hit, Mera didn't scream or hunch forward like her body was being torn in two. Instead, she held onto her best friends' hands, arched into Shadow, and closed her eyes as she let nature take its course.

"One more push," Gaster said softly, his earthy scent and energy dying off as he returned control to Mera. "You're so close."

A smile spread across her lips, so beautifully content. When she opened her eyes, it was to meet Shadow's flaming gaze. A gaze that had not left her face for many minutes. Fuck, who was I kidding... His eyes had been on his Sunshine from the first moment he saw her.

"I love you, Sunshine," he said. "You're a fucking miracle."

She laughed through tears. "This baby's first word is going to be *fuck.*"

Shadow shrugged like he really didn't care.

"And I love you too," Mera told him, her laughter fading as tears streaked her skin. Tears of joy and healing and hope. "You're the best thing that ever happened to me. You and our baby. Our family."

Now I was the one crying, seeing the full circle of my best friend's life. No longer would she know pain or rejection. She had a pack and family, and my heart soared in happiness for her. She deserved all of this and more.

She arched and groaned, and a stillness descended over the room as she pushed one last time. We were held in stasis then, until a single cry filled the air.

Gaster's waiting and capable hands received our newest blessing, and the moment the child entered this world, a massive tidal wave of power almost blew me off the bed. Mera's hold on my hand, though, anchored me to her side.

The baby let out another cry, which was followed by a second wave of power, not quite as strong as the first. A single, chiming note filled the air, lingered for a moment, then faded out. As if the worlds were finally settling after this new arrival of power.

"A baby born of power and fate," Angel said. "It felt as if the original energies realigned to make room for"—she looked down—"her. To make room for her new place in the power scale." Angel had been right; it was a baby girl.

Mera pushed herself up to see her daughter for the first time. Gaster didn't hesitate to pass the crying, bloody, tiny but powerful being up to her mother. Huge golden eyes met Mera's, and my best friend just stared and cried at her little miracle. "She looks just like you, Shadow," she whispered, large tears dripping down her cheeks.

The beast reached out, and I could have sworn his hand shook as he placed it on the mop of red hair, so thick no baby should be in possession of it. The baby's silent gaze met her father's, and she was no longer crying. Instead, Shadow and the baby wore a look that I could only liken to two ancient beings exchanging an understanding of the universe. It wasn't just her hair or direct gaze that felt unnatural, but everything else was as well.

Then that moment was over as Mera pulled her closer and the baby acted like a normal, fussy, boob-obsessed newborn.

"She's hungry," Shadow noted.

Mera went with it, moving the beautiful little girl to her breast, her loose white top easing down as she did. The child latched on immediately, which I'd heard wasn't always the case, but what did I really know.

Taking a step back, I took a moment to appreciate the perfection of the scene before me. Mera might think that the baby looked like Shadow, but I could see a lot of my friend in there too, from the red curls to the full lips and high cheekbones.

I mean, no doubt she had Shadow genetics with those otherworldly eyes and straight nose, along with the long limbs he was famous for.

"She's a perfect mix of Sunshine and Shadow," Angel said with a sigh, her thoughts aligning with mine. "What name will you honor her with?"

I honestly couldn't wait to hear what they called her.

Chapter Six

T urned out we weren't going to learn her name yet since there was an entire ceremony and blessing when a child of the Shadow Realm was named. Knowing I didn't have much longer with Mera, I crawled up to her side, lying beside her as she fed her daughter. Shadow let out a rumbling growl when I brushed against his mate, and I knew on instinct not to touch his child yet.

The possessive bastard would need time for that. Time before he could share the new female who had him wrapped around her little finger.

We were all fucked.

"Beast," Mera said with a soft laugh. "Calm. Simone is family."

His growl got louder, and as he crossed his arms and stared down at us, I knew this wasn't a battle she would win. Not today, when his emotions were raw and heightened.

"It's okay. I should give you both some bonding time with little... Shadowshine Jr."

Mera snorted. "Perfect name for her."

Shadow didn't sound as amused, but I was getting better at ignoring the scary, rumbling beast in the room.

"I'll inform the others of our strong, healthy, powerful girl's arrival," Angel said from where she was perched near the end of the bed. Her hands cradled her own belly, as if it had truly hit home to her that she would soon be a mom too. "And we will celebrate when you're ready."

Mera blew her a kiss. "Thank you for being here."

Angel returned the gesture with a kiss of her own. "There's nowhere else I would have been. Now rest up."

She left, and Mera turned to me. "You're not leaving yet, right? We haven't even had a chance to catch up. You have to meet my baby girl properly."

She glanced down and adjusted the feeding baby, who looked very comfortably snuggled into her momma.

"I'm going to stay as long as I can," I murmured, feeling the pressure of Valdor's summons hovering. "But I can't ignore the masters for too long. Lucien's running interference, but he's already done so much for me. It's time I faced up to the consequences of my actions."

It was time I stopped blaming him for my own bad choices in the vampire world. All of my growing up since then would be worth nothing if I continued to hide from the consequences of my screw-ups.

Mera jolted upright, and I could have sworn the baby let out a growl similar to her father's at being disturbed. "You don't have to do that on your own," Mera said, voice harsh. "If you go to Valdor, we all go to Valdor. It's like the Desert Lands. No one faces challenges or dangers alone in this family."

The fire suddenly spilling from Shadow could have scorched the damn oceans dry. Hoping I wasn't about to spontaneously combust, I reached out and placed a hand on Mera's shoulder to press her back into the bed. "Meers, you just had a baby. You need to rest and not worry so much about me. I don't even know what's happening yet or if it's serious. I promise I'll keep you updated though. If there's a possibility of danger, I'll take whatever help I can get."

I never forgot I was the weak one in this world. Shifters dominated on Earth, but in the rest of the Solaris System, I might as well be a human.

Mera didn't appear very convinced by my reassurances, but she wasn't really in a position to hunt me down. So when I dropped a kiss on her cheek and hopped off the bed, she didn't move two inches before Shadow was in her face.

Huge Shadow.

The version that topped out at fifty million feet tall or whatever he grew to.

"Mera..."

The low rumble of her name had the hairs on my body standing up, and since he'd used her real name, I knew it wasn't safe for me in here any longer. Gaster must have had the same thought, since he spluttered out some congratulations and well wishes before he scurried out of the room with me hot on his tail.

The door slammed behind us, and I felt the entire library urging us to fuck right off. As always, present or not, Shadow got his point across with ease.

With the birth of his child, the beast Mera had somewhat tamed was gone, and this new version was a touch terrifying.

By the time Gaster and I made it to the exit, we weren't alone. Angel and Reece, along with Len, Inky and Midnight were heeding the warning and getting their asses out of Shadow's direct domain too.

"Of course it had to be a baby girl," Len groaned with a dry laugh. "If we thought he was bad over his Sunshine, wait until we have that little—"

"Shadowshine Jr," I added since we didn't have the official name yet.

"Shadowshine Jr for sure," the fae snorted. "We're all fucked."

"My sentiments exactly," I said with my own weak laugh.

As we tumbled through the doorway and back into the white library, I found myself face to chest with Lucien, who'd clearly been standing there waiting for our return.

"Shadow had the entry locked down," he said in a low, ominous voice. "Is the baby okay?"

"Perfectly fine," Angel told him. "They birthed a beautiful, powerful little girl, whose presence has the beast's protective instincts... elevated."

Lucien nodded like he wasn't remotely surprised by this, and I tried to squash the mental image of his strong arms cradling a child. An odd thought since I'd all but decided that bringing children into this fucked up world wasn't for me. Still, Lucien would make one sexy father. Not just sexy, but caring and strong.

My father was the worst kind of role model, but I had a feeling Lucien's children would not feel the same as I did. One day that might happen for him, when he found the mate who called to his blood.

A thought that turned my stomach.

Nope. Nope, nope. I couldn't go there.

Luckily, a huge distraction crashed through the library, sending Gaster forward as an enraged howl left his lips. Energy whipped around us in the same instant, and I realized I'd spoken too soon about the "luckily" part. Vampires had a distinct and icy energy, and it was filtering through the library now.

Lucien was gone before I could blink, moving so fast he was a mere blur. Gaster disappeared too, and I took off in the direction of Valdor's door.

"Simone!" Len snapped, racing after me. "You're supposed to run *away* from danger."

He reached for me, but I pushed his hand away. "No! This is my fight, and I will never again cower in the face of a supernatural threat."

Angel, who was keeping pace with us, despite her belly, made a deep, satisfied sound. "Yes, warrior friend. We fight until the bitter end."

Reece, huge desert deity that he was, released a gust of red sand that swept around his mate and lifted her up into the air. "The rest of us fight. You grow my child and stay safe."

Oh, damn. We were about to have another battle on our hands. Between those two.

Part of me was sad that I couldn't stay to watch Angel kick his ass, but I had more pressing concerns. Like what the hell the vampires wanted with me that was so important they would risk Shadow's wrath. Even if they were able to enter the library under that bounty rule, they had come in with some real aggression.

They were not playing around, and it was clear that one way or another, I was going to Valdor today.

Chapter Seven

Valdor's door was familiar to me, with its red etchings depicting the Crimson City, where the most powerful tier one master vampires had their enclaves. There were many other cities in their world, but I'd never gotten to see any of them. I'd only heard about the golden gates of the Imbride Province, which was the closest in power base to Crimson City, and the purple fields of Hargin, which had the third largest population.

But I'd never been to either.

Vamps weren't real big on taking their food out for sightseeing.

Len remained at my side as we traversed through the library, his silver coat floating out gracefully behind him. When he kept pace with me like this, it almost looked like he was walking, since my speed had nothing on fae or vampire.

It took real effort for him to go slow enough to stay with me, and a trickle of warmth filled my gut at the concept of being protected and cared for, even if just as an extension of Mera. It really didn't matter to me what his reason was, just the fact that he was doing it meant everything.

As a latchkey child, with parents who'd made me a last priority on the regular, I'd never known a true "home" or pack, outside of Mera. For Len to give me a semblance of that, well... I kind of loved him a little. Probably also explained why I'd fallen so hard for Lucien. *Home* was an addictive feeling for one who'd never experienced it.

"You deserve an amazing mate," I told the fae, and as his silvery eyes widened, gaze clashing with mine, I knew I'd taken him by surprise. He didn't get to reply because we'd arrived at the drama.

Lucien and Gaster were facing off against eight vampires. They wore tier two master outfits, which were black with red armor molded to their breast, stomach, and thigh areas. I couldn't see any of their faces since black ninja masks covered their heads.

The eight stood in a V formation wedged between the shelves. We were alone in this section, all other inhabitants having bailed at the first sign of battle.

Lucien didn't turn my way when I arrived, but somehow, I still knew he was pissed off that I'd followed. Well, tough fucking luck, cupcake. He was the one who'd told me that there was no more hiding from this.

"Simone," the closest vamp called, his deep masculine tone mildly muffled by the mask. "You are requested to return to Crimson City by the council of tier one masters. We are here to accompany you."

He held out a hand, but before I could step forward or respond, Lucien moved, crashing into the male and disabling him in about a third of a second. A distinct snap of bone was heard as Lucien stomped on his arm for extra measure.

A silence moment stretched until Len chuckled, uncaring that his brother had just attacked a vampire.

"Lucien! What the hell, dude?" I snapped, and fuck if everyone didn't freak out at me addressing their powerful master like that. Not only was he a tier one, which was royalty to all the vamps, but Lucien's family was one of the oldest and most powerful. Their enclave, Crimson House, was never challenged, and its leader commanded the absolute highest respect. No one would dare to address him as I just had.

Not that I gave a single fuck.

"Release him," I said with another snap, moving forward. "This is not your fight."

He jerked his head up so I could see his eyes, dark sparks sprinkling the green as he snarled, his fangs visible between his parted lips. "They dared to step into this territory when I told them I would return you today," he rumbled. "They disobeyed my order, and I can't let that slide."

Well, shit. Seemed his actions had nothing to do with me and I'd just stepped into a pile of vampire politics when I shouldn't have. With another snarl Lucien moved, zipping between the black-clad vampires, taking them down like they were humans. They tried to fight back but were so outclassed in power and skill that it was fairly embarrassing for them.

Gaster, who was clearly growing more agitated at the mild destruction of this section of library, finally smashed his hands together, releasing a visible wave of power. It passed through me without causing any damage, but the vampires weren't as lucky as they ended up plastered against the very shelves they were disturbing.

Even Lucien appeared unable to immediately break free from the goblin's hold, and I had to say, I was impressed. Len crossed his arms, leaning back on a nearby shelf as he smiled. "No one ever expects the demi-fae to kick ass, which is generally their first and only mistake."

"I expected it," I said simply. "Shadow wouldn't have someone weak in charge of his library. Gaster was also the one chosen to deliver his child. Something tells me we haven't seen even a fraction of what our friend can do."

From my peripheral it looked like the goblin's thin lips curved into a smile before he returned his full focus to the vampires. "I'm going to release you now, but the second there's any aggression, I will simply toss you back into Valdor. Bounty or not, this is unacceptable."

He lowered his hands, and most of them crashed into the floor. Only Lucien and one other male landed gracefully on their feet. I had a feeling it was the male who had spoken first, demanding I accompany them.

When all the masters were once again standing, they had a terse conversation with Lucien before they finally left.

At that point Gaster checked in that I was okay.

"I'm fine," I told him. "Thanks for helping out."

He squeezed my hand, so much more affectionate than I remembered from my last time here. "I'll see you soon," he said as he left, and I took that as a promise since I had to hope this trip to Valdor wouldn't spell my last days in these worlds.

Len stepped forward to stand shoulder to shoulder with Lucien, both of them staring down at me. I couldn't read either of their blank expressions, but the vampire still had rage in his eyes, despite the once-again green color.

"So," I said casually, "seems my time is up? Should we head to Valdor now?"

Lucien's jaw tightened as he shook his head. At first, I thought he was saying no, but then I realized he was just gathering his thoughts. "The council ignored my message, and I have no doubt that they don't trust me to return you. They'll send more."

Great. Excellent. Fan-fucking-tastic news.

"It's not worth going to war until we know for sure they want her dead," Len said.

Lucien finally nodded. "Yeah, I agree. I have the power to get her out of there if the shit hits the fan, so we might as well just go forward and hope there's a simple fix."

"No way!" a voice snapped from behind us, and I blinked to find Angel was the one who'd spoken. I'd expected Mera, but apparently Shadow still had her tied down. Probably literally.

"I know you're powerful and influential in your world, Luce," Angel said stiffly, "but you have no idea what to expect. Someone is keeping secrets from you, and we've had too many world-ending battles lately for me not to assume this will be the same."

Lucien's gaze flicked up to Reece, who was standing protectively at Angel's back, before he returned it to her level. "They will not stop, and we don't know yet how bad it could be. I've managed to hold them off for months, but they've decided enough is enough."

"We can stop them," Reece said simply, like he didn't have a care in the world. Typical attitude of the gods.

Lucien met his brother's gaze again. "You want war? Before we even know what their summons is regarding? A lot of innocent lives hang in the balance, including our newest baby." His eyes dropped to Angel's stomach. "And the one soon to be born. War is always the last option."

Reece let out a huff, but he didn't argue. "Okay, then what's the plan if you get there and they decide to end Simone's life."

Right? What was the freaking plan if that happened?

Lucien didn't even frown. "I believe that if they wanted her dead, the bounty would be for her head. They also wouldn't have been put off for months. This is something more... like political machinations. Maybe even against me. For now, we should just play their game until we have all the facts."

Angel was still shaking her head, but in the end, it was my life to gamble with. "I agree to Lucien's plan. No one else gets to make this choice for me. I will face the consequences of my actions—the piper plays for everyone eventually."

"Mera would kill us," Angel said in a rush, her eyes wider and pinker than usual as she tried to appeal to my love for Mera. "And none of us want to see you hurt. You're part of this family, and we protect our family."

My chest was doing that stupid aching thing again, the unfamiliar burn of "family love" going to knock me off long before the vampires got to me. "You have no idea how much it means to me to be considered part of the extended Shadow family," I said, wishing I didn't sound so breathless. "I've been alone most of my life except for Mera, so... it's a lot. But I really don't want to go in there guns blazing, so to speak, and cause more issues—let's save the A team for a worst-case scenario. Unintentionally starting a war is the last thing I want to add to my daily goals."

Lucien let out a low chuckle as he stepped closer to me. So close that I could breathe in his crimson scent and see the many pigmented facets of green in his eyes. "I'm the A team, B, and you fucking know it."

"I've got two letters for you too" I told him with a smirk. "F and U."

He smiled. A perfect smile, flashing sparkling teeth and the hint of fangs. My body warmed more than I'd admit, even as I squirmed just enough to ease the discomfort low in my gut. Sexy vampires were apparently my Achilles' heel.

With his gaze locked on me, I felt Lucien's power rise. "You will come with me now," he said, his voice a low hypnotic buzz. My wolf attempted to surge up, but we were just too weak to fight his compulsion.

"There's no need to do that," Angel snapped from beside him; I couldn't move my gaze from Lucien to see her. "She said she was going to go peacefully."

Lucien reached out and wrapped a hand around my wrist, engulfing it in his strong grip. I couldn't look away, no matter how much I fought his power. Lucien had me completely under his control.

"I cannot have them questioning my loyalty at this point," he told Angel. "The reason they haven't filled me in on what this summons is about is because I've stepped in for Simone multiple times already. A shifter... effectively food. If I want to stay in the loop, I now need to act like a master vampire again."

The hand that had been around my wrist moved to circle my waist, and in the same breath, I was up and over his right shoulder.

His fucking shoulder. Like a piece of meat he was carting home for dinner.

Made sense since I was *food.*

Wait until I broke through his power, because given enough time, I'd figure out a way.

And then they'd all pay.

Chapter Eight

L ucien's hold on me didn't ease, not even amidst the protests from Mera's friends or when we stepped through the damn doorway and I felt the chill of the pathway between worlds, and definitely not when a familiar red washed over my vision. The red of my favorite wine and my favorite flower, which grew in Torma and was so rare I didn't even know its name.

Again, coincidences I did not want to look too closely at, but maybe both explained my obsession with Crimson City and the master vampire carrying me.

Last time we'd arrived in the Crimson City, I'd walked in of my own volition, naïve to my place in the world since on Earth a shifter was the top of the food chain. The vampires had cured me of that mistaken sense of worth.

Lucien had warned me to stay in the castle-like compound he called a house, but in my stupidity over his rejection of me, I'd stopped listening to him. Stopped using common fucking sense.

Being back here was triggering in a way that I expected and

hadn't had time to properly prepare myself for. My neck ached, reminding me that I'd almost died here. Almost died when I'd been convinced to enter the Master Chambers, a massive building at the center of this mazelike city. In that building I'd touched their sacred stone and changed the course of my future.

The stone's alarm had brought the guards, who ripped my throat out for breaking their most sacred law. I'd been bleeding out on the floor when Lucien raged in like a guardian angel. He'd shared his blood with me and saved my life, even if I didn't remember most of it since I'd been all but dead at the time.

And now I was heading back to the very place it'd all happened.

Desperate to speak, I pushed my wolf forward to bust through the compulsion, but she was as traumatized as I was and did nothing except whimper. It broke my heart to hear that strangled sound from her. The other energy resting on top of her, the foreign beat, swirled as if to remind me it was strong. This had to be the result of me touching the sacred stone, or maybe... it was Lucien's blood, still inside me.

He was vampire and I was shifter; our bloods were not compatible, and my body didn't know how to purge it from my system. His blood might have saved my life, but now it felt like it clashed with my shifter energy.

If I'd had a voice in this moment, I'd have asked Lucien about it, but of course, he wanted me going to the masters as a mute prisoner.

The city was set out like a maze, a zigzagging array of streets that went left and right and back and forth until eventually you found the center of the maze. *The Master Chambers.* Surrounding this building were dozens of entrances—or exits depending on your direction— each leading to a different section of Crimson City.

Last time I'd learned that there were about a million vampires in this city, which was the largest and most exclusive in Valdor. You needed permission to move to any of the enclaves here and a tier one master to take you in under their protection, or you'd quickly be ripped to pieces.

Lucien had told me there was one lone wolf—so to speak— vampire in this city without an enclave, but he was so damn powerful that no one bothered him. He'd refused to be a master or join any enclave after his family had been murdered in another Valdorian town.

Other than that, it was ten tier one masters, ten enclaves of vampires, and endless machinations and politics.

"I never wanted you back here."

His words startled me, at least internally since he still had my movements locked down. And while I understood the reason he'd used compulsion against me—he wanted to garner some trust again with his fellow masters—it didn't mean I wasn't pissed about it.

"And I know what you're thinking," he continued.

Doubt that very much, fucker.

"But I promise that if I didn't bring you in incapacitated like this, they'd come down so much harder on you. Do not remind them that you're a predator. Best, at this point, to appear frail and weak."

Man, if I could've moved at this point, I would've been swinging my leg like a prize fucking horse straight into his vampire balls.

Lucien chuckled, a low rumble, and I hated that tiny flicker of attraction I still felt when he went all sexy on me. "Your energy is strong," he said, sounding amused. He paused then, and his next words were slower. "Why do I feel it so strongly though?"

Can't answer your question, moron who compelled me.

Maybe it was best not to tell him my theory, just in case it meant more trouble for me. Lucien would probably try to drain my blood to get his back because we all knew that blood from another supernatural creature could be used against them.

He didn't question me further, instead picking up his pace as we headed deeper into the maze. The houses and streets themselves formed the walls of this circuit, and you had no choice but to continue along the path. Left or right was the only option, with no gaps between the buildings and shops.

Everything looked the same in the streets, with the only color variance the stones that belonged to each house. The master's houses were more unique and luxurious. Not that any of the vampires lived in slums, from what I'd seen anyway.

Shops were scattered between houses, providing the Crimson City citizens with bottled blood and plasma, a variety of foods, and other creature comforts. In many ways, this city reminded me of Earth, with similar levels of advancement and technologies, only there were no cars here since vampires could speed themselves around much faster than any vehicle would go.

Newcomers could be lost for weeks in this maze of a city, which left the masters safe and sound in their chambers in the center. The last to be attacked.

I hated when leaders let their "people" stand on the front line while they hid in their castles—a sentiment I was fairly sure I held in common with Lucien. Last time we were here, he'd talked about vampire politics, telling me he'd never wanted to be a master, but he didn't trust any other to keep his enclave safe. He'd also said that the tier one masters needed to be cleaned up since too many of them had been alive forever, abusing their power, which was one of the reasons he was only here when duty dictated.

The fact that we were both back here now was a slap in the face, and even if I wanted to blame Lucien, I couldn't. Once again, this was a result of my own actions when all he'd ever done was keep me safe.

The rest of the journey continued in silence, and though I couldn't see much of the landscape from my position over his shoulder, I did notice the brighter red of the sun lighting up the paved road below. It must be the middle of their awake cycle, which explained why there were more than a few vampires on the streets going about their business.

Lucien picked up speed at one point, and from there everything went by in a red blur. We would be at the chambers in minutes now.

"Are they going to kill me?"

For a brief second my wolf surged through his hold, and I

managed to speak. The compulsion locked me back down almost instantly. Lucien's speed faltered briefly, and I was able to see that we were approaching the outer layer of the Master Chambers.

His hands on my waist tightened as he lifted me off his shoulder so he could peer into my eyes. "How did you break my compulsion?" he questioned, pupils darting about my face as the green deepened until it was almost black.

Once again, he was asking me a question without allowing me to answer. It was almost as if he was trying to ferret the information from my mind, his energy seeping inside, but there were some things he just couldn't have.

My wolf made another surge, snapping at the invading power, and Lucien withdrew his energy. "Fair enough, B. I won't press again, but once we get through this next little performance, you're going to tell me everything that you've experienced since that night we shared blood. Everything."

I was back over his shoulder before I could blink—not that I could blink. If I wasn't a shifter, my eyes would have dried out and fallen from my damn head by now.

He continued on to the chambers. The guards, which were stationed at huge gates at each maze opening, opened them up before Lucien was even close.

As we moved into the outer courtyard of the chambers, I realized he hadn't answered my question. Probably because he had no idea if the masters wanted to kill me or not.

Here's hoping his words from the library were true and he had enough power to get us both out of here.

Before they ripped our hearts out.

Chapter Nine

The Master Chambers was at least six stories tall. I'd only been to two of those floors before, which included the entry level we were currently stepping into. This level was where they had their meeting rooms, a large ballroom, kitchen, dining area, and a circular atrium in the center, which showcased an array of their local plants.

Vampires ate a small variety of food to go with their regular plasma and blood, mostly fruit and pastries. So these plants were for aesthetics and flowery scents. The atrium garden was so huge that you could smell the slightly musky, earthy florae through the whole area.

No lie, I felt right at home with the notes of lavender and aniseed scattered throughout. I had no idea which plant was the "licorice plant," since it was best not to enter the garden. Just like the vampires, some of their vegetation wanted to kill you too.

Lucien wasted no time strolling toward a set of curving stairs behind the garden that led to the second and third floors. The ceiling here was open, so the floors above had a view of the deadly garden too. I'd been to the second floor, where they had the master's main sitting area. It was also where their Stone of Katu, their god, was kept. And where I'd gotten myself into so much trouble last time.

Floor three I hadn't made it to, but I'd heard it was another level of meeting rooms and ballrooms. Apparently these fanged assholes had a lot of dances to attend.

The floors above three were a mystery without access via these stairs.

Today it appeared that the second level was our destination as Lucien entered its wide, open space, the walls filled with windows to let the red sun in. I always likened the lighting here to a mix of sun and moonlight, and it never wavered, bright all day, with the sun shifting across the sky the only indication of time.

When their sleep cycle arrived, all houses were equipped with blackout shutters. Vampires were not forced to sleep at this time, but most of them did to keep their energy strong.

As Lucien strode farther along the second floor, I tried to lift my head and see if all the masters were gathered at the end waiting for us. I'd been to one meeting here, when the hall was filled with vampires, all wanting to air their current worries and problems to their tier one masters.

It reminded me of a court, masters perched in thronelike chairs atop a dais, most of them coldly dismissing the woes of their enclave members—just like my former alpha, who'd cared nothing for any shifter but himself. A leader should never disregard the wants and needs of their people. Never.

I couldn't see from the upside-down position I was in, but when we passed the huge stone in the middle, I knew we were close to the end. The Stone of Katu was taller and wider than me, shot through with reds, golds, and blacks, which made up the basic coloring of Crimson City and its surrounds.

All vampires who passed this stone touched it to reaffirm their bond to their god Katu. This god was said to have been born in a blood storm of the original worlds, and as it emerged, powerful, with six arms and four legs, its mouth was filled with fangs that could drain the other gods dry of blood and power.

When Katu was done feeding, it had created a world and birthed offspring... the ancient masters of this world, all of whom craved and required the same blood that powered their creator. Katu gifted all the masters their own stones, along with the Stone of Katu, which they used now for worship. It was this stone I'd touched last time without knowing the consequences for that action.

Apparently it was a crime for *food* to touch their sacred stone of the gods. I'd set off some sort of security blast of power, and before I'd even picked my ass up off the ground, vampire guards had me.

At least I could be assured I wouldn't see the guard with light blond hair and icy blue eyes again. Lucien had taken care of him after saving my life.

Two factors I was very grateful for. If only he could have saved me one last time so I didn't end up back here.

Lucien stopped moving then and lifted me off his shoulder. I was placed next to the stone and before the masters. There was no time for me to see if the six-foot-tall, perfectly smooth, oval stone that floated above a large bowl of trickling red "water" looked the same because all my attention was focused on the nine master vampires perched before me.

All of the tier ones were here. The big kahunas.

I was seriously fucked.

The tenth seat was open—Lucien's spot, with the red jewels that lined the edge of his ornate gold chair. Each of the enclaves had their own sacred stones that gave them longevity and power. Lucien's was red, which I thought was fitting, matching the sky and city.

Maybe that was part of the reason he was so feared and a hell of a lot more powerful than most of the masters. Or maybe it had nothing to do with the stones and everything to do with the vampire himself.

He left me standing on my own beside the Stone of Katu, its mild glow mocking me. I was still compelled, feeling alone and vulnerable, which only increased with the ten gazes locked on me, including Lucien's as he sprawled back in his seat.

The urge to kick Lucien's ass grew stronger within me. I might not be a particularly fiery female—that had been more Mera's redheaded personality—but I'd had enough of being pushed around by powerful assholes. The fact that my wolf was submissive at the moment didn't make the woman the same.

My blood was boiling.

The part of my blood that wasn't even mine was boiling too, swirling inside of me as I remained statue-like, staring at Lucien. He'd placed me right before his chair, which meant I could continue trying to murder him with my gaze.

The slightest smirk played across his lips as he settled in, shrinking the huge chair with his broad shoulders and long limbs. Gods, I wished I could smack that look off his face—a desire to save for later because apparently now it was time to fight for my life.

"Thank you for returning the *item* to us, Master Lucien," said the male on his right. He had dark blond hair cut at his shoulders and sharp grey eyes that were harshly assessing me. I could easily understand his words, the language of Valdor already installed in my mind by the Shadow Beast. Not everything translated perfectly from the vampire's language, but it was good enough to get by.

Lucien finally tore his gaze from me, turning a much harder look on the master beside him. "Don't think I've forgotten the way you sent tier twos in, Donovan, when I'd expressly told you I was returning Simone—a fact we'll be dealing with later. For now, let's just get on with whatever you need to say to the shifter. We're all busy and wondering what the hell this is about."

A few others made noises of agreement, so it seemed that Lucien wasn't the sole one in the dark. Only time would tell if that was a good or bad thing.

Donovan cleared his throat, straightening and smoothing out the white dress shirt he wore. He also had on black slacks, and the overall look was one of a high-powered businessman. If it wasn't for the flash of fangs he didn't bother to hide and the red liquid in the decanter in his left hand, there'd be no indication he was a vampire.

"Apologies, brother, about the retrieval team," he said in a deep voice. "We'd waited as long as we could, and I figured it wouldn't hurt to have the urgency reinforced."

Lucien's chest rumbled, but he didn't say anything. Maybe there was a second reason for my compulsion—to prevent me from raging at these fucking vampires because my temper was really flying at the moment.

Donovan focused his attention on me. "You have been summoned to Valdor for a few important reasons," he started, and some of my fury faded under nerves.

He stood and moved forward, stepping off the dais and stopping before me, blocking my view of the rest of the room. Our eyes met, and he almost seemed... curious as he examined me.

Until today, I hadn't really met the other top tier masters, but I knew this one by reputation. Donovan, master of Jade House. The stones lining his chair were not the jade color of earth, but a deep blue with flecks of red. He was a big male, like Lucien, but that was where the similarities ended. Lucien was a golden surfer god, with all that bronze skin, bright green eyes, and messily styled blond hair. Donovan's skin was a rich reddish brown, and his eyes were dark and cold. Physically he appeared no older than me, but there was an ancient feel to his energy.

A sixth sense told me he was the most powerful here, aside from Lucien, and since he was standing an arm's length from my defenseless body, I fought to not let the bubbling panic take over. "Release her," he said, and in the same instant, the hold on me vanished.

As Lucien's powers returned to him, that foreign energy inside tried to follow, almost lurching me forward. Luckily, I managed to stop before I crashed into Master Donovan and wrinkled his fancy suit.

As I shook out my tingling limbs, it took a few seconds before my shifter healing kicked in and got my blood flowing again. Time where

I tried not to look any of the vampires in the eye, especially the one right before me. Finally freed of compulsion, I did not want to go right back under. It might be a rare gift that only the most powerful had, but I was in a room with tier one masters.

Masters who wanted me here for a reason.

When no one spoke for a good many minutes, I finally had to say, "Why am I here? Shadow is not going to take lightly to one of his shifters being dragged into vampire politics."

Was I unashamedly reminding them that my god was accessible to me? Yep, I sure as fuck was. Not to mention Mera, who at times could be even scarier.

"The Shadow Beast need not concern himself," Donovan said softly, voice scraping over my nerves in a very uncomfortable way. "This is a vampire matter, and you... you are not completely his any longer."

What. In. The. Actual. Shifter hell? What was he talking about?

"See," Donovan continued, moving in a slow stroll as he circled me. His hand brushed the Stone of Katu, like he was mocking me with its presence. "When you were here last, you touched this stone. Do you remember?"

"How could I forget," I replied drily, following his movement with my gaze. "One of your guards ripped my damn throat out, no questions asked."

Donovan didn't react to that statement. "Turns out," he continued, "that not long after you touched our most sacred stone, sending out a unique energy due to your foreign shifter nature, we had a powerful vampire come forward to request a mate. Masters can make this appeal at any point, and then the best of the best are invited to participate in the Mate Selections. He demanded your presence a long time ago, but Lucien has been holding us back."

My eyebrows drew together as I pondered on what the hell he was talking about. Lucien had never mentioned a master wanting to meet me—he'd seemed genuinely confused about what the vampires wanted with me. So, it stood to reason he had no idea of this request.

I wasn't sure if that was good or bad news for me today.

"Step forward Master Carter," Donovan said, pausing to sweep his arm toward the end of the room, back near the stairs. It took a few minutes for a figure to appear and even longer for me to see him clearly. When he was close, I couldn't help but suck in a deep breath.

Master Carter was beautiful. As beautiful as Lucien, in a rugged, dangerous way. He was not quite as tall as some of the other vampires, but still well over six feet, towering above my height of five-nine. His shoulders were impossibly broad, and unlike most of the suit wearers, he was dressed like a hunter: camo army pants, tan boots, a rugged waterproof jacket, and a full beard that was the same dark color as the closely cropped hair on his head.

When he stood only a few feet from me, his bright blue eyes remained locked on my face. He held me in his gaze until someone growled. "What the hell, Donovan? He's not a master."

Carter's gaze went flat as he turned in the direction of that voice, which had come from one of the females. I hadn't seen which one, but the voice was soft and lyrical. "I can always prove it by challenging your position?" he rumbled, voice a deep rasp.

The hairs on my body stood on end at the unsuppressed anger in this male's voice. If it had been any other situation, I would have run in the opposite direction.

Carter was here for blood, and since he'd apparently *demanded* my presence, it stood to reason that maybe my blood was the one he was after.

Chapter Ten

Before all-out chaos ensued, Master Donovan distracted everyone by spinning on the spot and heading back for his chair, leaving me standing next to Carter. The beefed-up hunter-vamp hadn't attacked anyone yet, but if the look on his face was any indication, he wasn't far from it.

"If possible, all of us are more confused at this point," a different female said. This one sat on the other side of Lucien and had waist-length platinum hair. As she leaned forward from a chair lined with deep amber stones, her black dress, which was molded to her curvy frame, slid down to reveal perfect tits. Clearly uncaring that half her nipple was out, she waved her arms around. "Can someone fill the rest of us in so we can get back to our damn lives."

Her eyes, an icy silver color, met mine, and I could have sworn she licked her lips. Someone was hungry, and I was the only easy food in the room. Most of the time vamps drank bagged blood imported from other worlds they had long-standing deals with, since they could only be sustained by another vampire if they were in a true blood bond—which was rare. But every now and then, they had parties where live food was invited in.

They weren't supposed to kill them, but I'd heard stories during my time here. Horrifying stories. Around vamps, death was inevitable.

"It's simple, Julietta," Donovan said, like we were all morons, "if a master wants a mate, then we have to call a selection ceremony. Any eligible females or males, depending on their preferences, must be there."

A beat of silence and then the room erupted, vamps jumping to their feet with fangs out, ready to attack. I started to back up, knowing that I wouldn't survive a vampire brawl, only to find myself plastered against the new, scary "master."

Freezing to the spot, I couldn't move. My eyes locked on Lucien, who was half out of his chair, expression dark as he stared above my head, eyeballing this Carter, who didn't feel like a tier two master and yet clearly wasn't one of the mains.

With a squeak, I finally darted forward, only to find Carter's firm grip around my waist, holding me in place. My fighting instinct kicked in, and I swung at him, claws springing free from my fingertips as wolfish instinct took over. Growls ripped from deep in my chest as I slashed at his arm, but he didn't release his hold.

"Calm," he demanded in that same rumble of a voice. "I'm not here to hurt you."

Right. And I was just going to believe that because he said so.

Swinging my arm back again, this time I aimed for the throat because, vampire or not, no one got to just manhandle me without a reaction. Lucien would have gotten the same attack, except he'd been smart enough to compel me first.

Carter let out a deep sigh as I launched forward, but my arm caught on something, and I was thrown off balance. It was only when I got a whiff of *Crimson Heart wine* that I realized Lucien had joined the fray. Stupidly, it made me feel as if I wasn't quite alone.

If I had to choose my battles, then I also had to respect my allies.

He was the only one I had here, and I would take him over these assholes any day.

When he pulled me back into his energy, I didn't fight him, releasing my anger so that my wolf calmed.

"Why are you really here, Carter?" Lucien asked with almost no inflection in his tone, which to me was scarier than when he raised his voice. His icy control could cut you to the core. "You chose long ago to remain in exile in Crimson City. You chose to live in isolation, and out of respect for your age and power, we have left you alone to do so. Are you stepping in now to claim an eleventh enclave and head it as a tier one master?"

Well, crap. This was the lone wolf? The one strong enough to exist outside of the normal order and be left alone to do so? And I had been called here for some reason that had to do with him and his need for a mate? This was not good. Not good at all.

Behind us, the fighting continued, vampires screaming at each other, but since we were in our own little standoff, my focus remained firmly on our trio.

Carter sighed again, a huge gust of air that ruffled my loose hair. "I've been in mourning for a long time. My family... Well, you know the story. My emotions closed down after her death since it was the only way I could survive, but there was a moment..." His eyes met mine, and I tried not to squirm under the intensity of his gaze. "A moment when light broke through the darkness. You touched the stone," he whispered, "and sent out a ripple of energy. I was nearby that night, and I felt the power. When it hit me, I was alive once more, and that was when I knew I could no longer hide in shadows."

Finally, he released me from his gaze, and I felt like I could breathe again. "While I'm happy you're going to start to live again," I managed to say, "that doesn't explain why, specifically, I'm here. Surely, if you're looking to claim a mate at this selection ceremony, you're looking for a vampire mate?"

Carter's smile grew larger... predatory. "You're the first shifter to ever step foot in our world. Shadow Beast would never allow us to touch his creations, but now you carry the blood of us. Blood that hasn't destroyed you. I've been thinking about this during the time the masters asked me to wait for your return, and I've reached the conclusion that the reason Shadow does not allow shifters here is that you're compatible with vampires. As it stands, you already feel part vampire, and therefore, you can participate in the selection."

Before I could open my mouth to give him a little update on women's rights these days, which included choosing our mates and not being forced into an archaic competition, Lucien whipped me behind him, blocking Carter from view.

I didn't like having my back to the other vampires, so I turned, keeping the arguing masters in sight as I pressed into Lucien, still able to hear his conversation clearly.

"You can't just claim her," he was saying, and there was fire in his voice. "She has to participate in the selection and be the right match for you."

What the fuck, dude?

Carter didn't argue. "Agreed. She's here to ensure she would participate. With you continually protecting her, it's been an impossible task, but I finally reminded them of my strength to get this moving."

Lucien's body was vibrating against mine, a deep vibration building from within his energy, and pressed securely against him, I felt every motion. If I had to guess, I'd say he was about to explode, but then I was completely shocked when he suddenly raised his voice and said, "Call the selection. I will compete for a mate."

There was a beat of silence again, and then the room exploded.

For the second time.

Chapter Eleven

I had no real idea what Lucien's declaration meant, other than the fact that he was stepping in again to try and help me. "What the actual fuck?" I snarled. "I don't want to compete in a selection."

"You have no damn choice," he shot back. "They can still kill you for touching the stone. We have to follow through."

I felt there was more he wanted to say, but since this room had many ears, he refrained.

"You must love Mera a lot," I finally choked out, accepting his words, "to offer yourself in the selection to save her friend."

To my surprise he said, "I'm not doing this for her."

I spun, trying to move so I could see his face, but he stayed with me so I continued to be blocked from Carter. It was such a protective stance that my stomach filled with fluttering butterflies. It was dangerous to fall down this hole with Lucien again, but I had to ask. "Who are you doing it for?"

He finally turned so I could see his face, and the dark pitch of his eyes had me swallowing hard. "We need to leave," he said, ignoring my question. "They will call an official selection, so if you want a chance to update Mera, it has to happen now."

Carter let out a low growl, drawing our attention; I'd forgotten he was there. "She's not allowed to leave Valdor. She has been called."

Lucien moved so fast that all I felt was the wind against my skin before he was many feet away. His hand encircled Carter's throat as he lifted him and slammed the vampire against a nearby set of windows, cracking them right down the center.

Carter didn't fight back, just stared down the line of Lucien's arm as he held him against the cracking glass. As I raced closer, I heard Lucien snarl. "You get no say here. You cannot even claim master status until you bring a member into your enclave. For now, my word is the only fucking one that matters."

I gasped as he lifted his arm and slammed Carter all the way through the glass this time, releasing him two stories in the air. When I reached the Carter-sized hole, I stared down to find a grinning vampire on the ground. "See you soon, Simone," he said, confirming he knew my name.

Then he was gone.

These bastards moved way too fast for my liking. Not even in my wolf form could I keep up with them, and I hated that advantage.

Hybrid.

That word played around the back of my mind, but just because Carter had said it, didn't mean it would come true. Right now, I had a bit of foreign blood in my system, which was apparently enough to allow me into their selection. But that was probably as far as it would go. Right?

"Wait here," Lucien said shortly, his tone cold and without inflection. "I'm going to sort this out, and then we can head back to the library and wait for the official summons."

"Grea—"

I didn't even get to finish one word before he was gone, leaving me staring through a broken window to the shattered glass below.

Glass-like anyway. Most of the materials used here were similar to Earth's but not the same. It was just easier on my brain if I used familiar terms ... all of which I was overthinking so I didn't have to think about the mess I'd just found myself in.

Closing my eyes, I took a deep breath. *A vampire selection.* How did this shit keep happening to me? I was starting to think I might have been a little tough on my dates back in Torma. Horticulture and social media were starting to sound more interesting by the minute. Both certainly beat a date with a bloodsucker.

"Come on," Lucien said startling me from my messy headspace. "Time to leave before they decide that you're a flight risk."

I *was* a flight risk, but since there was nowhere I could hide from these bastards, running would only delay the inevitable. At least it seemed we got to go back to the library now and not only fill Mera in but come up with a game plan for the selection.

I still didn't have enough information to even know what was going to happen to me, but hopefully, Lucien would tell me every-thing I needed to survive.

When he took off, I followed as close on his heels as I could. "Wait up," I called, picking up the pace. My wolf stirred, feeling even more sluggish; she'd been worse since my arrival in Valdor, which was no doubt thanks to the swirls of vampire blood. Now that I knew it was Lucien's blood inside me, it made sense why it had been dormant for so long. Away from the vampires and Valdor, my wolf was stronger, but now the vampire was surging to life.

"Lucien," I called again, since he'd ignored my last request to wait for me. "Crimson!"

That stopped him in his tracks, and I swallowed roughly. The last time I'd called him that had been the night he'd saved me. I'd kissed him when I'd come back to life—hard—desperately needing some-thing in that moment that I thought Lucien could give me.

Turned out only one of us had been into it.

He didn't turn, but he slowed so I could catch up, and we were soon moving side by side down the stairs and out of the building. In the chamber courtyard, the red was brighter than when we'd entered, so the sun was heading toward their sleep cycle.

Lucien led us to one of the twenty gated exits, no doubt choosing the quickest path out of Valdor. The guards didn't stop us, opening the gates before we even reached them. Some of them had familiar faces, now that I wasn't hanging upside down and unable to move. These guards had been on duty last time, letting me in with one of Lucien's friends: Grant, tier two master of Crimson House.

Grant had convinced me to follow him and touch the stone.

Grant, who I'd flirted with to make Lucien jealous.

All I'd ended up doing was almost dying and getting Grant killed. Lucien hadn't taken kindly to his orders being ignored, especially by one of the few masters he trusted with Crimson House. Grant, with his easy smile, shaggy dark hair, and pretty blue eyes, had been very convincing when he asked me to break some rules with him. It'd never even crossed my mind that he'd been trying to get Lucien killed so he could step into a tier one spot.

Turned out I'd been stupid and naïve, and I was still paying for it today.

At the time I'd hoped that if I threw caution to the wind and took a risk, I might find a future like Mera had. Maybe even a mate like Shadow. The sort of love that destroys worlds.

Instead, all I'd found was pain, grief, and the realization that I was better off sticking to the fantasy stories in my books. There was no huge destiny out there for me, no matter how much my soul craved it.

"Are you sure there's no way for me to get out of this?" I asked as we moved through the maze of streets. Judging by the stones, we were in Crimson House, the red gems littering the pavements and embedded in the walls.

"There's no way without starting a war," he said shortly. "As you were informed the last time, touching our stone comes with a death penalty. It's within the masters' rights to demand it, and the only reason they didn't was my power. They can still enact the punishment retroactively, so it's the selection or death."

Choices, choices.

My chest and throat felt tight as I spoke again. "How many females take part?"

"I don't know," Lucien said, his jaw clenching as he spat those words out. "I won't know until the invitations go out. Unlike you, others have the option of refusing. We don't force our females or males into mating bonds here. For the most part, though, everyone wants a master."

Yeah, I doubted many would turn it down once they knew Lucien was involved.

"Why did you sign up for the selection?" I asked, and he let out a frustrated sound. His hands wrapped around my waist as he hauled me over his shoulder. At least he didn't compel me this time, as he raced through the streets and out into the vast plains that surrounded the city.

It didn't escape my notice that Lucien had gone very quiet and broody on me. I'd never known him to be like that in our previous time together—he had a playboy, joke-around nature in general. Now, darkness seeped out of his being, which was no doubt thanks to me causing continuous problems for him.

I'd done a lot of growing up in the past year, and it was time I gave Lucien the apology I owed him.

When he dropped me down to call on the doorway to the library, I grabbed his hand. He stilled as he stared down at where our hands were clasped. "I'm sorry," I said in a rush. "I'm sorry that last time I didn't listen to you and trusted the wrong vampire. I'm sorry that you had to break rules and give me your blood to keep me safe and that I took advantage of the moment and kissed you. I'm also sorry that I acted like a spoiled brat after that when you told me that there was no future for a vampire and shifter."

My grip on his hand was suddenly replaced with Lucien's strength as he pulled me close enough that our bodies clashed. My breath escaped in a huff as I tilted my head back to see his expression in the soft red light. "I was trying to protect you," he told me, voice biting. "Every step of the way you fought me, and now look where we are. You're in the position I fought so hard to keep you from: in the running to become a plaything for a vampire. Because I have no doubt... Carter will never love another. His mate that was killed was his everything. You fascinate him, but you deserve more."

If I hadn't already been breathlessly pressed against him, his words would have stolen every iota of air from my lungs. No one had ever told me I deserved more, except for Mera. "I'd rather be alone than a substitute for someone's true love," I choked out. "So how do we ensure I don't win?"

Lucien shook his head, and before I could ask him what the fuck that meant, he growled and tightened his hold on me, jerking my feet off the ground as his mouth slammed against mine. It wasn't a soft, gentle kiss but something hard and primal. A clashing of tongues and teeth as I lost myself. Lucien had intrigued me from almost the first moment I met him, and no matter how much I'd wished the feeling away, it had gone nowhere.

When he finally pulled back, we were both breathing heavily and I was trying to figure out what the heck was happening. "You can ensure you don't end up as a mate to Carter," he said, fangs descending until they were all I could stare at, "by making sure you end up as my mate. That's why I signed up. I am literally your last chance at not losing your freedom and, possibly, your life." He released his hold, and my legs barely managed to keep me upright as I landed on them. "So don't fuck it up," he growled.

Back and forth. Hot and cold. This was the same bullshit as the last time I was in his company. As he waved his hand, no doubt calling energy to open a door, I reached out and grabbed onto the black shirt he wore, twisting the material in my fingers for leverage to pull him closer. His eyes widened minutely as he stared down at me —my sudden burst of bravery had taken him by surprise.

"What happens if we do end up as mates at the end of this?" I asked in a quiet voice.

Lucien stared but didn't knock my hand away. "In the end, I can choose you as a mate. Then after some time, we can dissolve the mate bond. I'm a master and there are no rules for me."

Of course. Why would I think any differently.

"If you want to make it seem legit," I bit out, "you're going to have to work for it too. We must at least appear to be in this together."

"This isn't real—"

"I know that!" I cut him off. "But I can't handle your hot-and-cold, passive-aggressive bullshit for the entire duration." I waved my hands toward my face. "Like that kiss just now, which was, as always, followed by rejection. Just stop. Stop doing that. Either leave me alone and I'll take my chances with Carter or go all in for this selection."

"You want me to date you properly during the selection?" His voice grew lower, his eyes swirling with heat. "Do you want me to take care of your needs, B? Is that what you're telling me?"

Fuck me.

When his voice went all rumbly like that...

Shaking my head, I cleared my throat and attempted to pull myself together. "I don't know what's right," I finally said. "My emotions around you have always been complicated, but I do know that I can't deal with the mind games. Not when so much is on the line. I have to know I can completely trust in you."

Lucien was torn, that much was clear in his expression. "You can trust in me, B. I've only ever had your best interests at heart. As for the rest, I promise to stop with the mind games. You're right, we must stand together if we want a chance of walking out of this unscathed. Carter will not take lightly to his plans being shattered by another master, and the last thing you need is to be stuck in the middle of a vampire war. He has to believe it's real, at minimum, so he allows you to choose me at the end."

Has to believe it's real. Just so I never doubted that it was all pretend.

Exhaustion pressed in on me, and I was too tired to argue further. I'd have to just do what Lucien suggested and trust in him.

Hopefully, this time on Valdor worked out better than the last.

For all of our sakes.

Chapter Twelve

We returned to a library on fire. Literally.

"What the hell," I exclaimed as I hurried out of the shelving near Valdor's door and into the main area to try and see where all the billowing black smoke was coming from. "Who is hurting the library?"

The *who* in question came raging around the corner, and it was only because Mera dropped her flames at the last second that I wasn't burned to a crisp when she threw herself at me. Her hug was so firm that I felt my ribs rearrange themselves before settling back into place. There was no belly between us anymore, and it seemed she was already back in her normal jeans.

"Meers," I said, pulse racing. "Is our baby girl okay?"

She just held me tighter, and right when I was about to freak out, I felt Shadow close in on us. He came from the same direction as Mera, so I could lift my head and see he held their daughter, clad in a black jumpsuit, comfortably in his huge, tatted arms. The baby was sound asleep, clearly uncaring about the chaos Mera was causing, and I'd have to say she looked content being held by a creature that gave most of us nightmares.

"Simone!" Mera snapped as she pulled away, drawing my attention to her face. "How could you go to Valdor without us? You had no idea of the dangers you were facing, and everyone just let you leave!"

Ah, the flames were starting to make more sense, and at least it seemed with Mera wielding them, none of our books were destroyed. It was just her body spontaneously combusting.

"I told the others to let you know we were leaving," I reminded her. "Plus, I had Lucien with me."

Mera didn't seem to think that was an adequate response as she shook me. "You had Lucien with you last time and some horrible shit still went down. Shit that none of us even know about!"

I felt the brush of Lucien's energy against mine as he moved closer, and his blood responded inside me by swirling in hot arcs. "I think it's time to fill you in on what happened with Simone in Valdor. She's under a compulsion from many masters that I can't lift alone, but I'm under none. Best we are all on the same page moving forward since things have escalated past what I expected."

Mera was trying to kill him with her glare. "You better fucking start talking, Lucien, or I will rearrange your internal organs, starting with your balls."

In case anyone was wondering, Mera did fail biology in school, but that felt like a deliberate mistake.

I turned my head in time to see Lucien's lips twitch. "Fair enough. Let's get comfortable."

Mera didn't release me, not even as we made our way to the dining room and sat at their usual table. Angel and Reece weren't here, and neither were most of the other males that made up Shadow's inner circle. It was just Mera, Shadow, Lucien, and me. Oh, and the baby. Speaking of...

"Does she have a name yet?" I asked as Mera let out an exaggerated huff.

"She does. Don't change the subject. The naming ceremony will not go ahead until you've dealt with your Valdor issues. Which you will tell us about now."

The short, sharp sentences were all we needed to hear to know that Mera meant business. She would not let this slide again, and I was secretly grateful that all the information would finally be out in the open.

Lucien, who sat across from me, leaned back in his chair and crossed his arms over his chest. He looked somewhat relaxed, but I'd spent enough time watching him to notice the tension in his broad shoulders and defined jawline. "When I took Simone to Valdor to protect her from what was happening in the library, my plan was for her to just stay in my house and lay low. As a tier one master, no one enters my domain without my permission, so it was the best way to ensure she remained safe and..."

"Uneaten?" Mera suggested when Lucien appeared lost for an appropriate word.

He nodded, flashing his perfect, white teeth. "Exactly. Valdor is not a world that any enter except vampires and occasionally..."

"Food."

Mera was on fire with finishing his sentences tonight, but he never snapped at her. For alpha males, they were surprisingly okay with alpha females too. Unlike many of the Torma shifters I knew.

Lucien hurried on with his story. "The problem we ran into is that Simone is a strong, intelligent, wild creature, and keeping anyone like that caged for long was obviously going to be an issue. She started to push back against my rules. At first it was just exploring my yard, but then she wanted to see Crimson City and to meet other vampires and to live her life on her terms."

I'd brought everything on myself. We all knew that. Lucien was trying to make me sound less like a stubborn dickhead than I'd actually been.

"I've changed since Valdor," I told them all, relieved that I could say that much. "I don't rush in like I used to. I'm more measured in my response to what life throws at me because I fucked up bad there."

My mouth was shut again, but I'd managed to get that sentence out.

Lucien shook his head. "It was not all her fault. I'm rarely in Valdor, so when I am, I have to deal with enclave and master business. I left Simone alone, relying on trusted friends to keep her safe. And that was my mistake. Grant, a tier two master who often helped with enclave business, decided he wanted my position. He saw Simone as a weakness to use against me, and when he convinced her to let loose and have some fun, he took her to the Master Chambers where we keep the Stone of Katu, our most sacred rock from the vampire god."

Mera gripped my hand tighter as the story went on. Shadow, meanwhile, looked to be reserving judgement as he slowly patted his daughter's back as she snuggled against his huge chest.

"Simone touched the stone."

That meant something to Shadow but not Mera, judging by their expressions.

"It carries a death sentence," Shadow rumbled, and that was when his mate gasped and just about broke my fingers. She ended up jumping to her feet, looking furious.

"Yes," Lucien said quickly. "The guard ripped her throat out on sight, but I got there in time to save her and destroy Grant. He'd been hoping Simone would die and he could blame it all on me so that I'd have the death sentence, but he underestimated this shifter's will to live. She held on until I arrived and could save her."

"What happened next?" Mera bit out, her face pale.

"The masters agreed to free Simone, as long as she didn't return to Valdor again."

"And I never planned on it," I got out drily.

"They called her back though," Mera pushed.

Lucien let out an annoyed rumble of a sound. "Yes, apparently when Simone touched the stone, she sent out a pulse of energy that called to a master without an enclave, a powerful, ancient being who is strong enough to challenge even me."

"Really?" Shadow shook his head. "I find that hard to believe."

Lucien shot his brother a smirk. "Look, I can't be sure since he's never challenged me, and I haven't seen him in action for centuries. After his mate was killed, he went into hiding. He takes no enclave and claims no land, but we knew he was in Crimson City somewhere. He's been left to exist, since no one wants to challenge him and find out exactly how powerful he is. But now he's suddenly decided that he wants to rejoin vampire society. He's called for a selection to find a new mate."

"And what the hell does that have to do with Simone?" The pitch in Mera's voice was growing shriller, which appeared to be the one thing that could disturb Shadowshine Jr from her peaceful slumber.

The tiny baby stirred, waving little hands around, the black jumpsuit highlighting the shimmery bronze of her skin. Golden eyes met mine, and I managed to hide my flinch at the spark of awareness present within them. Mera reached down to scoop the baby up from Shadow. He didn't protest, but when she turned around to hold the child out to me, a rumble escaped from the beast.

Mera shot him a glare over her shoulder. "Come on, you possessive bastard. You're going to have to let her go eventually. Our daughter will be ten and unable to use her legs."

"She will be perfect," Shadow shot back in a huff of smoke, eyes tracing from his mate down to his baby. Mera was vastly underestimating his possessiveness and how long it was going to last. This beast was a goner.

We all better hope their kid liked us, or Shadow would be arranging our funerals without a second thought.

Chapter Thirteen

Shadow calmed when Mera brought the baby to her chest and started to gently rock her. "Anyway, back to Simone. What does this selection ceremony have to do with her? She's a shifter, right? Surely, there's no reason to call her back for this event. Does she have to touch the stone again or something?"

Lucien dropped the relaxed pose, leaning forward and pressing his hands against the table. I couldn't help but notice how much space they took up, big, strong hands, reminding me of a shifter. Vampires were not like those in human lore, refined and sophisticated. Valdor vampires were built like warriors, with the rumbly personality to go with it.

"When I saved Simone," Lucien started slowly, "there was no option but to use my blood and hope it healed her. I'd never fed a shifter before—or any being for that matter—so I had no idea what would happen. But she was going to die either way, so I had to give it a shot." His gaze met mine, and I swallowed hard as the memories of his mouth on mine returned. "Turns out shifter and vampire blood are.... compatible." His voice lowered. "Simone still has my energy within her, mingling with her own. It's growing stronger as time goes on, and at this point, she can no longer be considered fully shifter."

I waited for this to blow my damn mind and send me into a crazed state, but it just didn't freak me out like it should.

Somehow I was adjusting to the new level of crazy better than expected.

"For a while now," I managed to say, "I've felt like my wolf's energy was being suppressed by this cloud of power inside. Now we know it's Lucien's blood."

Mera looked like she wanted to scream, but when Lucien continued talking, she managed to remain quietly vibrating in her rage. "For now, the vampire blood inside her is a technicality that will allow her in the selection, and since Carter requested it as part of his mate call, the masters were inclined to force the issue. They want him to step up as a new tier one master, bringing more power to Crimson City."

"Why didn't you just say no?" Mera snapped. "There must be a right to choose."

"There is," Lucien agreed. "And under normal circumstances that would have worked, but they could still decide to punish her for touching the stone, so it's enter the selection or die."

Before Mera could explode, Shadow leaned forward. "The vampire blood is weakening your wolf?" he rumbled.

I shrugged. "It feels like she's wading through jelly to rise up, and I don't have the same urge to shift as I used to."

Mera looked absolute horrified. "What if Shadow went there and reminded them that shifters are his and pissing him off is a really bad idea? Not to mention pissing off his mate." She bared her teeth as the air grew hotter around us.

Shadow was on his feet in the next second, moving around his mate and daughter to stop behind my chair. As I tilted my head back to see what was going on, he wrapped one huge hand around my head and cheek, and I gasped as the burn of his power zipped under my skin. For what felt like an eternity, I couldn't move, trapped in his hold. The only part of me reacting was my wolf as she surged forward, desperate to frolic in the energy of our creator. Our god.

So freaking weird that he was also my best friends' mate.

When he finally released me, I shook my head. It took a few second for my scattered thoughts to realign enough for me to notice that a big body stood between Shadow and me. It took another few seconds to figure out who it was: Lucien.

He'd been the one to break the hold.

"What the fuck are you doing?" Shadow roared. "You dare interfere?"

Lucien's body grew larger to match Shadow's, and though I couldn't see his face, I had no doubt he was black-eyed with fangs out as he faced off against his brother. "You don't handle Simone like that." A rumbling rasp of words. "Not now. Not ever."

A fucking feather could have knocked me off my chair. Lucien was defending... me? Against Shadow, his oldest friend. I expected it from Mera, but the vampire would never have challenged Shadow for me before.

Turning toward Mera in the hope she had some information I was missing, I found that she looked as wide-eyed and confused as I felt. It didn't stop her from springing into action, moving between the two growling, furious alphas.

I heard some scuffs of shoes and chairs moving across the floor and knew the rest of the room was bailing, smart enough to know that a god battle was no place to hang around.

"Mera!" Shadow roared again. "Take our baby and get away from Lucien."

Shadow's command had no effect on Mera at all; she stood her ground and glared at him. "You need to take a quick walk and cool off," she snapped. "I'm doing my best to work around the parts of your beast that are out of control, but hurting my friends is where I draw the line. All of my friends, including Lucien."

Shadow's next roar shook the damn walls, but for once, he did as he was told and turned to leave. When he was near the exit, he paused briefly to say, "I can't stop the vampires. Unless she can rid herself of Lucien's blood, Simone is as much theirs as she is mine now. It would mean war to pull her from the selection—which we can do. But working out how to fail out of the selection is a better plan to start with."

Then he was gone, taking much of the tension with him.

Mera and Lucien both returned to their seats, and I tried to calm the pounding in my heart and the restless energy of my wolf. Shadow's power had kick-started hers, and she wanted to run. I hadn't shifted in so long, but now was not the time.

A fact my wolf gave zero shits about.

Lurching to my feet, I moved away from the table and chairs and shook out my body. "Are you okay?" Lucien asked, at my side in a beat.

I waved him off, unable to speak as my wolf surged forward. Turning my back, I jerked my shirt off, kicking my shoes aside at the same time. "She's about to shift," Mera told him.

She might have said more, but my ears turned off as I lost myself in the change. Within seconds I'd shaken off my human side, feeling at one with my beast for the first time in months. My wolf was above average in size, her black hair shaggier than many wolves, and I never felt cold in the winter, even during the deepest chills.

Tipping my head back, I howled out a loud call of joy. "Shadow stirred her shifter energy," Mera said, and in my monochromatic vision, it appeared as if she had glowing flames around her. The brightest flame of all was the baby girl in her arms. The child's eyes met mine and held for many long seconds.

Wolf.

I heard the voice, an echo of power in my head, and I didn't freak out because why the hell wouldn't Mera and Shadow's child be able to talk to and—

Come.

My feet were moving before my brain could catch up, and apparently talking in my head wasn't the only thing Shadowshine Jr. could do.

Mera must have felt the use of power because she looked down as I curled up at her feet. "Did you do that?" she asked the baby, reaching out to run a finger down her child's cheek. "We don't control other beings, little one. Give Simone her free will back."

Since I was being held against Mera's legs, I couldn't really see what was happening, but she must have gotten through to the baby because just as quickly as I'd been called, I was released. Shaking off my fur, I backed up a touch, and when I met my best friend's eyes, I called my human side and shifted.

Once upon a time my wolf would never have let me go so quickly, but she was still weaker. What Shadow had done was already wearing off. It had been a temporary fix of shifter energy, but Lucien's vampire blood was strong and unwilling to release me.

Standing there naked and shaking, I dropped my hand to the table to support myself. Mera moved toward me, but I flinched as the child got closer. I saw the hurt on my best friend's face, but my reaction had been instinctive. This baby was not even a day old, and already she could talk in my mind and force her will on me.

"She only wanted to touch your wolf," Mera said softly. "Shadow is her father, after all."

My heart ached at the pain I'd just caused her, and as I straightened and attempted to pull myself together, a warm shirt was slipped over my head. With a jolt, I turned to find Lucien with a huge expanse of golden skin and muscles on view since I was now wearing his shirt.

His body heat engulfed me, while the scent that wafted from the shirt made me dizzy. But there was no time to lose myself. Tearing my eyes from Lucien, I faced Mera. "I'm sorry for flinching, Meers," I said, taking a step forward and stumbling. My body was exhausted, and if I didn't rest soon, I'd just pass out where I stood. "My reaction was instinctive. Self-preservation. It's natural to fear someone as powerful as she is, but you know I'll always love you and your child. Even if she's as strong and scary as her father."

I tried to it make a joke, but it fell flat. Mera, thankfully, was an understanding person. "I'm sorry she did that. I think you just reminded her of a big fluffy puppy, and she wanted to play with you. I promise that we'll spend a lot of time teaching her power boundaries."

Lucien, who remained close by—so close I could feel his energy tingling over my skin—said, "She's very aware and strong for a newborn. I can't wait to see what she can do when she's older."

Mera let out a choked laugh. "Terrible twos are going to be interesting."

"Understatement of the year," I managed to say. "But you and Shadow are more than capable of handling whatever your baby or life throws at you."

The door opened with a bang, and we all turned to see Reece fly through.

"Angel is having her baby," he barked out. "Or, at least, she is refusing to until you're all there."

He waved in a manner that indicated if we didn't move our asses, we would be swept up in a desert storm.

"So soon, is everything okay?" Lucien asked the desert deity.

Reece nodded in jagged movements. "Yes. Our child is ready."

Simple as that.

"Looks like you won't be facing the terrible twos alone," I whispered to Mera as we headed toward Reece.

All I got in return was her laughter, and when her baby's unusual eyes met my gaze, I had to laugh too.

Here was hoping that their sense of humor remained true.

They were going to need it.

Chapter Fourteen

Compared to Mera's pregnancy, Angel's had been relatively short and uneventful. There had been no wars or an end of the worlds to deal with, and it appeared to be a very short gestation for their child.

But one part of her pregnancy was similar to Mera's—this child was also a first of its kind. The first to be born of a Desert Land deity and an Honor Meadow transcendent. The first born of power beyond the normal, conceived in a grotto of gods. The silver sands there, filled with original magic and creation, would be its legacy.

Mera's child was scary, and I had a feeling that Angel and Reece's would be exactly the same.

Reece hurried through the Library of Knowledge and toward one of the doors that I could only assume led to the Honor Meadows. He didn't look back as he powered on, and I was finding it hard to believe that Angel had even convinced him to leave her side to find Mera.

"It's weird," Mera said as we raced between the shelves. "But I didn't feel her through our bond. No labor pains, no call to me, and even now there's nothing. What does that mean?"

She closed her eyes, lifting her child against her chest. "Is our bond damaged?"

Shadow appeared from wherever the fuck he'd gone, and somehow, he knew I needed pants, which he handed to me. As I pulled on black sweats under Lucien's shirt, I watched as Shadow hugged Mera against him. They didn't squish the baby, not that I was worried; she was far less fragile than her newborn appearance indicated.

"The energy required for this birth will take all of Angel's focus," Shadow answered her question from before, then breathed in her scent like the five minutes he'd spent away from his mate and child had hurt him. "Your bond will reaffirm itself as soon as you have both recovered from birthing god-children."

Mera lifted herself up to press her lips against Shadow's, but he didn't allow her the quick kiss she'd been aiming for. Changing the angle, he slanted his mouth against hers so he could possess and dominate her completely.

As I turned away from them because, *hot damn*, Lucien filled my vision. He was closer than I'd thought, and in my next breath, cherry and oak invaded my lungs. It continued to sink into my body, swirling and joining his blood inside.

I'd never felt like this with any other being, not male or female, shifter or supernatural. The insane need he created within me was so strong that it had almost crumbled my world last time. Being away from him hadn't lessened it, even as I'd fought to move on.

There had been no moving on, and I wasn't sure what to do now.

Lucien had made it no secret that we weren't compatible, and while he might be participating in this fake relationship to save me from Carter, I knew it would end as soon as the selection did. And I would be crushed.

"Come on," Reece all but roared, his patience completely shot. "Otherwise, I'll leave your asses and you can figure out how to find us."

Thankful to have a distraction from the vampire, I hurried toward Reece. The others did the same, and Shadow didn't appear remotely upset with his friend's outburst. If there was one thing the beast understood, it was losing your shit over your mate.

Lucien was right beside me, his presence both comforting and mild torture. "We have time for this, right?" I asked him. "I want to be there, but I don't want to bring war to their door if the vampires get pissed off because we're late for the selection."

Reece was at the door now, holding it open so we could all step through. Lucien caught my hand at the last moment so that I wasn't crossing without his help—useful since I had no idea how to control these doorways. "We have time," he said. "There's been no official call yet, and it will take them a day at least to send out a summons for the opening ceremony. I believe you were brought in early to ensure that I would no longer stand in the way of their request."

"Bet none of them expected you to sign yourself up for a mate too," I said with a strangled laugh just as we stepped through to the Honor Meadows.

Lucien's response was lost in the swirl of energy from the doorway. It felt stronger and drier than the previous doorway as we arrived in a golden field. The grass itself was what gave the world a golden sheen, and it reminded me so much of the golden fields outside of Crimson City.

Everything smelled fresh, the low light was akin to dusk back in Torma, and the feel of a summer afternoon permeating the air.

Reece took off into the field, stopping a few hundred yards from where we'd started, at a point that looked the same as every other part of this field. "She only has a few levels built up," he said as he dropped to his knees.

I was just wondering what he was doing when he slammed his hands into the dirt.

What in the...? I knew there were levels of power in this world, but was Reece *digging his way to the next one?*

I stared wide-eyed, wondering what was going to happen next, and then he appeared to grab two sides of the small hole he'd made, and he... tore the land apart. The golden grass moved under his touch, and when he was done, there was a deep chasm in the earth.

Reece stepped through first and then Shadow and Mera. As I went to follow, a firm grip stopped me from moving and *my stupid heart jumped* as Lucien took hold of my hand again like we were a damn couple or something. He was really taking this "fake mate" thing seriously.

For so many complex reasons, part of me wanted to tug my hand away. But I also knew that would make me look petty and juvenile, so I bit back my fears and insecurities and settled into the moment. Best to focus on the fact that we were about to be present for another monumental birth.

An experience I never would have had back in Torma.

These were the moments that I had to live for.

In case they were my last.

Chapter
Fifteen

T urned out that in the Honor Meadows, all the layers of the world felt real and whole and complete. We stepped through the golden field to find ourselves in an ocean land with limitless blue sky above. It was warm with a salty scent in the air, and when I crouched down, the sand felt real and hot.

There was no way for me to decipher the illusion here. Even when my wolf prowled to the surface, curious about this new energy, she found no scent other than salt and sand. "This is unbelievable," I murmured, turning slowly to take it all in. "How is it even possible?"

Lucien, who'd let go of my hand at this point, watched me closely, like I was more interesting than the layer of magic we were in.

"Honor Meadow energy is very"—he paused, as if to consider his next words— "elemental. Built from the power of original creation. It allows them to form realities which are in no way illusions."

I was finally beginning to understand the deferential way Angel had been treated back when Mera first met her. Back when she was robotic and cold but also feared.

"She had thousands of these layers?" I shook my head. "How much power would be needed to created even one?"

"A lot," he told me. "An incredible amount. The fact that she's been able to gather enough to build even a few layers in this short amount of time, speaks of her internal source of power. Not to mention what she gained through her bond with Reece and ability to hold the silver sands."

"Reece gained too," I shot back. Angel had sacrificed her power and life for him, and that should not be downplayed.

"He gained everything," Lucien said, his voice growing deeper with emotion. "He's one lucky male to have found a female like Angel. I will never discount that. I just meant that together they have built on their base energy. A team effort."

He turned then to make his way into the next level, and I wasn't sure if I'd annoyed him by snapping about equal rights. The moment felt too awkward to ask, so I simply followed as he moved along the beach. We were a few minutes behind the others, who had already left this level, but the opening remained.

When we stepped through, I still had to close my eyes, even though I knew the drop was no more than a short step to the next level, which was a jungle. In here, all signs of the ocean were gone. That light breeze was replaced with a heavy humidity, the briny scent now rich and earthy.

There were predators in this level—my wolf was aware enough to recognize their distinct scent and energy—but at least they felt mostly curious versus murderous. "Is this the level?" I asked Lucien as we stepped into the dense jungle, undergrowth crushing beneath our feet. I was still in my black flats, and it felt like a million years ago I'd wanted to throw my phone as it rudely awoke me.

How long since I'd even eaten or had a drink?

No wonder my wolf was weak, but apparently there was no time for anything other than childbirth and vampires today. Sustenance would have to wait.

"This is the level she'll be on," Lucien said. "Angel's energy is strong here, and I know this is her preferred home base."

We wandered until we heard voices, and not a minute later, we came upon a cabin that blended almost seamlessly into its environment. Mera and Shadow were standing out front, and as my bestie turned toward me, I noticed that she was feeding her baby, its small face almost engulfed by a massive boob. "If I don't feed, my tits feel like they're about to explode," she groaned.

I had to chuckle. "Hopefully, your little one is hungry because, damn girl, your boobs are... I mean, that almost looks painful."

She shook her head, face pulling into a grimace. "It's the weirdest, most uncomfortable feeling. The pressure builds up... and yeah, anyway. She's feeding well, so hopefully I can switch her to the other side in a minute and save us all the risk of a milk shower."

A look of intrigue and *something darker* crossed Shadow's face. I really didn't want to delve into the darker side because there was a decent chance he'd just developed a new kink. But to each their own. With the way my dreams had been for the past many months, I was in no position to kink judge anyone.

"Is everything okay with Angel," Lucien asked, facing the cabin. There was no sign of life inside, even though I had to assume Reece and Angel were in there.

"Reece is just letting her know we're here," Mera said. "We thought it was a bit rude to all barge in on her at once."

"Do transcendents birth children the same way as shifters?" I asked.

"As far as I'm aware, it's the same basic concept," Mera said.

She'd told me a while ago that most of the inhabitants of the worlds connected to the Solaris System had a similar reproductive process to shifters. That didn't mean all of us supernaturals were compatible to create life together, but it helped in understanding the biology of how it worked.

For me, when travelling to these fantasy worlds, I enjoyed when there were aspects that made sense straight away. It was how I liked my books too, which was probably why my favorite stories were urban fantasy. Elements of familiar intertwining with the fantastical.

Stepping through these layers of the Honor Meadows was so new and mind-blowing that if I'd had to figure out the landscape as well, it would be too much. But an ocean and a jungle were familiar, so my brain could deal.

Before I could spend any more time contemplating the nuances of my personality, the door was flung open as Reece exited onto the wood porch. "She's close now," he snapped, sounding stressed. "And she's asking for Mera."

Mera didn't even hesitate, rushing up the stairs and into the house with the baby clutched to her chest. Shadow, for once, didn't charge after her. Even the big bad beast knew better than to challenge an in-labor Angel. "I'll keep you updated best I can," Reece said as he too stepped back toward the open door. "With any luck, we will need no additional assistance and our next member of this family will arrive safe and well."

"We are sending energy your way," Shadow said simply.

Reece nodded, and it was clear that meant more to him than I understood. He was gone in the next minute, and that left the three of us to cool our heels while we waited for more news.

Chapter Sixteen

The first ten minutes in the clearing were quiet. Shadow and Lucien were well versed in sitting in silence without fidgeting, while I, on the other hand, was more than a little uncomfortable with a beast-god and a master vampire on either side of me.

This was going to be a long afternoon.

"What's the plan for Valdor," Shadow said, and I was grateful for the distraction, even if the subject wasn't my favorite.

"The plan is to get Simone through the selection alive and without ending up as Carter's mate." Lucien's response was sharp—he wasn't happy about this situation still.

That made two of us, buddy.

"Lucien nominated himself as a master looking for a mate," I added.

This took Shadow aback. The beast didn't let his real emotions slip much, but I saw confusion and surprise briefly crease his brow. "You were determined never to mate or have a family," he said to

Lucien. "You've never even drunk from someone or allowed any to drink from you in worry that would trigger something. Have you changed your mind?"

Now I was the one surprised. Lucien didn't want a mate or a family... ever? I'd thought it was just about me being a shifter.

"I haven't changed my mind," he told Shadow. "I've lived a long life, and in that time I've witnessed much darkness. I'm just not sure I can risk children in this world."

His eyes drifted toward the cabin. "Though I will admit to a slight pang in seeing young born into adoring families."

"The fear is there too," Shadow admitted gruffly. Reluctantly too, if his harsh exhalation was any indication. "I've always been untouchable. No one could hurt me because I had no weak spots. Then Mera came along, a damn sun that scorched through my shield and filled me with softer emotions I didn't think existed within my being."

"And your daughter," Lucien said. "Has she changed you too?"

"Beyond anything I could have ever imagined," Shadow admitted.

"I'm not sure I can handle it," Lucien said softly as his eyes met mine. "It has taken me dozens of shifter lives to get my emotions under control. Vampires feel strongly, ten times amplified. The highs are incredible, but the lows... they're not always survivable."

I sensed there was some backstory there, and I hoped before this was all over, I'd at least know that part of him. The reason he remained eternally alone.

"Back to Simone," Shadow said, clearing his throat. "How can you ensure that she will end up with you and not Carter? I assume this selection will take into consideration more than just your choice on a mate. There'll be trials?"

Lucien started to pace. "The selection is a compatibility contest, and to ensure that, there are some trials. Selected females are eliminated throughout, and there's the possibility Simone will be knocked out early, and then I'll be able to bow out. But I have a feeling Carter will ensure she makes it through to the final round, so the stronger plan is to convince him and all the masters that Simone and I are the best match. They already know how protective I am of her, so I think this can work."

"Do vampires have true mates like shifters?" I asked.

He shook his head. "Not really. We have what we call a blood call bond, where we find someone with compatible blood that can sustain us. It's so rare. And you won't know until you exchange blood and feel strengthened, not to mention a pull toward each other."

"It speaks of a compatible soul," Shadow added.

Lucien nodded. "Yep, it's our deepest level of connection, but very few even look for it these days."

"Sounds like a true mate bond to me," I murmured. "The pull toward each other and the need..."

Lucien shrugged. "I mean, I guess it could be looked at that way," he said. "I've seen enraged, blood-call bonded partners destroy cities when their mate was threatened. I've also heard the loss of such a mate is not survivable by the other."

Shadow's laugh was dark. "I can relate."

"Me too."

They both looked at me again, and I realized that I'd let my inside thoughts slip out. In a rush to explain, I added, "I relate in the way that while I don't have a true mate, I understand why they destroy cities. I think it's perfectly reasonable to lose your shit for those you love. I don't even have to be mated to feel that primal drive. In a way, you're fighting for your own life since you wouldn't survive without your mate, and self-preservation is one of our strongest instincts."

Two sets of eyes burned into me, one filled with flames and the other green, streaked in darkness. What I'd said had resonated with both of them, no doubt for different reasons, but it did make me squirm to be under this level of scrutiny.

The urge to fan my face was strong.

Angel better have her baby sooner rather than later because I wasn't sure how much longer I could hang with all of this intense alpha-ness and keep my sanity.

"I understand why you are Mera's best friend," Shadow finally said, and he couldn't have given me a greater compliment. "You will make a worthy mate and are the best example of what I expect shifters to be. Not the shame that many have brought on themselves."

He patted me on the head, and fuck if I wasn't his pet wolf now. *Worthy.*

Thanks, oh master of mine.

Even Lucien grinned at that, and once again, I was stuck ignoring fire in my belly and need in my soul. His definition of a blood-call bond felt like what was happening inside me right now, his blood taking up residence while need for him drove me almost crazy.

I knew better than to say anything about it, but maybe there was a deeper reason for the pull I felt to the vampire. Maybe our souls were more compatible than he thought.

Or maybe I was in so deep that, this time, I would lose my heart for good.

Chapter Seventeen

The next little while was spent discussing the selection. Lucien gave us an indication of the trials that would occur, which included hunting, scavenger trials, home visits, and dates. "B will just have to ensure that she repels Carter to the best of her ability," he continued. "He already expects they have a blood compatibility, thanks to her touch of the stone activating his energy and breaking through his darkness."

"Why did that even happen?" I asked.

"I have no idea" Lucien admitted. "No one has ever touched the stone who wasn't vampire. Maybe that's just a normal burst of power from its securities, and Carter was simply in the right place. Or maybe you truly are compatible to vampires, hence why your energy called us. I know it was how I found you in time to save you."

He'd never told me that before, and I found it mildly comforting to know it wasn't just crazy-ass Carter I'd called. "I've felt a pull toward Valdor ever since that night," I told him.

Shadow shifted closer, his gaze moving between Lucien and me. "Are you sure it's Valdor calling you back?"

None of us could miss the implication there, but Lucien and I maturely ignored it completely.

"Just remember," Shadow continued, "that while I can't interfere in a political manner, I can still be there as Simone's family. Mera considers her a sister, and so do I."

My stomach jumped at being claimed as family by a being we'd always worshipped as a god. *Whose life am I living?*

"I protect my own as well," Lucien growled back.

As odd as that response was, it reminded me of a shifter's possessiveness, and I understood where it came from. At the moment I was Lucien's responsibility, so he'd taken offense to Shadow's words, as though they were a slight against his ability to take care of this situation.

Typical alpha male bullshit.

No way did my damp panties have anything to do with that. It was... hormones.

"My offer in no way takes away from what you're doing to protect her," Shadow said without heat. "As with Reece and our last foray into the Desert Lands, sometimes situations end up being more than expected, and a little backup never goes astray."

Lucien relaxed as he nodded, leaving that conversation there to die.

I was fairly certain all of us were relieved when Mera appeared in the doorway. "She had a boy," she cried. Shadow was up on the porch and by her side in a heartbeat. He took their baby from her, cradling the tiny child against him and freeing up Mera's hands.

I followed, making sure to keep my distance now that beastie Shadow had his child back in his possession. "Baby and momma okay?" I asked.

Mera threw her arms around me, hugging me tight. She smelled like energy and milk, giving off a true mother-earth vibe. "They're amazing. I can't get over the adrenaline shot of bringing life into this world. Now that I'm not the one getting my vagina ripped in two, I get to enjoy the other parts."

Shadow lifted their daughter, moving her closer to his face, and when she reached out and placed a hand on his cheek, that freaking beast actually smiled. A true smile.

What was happening?

Mera started to drag me toward the door before I could further observe the personality transplant her mate was going through. "Angel asked that you all come in to visit so she can thank you for your positive energy and thoughts."

Inside the cabin, Mera moved so fast that I barely had a chance to notice the sparsely decorated space. We walked through an entranceway and past a few rooms that mostly appeared to contain weapons. When we ended up at a bedroom, Mera didn't pause at the threshold.

The wood-lined room was simply decorated, with a large bed, a few pieces of armor on the walls, and a thick, fluffy rug under our feet. I really wished I'd had time to take my shoes off because the white, wool-like material was not forgiving when teamed with shoes and a forest floor, but Mera never gave me the chance.

When we reached the bed, it was to find Angel laid back against a bunch of pillows, her long hair fanned out around her. There was no sign she had just given birth; her face was clear and relaxed and her stomach no longer swollen, which I could see clearly as the sheets were around her waist, while a tiny boy nestled against her breast, already feeding.

She looked up as I leaned over the side of her bed. "Simone," she cried. "Thank you for being here."

I reached out and brushed my hand along her arm. "Girl, he's absolutely stunning. I can't even with you and Mera having such perfect and amazing babies."

Reece, who was on the opposite side of the bed to where we sat, reached out and placed his huge hand on his son's back, almost completely covering the child. There was a swarth of dark hair on the baby's head, with just the slightest curl to it. His skin was darker than Mera's baby's, a deep rich brown, and I wondered if he would have his father's bright blue eyes or Angel's pink tinged ones.

I couldn't wait to find out.

Mera was right; there really was a buzz in this creation of life and seeing the results of mixing power and genetics. Children born of true love and mate bonds.

It was a new kind of high.

Shadow and Lucien pressed in behind Mera and me. The air was hotter than it had been before as all of us crowded closer to celebrate this new life. After another minute, their baby stopped feeding, and Angel used energy to clothe herself as she sat up to lay him on the bed, secure in the space between her legs. "We are honored for you all to meet Damon, named for the warrior god recognized in both our races. Born of meadow and desert, a bridge between two worlds, and the miracle that we never expected."

"You said his name," I gasped. Multiple gazes turned my way, and I hurried to add. "Which I love, of course. It's just we're still calling Mera and Shadow's baby Shadowshine Jr because we need a naming ceremony."

Angel chuckled. "We don't have naming ceremonies in our culture. I do need to take Damon for a blessing from Tholi, our spiritual guide. Plus, he must be honored in the Sacred Lands and silver sands of the grotto, but there's no need to keep the name hidden before these blessings."

Shadow leaned over, and I wasn't the only one to gasp when he placed the little girl on the bed, gently settling her beside Damon. The fact that he'd willingly let his child out of his or Mera's arms was also a miracle.

We all stared down at their overwhelming cuteness. Mera's child was no bigger than Angel's, despite the difference in gestation periods. "Were they technically born on the same day?" I asked.

"Yes!" Mera and Angel cried together.

"Couldn't have planned it better if I'd tried," Mera continued, her voice high with emotion.

"Twin souls," Angel murmured. "Just like their mommas."

I tried not to let that settle as an ache in my heart. Mera was my best friend and sister, but I didn't own her. It was just... I wished to one day be in the middle of the joy and not hovering on the outside.

Today was not the day to dwell, though. It was a day for celebration. "They're pure perfection," I said with a sigh, pressing a hand to my chest. "I've never wanted children, but you could almost change a shifter's mind with these two."

I blinked as Damon reached out his hand and grabbed onto Shadowshine Jr's. Before anyone could make a sound, a burst of power slammed into us, and I would have stumbled back if Lucien's bulk behind me didn't keep me standing.

"Shadow—" Mera got only his name out before both the babies vanished in a flash of dark mist and red sand.

Well, shit.

S hadow and Reece reacted in a heartbeat, swirls of red dust and shadows exploding in the room, just like from their children. They vanished too, presumably after their offspring.

Turning toward Mera, I was surprised to see her looking calm. "What just happened?"

"They've bonded to each other," Angel told me, also relaxed. "They'll be back shortly. This is just a short power journey—we can feel their energy close by."

Mera hopped up on the bed and stretched out beside Angel, the two of them waiting patiently for their babies to return. Sure enough, a moment later, there was another burst of power, and the babies were back in the room, snuggled on their mothers' chests.

Shaking my head, I had to laugh. "You do realize how insanely insane this is, right? Newborns shouldn't be able to do any of this."

Newborns shouldn't even be able to hold their heads up and look around, let alone transport themselves off to places unknown.

Mera and Angel joined me in laughing, but I was fairly certain we were all amused by different parts of this moment. The room filled with dust and smoke and, a beat later, Shadow and Reece all but landed on their mates and children. "Getting a little slow in your old age," Mera joked, then let out an amused shriek when Shadow's smoke engulfed them completely.

A second later, there was no sign of my oldest friend.

"They outran us," Reece rumbled, but he didn't sound angry... he sounded proud. "Their energy is beyond anything I've ever expected."

I backed up a step, sensing that it was time for us to leave. New parents need to bond with their babies—or so I'd heard. My parents had probably thrown me into a cot and left me there until I cried. But Angel and Reece were not like that.

Lucien must have had the same thought, staying with me as we moved toward the door. "Congratulations again, guys," he called as we walked. "Your baby boy is just incredible, and I can't wait to see what he does in life."

"Enjoy your time bonding," I added. "We'll be back soon to see what Damon and Shadowshine Jr achieve, but first we have to head to Valdor for a little vampire bachelorette."

Reece and Angel pulled their attention from their super-powered baby for a moment, but they didn't stop us. "Keep us updated," Angel said when we were almost at the door. "We can be there in a heartbeat."

"I will send messages back through the library," Lucien told them. "It should be okay, though. Best that you enjoy your time as a new family."

We were out the door then, moving across the porch and into the forest.

"Do you know how to get out of here without Reece?" I asked.

Lucien's smile was broad, and I tried not to fixate on the slight points of his fangs. "You underestimate me once again, B. I'll get us out of here without a problem."

I barely heard what he said, so focused on the urge to press my hand to the throb in my neck. Not just that, but I was also focused on the pulse in Lucien's.

The blood inside me had to be forcing this obsession I felt to taste his blood again. Right?

Since I was frozen, Lucien just scooped me into his arms without permission and carried me wedding style for a change. He moved at a speed that had my head spinning, and with the blood pulsing inside me, it was a miracle that I didn't vomit on him. He zoomed up through the layers until we were back in the sunset meadow, where the lighting was exactly as it had been earlier when we entered.

Lucien dropped me to my feet, his hands seeming to linger on the bare skin of my arms as he released me. My body reacted as if he'd grabbed me, fingers biting into my skin as he pulled me toward him, lips crashing into mine, while he—

Fuck.

A low groan escaped me. I could not keep having these out-of-control sexual thoughts about a vampire who'd made it clear that I was a duty. Pressing my thighs together to help ease the ache, I forced myself to focus. I needed my head on straight for this next Valdor adventure.

"I have a question," I said to Lucien, grateful I sounded normal, even if I didn't feel it. "Why would Carter want a mate who will die in a fairly short time compared to your immortal life?"

Lucien, in the process of opening a doorway, turned to meet my gaze. "I believe that if he bonds with you, you'll live the same lifetime that he does. His blood will sustain you."

Vampire blood didn't sustain another vampire unless they had a blood call, but I wasn't a vampire. "I'd have to drink his blood for the rest of my life?"

Lucien nodded. "Yes. Since it appears shifter and vampire energy are compatible, you'd eventually become a full hybrid. I'm not sure, then, if you'd need vampire blood or the imported blood we drink, but either way, your life should extend as long as you want."

"Or as long as Carter wants," I replied drily, "since I'd basically be his pet."

The fact that Lucien spoke so casually of me being a hybrid and I didn't even freak out about it told me that already the changes inside were affecting me. It didn't feel weird to talk about drinking blood, which explained my reaction a moment ago in the forest.

"All of this is redundant, anyway," Lucien said. "Carter will not claim you as a mate while I'm alive and my blood resides within your energy. We are prepared, and we will be even more prepared by the time the official summons arrives."

I could only hope he was right.

"Please tell me being *more* prepared means food and sleep," I said. The moment I mentioned sleep, a yawn nearly split my face in two, exhaustion pressing in on me.

It had been a damn long day, and I hadn't even been the one to have a child. Just thinking about that reminded me of the twin souls. Baby and moms.

"Your energy wanes when you're sad," Lucien said suddenly.

Wait, what?

I blinked at him. "You can feel my energy? I mean, to the degree that you're noticing it waning?"

His nod was brief, even if his expression remained closed off. "The more time we spend together now, the stronger my blood feels within you. I had no idea it would be like this."

"Have you never shared blood before?" It had been mentioned earlier, but I wanted more information.

"I've never shared my blood with another being."

I snorted. "Are you a virgin too?"

Whoops, that shouldn't have slipped out. That was an inside thought.

Thankfully Lucien chuckled. "Sharing blood is an intimacy beyond what most would understand. Sex is one thing, but blood is deeper. You're giving and taking of your energy and essence. It's the lifeforce that keeps us all alive."

And now I really wished I hadn't brought it up, because when a sexy vamp locks glittering green eyes on you, crowding his big body into yours, there's really no place for your mind to go but the gutter.

As Mera would put it: slutterbrain.

I had a really bad case of slutterbrain.

Lucien appeared to enjoy the burning heat in my cheeks, and let me tell you, it had nothing at all to do with embarrassment. Eventually he took pity on me and headed toward the nondescript white door leading back to the library.

That was all it took to remind me that I was about to head into Crimson City again. To compete in a contest that was designed to strip me of my freedoms.

No matter what Lucien said, a part of me worried that the masters had already rigged it to get what they wanted. Or more accurately, what Carter wanted.

If that was the case, our plan would go up in smoke.

Or blood.

Chapter Nineteen

Even though there'd been no official summons yet, Lucien decided it would still be best to return to Valdor and rest at his home. "There's a decent chance they won't allow you to stay with me during the selection," he said as we wove our way through the maze. "Carter will cite it as an unfair advantage, since I am now in the running for a mate as well."

"Where will I stay?" I huffed, struggling to keep up with his pace but determined not to slow us down. "And will I be safe there among vampire females competing to be chosen?"

Lucien caught an arm around my waist and lifted me into his side as he took off, whipping past many curious onlookers, who were no doubt wondering why I was in their city. Until the selection was called, it would be big news that I was wandering around.

"My one stipulation," he told me, voice not even remotely breathless, "is that you have security of my choosing."

Security he'd hopefully be more selective of than last time, seeing as his friend had been the one who'd almost gotten me killed. I would also choose to be less of a fucking moron this time. With any luck, that would keep me alive through this selection.

When we reached Crimson House territory, Lucien slowed and spent some time talking and interacting with the vampires in his enclave. More than a few curious looks were shot my way, but no one mentioned my presence. They knew better than to question their top master.

One thing I appreciated was that no one in Valdor appeared to be homeless or poor. They didn't even have such concepts, with the many provided for by their masters. Lucien, despite all his dislike of being a master, appeared to look after his vampires very well.

It was clear that they adored him.

By the time we reached the large, gated compound where he lived, I was so exhausted I could barely keep my eyes open. My wolf was basically nonexistent inside, and I needed to address whatever was happening to her energy as the vampire energy grew stronger. Being back in Valdor was affecting me. I'd been keeping Lucien's blood at bay all those months in Torma, but here, I could no longer stop its swirls from taking over.

Lucien opened the gates, and we stepped into the front courtyard, which was paved and filled with three large, spouting water fountains, each a depiction of a different god carved from the crimson stone of Lucien's enclave.

Being surrounded by my favorite color always made me feel better, and even when the large gates closed, all but trapping me inside, I'd never felt as free as I did in Lucien's home.

I'd never told anyone this, but Lucien's compound was my secret happy place.

A sanctuary from real life and the dangers that were always around.

"Are you okay?" he asked, too damn observant as always.

"It just feels a little weird to be back here," I lied. "But also, not weird." And there was the truth.

"It felt emptier when you were gone," he admitted, and then he shook his head and strode off, like he hadn't expected to say that out loud.

I followed slowly, trying not to let those words settle into my heart as I stared up at the white, two-story house. Torma had no homes like this, not even among the very elite and richest shifters. The best way to describe it was a mix of contemporary and colonial. It had clapboard in some section, smooth panels in others, and a small front porch led to a door that was twice my height and width.

Huge windows lined the front façade, with more out the back, along with a very large deck looking over a few acres of land. Unlike most of Crimson City, Lucien had plants and herbs and flowers in his garden. He'd spent decades bringing touches of other worlds to his.

"Come in," he called, and I tore my gaze from the house and moved toward the door he held open. Stepping inside, I realized I'd forgotten how vast and impressive the entryway was. It spanned the full two stories, and the ceiling above contained well-placed skylights, giving it a bright and open feel.

The entry was circular in design, with curving stairs that led to the second floor. His massive house had multiple living areas, a huge kitchen, an atrium with glass walls for a full view of the garden, a gym, and theater. The last was not a normal addition to homes in Valdor, but apparently Lucien appreciated the arts and, like with the garden, his home had imported elements from other worlds.

The perks of being best friends with the god who created the Library of Knowledge.

"Your room is just as you left it," he said, and I tried really hard not to react to *your room*. Instead, I pasted on a neutral expression and followed him up to the second level, which housed the dozen or so bedrooms and bathrooms in this place.

The long hall led to Lucien's master suite at the end, which I'd never seen but had spent way too much time thinking about. This time, though, I had a focus and a mission to occupy my thoughts: make it through the selection *not* mated to Carter.

When we reached the room I'd used last time, I entered to find that Lucien was right. Nothing had changed. It had pale blue walls, a large four-poster bed with cream bedding, and two doors that led to the closet and the bathroom. One large bay window let in rays of low, red light, and I wondered if it was close to the sleep cycle. Shutters would close over the windows at that point, and the inside would turn pitch black if you didn't use fake illumination.

Valdor didn't have the same plumbing or technology as Earth, but it was close enough that I never felt completely out of my depth.

As I walked in and collapsed my exhausted ass on the side of the bed, I couldn't get over the sense of calm that filled me. I mean, I should be panicked about being back here, panicked about the selection, and panicked about vampire blood turning me into some sort of hybrid.

But I felt none of that.

"Why does Valdor feel like home to me?" I asked, needing to understand.

He moved closer and, to my surprise, took a seat right beside me—close enough that I could sense his energy swishing across my skin.

"I wish I knew," he said quietly, and there was this odd catch in his tone that had me turning to examine his features. "I also wish I knew why it feels right to have you here and why it was empty when you left. You're a shifter, but it has never felt like there's any difference between our races."

I swallowed roughly. "Is there a chance that Carter is a true match to me then? Should I actually participate in the selection and just see what happens?"

I had no idea why I asked those questions when I knew in my heart that Carter was not the one I wanted.

"He's not for you, B," Lucien said, an edge to his tone. "Trust me on this. I said I would protect you last time, and I failed. There's no chance of that happening again. This time you will obey my rules and stay alive. No exceptions."

Frustration rose inside me for so many reasons. "Stop calling me by my damn blood type," I snapped. "And also, I said I would follow your rules, but don't think you can tell me who is for me. You don't own me."

He reached out and in one swift move turned me so that we were now inches apart, facing each other on the bed. "I don't just call you B because of your blood type," he rumbled as the black crept into his eyes again. "At first it was due to the damn buzzy nature of your personality. You were always everywhere, buzzing around, distracting me from life."

Great, I was an annoying bumblebee. So much better.

"But then" he continued, and I forced myself to breathe through gritted teeth, "I started to understand the true importance of the bee. You see, Earth could not exist without it, a fundamental creature that performs the most important task: creating new life. I didn't understand until you were gone and everything suddenly felt empty. So now, it's *Bee* for more than one reason."

My throat was tight, and in my head, I'd already adjusted my thoughts to *Bee* instead of *B*, because that was actually... kind of perfect.

"Okay," I found myself saying. "I guess *Bee* can stay."

His lips twitched, and he closed the distance until our legs were touching, upper bodies close enough that I could smell every note of cherry. "As to your other point," Lucien continued, leaning in so I was all but engulfed by his huge frame, "about not owning you... While you're here in Valdor, you do belong to me. Mine. Mine to protect and control."

Before I could respond, he leaned over and scraped his fangs slowly across my neck, dragging those tips with such exquisite care that he never broke the top layer of skin. There was no scent of blood, and I almost jerked into him, needing to feel those tips enter my body.

The vamp blood inside me surged as my body pulsed with need. Lucien let out a rumble and was gone from the room in a second. The door slammed closed after him, and I fell off the bed onto my hands and knees on the soft rug. My body trembled as I dug my fingers into the wool, the swirling blood surging and filling my insides until I thought I was going to explode.

I muffled a scream as heat engulfed me. *What was happening?*

Somehow, I managed to drag myself into the bathroom and get the door closed before I continued across the tiles. When I got to the shower, I hit the lever to send freezing cold water onto me. Without thought, my hands scraped at my clothing, getting them off so there was nothing on my sensitive and burning skin.

All the while I prayed the freezing stream would cool me down.

Only it didn't. The heat continued to build, and even though the shower stream soaked me, I knew that the damp heat between my thighs was pure arousal. Pure need. My pussy throbbed with no relief in sight.

My hands slid down my stomach and over the junction of my center; I needed to find relief from this pleasure-pain fire.

I really fucking hoped Lucien was out of earshot by now. Even if it was his damn fault—triggering me with fangs at my throat—I didn't want him here to witness this.

Him taking care of what he'd created was a complication we didn't need, so for now... I would have to take care of it myself.

Chapter Twenty

The icy water against my skin felt like it was awakening pleasure points I'd never even known existed. It wasn't like I was completely naive when it came to sex and arousal. I was a shifter, after all, and we are big on celebrating all of our base instincts—it would be considered odd to make it past your first shift and be a virgin.

I wasn't a virgin. I'd had sex with two males and a few fun sessions with a female. But afterwards, it always felt empty, so I'd decided to wait to find a real partner to learn and grow sexually with. Hence all the first dates and no sex to show for them.

Which, of course, made me a damn expert in getting myself off. But my body had never felt like this before, where my own touch was almost too much stimulation, making the burn worse. It wasn't fading; the blood continued to pulse against my skin like it wanted to expand or explode.

Running my hands across my skin again, I remained sprawled in the huge shower, my breathing harsh and fast as I stroked my clit before sliding one finger and then two inside my pussy. I cried out at the sensation, nerve endings firing and pulsing in time to the blood, and there was no way I could stifle the moans.

Moisture pooled under my fingers as I mindlessly thrust, desperate for any release, but no matter how close I got to orgasm, I could never push myself over the edge. None of my usual tactics worked, not nipple stimulation, clit stimulation, or my favorite: the G-spot.

As I tore my hand free, arousal coated my fingers in a way that told me I should be orgasming by now. *Gods, please fucking help me.*

The pain was too much, and as I curled in on myself and sobbed, I wondered if I was dying. What the hell had Lucien done to me?

Hands that weren't mine stroked across my sensitive flesh, and I cried out, jerking my head up to see piercing green eyes. "What's happening to me?" I screamed, too far gone to be embarrassed.

His face was tense, expression serious. "We ignited the blood inside you. It's been dormant for too long, and you need that blood removed and then replaced."

At this point I could barely understand what he was saying; darkness pressed in on me, even as I was still trying to reach down and relieve the pressure. Lucien caught my hand. "That won't work, Bee. You need to listen to me."

My ears were barely cooperating, but those words registered, so I nodded.

"I'm going to bite you," he told me in quick sharp words. "I'm going to do it as quickly as I can, and it will hurt at first, but then it'll feel good. I need you to stay still so I don't lose control."

I was nodding again, so desperate that I didn't care if he had to kill me. I'd take that over the inferno inside.

Lucien's growl was long and low—and deep enough to nearly rumble the walls of the shower stall. My eyes were glued shut as I waited for him to lift me from the shower; instead... he got in with me.

Somehow, I opened my eyes in time to see black irises burning into my face as he lowered his head between my legs. "Wait—?"

I got that one word out as his mouth landed on my aching pussy, and even though he'd said he was going to bite, his tongue swiped across all the moisture there. I wanted to stay still as promised, but... fuck. My body jerked and arched into him because, unlike my hand, his mouth felt amazing. Felt like exactly what I needed.

His tongue swiped through my arousal again, and I didn't imagine his groan. "Hold on, baby Bee," he rumbled, and then there was a sharp scrape as he buried his fangs in my upper thigh, right near the femoral artery.

The prick barely hurt, but the first pull of blood from my body increased the burning, and I screamed so loudly that I heard my voice crack. As he settled in between my legs, half of his frame out of the shower, he held me down as he drank more of my essence in.

With each pull, the fire eased, and I arched against him as pleasure took over from the pain. Unable to stop myself, the tight bud of pleasure in my center spiraled out of control, and I came so hard that I smashed my head on the floor as stars danced before my eyes.

Lucien didn't stop there, continuing to feed from my leg as he lifted one hand and slid his fingers through my folds and inside me. One finger at a time, he pushed through the tight muscles, scraping every pleasure point.

With fangs and fingers inside me, I rode his hand, lost in the absolute bliss he was creating. I'd never felt anything like this before, and I would do a damn lot to feel it again. When he was finished with my thigh, he swiped his tongue across the wound, and just as I was hit with sadness to know that it was over, he slid his mouth down my clit once more, taking the tight bud between his teeth.

Holy fuck, thank you shifter gods.

He tongue caressed me as I cried out and sought to find traction on the bathroom floor. The tiles gave me nothing as I scraped and clawed at them while another explosive orgasm sent me into pleasurable convulsions that Lucien controlled with his firm grip on me.

The scent of arousal and blood was strong in the air, and oddly enough, there were no metallic undertones that I normally associate with my blood. It was more floral, like lavender.

"How's the burning?" Lucien asked as he lifted his head, and I was caught in the dark swirl of his eyes, overwhelmed by how damn good he looked between my legs.

He was fully dressed, hair slicked back as the water ran over him, and I was in so much trouble. "It's still there," I admitted breathlessly, "but a hundred times better than before you"—I cleared my throat—"helped. It's manageable."

"Manageable is not good enough," he shot back, fangs appearing again as he lowered his head. This time the anticipation almost sent me straight back into an orgasm.

Our gazes remained locked as I felt the prick against my clit, which must have been engorged with blood because the moment Lucien's fangs hit it, he released a deep, rumble of desire.

The animalistic rumble was the sound a wolf made when it wanted to fuck or fight.

I definitely knew which one was hitting Lucien.

And me.

The fact that this was a bad idea and would make a complicated situation a zillion times worse faded under the intensity of this moment. The fallout of this was future Simone's problem, and even if a breakdown was imminent, that didn't mean I couldn't enjoy the now. Because the now was mind blowing orgasms, and I was a greedy bitch who needed all of this to continue.

So, so greedy.

Chapter Twenty-One

L ucien moved his mouth against me, taking in my slick heat, drinking down everything my body had to offer until the entire shower stall was drowning in my scent. Blood, arousal, want, lust, need... it all blended into a potent cocktail that, even without a pussy full of vampire fang, would still have me on the edge of orgasm.

"Crimson," I moaned, tilting my head back to cop a full face of cold water. Spluttering, I almost suffocated, and it would have totally been worth it.

When he lifted his head, the sight of my blood against his lips shouldn't have had my body jerking toward him. Blood play had never been my thing, and yet, with this particular male, it hit me like a shot of lust to my center.

As I jerked again, Lucien rumbled, not an iota of green remaining in his eyes. They were intense in their darkness, and if I hadn't known emphatically that I was here of my own free will, I'd have thought he was compelling me.

There was no compulsion needed for me to be into this vampire. That was the honest truth.

Without breaking eye contact, he reached up and shifted the temperature control to bring warmth into the waterfall of water.

"Crimson," I said again, the nickname feeling right, here in this shower stall with his scent mingling so deeply with mine. "Aren't you wearing a few too many clothe—"

I didn't get to finish that sentence before a loud chime echoed through the bathroom. I remembered from last time that meant someone wanted to contact Lucien through the speaker at the front gate.

Lucien stilled, his breathing deep and ragged. For a moment, it didn't seem he was going to bother checking who it was, but then he shook his head and pushed himself up from my body.

"The official summons," he bit out. He towered over me, looking down at where I was still sprawled before him like a damn offering to the gods.

Scrambling up myself, I didn't bother to hide my nudity. Lucien had entered my shower and then proceeded to give me multiple mind-blowing orgasms. We were definitely past the point of being shy.

"You still have the fire of vampire blood inside you," he said shortly, eyes lingering on my face. "All I did was take the edge off, but there's a chance the need will return. I will have to share my blood with you next time, but this should tide you over for now."

"What can I do to help myself if it happens again?"

Lucien shook his head. "You can't help yourself. This is a vampire need, and only feeding will stem the fire."

Great. Just fucking great. The last thing I wanted was to be in the middle of a vampire enclave and get hit with this level of need. "You triggered it, though," I reminded him. "So, if you just refrain from brushing those"—fucking addicting—"fangs anywhere near my skin, we should be okay."

Wishful thinking at its finest.

"You should be careful," Lucien shot back just as the house let out another chiming sound. "As your blood and my blood mingle further, more changes could take place."

There was another chime, and with a growl, he took off at vampire speed, leaving me naked and very confused. Since this was the summons and I couldn't rock up to the Master Chambers naked, I jogged to the shelf that held the towels and lifted one of the huge pieces of material.

Wrapping it around me, I took a moment to breathe in its clean, fresh scent, still amazed that everything in this house was cleaned and maintained from the energy of the crimson stones embedded in the walls and floors.

If I dropped this towel on the floor, it would be gone in an instant.

Very convenient, especially when you were a master vampire who didn't like other beings in your house. It was still a wonder he'd allowed me in here for so long.

Moving to the sink, I opened the drawers of the white cabinet beneath and found a full selection of items, just like the last time I'd been here. Many of them were familiar Earth brands, including toothbrush and paste, a hairbrush, and even makeup.

Scrambling through, I used the items I needed but didn't bother with makeup. My aim was to be as unappealing as possible for Carter. Though, considering how bad I was at applying makeup, maybe I should give it a whirl and go with the whole clown look.

By the time I was done in the bathroom, which included hanging up my wet clothing, just in case it was the only set I had here, Lucien still hadn't returned. Moving to the bed, I sank down onto the soft surface, enjoying the clean scent of the bedding.

After some time, exhaustion pushed against me, and I closed my eyes, needing a minute to get my energy back. My wolf stirred weakly inside, less compressed by the blood but nowhere as strong as she used to be.

Sorry, girl. We will figure out how to bring your strength back, I promise.

112

Blood lust or not, though I was craving more of Lucien's touch, I wouldn't sacrifice my wolf for it. There had to be a way to merge the two.

A whirring sound filled the room, and I turned my head to see the shutters slowly descending, wiping out the last of the red light until darkness engulfed me. Sleep took me away, as if my body was trained, just like the vampires, to rest during the sleep cycle. Despite my expectation of a short nap, I crashed out so hard that it had to be hours later when I was jolted awake by a hand on my arm.

I came to, screaming and swinging, the same response my phone got when it woke me up. Lucien caught my fist before it could connect, and a snort of laughter escaped him. Through my blurry vision in the low, red light of the room—I'd definitely been asleep for a long time if it was the awake cycle again—I could see that he was more than a little amused. "Still a morning person, I see."

"Fuck off," I snarled, before a yawn overtook me. "It's been forever since I slept." Forever and multiple journeys through the worlds.

Whatever mirth had been in his gaze faded. "Unfortunately, there's no time for more rest. Your guard and escort are here to take you to the room you'll use for the duration of the selection. From there you will be afforded the best in clothing and accessories."

If anything was going to bring me awake fast, it was that statement.

"Did we work out a proper plan?" I gasped, sitting up, completely naked and freaking out. "What exactly do I do to ensure I'm either eliminated from the selection or chosen only by you?"

Lucien hauled me off the bed in a blink, standing me on shaky legs. Before I could ask another question, he reached over to pick up a pile of clothing that must have been sitting on the other side of the bed. "Put these on for now. We will discuss a plan later, but for the most part, let's take it one event at a time. Your first job is to be unlike-able to Carter. Think you can handle that?"

It was my turn to snort out a laugh. "I can get you many references from bad dates to confirm my general lack of appeal."

Lucien didn't appear to find my joke funny, and I wasn't sure which part put that grim look on his face. "Get dressed," he repeated. "We'll be downstairs waiting for you."

He moved away as my pulse and heartrate spiked. I remained like that until his broad shoulders disappeared through the door and I was the only one left in the room.

Me and a pile of clothes.

Just as I reached for the top piece, Lucien appeared in the doorway again, and I froze with my hand wrapped around a shirt. His gaze locked on mine, burning into me. "Anyone who touched you and didn't appreciate the fucking gift they were given deserves to die."

Then he was gone, and I was left breathlessly wondering why he'd made the effort to return and tell me that. And why it affected me so much.

Lucien had warned me to repel Carter, but he should have said the same thing about himself. I could not fall in love with that master vampire again.

No matter how he made me feel or how my body responded, I wouldn't survive the heartbreak again.

That was a fact.

Chapter Twenty-Two

My limbs felt weak as I hurried to pull on the clothing I'd been given. The plain black shirt, clearly Lucien's, fell below my thighs, and I breathed in the crimson scent before forcing myself to keep getting dressed. The next item was too-big-for-me sweatpants, but I managed to tighten the drawstring enough to keep most of my parts under wraps. There was also a pair of socks, which I put on, and then I hurried into the bathroom to brush my hair. It would be a mess after my sleep.

The reflection in the mirror was one of wide eyes and dilated pupils, flushed cheeks, and lips that looked fuller than usual. For no damn reason at all.

In truth, I looked like a woman who'd just had a long night of hardcore sex resulting in dozens of glorious orgasms. Which was definitely not the case.

I mean, I'd had the glorious orgasms, but that was hours ago, which meant all of these physical changes had to be my close proximity to the vampire and the way he was stirring both his blood and mine inside me.

After running a brush through my hair, I quickly braided it to keep it off my face and decided that was the best I was getting, since I was already late.

Racing out of the bedroom and into the hall, I moved toward the stairs. Toward the pull of power.

To find Lucien and Len in one of the sitting rooms.

"Len!" I cried, heading straight for the fae. "What are you doing here?"

He got to his feet and met me halfway as he moved in the graceful way of a faerie, like their limbs and muscles weren't built the same way as the rest of ours.

"Hello, little wolf," he said with a broad, silvery smile. Everything about this male was larger than life, including his size and how other-worldly and handsome he was in the silver color of his race. "I'm here to be your bodyguard since our young Lucien cannot guard his wolf due to a conflict of interest."

Lucien didn't comment on the "his wolf" remark, and I had no idea what to do with it, so I shoved it aside and focused on what I could: Len was my bodyguard.

A sense of relief hit me. The fae was someone I knew and trusted, which would make this entire selection so much easier to handle.

"The masters are okay with an outsider being with me through this?" I had to double-check because it seemed too good to be true.

"I have more than a little influence with the masters," Lucien said, seeming relaxed. "The rules state that as long as it's not me or someone else competing for your mateship, you can have any security."

Letting the last of my anxiety rest, I nodded. "Should we get going then?"

"Yes, follow me. The guide is outside," Lucien said.

Whatever joy he'd felt at seeing his friend was gone, and he was all alpha again, hiding his emotions and taking the weight of the world's responsibilities on his shoulders.

It hit me then that I'd once again been selfish in thinking only of myself and how this all affected me. Lucien had really gone to bat for me, stepping up for the selection and even earlier in the shower. He'd been helping me, keeping me safe, protecting me for a long time. It was time for me to start showing my appreciation by following his rules about the selection and not making his job more difficult.

The sooner this was over, the sooner we could all get back to our lives.

When Lucien and Len headed out of the room, I trailed a few steps behind. They were having a discussion in rapid whispers, but it was too quiet for me to hear more than a few words. I heard enough to know it was about my security and what Len could expect from the guards and masters—information I probably should have listened to, but I just couldn't find the energy to force my way into the conversation.

Sleeping had helped, and the vampire blood wasn't burning any longer, but I felt a little flat. I wondered if this was part of the "you'll need to feed too" thing Lucien had mentioned. I mean, what was I supposed to do if that happened for the rest of my life? Would bagged blood work?

As gross as it sounded, at least I knew it would keep me alive as long as Mera and the others. Or maybe my aim should be to figure out how to rid myself of vampire blood once and for all and go back to my normal life. Of course, I had to make it through the selection first to ensure that I even had options to consider.

When we exited the security gates, Lucien paused his conversation with Len and looked around. "Hmm, I told the guide to wait for us at the Chambers, but I figured he'd ignore me."

Clearly he'd known better than to ignore the Crimson House master.

"Everyone listens to you here," Len said with a low laugh.

Lucien took another look around before he waved us forward. "It wasn't an order, and I expected the other masters would insist on his presence, worried about Bee being a runner."

"Or a flyer," I said drily, since my nickname had a new context to it now.

Lucien's gaze was filled with a low simmering heat when it met mine. "Or that."

We pushed forward, walking through the Crimson House streets before turning out of this section into another part of the maze. Lucien was clearly taking the shortest route today.

Len remained with us, seeming not at all curious about the design of the mazelike streets, which told me he'd been here before. "Do you know how to find your way out of Crimson City without Lucien?" I asked him. "Just in case we have to run or hide during the selection."

The fae shot me a wink. "I think I can work it out; I've been here more than a few times."

Lucien slowed his pace to match mine. "If you get into trouble, call for me first. Don't try and take on the vampires alone. Even Len will struggle against the full force of the ten masters, including Carter and guards."

"How do I call you?" I shot back. There were no phones in this world, hence why mine was back in my desk drawer in the bookstore.

His expression didn't change. "Len knows how. And since he'll be with you at all times, there's no need for you to know."

I fought the urge to roll my eyes. "All times, eh? So, even in the shower?"

Hands wrapped around my biceps so fast that by the time my gasp escaped, I was already dangling off the ground. Vampire speed was so fucking unfair.

As I snapped out of my shock, I kicked out as hard as I could, but the bastard managed to side-step my strike. My shoe scraped along the side of his pants. "Stop fucking manhandling me," I snarled, fired up.

He brought his face close to mine. "No one touches you in the shower, Bee." His irises were darkening, gaze burning into me, and all

I could breathe was his scent. Oxygen vanished, replaced by cherries. "If you need someone in the shower, you will summon me and no one else." His grip tightened; the firm hold on my skin doing things to me. "I don't share well, and we struck a deal that for your time here, you belong to me."

With my head spinning, I struggled to remember when we'd struck such a deal, but there was clearly no point in arguing with him. If my traitorous vagina was any indication, Lucien temporarily owning us sat just right with her. It was an archaic concept, but not one I was unfamiliar with, since shifters were all about the animalistic claiming. I just hadn't expected it from a vampire.

Arching under his touch, my head filled with memories of his fangs in my thigh and clit, and I was left staring into piercing green eyes while breathing embarrassingly heavy. Lucien's expression gave nothing away, but he hadn't released me, which told me he was waiting for my agreement.

"Okay," I finally said. "I won't invite Len—"

His chest rumbled, loud enough to interrupt me.

"Len or *anyone else* into my shower," I growled back, frustration biting at me.

My feet hit the ground as I was released, and we both turned to find a smirking Len watching us. Lucien didn't say anything to his friend, marching off at a pace that had me scrambling to keep up. When we reached the set of guards on this entrance, Lucien addressed the closest one.

"She needs to be escorted to her assigned room for the selection. And note that her fae security is to stay with her at all times."

The guards, both smaller and way less intimidating than Lucien, nodded in a few quick jerks of their heads. "Yes, Master Lucien," the closest one said, running a hand over his completely shaved head, showing discomfort. "We will ensure that everything is taken care of."

Lucien didn't seem that satisfied by the answer, as he shot me a quick glance—a final wellbeing check, by the looks—before he turned and left. Len moved in closer behind me, effectively guarding my back. "Follow us," the bald vampire said. "All of those called for the selection are being housed on the top level of the Chambers."

Well, that answered one of my questions about what lay above the two levels I'd seen.

The guard, whose name I learned was Galco, chatted about the selection as he led us through the building and up a set of stairs I hadn't even known existed, hidden as they were behind a door on the ground level.

"I've been working for the masters in security roles for most of my three hundred years," he said, his hazel eyes shining with enthusiasm. "I'm young for a vampire, and working for the masters is a stepping-stone to becoming one. They only let those with a decent level of power guard the front gates, so I'm hoping this will lead to big things for me in the next few thousand years."

"Do all vampires live forever?" I asked him.

Galco turned back from where he stood on the stairs, seeming a touch surprised by my question. It was odd, but in my last time here, I'd never asked that question. I'd just assumed they did because Lucien was ancient as hell, but maybe not all vampires were as long-lived.

"Not all," Galco said, confirming that thought. "Only the strongest and oldest bloodlines will regenerate forever. But we all live a long time. Even the weakest will live a thousand years, and those that are masters live forever." He shrugged. "Well, they do if they don't piss off Lucien and he wipes them out."

Galco resumed his journey up the flights of stairs, and I was reminded that if I didn't turn into a hybrid, I would only live for a couple of hundred years. I'd be out of Mera's and Lucien's lives in a mere blip of time.

For some messed-up reason, my chest ached at the thought of leaving this world so soon. I'd leave everyone I loved.

They'd go on and live their lives and have adventures, and I would be in the afterlife wondering if any of them would ever cross to my side of the veil.

Dammit, I couldn't dwell on this right now. Worrying about the future would have to wait, and maybe it was worth remembering that even an eternals' existence could be cut short. Alistair, Lucien's brother, had been killed in the Desert Lands.

Life was short, so I would focus on fighting to enjoy every second I had.

Chapter Twenty-Three

Galco continued to ramble as we followed him up the nondescript stairs—he was legit the friendliest vampire I'd ever met. I was starting to think the rest were just cranky old fucks.

Len remained in a silent, protective, swath of silver at my back, and I felt better knowing he was there. By the time we reached the door, I felt as if I'd made a new friend in Galco. "You find me if you have any trouble, Ms. Simone," he told me with a broad smile, a hint of fangs all I could see. "And between you and me, I'm really hoping you win this thing."

He left before I could tell him that winning was the last result we wanted from the selection. Then again, one option was to "win" Lucien, so maybe I'd take his hope after all.

The room I'd been assigned was a decent size with a bed topped by a wood headboard. Ornately carved patterns in the reddish-brown timber were offset by forest-green bedding, not to mention the dozen or so pillows in varying shades of green, all of which gave the bed a luxurious but also comfortable feel.

Off to the side was a small sitting area, along with two open doorways, one of which I could see white tiles through. Having my own bathroom was a huge relief—no one could ambush me naked, since apparently Len was not allowed quite that close to guard me.

The fae did a quick check of the room before he relaxed in one of the tan leather couches "You can never be too safe," he said as I moved closer. "From now on it'll be best if you don't even sneeze without checking with me first."

I narrowed my eyes and crossed my arms, drawing in the wide sides of Lucien's shirt. "Are you going to taste test my food before I eat it?"

I'd been half joking, but he took the question very seriously. "If I have to, I will. I'll place some stones in this room for now, which will keep this area safe... or at least alert us to danger. But outside there are too many variables. Best to just approach all situations with caution."

Standing again, he opened his coat and pulled stones from within the inner pockets. Moving around the room, he placed them at differing intervals, including a couple under the pile of pillows. As he dropped each stone, tingles of energy rushed over my skin.

"Amazing," I said. "Thank you for sharing your fae power with me. Kind of wish I'd had some of these gems on Earth to watch my back."

There was a flash of confusion on Len's face. "It's that dangerous on Earth?" he asked.

"Yes and no." I shrugged. "Humans are vulnerable, and often hurt by nature itself. Even worse, they hurt each other. Shifters do that too, but we are far less breakable. If you have a shitty pack, though, life can be really rough."

Mera could attest to that. And in their own way, my parents had made my life hell.

Len mulled over my words before he shook his head. "I feel this call to Earth, which I've been ignoring for a long time. I always figured it had to do with Shadow, but the longer it goes on, the less I believe that. I will have to think on journeying there and following the call of power. Maybe when we're done here with Valdor, you can introduce me to shifters and humans."

"I can do that."

Len nodded his thanks before retaking his seat on the couch. "Since there's only one bed," he said, "I will sleep here."

"Appreciate that gesture," I said, before taking a deep breath, "but if you want to share, it's okay with me. That couch doesn't look large enough to be comfortable."

Not for a being of his size.

"And the bed is huge," I added.

Sleeping in a bed with a stranger was not my idea of a good time. I mean, reading about it was one of my favorite tropes, but in real life, it just felt kind of awkward. That probably had more to do with the fact that I wasn't attracted to Len, so there was no chance of any fun night snuggles.

No doubt I'd feel differently if it was Lucien.

Don't go there.

Len's laughter distracted me. "To save myself a solid ass kicking, I regretfully have to decline that generous offer. I'll be comfortable here, thank you."

I didn't ask who'd kick his ass because we'd both witnessed Lucien's little scene back in the street. He'd claimed me while I was here, and Len would never go against his friend.

"Probably for the best," I agreed. "I've never shared a bed before... Who knows what I do in my sleep."

Len's laughter warmed me again; apparently, I enjoyed making a fool of myself and amusing these ancient, powerful males. But there was no more time for that. I needed to get my game face on and work out how I was going to convince the Stone of Katu, and the other masters, that I was either *not* Carter's mate or that I was Lucien's.

Lucien's blood inside of me was a good start, but it would take more than that.

I needed to know him; I needed to research.

Lucky for me I had the best Lucien resource at my fingertips: Len, his best friend.

Len might have signed up for bodyguard duty, but now he was also on encyclopedia-of-Lucien duty because this was one class I needed to ace.

No excuses.

Chapter Twenty-Four

No one bothered us for the next few hours, and I spent that time quizzing Len on every aspect of Lucien's personality. He knew a lot about the master vampire, from his favorite colors: teal and black; to his favorite food: blood, of course, and apples from Earth, of all places; to the fact that he had no blood relatives alive. He was the last of his bloodline, which made me sadder than I expected. "His family all but built this town," Len told me. "Hence why Crimson City is the official-slash-unofficial name."

"I had no idea," I said, feeling stupid for never even asking about the fact that the town and his house had the same name.

"Oh yeah, he's royalty in this world, not that he's ever wanted to claim it."

That was true. If anything, Lucien wanted to live the most under-stated life he could manage. Unfortunately, his shine was too bright for him to hide.

"He loves well-aged scotch and whisky," Len continued, not realizing my thoughts had drifted off. "And he has a weakness for shiny, powerful objects. He manages to control it easily now, but when we were younger, he'd challenge me for my stones all the time."

Learning these little secrets about Lucien felt like a gift, even if they were only needed to get through this selection and possibly be out of his life.

"What does he like in females?" I asked. "Is there a 'type' the masters expect him to go for?"

That gave him a moment's pause. "Actually, Lucien, for all of his playboy personality is very private with his love life. I've never known him to seriously date—none of us ever have, to be fair. But Lucien doesn't give enough of himself to invest even temporarily in a relationship."

"Why?" I asked, somewhat surprised. I'd figured that Lucien wasn't dating at this point in his life, not that he'd never really dated. I mean... he was old as dirt, so how was that possible?

"His parents had a blood call bond," Len said softly. "I don't know the whole story, but I believe searching for a way to have more children is what destroyed his mother, and then his father followed."

My heart ached as I pictured Lucien as a young tow-headed child, even though he'd probably been four hundred years old when it happened. I wondered if he'd felt that he wasn't enough for them.

I could relate to that.

Maybe one day he'd trust me enough to share the story, but considering even Len didn't appear to know the finer details, the odds were low. It did give me some insight into comments Lucien had made about not wanting a mate or offspring, which gave me an even deeper appreciation for his willingness to enter this selection.

I knew he didn't plan on finding a mate from it, not a true one anyway, but it must have been somewhat triggering for him just to sign up.

A low musical chime echoed through the room, interrupting my thoughts and the information-gathering session. Len was up and off his couch in a flash, and at the door before I even got to my feet. When he opened it, I was close enough to see a petite female there.

She wore a tight black dress, sky-high black heels, and a seductive expression as she eyed Len up and down, tilting her head back so her dark, flawless curls tumbled down her spine.

Everything about her was attractive, from her almond-shaped brown eyes to her full pink lips—all of which barely seemed to register with Len as he observed her with caution.

"Can I help you? he asked, tone hard.

"I really hope so. I'm one of the selected." Her voice was soft and accented with a purring sound as she rolled her r's. "Came across to introduce myself and see if there've been any announcements I missed."

She reached out a hand as if to touch Len's coat, but he moved aside so fast there was no chance for her to sink her red-tipped claws in. I looked down at my naked nails and too-big clothing and figured that this selection should be a breeze to lose.

Easing around Len, I shot her a smile. A fake, fake smile.

"So lovely to meet you," I said overly cheerily. Occasionally, my acting abilities really came in handy. "I'm Simone. And we haven't heard any announcements yet."

Those pretty brown eyes met mine, and I was surprised when she didn't sneer or shoot any mean-girl comments my way. Instead, she smiled brighter. "Simone." She exclaimed. "That's a lovely name. I'm Hattie, and I'm desperate not to be in this selection. Please tell me you feel the same?"

You could have knocked me over with a damn puff of air at that announcement.

I blinked at her so many times she probably thought I was seizing. "You don't want to be part of the selection? Why are you here then? I thought vampires had a choice."

She swallowed roughly, her perfect, white teeth and cute fangs disappearing. "My family doesn't have much power. My madre believes I'm their key to stepping up the ladder of success. There was no choice for me."

"Me either," I admitted, feeling a strange sense of kinship with this confusing chick. "I'm not even a vampire."

Hattie nodded. "Yes, I heard that. And in all honesty, that's why I chose your door to knock on first. The others are all here to win and will backstab and claw their way, fang and nail, onto a master's cock. Meanwhile, I'm in love with the boy next door and will do literally anything not to win."

A snort escaped me. She reminded me of Mera, and feeling homesick for my best friend, I reached out and grabbed Hattie's hand. "Okay, you and I are about to become selection besties," I said, relaxing. "We can help each other. Stick together."

She nodded. "I would really love that. I've never had many friends—no one likes the weak family."

Ugh, vampire politics were so similar to shifters'... I hated it all.

Giving her hand one more squeeze before releasing her, I said, "You never have to worry about that with me. I'm not a power chaser."

Before she could reply, another chime filled the area, but this time along the entire hallway. "The opening ceremony will commence in four sun movements," a robotic voice announced through the area. "Items will be delivered for you to wear. If you do not show up, you will be eliminated."

Hattie turned to me. "If only it was that simple for me. If I was eliminated in the first round through my own actions, my parents would disown me."

"I also can't be eliminated that way," I said with a sad laugh. "Or they'll eliminate me permanently. My only hope is to either be rejected by the stone or to be chosen for Lucien, who agreed to release me after." I wasn't going to go too deeply into the plan, but mentioning it shouldn't be an issue.

Hattie straightened, her eyes growing wider. "Lucien? As in... Master Lucien of Crimson House?"

When I nodded, she opened her mouth in a silent scream. "He's like the most eligible bachelor in the fucking world," she whispered through her freakout.

Right. It wasn't as if I'd forgotten that, but sometimes it still took me by surprise. Lucien was a big deal here. Like... a big, *big deal.*

"They seriously don't tell you who the masters are?" I asked her.

She shook her head, a snorty laugh escaping. "Like they would tell us anything. Most females don't even care. Only a few with enough power in their family or a mate already would say no. And since they never send invites to mated females, it's always a hundred percent turnout."

All of the doors in the hallway banged open then, thirty or so at a quick count, and from these doorways, female vampires emerged, most of them dressed like Hattie. Or more extravagantly. Hattie's boobs and ass were at least somewhat covered.

"What are they doing?" I wondered out loud, glancing back at Len, who remained quietly at my back. "They said four sun movements." Which was about four hours, from what I remembered.

Before anyone could answer me, my blood sizzled as a spark of energy traveled down the hall, and Len yanked me into the room as a large, wood trunk landed in front of my open door.

"Our clothing has arrived," Hattie said with a sigh. "Looks like we're out of excuses to not get ready."

Since my new vampire friend already looked like she was ready, I had no idea what she was going to change into. Apparently, there were sexier outfits in here for us.

Sexy enough to impress our possibly new mates.

Our new masters.

Ugh, vampires sucked.

In more ways than the usual.

Chapter Twenty-Five

After Hattie promised to find me at the opening ceremony, she left for her room a few doors down, effortlessly carrying her trunk inside. I reached down to grab mine and found that I couldn't even lift it one inch. "What the fuckery?" I snarled, pulling harder on the side handle. "What's in here? It has to weigh ten tons."

It wasn't even that large of a trunk, and yet shifter strength couldn't budge it. Len let out a low chuckle as he pushed past me and grabbed the handle. Show-off that he was, he managed to lift it with almost no effort.

"It's the magical essence surrounding the case that's weighing it down," he told me as I glared. "You have to counter with your own power, but as a shifter, it's harder."

"I'd have figured it out," I grumped, not liking that I was so much weaker than even the smallest vampire female. If I were really competing in this selection, I'd be in some real trouble.

Len set the trunk down near the small room that was lined in shelves and hanging space. I clicked open the two huge brass levers on the side and, thankfully, was able to lift up the lid without fae help. The contents made me blink; the weight of this beast was starting to make sense. "How the heck did they fit this all in?" I asked.

Len reached out and brushed his hand over the side. "Magic," he said shortly. "They've enlarged the inside, even if the outside still looks like a normal trunk."

Clever trick.

It took us the better part of an hour to unpack everything: puffy ballgown dresses, casual clothing, toiletries, and some items that I could only assume had been included for me as a shifter from Earth.

"Vampires don't need tampons, right?" I asked Len, and all credit to him, he didn't freak out at the concept of blood gushing from one's vagina after a shifter's heat cycle.

"I believe they do have a similar reproductive cycle to you," he told me. "Shadow based much of the shifters' makeup on his own knowledge, which included attributes from other races connected to the Solaris System."

Which explained our compatibility with other worlds, including the ability to breathe their air and understand some of their languages.

"Do you think it's formal tonight?" I asked brushing my hands over the many gorgeous dresses. Vampires had good taste, and don't even get me started on the shoe selection. I really needed to figure out how to take these clothes with me as payment for their bullshit agenda of pulling me into this.

"Opening night is definitely black tie," Len said. "Do you want any help choosing an outfit?"

I shook my head, having already decided on what I wanted to wear. "It has to be this dress," I said, reaching for a crimson-red number. My favorite color. "This baby is getting worn tonight, just in case I die tomorrow or some shit."

"Never gonna happen," Len said with a smile. "But that's a great choice. I'll give you some privacy to get ready."

I grabbed his arm as he moved past, and when he turned to meet my gaze, I smiled. "Thank you for being here, for giving up your valuable time to keep me out of the vampires' clutches. I really appreciate it."

He examined me for a few uncomfortable seconds, and I barely managed not to squirm. It was disconcerting how these males looked into your soul. "You've never had a family, have you?" he asked in a soft tone that stabbed into all my broken parts.

"I had parents," I got out. "They were just more interested in the pack than me. Mera's been the only one to ever truly have my back, but she's always had so much shit to deal with that I've mostly kept her out of my issues."

Dammit, why was my lip quivering? My eyes burned as I fought for the resolve to not cry in front of a gorgeous, powerful fae. "I made it on my own," I finally choked out, hoping that ended the conversation.

Realizing I was still holding onto him, I released my grip, but Len didn't move. "You have a pack now," he said in his low hypnotic tone. "This is what we do for each other, no questions asked and no need to thank. We stand together so none of us will ever fall."

Dammit. Motherfucker was definitely going to make me cry.

Thankfully, he left before I could lose my shit, and I escaped into the shower to release the few tears I wasn't able to keep down. Hot water was amazing for washing away pain when it wouldn't stay inside.

I considered myself an expert at compartmentalizing situations, which was how I ended up in this position without losing my mind. Selection and blood lust and possibly turning into a hybrid was no biggie when I could slot it into a box in my brain and close the lid. Somehow, though, Len had all but torn me open with no more than a few sentences.

Or maybe Lucien had started that when he devoured my body and claimed my fractured soul.

By the time I'd scrubbed myself down and used the provided

toiletries on my hair and face, along with brushing my teeth, I felt much better. And definitely much cleaner.

Using a selection of hair tools and makeup, I got to work on myself and within thirty minutes had long, shiny curls, mascara and kohl on, and red, full lips.

After I ducked out in my towel to grab panties and the dress, I held it up in front of the mirror. The crimson dress was a deep, rich color, and it complemented my olive complexion nicely. There was no way to wear a bra with this style, so I pulled on a red thong and let the dress slide down over my head. Once it was on, I adjusted my middle-class boobs—C cup all the way—so they sat up nicely.

There wasn't a ton of support in the slinky number, with no back at all and the bottom material starting just above my ass, but everything appeared to be in place. I went up on my toes to see more of my reflection. Mirrors here weren't made from the same material as Earth mirrors, but the slight distortion didn't bother me.

The silky skirt swished around my bare feet; it was a touch long, but add in heels and it would be perfect. Apparently vamp energy knew how to size up a shifter without even touching them. Creepy but convenient.

With a swish of my curls over one shoulder, I took a deep breath —I was as ready as I'd ever be. It was time to get my ass out there and act in the most important role of my life.

When I left the bathroom, I found a set of stunning silver heels among the many shoes I'd been provided. They had a slightly thicker heel than a stiletto, which made it so much easier for this shifter to walk in. I'd really like to not end up on my face tonight.

As I stepped into each one and straightened, I heard a low whistle. I turned to find Len in a black tuxedo, looking like a shiny god. The silvery details in his hair, skin, and eyes were highlighted by the dark suit. His shoulders looked broader, his legs longer, and even with my heels, he towered over me.

"Thought the plan was to not get yourself chosen," he told me with a twinkle in his eyes. "You need to talk to Mera about what happened when she tempted the beast in a red dress. You should probably change."

I laughed, feeling unexpectedly happy with his compliment. I was vain, whatever. But in truth, I knew that I would never stand out among those beauties.

"I've seen the vampire females," I reminded him as my laugh dried up. "I don't think there's any reason to worry about me making an entrance. Mostly, though, a nice dress and makeup can be as good as armor at events like this. Tonight, I need all the protection."

Len shook his head before he held out a hand to me. "I've got your back, beautiful. You just go out and show the vampires what shifters are made of. Their underestimation of your strength will be their downfall."

I slid my arm into the crook of his elbow and said, "You're a pretty good wingman."

It was on the tip of my tongue to ask why he didn't have a mate to protect and adore, but I was worried his story was very personal, and maybe we weren't quite at that point of sharing yet.

Shadow and his friends had all been without mates for a very long time, each for their own reason. Two had fallen now though, so maybe they'd all soon start finding the one to tame their ancient hearts.

Or maybe I'd been reading too many romantic fantasy stories and should focus on the selection.

When we entered the hallway, only a few other vampires were leaving at the same time, and none had an escort like me. No one spoke to us, and I tried very hard to ignore the assessing looks thrown my way. Clearly, no one was surprised by the wolf's presence, but they weren't happy about it either. Not if their expressions were any indication.

But thanks to Len at my side, no one approached me.

Following the others out of the hall of rooms, we made it to the stairs and descended to the ground floor, where their largest ballroom was located. My heels weren't the easiest stair attire, but under Len's steady hold, I didn't falter once.

I did, however, feel like there were multiple metaphorical daggers in my back by the time I got to the bottom. Thankfully, no literal ones.

At least not yet.

Let the motherfucking selection begin.

Chapter Twenty-Six

S tepping into the vampire ballroom was like stepping into a fairytale. A dark, delicious, possibly twisted fairytale. Heavy black and gold curtains spanned the room, the shiny marble floors reflecting their colors, which were highlighted by the many lanterns flickering around the edges. Above our heads a massive chandelier sparkled in silvers and golds, and I'd never seen anything as ornate as that piece, which spanned half the room.

Everything was lit up in a soft, romantic glow, and all I could see were shiny dresses and shinier vampires.

Along with the dozens of females in the selection, there appeared to be many other vampires in attendance as well. Couples twirled around the dance floor, while others chatted, standing near a bar and table of food.

My stomach rumbled since I'd gone at least a day without food. As a shifter, that wasn't going to kill me, but I would need nourishment soon to build up strength.

Looking around, I saw no signs of Carter or Lucien and figured they were due to make a grand entrance at some point. That was when everyone would really flip their shit.

I wondered how Lucien was feeling as he stood in the wings, about to be part of a selection he'd never have normally signed up for. Unease filled me at the thought of him experiencing any anxiety or emotional upheaval, especially when I was the catalyst. It was hard to tell what Lucien was thinking, but I really hoped this wasn't weighing too heavily on him.

We could get through it together, I truly believed that.

Len led us in the direction of the shiny gold bar, and I tried to ignore all the attention we were drawing. "Would you like a drink?" he asked.

"Holy fuck yes," I said in a rush. "There's literally no way I'm getting through this night sober."

His laughter caught the attention of a few females nearby, and I was grateful that all the attention I'd felt earlier was now on my male bodyguard, allowing me to fade into the background.

When we reached the bar, with its gold filagree pattern across the shiny surface, Len released me. He appeared to be perusing the drinks lining the shelves on the back wall, and I did the same until I was surprised by a familiar bottle. "Crimson Heart!" I gasped. "That was my favorite sneaky beverage back in the day, but then we stopped getting it in Torma."

Len turned in the direction I was pointing, to the bottle that was the same color as my dress with a single flower on the front. "That's one of the vampire's special elixirs," he told me, raising his eyebrows as he met my gaze. "It should never have been in Torma."

I swallowed hard. "A vampire wine?"

"Yep. They're quite famous for it, with its hints of cherry blossom and blood."

I stood there blinking like a crazy fucking person because it turned out I was into the blood thing after all. "Do you want a glass?" Len asked me.

I nodded. "Yes, I'd like to know if it tastes the same."

If it was the same, it could explain why it was one of the only wines to ever get me wasted, when human alcohol was burned off fast by a shifter metabolism. But how the hell had it ended up in Torma?

Maybe someone there had been secretly banging a vampire. Weirder shit had happened.

While Len waited to be served, I turned to take in the room. It was filling up fast now. Vampires poured in through the front door, and the masters were congregating in a section of the room that was slightly elevated from the rest.

Their platform was bare of any seating, but clearly there to showcase the tier one masters.

"Here you go," Len said, just as the lighting from above dimmed and the room started to quiet down. I took the heavy crystal wine glass, lifting it to smell a very familiar cherry-and-oak scent.

Well, slap me on the ass and call me a piñata. It was the same.

I took a sip, moaning as the rich taste burst across my tongue and down my throat. It was delicious, the cherry tart enough to bring my tastebuds to life and the oaky fire adding a unique blend; it was so damn good.

Taking a larger drink, I enjoyed the burn of whatever alcohol or magic was in this, and it didn't even cross my mind to be grossed out by the traces of blood Len had mentioned.

When in Rome and all that, and there was a reason this wine had been my favorite for years. I'd mourned so hard when it disappeared.

Focused on my drink, it took me a moment to notice that the music was dying down. On the platform across the way, one of the masters stepped forward, and I recognized Donovan of Jade House. "Welcome," he called, his voice projected and bouncing around the walls. "We're pleased to see so many of you show up to support the selection."

There was a short cheer from the crowd that died off almost immediately.

"As you all know, we have two tier one masters who wish to find a mate and bring power and prosperity to their enclaves. We have offered thirty invitations to the most eligible vampire females in Valdor." He paused slightly, and I could have sworn his gaze drifted to me. "And one wolf shifter who was called by the gods." Okay, yep. Definitely looking at me. He wasn't the only one either, but thankfully, most of them turned back to face Donovan when he continued. "Let's bring in our two masters."

He waved his hands toward a set of double doors I hadn't noticed on the opposite side of the room from the entrance we'd used. When the doors opened, the lights brightened above, a spotlight of sorts landing on Carter. Gasps rang out around the room, and I had no doubt that those thirty vampire females were pushing forward for their first glimpse of the eligible bachelor.

As I took another drink, I observed him over the rim of my glass. When I'd seen Carter last time, he'd seemed broad and intimidating with a lumberjack vibe. Tonight, dressed in a black tuxedo, he looked even broader. Handsome, but there was no stirring inside of me.

It was like looking at a pretty doll. I could admire the overall image, but I still didn't want to take it home with me. In truth, I fucking hated dolls. They creeped me out.

"Master Carter," Donovan called out. "He's beginning his integration into Crimson City, ready to build his own powerful enclave: Silver House."

Carter didn't look at Donovan or even acknowledge what he was saying, instead he paused, silently scanning the crowd. Thankfully, that piercing stare never made it to where I stood in the shadows with Len, and for that I was grateful.

"The second master in the running for a mate," Donovan called, and for some reason, a deep shiver of energy filled the space. The crowd was hanging on this announcement. Or maybe they'd done the calculations about which master was missing from the platform right now. "Is Master Lucien of Crimson House, one of our strongest and most eligible bachelors."

The noise was near deafening, vampires losing their shit as they screamed, and when Lucien stepped out... Fuck. Me.

I didn't realize I'd murmured that out loud until Len laughed at my side, but I was too busy devouring Lucien to even turn his way. Carter might not have stirred anything inside of me, but my entire body was on fire now that Lucien had arrived.

He wore a fancy suit, just like the others, but he'd forgone a bowtie of any description, leaving the top couple of buttons open to showcase golden muscles. The rest of his outfit was perfectly tailored, and even from over here he looked like a giant with impossibly broad shoulders. I couldn't see his eyes, but I could guess at their piercing green taking in the room around him.

Lucien didn't appear happy to be here. There was no welcoming smile or gracious wave; instead, that coldly still expression remained on his features as he moved through the crowd.

Guilt splashed through the arousal I'd been feeling. I'd done this. I'd forced him into this position he'd never wanted, and there was nothing I could really do to help him out. Except ensure I was the female chosen for him.

I was the only one who would respect that he didn't want a true mate and leave him alone. No matter how delicious he was or how difficult it would be to walk away.

We were not meant for each other.

The sooner I wrapped my head around that, the better it would be for everyone.

"Holy gods above," a female nearby groaned, jarring me from my thoughts. "Master Lucien is the second master? That's... It's going to be a bloodbath among the selected females."

A quick glance told me she was chatting to a friend and was clearly not competing for the master's hand. I got the feeling she almost wished she were by the way she hungrily stared over at Lucien.

With a shake of my head, I took another drink only to find my glass was empty. Well, that went down faster than expected. Len took the empty crystal from me and turned, hopefully to get another.

He was in the running for my favorite date in months, bringing me wine on tap and no horticulture or social media talks.

But... there was also no chance of getting felt up at the end of the date, so maybe not quite perfect.

A hush grew around us, and I turned from the bar to see what had caused the commotion, only to curse in surprise when I found Carter standing practically on top of me. He was so close that if I stepped forward a foot, we would be touching.

His hungry gaze stared down at me, and no lie, I kind of wished I still held the heavy wine glass. It might be empty, but it would have made a decent weapon.

Chapter Twenty-Seven

"Simone," he purred, blue eyes a hypnotic swirl as he ran his gaze over my face and then down the lines of my semi-revealing dress. "The female I've been waiting to see."

I coughed before shaking my head to cover up my unease and annoyance. "Can't say the same, Carter, old buddy." I worked really had to appear unconcerned and uninterested in him. "I'm here against my will. Or have you forgotten your little demand?"

His eyes flashed, the color growing brighter, but he didn't snap back. Instead, he smiled. "Ah, your fire is exactly what I want in a mate. You'd never survive with me if you were a demure wallflower."

Letting out a long sigh, I realized this was going to be tougher than I'd expected. Closing the remaining distance between us, I channeled Mera when I stabbed my finger into his hard chest. "Listen here, you chauvinistic vampire. I am not fire, I'm a wallflower. I prefer reading to fighting. I own a fucking bookstore. I do not"—I jabbed him again—"I repeat, I do not want to be your damn mate."

Carter didn't move or react, and it seemed that he was immune to my personality flaws. Clearly, I needed a stronger plan to put him off because if the Stone of Katu decided I was a good match for him, the only being who could veto it was the vampire himself.

Masters still held the power to veto a match, which was the only thing keeping me from feeling too guilty about Lucien. He might be miserable, but in the end, he still had all of the power and control. Unlike me.

Carter, who hadn't moved, despite my finger pressing against his chest, smiled again. His fangs appeared, and I wasn't imagining the way his gaze landed on my neck. "Your blood smells like energy and life," he closed his eyes briefly. "When you're angry, the fire fills your scent. I can't wait to taste you—"

He didn't get a chance to finish that disturbing as fuck sentence before there was another round of gasps, and I felt a new powerful presence. As I stepped to the side to see who was here, Carter reached out and grasped my arms, holding me in place. "We were just getting to know each other," he rumbled, leaning down as if to kiss me.

In a panic, I jerked my knee up in the hopes of smashing his balls into his throat, only for him to fly off me before I could make contact. I watched with a slack jaw and wide eyes as Carter flew across the room before Lucien stepped into the spot the other master had just occupied.

Our gazes locked, and I didn't miss his black eyes or the way his chest heaved. A rumble escaped him as his fangs appeared. He stepped closer to me, keeping me locked in his animalistic stare. "Crimson," I said softly. "Are you okay?"

No reply except another rumbling growl. I wasn't sure if I should touch him or not; I didn't know how to diffuse this situation. "Lucien," I tried again. "I'm okay. Perfectly fine. You can't just go throwing vampires across the room."

I caught sight of the crowd parting behind us, and I knew exactly why all the onlookers had moved. Carter was on his way back, and he looked pissed.

"Carter's coming," I said in a rush, but Lucien seemed completely unconcerned, his gaze remaining on my face, like he was memorizing the damn thing. It was only at the last second, as I braced to be collateral damage between two clashing vampires, that Lucien spun and shot one palm out, smashing Carter in the chest and sending the other vampire back across the room.

At this point, the tier one masters got involved. Len dragged me out of the way as Lucien snarled his annoyance to Donovan—Carter had broken the rules by grabbing a female without her permission.

"Looks like you're going to need this," Len said, handing me two glasses of wine. I took them both, gulping the first down in one go before moving a little slower with the second.

The fae remained at my side and kept everyone else away from me. "Sorry I didn't step in when Carter first approached," he finally said. "I figured you wanted a chance to update him of your annoyance at being here, and I didn't expect he would try anything in a room of witnesses."

I patted Len's arm. "You did nothing wrong. My job here is to repel that bastard, and I was trying my best. Unfortunately, he took my annoyance for fire and seemed to like the insults."

"I also saw Lucien coming," Len added. "And I could tell he was on a warpath. Told you wearing the red dress was a bad idea."

I snorted, a buzz building in my body from the potent wine. "It was a pissing contest and nothing else. I could be standing here in a sack."

"Yes, you could have been," he said, and his tone indicated that he was taking the sack theory in a different way than me.

The masters got their shit sorted eventually, and the music started up again, drifting around the room, even though I could see no speakers or live band.

"Would you like to dance?" I asked Len. I loved dancing, having taken lessons in Torma when I was younger. Shifters were into dances and pack mixers, and my parents had demanded I be well trained so as not to embarrass them or our alpha. The joke was on them because it didn't end up being a chore or punishment. It was my escape.

"Uh, it's probably not the best idea right now," Len said softly. "We don't want to push a certain master over the edge again."

I had no idea if he was talking about Carter or Lucien, and since I was three glasses deep into blood wine, I snorted as I said, "What do you mean by that?"

His lips twitched so briefly I barely caught it. "Lucien is showing common traits of vampire possessiveness. I've never really seen it from him before, and while it could be a product of you being under his protection, there's a fire there that indicates something else is going on. In that regard, it's best not to antagonize him."

I swallowed roughly, thinking about the fire that had almost consumed me in the shower earlier. If Lucien hadn't... uh, come to the rescue, I would probably have combusted into a small pile of ash.

"It's probably his blood still within me," I choked out, pressing my thighs together. "Forming a connection between us."

Len slanted a look at me, eyebrows raised, but he didn't argue, at least. I had no idea what to do with the idea that there might be more between Lucien and me. I'd felt a pull toward him from the first moment I met him, but he'd done a very good job ensuring I never considered him mate material. Going back there again was dangerous for my heart.

Donovan's voice rang out. "All of the invited females, please make your way to the front to officially meet the masters."

It was a distraction, but not a great one. "I'm being paged," I said, my mood dropping.

I threw back the rest of my drink and took a step forward, stumbling on the unfamiliar heels and buzz of wine. Len came to the rescue, taking my glass and setting it down before he linked our arms again.

"Ignore the mind games," he murmured as we moved forward.

"Ignore the other females and whatever the masters say or do. You're here to make a bad impression, and then we can head back to your room to regroup."

Right. Just ignore all the powerful vampires in the room.

Piece of cake.

Actually, cake would be really awesome right now, but first, I had a meet and greet to attend.

Chapter Twenty-Eight

Outside of Hattie, I hadn't really seen or interacted with the thirty females in the selection. Now, though, we were being herded together like a line of cattle to the slaughter, and as I fell in near the back, I was able to observe all of them.

I spotted Hattie about halfway along, animatedly chatting to the female in front of her. Both were dressed in the same pale pink, puffy ballgown with their hair intricately styled in curls and pinned on top of their heads. I noticed that most of the others in the line had also opted for the over-the-top voluminous dress. In varying shades and styles, but the puffy skirt was a staple.

As the line started to move, Len stood off to the side, leaving me alone. More than one female shot me a dark stare, and it was clear that Carter and Lucien's little altercation had been seen by all. Bastards had put a target on my back by making it extra hard to convince the females I was no threat.

We moved forward slowly as each of the females spent time chatting to the masters. This was legitimately so boring I couldn't understand why the other vampires in the room were standing around watching like it was the best show they'd ever seen.

Hopefully, they'd get the music and dancing going again shortly.

By the time it was my turn, my feet hurt and I'd almost fallen asleep standing up. Moving to Carter first, I stared up at him, my expression completely neutral. "Simone Lewison, of the Torma pack shifters," Donovan announced from the side. "She's here at the request of Master Carter and also due to her affinity with the Stone of Katu."

Thanks, Donovan, you old fuck. Why don't you add another five targets to my back? At this stage I wouldn't have to worry about losing... someone would take me out long before then.

"Simone," Carter said in his deep voice. "Pleasure to officially meet and welcome you to the selection."

He held his hand out, and I tried not to look at Lucien, who was standing about six feet away watching us closely.

As I placed my hand in Carter's, I leaned in. "I don't want to be here. Just let me go now."

Those close enough to hear gasped, but Carter just smiled. "Why don't you give this a chance. A real chance. If by the end of the selection you haven't fallen for my charms, then I will gladly choose another."

His words were exactly what I wanted to hear, and yet I sensed that he was leading me down the path of false security so I would drop my guard.

"I won't change my mind," I told him firmly, removing my hand from his warm grasp.

He just nodded. "Challenge accepted."

Dammit. I should have known better than to throw a definite *no* his way so early on in the selection. Ancient, powerful supernatural beings were used to getting what they wanted. I'd just given him extra incentive to win.

Before I could attempt to repair the damage I'd just done, Donovan was ushering me across to Lucien. When I stood before him, I took a few calming breaths and lifted my gaze to meet his. The rush of air in my lungs ceased as I stared into black pits.

Lucien might be standing here, expression blank, arms relaxed, but there was a war raging within him. I made the first move, reaching out to place my hand on his chest, hoping I could calm him before he ripped this room to pieces. "Crimson," I said softly. His eyes never left mine, and even I was feeling an urge to run and hide from this predator. "It's okay. Remember the plan."

His jaw grew even more rigid, and I had no idea what I'd said to upset him further.

Maybe touching him had been the mistake.

As I went to pull away, his hand shot out and slammed over the top of mine, holding me in place. It didn't hurt, but I jumped all the same from that unexpected move. Lucien leaned over, keeping me captive with his firm grip. His lips grazed across my cheek, and I fought the urge to collapse in a puddle of arousal. I'd clearly had too much wine for this because I was legitimately wondering if Lucien was going to rip my throat out, and if I'd even care if he did.

"Bee," he said, voice a rasp of dark energy. "If Carter touches you again, I'm going to kill him."

There was a moment where I wondered if my ears had malfunctioned. Did Lucien just say that? This was a selection, and I would no doubt have to go on dates and dance with Carter. There was no way I could avoid touching him completely.

"That's not possible?" I spluttered.

The scrape of his fang across my throat was enough to have my knees trembling. His hand tracing across the bare skin of my spine made the tremors even worse. "Obey me in this," he rumbled again, "or Carter will die and you will be punished."

"Not much incentive there," I managed to choke out.

Lucien's laugh was not a nice one. "Don't test me."

I pulled away from him, trying to figure out what had happened to the laid-back surfer-vampire that I'd first met. This was the vampire of nightmares. A true monster.

And why in all fucks was I wet enough to feel moisture along the top of my thighs?

If anyone had lost their mind here, it was me.

Lucien released his hold on me, and I stepped out of his orbit, desperate to calm my energy and the blood pulsing within me. Both of us needed a timeout, and then we could talk more on this later because there was no way I could agree to his demand.

Tonight, though, I would have to figure out something because Lucien was a loose cannon.

A mix of curious and disgusted expressions followed my path through the crowd, but I managed to easily ignore them as I looked for Len. He would know what to do about his friend. The fae emerged from the shadows, silver eyes meeting mine. "What happened with Lucien?"

"He's furious still," I said quickly, keeping my voice low. "Warned me not to touch Carter again or he would kill him." I swallowed roughly. "How the hell am I supposed to manage that when Carter is the other master in this selection? I'm sure we're going to be asked to dance in the next five seconds."

I paused to give the universe a chance to back me up, but to my surprise, there was no immediate announcement. Typical freaking vampires, always a pain in the ass—

"Selected, please make your way to the dance floor."

Ah, there it was.

I turned my panicked gaze on Len. "Any idea what I should do now?"

He looked around, possibly searching for Lucien. If anyone could talk some sense into that hotheaded vampire, it was one of his brothers. "I'll see if I can find him," he told me. "Stay here, and whatever you do, don't touch Carter until I return."

He was gone before I could reply, and taking his advice seriously, I made my way in the opposite direction of the dancefloor, determined to be the last in line. Unfortunately for me, I was well known in this room. "Wolf, you need to go that way," a male vampire said, blocking my path.

"How does *fuck off* sound?" I snarled not even looking at him but seriously in no mood for this dude who was most definitely not the boss of me. Stay in your goddamn lane, asshole.

His hand shot out to grab me, and as I focused on the vampire—who was not much taller than me, with a head full of golden-blond hair and angry, slanted grey eyes—I snarled.

"You've clearly got a death wish," I said as I struck hard with my left hand, cracking the heel of my palm into his nose.

He hadn't been expecting that attack and stumbled more than a few steps before he zoomed back toward me, both hands out this time. My wolf surged up at the last minute, weak but there, and she gave me the extra speed and strength I needed to spin and slam my shoe into him. My foot came free, leaving the spike of the heel embedded in his chest, which had the guy shouting and jumping around.

Kicking off the other shoe, I backed away as the vampire's fangs sprang free. My back landed against a hard surface, and in a blind panic that it was Carter, I spun to find Donovan behind me. Which might be even worse.

His gaze went to the heel in the blond vamp's chest and then back to me, and I wondered if I'd just signed my death warrant by attacking one of his own.

Chapter Twenty-Nine

"Someone better explain immediately what is happening here," Donovan said, expression drawn.

"She attacked me," the vampire snarled, the shoe still lodged in his chest backing his accusation.

Donovan spun on me. "Is this true?"

"Yes," I said without hesitation since there were plenty of witnesses and I was standing barefoot. "He grabbed me and tried to force me to follow him. No one gets to lay hands on me without retaliation."

Despite recent circumstances and evidence to the contrary, I was still a wolf shifter with an animalistic nature and hand-to-hand fight training. Relying on powerful males had become a common theme in my life lately, but it needed to stop. One day soon they would all be gone, and then it would only be me left. The one I'd always relied on.

"Is this true, Flarion?" Donovan asked, turning back to the vampire. "Did you grab one of the selected without permission? Have you all learned nothing from Carter's actions not one sun movement ago?"

Flarion started to splutter and rage as the metallic scent of his blood grew stronger. "She was heading away from the dance floor. Stupid wolf thought she could ignore the summons. If you want my opinion, the vermin should be flayed and turned into a rug for my floor."

Seeing red, I surged forward again, only to find strong arms around my shoulders holding me back. As the scent of crimson wine filled my senses, relief hit me—Lucien held me. I turned to find his green eyes locked on Donovan.

Thank fuck. Whatever Len had said to him, the surfer-vamp was back in control.

"Flarion touched one of the selected without their permission," Lucien said calmly. "I believe that warrants time in the pit. Let's see that it happens."

Donovan nodded his head, and then guards appeared from the shadows, taking hold of Flarion. The vampire spluttered and shouted, fighting against their hold, but the guards didn't seem to care, hauling him out of there with ease.

"Back to the dance floor," Donovan said, clapping his hands together and then straightening his dark blue suit.

Lucien tried to lead me away then, but I tugged on his arm to stop him. "I have no shoes," I said, waving at the puddle of red silk on the floor. "I can't dance in this dress without them."

Lucien shot me a slow smile, and I fought to remain angry with him for his shit from before. This side of him was as charming as the other side was terrifying... and both sides were sexy. They were also part of the reason I was in this mess.

"I'll find you something. Size nine, right?"

Should I be surprised that he knew my correct size? "Right."

He disappeared as a new song started, and through gaps in the crowd, I could see lots of couples dancing, including Carter. Len appeared in my peripheral, and I turned to give him a smile and nod. He'd saved the day by calming Lucien down.

Speaking of, the master returned a moment later, holding a pair of silvery heels, which were almost identical to the ones I'd used as a weapon. Like the gentleman he wasn't, he held an arm out and allowed me to use him as a support while I slipped on the shoes. The moment I was done, I released him. "I think you're wanted on the dance floor," I said shortly.

He didn't leave, stepping closer instead. "I won't apologize for what I said before, Bee. Carter should not have touched you. None of them should be fucking touching you. You stand here"—he waved his hand across the silky material—"looking positively edible"—his fangs descended, and I was trying really hard not to react—"and no one should be touching you."

He moved so we were touching. "Until this selection is done, you belong to me. Remember that. We made the deal."

I couldn't remember my own damn name, let alone this deal he kept referring to.

"I can't get around touching Carter," I managed to say.

I waited for darkness to fill the green of his eyes, but he controlled himself. "Yes, Len pointed out that demand might be an impossible one. Touch him only when necessary, in the official capacity of the selection. I think I can keep my vampiric nature under control if it's clear you're doing a job and nothing else."

My name was called over the speaker, ordering me to the dance floor. Lucien's name was next. We didn't move though, the moment and confusing feelings holding us in stasis. "I know we're playing this game to win," I said with a sigh, my chest tight, "but it doesn't—"

"Feel like a game," he finished.

I nodded. Lucien was not acting as I'd expected. Last time I'd been in Valdor, he'd been coldly holding me at arm's length. But this time... this time he was burning hot.

"Your blood is calling to me," he said so softly that I almost didn't catch it. "I'm in too deep to back away. Game or not, let's just see how it plays out."

My throat was too choked up to reply, so I just nodded my head.

Lucien led me to the dance floor, and he stepped right into the role of master looking for a mate, moving toward the selected who were waiting for him. The first up to the plate was Hattie, and I laughed when she saw me and jumped and waved. "Where the hell have you been?" she mouthed as Lucien approached her. She didn't wait for my reply though, stepping into his arms and smiling up at the handsome vampire.

Now I was the one fighting the urge to threaten bodily harm if he touched another female. Which was ridiculous. Sure, Hattie—and all the others—were beautiful. Tall and svelte with a range of skin colors from the whitest white to many dark-skinned supermodels. I appreciated the beauty of the female form, and in this room, there was a prime selection. Not that any of us should be viewed like a slice of beef to be bought.

Forcing myself not to watch Lucien, I stepped up to join the end of Carter's line, silently fuming for so many reasons. I should be back in Torma opening my bookstore and living my boring life.

Boring.

The word bounced around my head, and almost instantly I rejected the very notion. It was time to change my mindset. Time to stop being angry and start finding my blessings. No matter how hard this selection was, it was still better than an empty life. In truth, since Inky picked me up from Torma and took me to the library, I'd been on a nonstop rollercoaster adventure, and it wasn't over yet.

It certainly wasn't easy, but I'd felt more alive in the last few days than in all the months before. I'd spent so much time hiding from myself. Hiding from Lucien and the pain of almost dying. And his rejection.

I'd simply stopped living.

But there was only so long you could hide from the truth.

My truth: Lucien was under my skin. Denying it was like denying myself... I couldn't do it any longer.

I knew a time would come very soon when the selection was over and I would once again be back on Earth, once again mourning his loss, but until then I was going to embrace this life. Every dramatic, angsty, emotional piece of it.

After all, it wasn't every day you got to participate in a vampire selection while the sexiest master in existence drank your blood.

Turned out I was living a story worthy of an urban fantasy heroine, and curse my soul, I was going to enjoy every second of it.

Chapter Thirty

When it was my turn to dance with Carter, I stepped up into his arms without hesitation. Lucien had told me to treat this as a job, and I was going to follow his advice. "I'm not the monster you think I am."

Carter's opening sentence took me by surprise as I tilted my head back to meet his gaze. "I've never said you were a monster. I just don't appreciate being dragged into a selection that I didn't ask to be in. Every other invitee had the option of refusing, but I've been forced. I don't really know what you expected."

That appeared to stump him for a moment, his brows creasing as his lips thinned. Finally, he shook his head. "As I told you before, I promise not to force you. If in the end you decide that I'm not the mate for you, I'll respect that. But to decide, you need to give it a proper chance."

"What if I don't want a mate?"

I wasn't anti-mate, but it also wasn't the sole focus on my existence.

Carter leaned in, and for once his voice was gentle. "I had a mate. She was the most precious being in the world to me while she was alive. I would have died for her in a heartbeat. Killed for her without hesitation. Bled so she didn't have to. You deserve a mate just like that."

My throat grew tight as I nodded. "Yes, I do. But see, you've already had that with a vampire. I would always just be second place. I've always been second place in the lives of those who were supposed to love me." He opened his mouth, but I went on before he could interrupt. "I'm not saying that for sympathy. I came to terms with my truth long ago, but when it comes to a mate, I want to be first. The same way they would be for me."

Carter was watching me so closely that I felt almost naked under his gaze, but I wasn't quite done yet. "You talk of dying and fighting and loving your mate," I said softly, "and I have no doubt that every day of her life was amazing. I'm sorry she's gone now, and I hope for your future happiness. But I'm not the one for you."

Carter's smile was sudden and brilliant... and completely disconcerting. "That's why I called you to this selection," he said. "You are perfect for me. A true partner."

Was this vampire for real? "What part of I *don't want to be second* didn't you understand?" There was more bite in my tone now. Some dudes apparently needed to be hit over the head with the truth to actually hear it. "I won't compromise on that, not now or ever, so you might as well focus your attention on one of the others."

Carter stopped moving, even though the music wasn't quite done. "I need you to understand, Simone, that when my mate died, I did as well. My heart and my soul and the parts of me that gave a fuck about anything died. It wasn't until you touched the stone, sent out the burst of energy, and shocked me back to life that I was reborn. The way I see it, this version of Carter can make his new mate number one. This is my rebirth, and I plan to embrace it fully."

He lowered his head and pressed his lips to my cheek, the heat of his energy tracing delicately across mine. "Give this a chance," he murmured.

I didn't even know what to say. This stubborn asshole was clearly not going to give up easily, so I needed to figure out another way. "I'm here aren't I," I said to placate him for now.

Carter nodded. "You are, and I'll see you tomorrow for the first round."

When he was gone, I forced myself to breathe deeply a few times, needing to clear my head. "Simone."

Lucien appeared beside me, and he must have seen something odd in my expression because his hardened immediately. "What happened?" he snapped, looking around for Carter, no doubt.

Grabbing his arm, I shook my head. "No, nothing. Carter was just going on about true mates and being number one... I'm just all caught up in my thoughts."

Lucien muttered under his breath but didn't leave me to go kill the other master. We were both making progress, apparently. He did reach out and pull me into his arms, and I settled against him as if we'd been dancing together for years.

Our bodies moved in sync, always so compatible, even when both of us might have wished differently.

"Carter could be using a subtle compulsion on you," he told me as we moved.

I blinked, not having expected that. "I mean, it's not like I want to be his mate now or anything. I still actively tried to talk him out of choosing me, but... I was rather relaxed, now that I think about it."

Lucien nodded, muscles tensing under my arms. "Yes, that's what I was worried about. He will start slow and low before trying to force more of his will on you later. You have to learn to block his energy."

"How do I do that?" I asked, a little pissed about how easily these vamps could take another's will away.

Lucien tightened his hold on me, hand completely splayed across the bare skin on my lower back, touch burning me like a brand. "Normally, I'd suggest your wolf," he murmured. "But she's too weak at the moment. Your best option is for us to finish what we started earlier. You need to feed from me again, take my blood and use it to strengthen yourself."

Thoughts of *what we started earlier* had moisture pooling low in my center. My thong was definitely not adequate coverage to handle my need tonight. "Won't that weaken my wolf more?" I rasped.

He spun me, our feet moving faster in time to the beat as we settled in with the other dancers. "Your wolf will always be part of you," he told me. "Feeding from me now shouldn't create more of a bond than the one that's already formed. Certainly nothing worse than finding yourself mated to Carter because he clouded your judgement."

Leaning back, I stared up at Lucien, about to ask a very personal question. Maybe it was the wine talking or maybe I just had to know if Len's guess was right. "Why are you so against true mate bonds? You're not like Carter, having lost a true mate already, so why?"

Lucien let out a dry laugh, but to my surprise, he answered. "I don't really talk about it because it's best to move forward and not dwell on the past. But I feel I owe you some truth. My parents shared a blood call, the true bond I told you about. The problem was they could never extend that love to any other. I was their only child, born to keep my mother happy, but ultimately ignored.

"Then she wanted another child, and another, all of which was impossible due to the very rare nature of vampire pregnancies. My father was killed by a rival enclave when he attempted to take one of their young. Destroying them both. For with a blood call, one cannot survive without the other."

His sigh was so low I almost missed it. "From where I stood, that sort of dependency on another did more harm than good—especially when children were involved. It's why I made the decision to avoid serious relationships."

Len had some of the story right and other parts wrong, but it really didn't matter since the end results were the same: Lucien did not want a true mate.

He swirled me again, but I barely noticed, so focused on him. "What do you think of Shadow and Mera? Or Reece and Angel?" I asked. The first of their brotherhood to break the eternal bachelor cycle.

Lucien's expression brightened. "I'm truly happy for them. My damage is my own, but I see their joy and contentment. I mean, I barely recognize either of them these days, and it's all for the better. What is written in my future is not for them."

"You know your future can change at any point you want it to," I told him. "And you are not your parents. If we don't learn and do better, then what is the point of living at all?"

I'd learned to step away from my parents at a young age, and it was one of the most freeing things I'd ever done. He sobered. "At times I find it hard to believe you are so young when your soul is so wise. I'll think on your words, Bee."

Tonight had been a mess, but this part felt kind of right. Lucien and I had taken a step forward in our relationship, and maybe now, the future wasn't quite so defined.

For either of us.

Chapter Thirty-One

T he next morning when I dragged myself out of the supremely comfortable bed, my stomach raged at me, reminding me that I'd bailed after my obligatory dance with the masters and hadn't ventured near the wall of food.

Going on two days without eating, with wine and a few mouthfuls of water my only sustenance, there was no way I could miss breakfast. It had to fit into my schedule no matter what.

"They dropped off this envelope early this morning," Len said as I stumbled toward the sitting area. Peering through slitted, blurry eyes, I noticed how awake he looked.

"I hate you," I groaned. "No one told me you were a morning person."

Len laughed, seeming to take no offense in his cheery mood. Seriously, morning people were the worst. Straight up sociopaths.

"I haven't slept at all," he said. "I find that's the best way to avoid the dreaded early morning wake-up call." He nudged the large, cream-colored envelope toward me, and I snatched it up.

"How long can you go without sleep?" I asked around a yawn.

"Weeks," he replied. "I use energy from my crystals to power my own internal magic. I won't take a risk with your safety while on duty."

I waved him off as another huge yawn took over my face and made my eyes water. "You can sleep. I don't think the danger is that high."

He smirked and crossed his arms over his chest. "I stopped two of the selected from ripping your throat out last night. They got into the room, moving at vampiric speed. It was lucky I had those stones set to give me a head's up."

Okay, that had me waking right the fuck up.

On instinct I put my free hand to my throat. "What did you do with them?" I asked, turning toward the front door, which was securely closed with no sign of forced entry. "How did they get in?"

How had I missed the attacks? Sure, I'd been tired and a little drunk, but that was no excuse. My shifter instincts were suffering badly, and it could have gotten me killed.

"They appeared to have the entry code," Len said. "I've had it changed." He rambled off some numbers, which I immediately forgot. "Lucien took them away. Seems the competition is already down to twenty-nine, so you're doing well."

I laughed. "And yet I'm not supposed to be whittling away the contestants to make it easier for me to win. Maybe I should attack someone and get myself thrown out."

Len shook his head. "Judging by the look on Lucien's face, I don't think that was their only punishment. I wouldn't suggest it as a viable plan."

Of course, it wasn't. Why would an actual plan fall in our laps.

Taking the letter with me, I made my way into the bathroom, wincing at the bright lights filling the ceiling. The red of the sun filtering through the bedroom window hadn't hurt, but fake fluorescents always annoyed me.

Dropping the letter near the sink, I decided to read it after a refreshing shower. Closing my eyes, I stood under the hot spray, my body begging me to reach down and relieve the tension that had been building since Lucien lost his shit at the dance. Sexy, angry vampire was apparently my aphrodisiac.

I'd learned the hard way that I couldn't ease this need, so I refrained from even bothering. Stirring up the arousal and blood inside was a surefire way to send me back into the screaming fit. And we had no time for that.

When I couldn't avoid life any longer, I finished by brushing my teeth, shaving hairy parts, and washing other parts, then got out of the shower to prepare for the day. Ignoring makeup, I went for a bare-faced look and brushed my hair up into a high ponytail. My mane of dark hair was longer and thicker than ever, which I mostly noticed because the hair tie barely got around twice.

"Vampire blood," I muttered. Being back here had the blood inside me reacting to the vampire energy, and I couldn't deny that it was changing me. Lucien wanted me to feed more from him, and while the anticipation of that had me feeling *all kinds of things,* a part of me still worried that I'd lose the last of my wolf.

She lifted her head then and let out a sad howl that made me want to cry. "I'll free you," I promised, saying it out loud while staring at myself in the mirror. "We might need more blood to strengthen us, but I will not allow you to vanish under it."

Wrapping the cloth around me, I left the bathroom and made my way to my wardrobe. I still hadn't bothered to read the itinerary yet, but since I really didn't give a shit what was expected any longer, I decided to just wear what I was comfortable in: skinny black jeans, low-heeled boots that zipped up to my calf, a plain white shirt, and a black jacket.

It wasn't cold in Valdor, with their spring temperature, but I'd be fine in a jacket and boots. Back in the bathroom, I picked up the envelope and opened it. Pulling free one piece of thick parchment, I saw fancy cursive writing.

There are twenty-nine selected remaining in this competition.
Five more will be eliminated today.
Please note the events in order below. Do not be late for any of them.
First: Breakfast in the great hall. Refuel for maximum strength.
Second: Blessing from the Stone of Katu. Strive for acceptance.
Third: Obstacle course to determine fitness levels and agility. Strive for
victory.

I BLINKED AT THREE. Was fitness level really an important factor in a true mate? Did they want a lovely long-distance runner who could do a backflip in her sleep?

At least an obstacle course would be an easy one to fail since I would struggle to keep up with a vampire for even a short period of time.

As I exited the bathroom, there was a chime through the room, and Len was at the door in a heartbeat. When he opened it, I couldn't see who stood on the other side until they stepped inside.

Lucien.

Moving toward him, I wondered why he was here. "Everything okay?" I asked.

He nodded, and I took a second to look him over. He was dressed in black army-style pants, black shit-kicker boots, and a dark green shirt that made his eyes a deeper green than normal. He looked good. Really, *really* good. This would be so much easier if Lucien didn't always look so damn fuckable.

"I want to start the process of building your mental and physical barriers," he told me, and somehow, I found the strength to focus on his words. "Carter is going to do everything in his power to ensure you make it through to the next round so he can continue to influence you. We need to start building now, before it gets any worse."

I nodded. "Yeah, and if we could ensure I wake up before my throat almost gets ripped out next time, that would be great too."

For the first time there was a flicker of emotion in his face. "That too," he said gruffly, "though I've sent out a warning to the other selected advising them of what happened to the two who attacked during the sleep cycle."

I snorted. "Think that will work?"

Lucien straightened, expression confident. "If it doesn't, the next punishment will be much worse."

"Okay, then. So, what do we need to do this morning?"

He stepped closer, and his scent was strong as it filled my nose, drifting down inside me. The blood he'd eased in the shower started to swirl again in heated arcs, and I tried not to think about what was about to happen. I wasn't even sure what I wanted to happen.

The door to the room opened, and I heard Len call out. "I'll give you two some privacy."

Neither of us responded or looked his way. I couldn't tear my eyes from Lucien, even if I wanted to, and I was starting to wonder if maybe taking more of his blood was a bad idea. It might help me resist Carter, but it was getting harder every damn day to resist Lucien.

At this point, though, he was the lesser of two evils, so I'd just have to hope that this wouldn't come back to destroy me later.

"Do you want to bite me?" he asked. "If you call up your wolf, you can take control."

I swallowed hard, trying to find moisture in my mouth. "I can try. She's buried deep, and I don't think she's too keen on more vampire blood, but it's worth a shot."

"Take the shot," he murmured, and I wondered if all the moisture missing from my mouth was in my underwear, because goddamn.

This girl was ready for some action.

Chapter Thirty-Two

Lucien remained where he was, expression neutral, even if his eyes hadn't moved from my face. I wondered if he was letting me take the lead because he didn't trust his vampire energy not to go berserk, like at the dance. Or maybe he was just forcing me to find my own inner strength, which I was more than willing to try.

Closing my eyes to block out his beautiful and distracting face, I coaxed my beast forward, reminding her that we needed to feed and strengthen ourselves. *To get through the selection.* She was beyond reluctant, the slow trickle of her energy barely even registering, but she was still there. I wouldn't give up until I got her moving.

Finally, she stirred, and as she moved through the heat of the vampire energy, I pushed for a partial shift, wanting just my teeth and jaw to change so we could break through the vampire's skin.

As the shifter magic overtook my body, I cried out and felt the force of a full shift coming over me. *No.* I attempted to pull her back because there was no time to be stuck in a wolf body when I had a selection to get to.

"No," I growled out loud this time. "We can't fully shift."

My wolf was beyond listening to me, and as I fell forward, Lucien caught me. My skin had been stretching with the wolf, but as soon as his power surged into mine, her fight died off, and with a whimper, she rolled over inside, metaphorically exposing her belly. At first it destroyed me to think she was hurt, weakened by his presence, but as she continued to lay on her back, I searched deeper to find...

She wasn't hurting at all. She was submitting. She was treating Lucien like he was our—

"Alpha," I breathed. "She considers you her alpha."

I tilted my head back to see his breathtaking face, glowing skin near blinding in its intensity. "That's one of the reasons she's subdued around you. She's giving you the lead."

I'd never felt her like this, even with Alpha Victor in Torma—part of the reason I'd always considered myself packless, except for my bond to Mera.

"I don't understand why your shifter side is reacting like this," Lucien said, still holding me close. "Your energy is strong enough to be an alpha yourself."

A strangled laugh escaped me. "I used to think that too, but as I've gotten older, I've come to realize something: I'm not alpha. Or even beta. I'm an omega."

Lucien tilted his head to the side, and I could almost see the gears turning in his brain as he put it all together. "Omegas stand outside of the pack hierarchy, right?"

"Yep," I said, finally sharing my secret. "It's the reason I've always felt like an outsider in Torma and how I was able to resist an alpha command for a long time. I pretended I was controllable because being an omega is not always the safest position in a pack."

Lucien didn't like that, his brows drawing together as he snarled. "You should be the most protected pup of all. Omegas can create peace where there's violence, bring hope when there is none, and prevent wars."

My laugh was bitter. "In Torma, they desired none of those things. I was just lucky that my parents kept me somewhat isolated from the alpha. Victor would have killed an omega for sure."

I'd always hoped that my parents kept me out of shifter life to protect me—that a tiny part of them loved me enough to shield me from the insane alpha. But as I got older, I realized the truth: They didn't know I was an omega. They were embarrassed that I was a pathetic, submissive wolf, and for that, I was hidden away.

"I bet it's also the reason you and Mera work so well," Lucien mused. "She's beyond alpha, and you would calm her nature."

"Mera's strong energy did mask my own," I agreed. "It got harder when she was gone, but I just acted like I was in mourning and barely left my house. My parents backed me up. Eventually, the leaders of Torma were usurped, and it's been quiet ever since."

"You never have to go back to that," he told me, the rasp of his voice stirring his blood inside. "You will leave Valdor stronger. You will forge your own path and future, and whatever that ends up being, you will be safe."

His fiercely protective side knocked some of the air from my lungs, making me feel a touch breathless. A moment of peace and clarity followed, and I was able to bring forth my wolf and do a partial shift.

Lucien leaned forward so I could reach the smooth expanse of bare skin at his throat. I felt no hesitation as my newly sharpened teeth sank into him. All rational thought vanished at the first pull of blood into my mouth, and even though I couldn't remember the other time I'd drunk from him, this memory would stay with me forever.

I'd expected a sharp, metallic flavor, but Lucien was delicious, reminding me of Crimson Heart. His blood was warm and rich with hints of cherry—his scent made perfect sense now. I groaned at the next pull of blood, drinking in more than just the liquid. I consumed his fire and power with each sip, and damn, it was more than a little addictive.

Eventually, Lucien had to cut me off, and as I pulled away, I noticed the slightly ravaged section of his skin was already healing.

My wolf sank inside me, feeling all blissed out, and I was the same.

"Well, fuck," I murmured.

Lucien laughed, and my eyes focused enough to see he remained strong and glowing, with no sign my greedy drinking had stolen anything from him.

"What happens now," I asked, head still spinning as his blood literally pounded in my veins, burning through me.

"Now, you let it settle," he told me. "And I get my turn."

I blinked at him. "You're going to feed from me too? Will this form some sort of bond between us if we keep this up?"

Lucien nodded. "It could, if we did so touching the Stone of Katu. But for now, we're just sharing blood. It should be relatively simple."

"You hope," I responded drily. "Since you've admitted to being a virgin."

He barely hid his smile. "Not where it matters, Bee. Not where it matters."

He stepped closer. I went to push myself up from where I'd half collapsed in my bliss, but he swooped in and wrapped his arm around me before I could move, lifting me up and into his body. My wolf howled, and I did the same, letting the sound ring out through the room. Lucien growled, and despite his words from before, it felt like the animalistic natures inside both of us were bonding.

When his fangs sank into my neck, my howl died off as a low moan escaped. Every part of me came to life, and I rocked against Lucien. He adjusted his hold so my legs could move around his waist, and I cried out as his hard length pressed into my sensitive center.

With his mouth still against my throat and the fire of his blood in my body, I desperately scrambled to get his pants undone, my hands sliding along firm muscles as I fought for more. "Lucien," I moaned, "I need... to feel... you. Please."

His rumblings increased, chest rocking as he shifted his lower half so I could get his pants down and free his *holy fucking hell*. I couldn't see it, but I could feel that his cock was thick and long, and moisture beaded under my thumb as I ran it across the slit on top.

"Lucien," I cried again, and with each pull of his mouth against my throat, I felt the same pull at the junction of my thighs.

Somehow, without removing his mouth from my neck, he got my pants undone and his fingers slid through my folds to find me soaking wet. The scent of my arousal spread up between us, and it turned me on even more as I lost myself in the sensation of rocking against Lucien's hand.

"More, Crimson," I demanded, and with my hand wrapped around his cock and his buried in my pussy, there was no way either of us could resist. There was also no need to worry about pregnancy, since I wasn't fertile, which meant there was no reason to stop. At least none I was ready to think about at this point in time.

Lucien pulled away, tongue swiping across my neck to chase the last drops of blood, while the head of his cock entered me. The burn of the first stretch so delicious that I was panting as he slid inch by delicious inch inside me. I was tight, but my arousal soon smoothed the path, as Lucien hit every damn nerve ending I didn't even know existed.

Pulling out of me slowly, he drew out the pleasure again, and I was screaming when he thrust roughly into me. "Bee," he groaned. "You're so fucking tight."

The fire inside forced me to move against him before I could speak. "I've only had sex twice, and you're huge. Also... don't ever stop fucking me."

He stilled, a deep growl escaping as he stared down into my face, and I wondered if that last line had freaked him out. Thankfully, he didn't stop, because I was almost a hundred per cent certain that if Lucien stopped before I orgasmed, I would combust.

Literally.

Chapter Thirty-Three

I'd always wondered if I'd ever experience the sort of mind-blowing orgasms that Mera described in her long-winded chats about Shadow and his prowess as a lover. My few forays into sex certainly had been nothing like that.

Then I'd met Lucien. Felt the pull of his mouth on my body, and I'd finally understood what had addicted Mera to her beast.

As I arched my back, Lucien's grip tightened on my skin, and I could feel every indent of his palm on my ass and thighs. His powerful thrusts never eased, not even as my head spun, and I wondered if I was about to pass out.

When the swirls of pleasure in my gut grew too intense, I tried to hold back, but there was no hope. It would be like trying to stop a raging storm with an umbrella. The power was too great, and I had no choice but to tumble over the edge, screaming as I went.

Lucien groaned against my skin, and I heard him rumble, a desperate edge to his voice, "More."

I had no idea if he meant blood or sex since, in this moment, it felt like they were one and the same. I didn't care, either, because I would do anything to keep feeling all of this. Lucien filled my body and soul. Rebuilt me until I didn't recognize who I was anymore. The sort of rebirth that I thought was reserved for Mera and Angel.

I'd never be the same after this. I knew that as surely as I knew my own name.

There was no time to worry about what state I might be left in, as Lucien captured all of my attention. His lips slid across mine, tasting my mouth, his tongue lazily demanding entrance as it swiped across my own. There was a hint of blood mingling between us, and it only turned my desire tenfold.

"Stay with me, Baby Bee," he whispered against my lips, thrusting harder, and I found myself moving against him faster, chasing my next high. Lucien laughed a low, deep rumble as his hands pulled me up on his body, giving him a better angle to slam into me.

This time when I came, my cry was hoarse, after having nearly screamed myself into silence. Lucien made a guttural sound as he slowed, his cock swelling as he sent me over the edge again, and we came together like a perfect fairytale.

Only I was in vampire town, where fairy tales died and nightmares were made.

Not that I cared—I'd choose this dark, bloody world over Torma every single time.

When my body finally stopped trembling, I loosened my legs around his waist, expecting he would drop me back to my feet.

Only he didn't.

He walked us into the bathroom. "What are you doing?" I rasped, throat still raw as hell.

"Taking care of you."

My heart definitely skipped a beat. "Why?"

My only response was a growl, and then he was stripping off whatever clothing had made it through sex, until we were naked.

This was the first time I'd seen him without some covering, and I was starting to think I could easily go another round.

Or ten.

Shifter males were ripped—females too—but Lucien was a step above. He had a warrior's body, just like the others in Shadow's merry band of assholes. All of them were huge specimens of the male species, with extra muscles and height, because they were legit warriors.

They'd clearly never spent the day in bed watching crappy movies and eating bags of chocolate and licorice, and it showed. Lucien was all defined lines across his chest and abs, and the huge valleys and peaks in his biceps and triceps moved as he shifted us under the water. Not to mention his thick thigh muscles, keeping both of us standing.

I mean, the strength just to hold me with one hand so the other could strip my clothing before... impressive.

"I think you fucking killed me?" I whispered, wishing my voice wasn't all rasp.

Lucien's eyebrows drew together as he examined my face. He slowly lowered me to the tiles and lifted his hand to scour across his wrist with his fangs. "Drink."

A stronger chick would have hesitated—good for her. But I needed my fix.

Move over licorice, there was a new obsession in town.

By the time I'd swallowed his blood, my throat was back to full strength, and the rest of me felt fucking amazing too. Vampire blood was potent with healing and regeneration, and I was already anticipating the next time I'd get to taste him.

Lucien took a step back, the water from the multiple showerheads beating down on him.

Slicked back hair and water dripping along golden skin was a good look for him.

"What happens now?" I asked, fighting to keep any vulnerability from my tone.

"You will need to drink from me again," he said softly, "to keep building your barriers, and I will need to from you, to ensure the fire of the blood doesn't burn out of control until it all settles within you."

"You don't seem upset about it," I noted.

His hands brushed across my side as he pulled me closer. "I've tried to deny it, but your blood calls to me. The fact that we have to continue to share for the duration of the selection doesn't bother me. However, if you want me to find another solution? Bottled blood—"

"Nope," I cut in quickly. "No need for any other solution. I'm happy to keep this little arrangement up for as long as needed to get through this selection."

Or forever.

Not that I'd ever say that out loud. My blood might call to him, but that didn't change Lucien's view on mates. At least I could anticipate more feeding and fucking for the time being, and I was okay with that.

Part of me was starting to hope the selection lasted for a few years.

It was the least the gods owed me.

Chapter Thirty-Four

Lucien stuck around to thoroughly clean me up... and down. When I could stand again, I knew we had to be seriously late for the morning events.

"Do you need anything else?" he asked as I stepped from the shower.

For some reason my next words stuck in my throat. Why did it destroy me so thoroughly when someone gave a shit about my needs? I didn't know how to deal with the rising wake of emotions that ensued from such a statement. "I'm fine," I choked out.

Lucien didn't just take me at my word, striding forward, unconcerned with being naked and wet as he took a towel and stroked it over my body, drying me. "You need to get dressed now," he said when he was done. "When you're naked, I have a much harder time controlling myself."

"That goes for both of us, Crimson," I said with a strangled laugh. "Your weapon of mass destruction is waving around about to start another battle."

He tilted his head like he was trying to figure out if he'd heard me right. But seriously, his cock was impressive enough that if he didn't want me to jump on it again, he needed to lasso and contain it.

Before anything could happen, the doorbell chimed, and Lucien let out a curse as he strode from the bathroom. "Still naked," I called out after him, but he gave zero fucks.

Weirdly enough, my wolf was rumbling in my chest because, apparently, I did give some fucks about another vampire seeing him naked. This possessive shit needed to be brought right under control and soon because Lucien had made it perfectly clear that when this was all over, he was done.

He wanted nothing to do with long-term relationships, mate bonds, or children.

As hard as it was to accept, I had to respect his wishes—even if he did give me the most mind-blowing orgasms of my life and said heart-clenching things like I reminded him of a bee, the one creature literally essential to Earth's survival.

Sadly for me, the essential part I filled in his life was on a time limit, so this was an enjoy it for now and walk away when it's done situation.

Len's voice reached me, and I realized he was the one who'd chimed the bell to let us know he was returning. I relaxed my hands, which had partially shifted into claws, and was about to walk from the room clad only in the bath sheet, when Lucien appeared in the doorway. Blocking my exit.

His expression was dark, and my mind immediately started throwing terrible scenarios at me. "What's wrong?"

His expression didn't ease. "Nothing is wrong. What clothing do you need?"

I shrugged, inching the top of my towel higher. "I can look for myself. You should get to the breakfast or whatever we've missed."

He didn't move, even as I sort of nudged him out.

"No."

I stilled. He didn't sound angry; it was a simple statement.

"Excuse me?"

"You do not dress in front of Len. You do not walk out in a towel if he's in the room."

I started to splutter and protest because *what the actual fuck,* when he wrapped his hand around the lower half of my face. He tilted my head back and leaned over to press a long, lingering kiss to my lips.

"Until the selection is done, you belong to me, Bee. And I never share."

Clarity and sanity returned in a blast. "I thought we went over this last night at the dance," I said in an angry hiss. "We might be fucking, but—"

My words were cut off as his hand slipped under my towel and he stroked through the newly pooled moisture between my thighs. Yeah, I was a hot mess completely turned on by his dominance, but that didn't mean he got to know that.

"Seems we agree on the terms," he said, sliding across my swollen, aching flesh once more, and I barely stifled a groan.

His hand was gone in the next second and then so was the vampire, the closed door of the bathroom staring me in the face. "We'll wait outside in the hall for you." His words drifted through to me, and I slumped against the door, my forehead cracking onto the wood as I lost the ability to hold myself up.

I was in so much trouble that it wasn't even funny.

How did this happen? How did I find myself tangled in romance and drama like I was starring in my own paranormal romance novel? Leading lady roles were for other supernaturals... like Mera. I was more of the quirky sidekick.

It was almost as if her leading role had spread like a virus into my life, and now I was going to be navigating a story on my own. Just as she had.

"Am I strong enough for this?" I asked the still closed door. "Seriously?"

No one answered, thankfully, because a talking door would have been fucking terrifying. Just like Mera's talking cloud of smoke. Tilting my head back, I stared into the ceiling above and scowled. "Don't you be sending me any animal, smoke, or goblin sidekicks. This is not a fairy-tale story. I repeat. Not. A fairy tale."

With that statement made, I opened the door and headed for the wardrobe. I took out a nearly identical outfit from before, only the jacket this time was a deep burgundy color made from a velvet-like material. When I was dressed, hair smoothed back again and game face on, I left the bedroom and exited into the hallway. Len moved forward from where he'd been leaned against the wall, face nearly expressionless, except for a small smile playing around his lips. "Ready to go, princess?" he asked.

"Not a princess," I shot back. "No animal sidekick or leading-role potential in sight, thank you very much."

To his credit, he managed not to look surprised by my crazy outburst.

"Not sure Lucien would agree," he said. "I mean, he's got you in a starring role at his side."

I resisted the urge to punch the enigmatic and powerful silver fae. "Shut up."

His laughter followed me down the hall as I took off, but he soon caught up to me. "Seriously, you have no idea what you've gotten yourself into."

That did give me a moment's pause. "What do you mean?" I finally had to ask when it was apparent he wasn't going to continue on his own. "And where is Lucien?"

He'd said *we* would wait in the hall.

"He was called ahead to view the obstacle course, and he wants to ensure it's safe for you," Len said without hesitation. "And I'm telling you, Lucien has your blood scent now, and I've never seen him like this. Truth is, my friend has a big heart and an obsessive tendency to go in full throttle when his emotions are involved."

None of this was new information to me, and I didn't care about the obsessive and possessive nature of the master vampire. If I was only going to have him for a short period of time, then I sure as hell wanted a hundred and fifty percent of him. Nothing less would do.

"I'm all in, but I have to remember that it's not forever," I told Len quietly. "Lucien and I are fucking and feeding for the duration of this selection because it keeps me strong and all of our urges under control. But after this is over, so are we. I just have to figure out how to deal with whatever is happening to me as a hybrid wolf-vamp."

"Right," he replied softly, clearly not believing a word of it. "Crimson and Bee, just partners in crime."

I elbowed him, but he was made of steel, and all I did was bruise myself. Luckily, I was all hopped up on vampire blood, Lucien's power sloshing around inside me and filling up my wells of energy. I was healed before the true pain even kicked in.

When we reached the ground floor, we exited into the area where the breakfast was supposed to have been. At first, I couldn't see the other selected, but then we followed the voices, moving through a doorway and into a much larger room with windows spanning three sides.

It sounded like they were finishing up, which probably meant I'd missed breakfast. Again. Well, I guess I did eat already, if you counted that little blood exchange.

As much as I loved food, I wouldn't have missed this morning with Lucien for all the pancakes in the world, even if I starved to death in the process.

Some experiences were worth dying for, and sex like that... might just be one of them.

Last time I'd been here, I'd felt pathetic throwing myself at a vampire who didn't want me. This time was all different.

Lucien wanted me, so I would embrace it all.

Until that time ran out.

Ticktock.

Chapter Thirty-Five

We approached the selected, who were gathered together listening to a speech. I couldn't see who was talking from where I stood, but for once it wasn't Donovan. This voice was feminine, rich and throaty, and it was vaguely familiar, making me think it was the master female Julietta, with the long platinum hair, who'd spoken that first day.

"...great honor that you've been invited," she was saying. "Forming a matebond with a master is a rare opportunity, and you will be richly rewarded. Do not take this task lightly. Do not squander the chance you've been given. Now it's time for us to head to the Stone of Katu for your blessing by the gods."

"Can you see any food?" I whispered to Len as everyone started to move. "Their advice to refuel has me a little worried. I haven't eaten anything for days."

His lips twitched. "Are you sure about that? I could have sworn—"

Before I could think about how stupid it was to hit the fae again, my fist was slamming against his arm. "Ouch, fuck," I snarled, shaking out my throbbing hand. It healed in a few seconds as Len laughed, thankfully not wanting to murder me on the spot.

"Let me have a look around for some food," he told me, expression sobering, though his eyes were still filled with amusement.

"Thank you," I muttered, clearing my throat to force a smile. "Appreciate it."

With a wink, he was gone, heading toward the far set of windows with the long table beneath. As I waited and tried not to think about all the "eating" that had happened this morning—thank you fae for bringing that back up—a familiar face popped up in front of me. "Hattie!" I said with a smile.

She threw her arms around me, pulling in for a strong hug. Usually when a vampire *or Mera* hugged me, it was a somewhat painful experience, but today I felt like my body held up much better against it.

"I've been waiting for you all morning," she said. "Stay right here; I saved a plate for you."

She hurried off to another set of small tables that I hadn't noticed until now and grabbed a plate. She was dressed simply today, wearing a plain white button-up shirt, black leather pants, and black flat boots. Her hair was slicked back in a ponytail and her face appeared free of makeup. She honestly looked even more beautiful than she had in her ballgown.

"Here! Eat!" she said, thrusting a plate into my face. My stomach grumbled so loudly that I would have been embarrassed if I wasn't beyond hungry.

"Thank you," I murmured, feeling overwhelmed by her caring enough to save me some food. "I was a touch concerned that I might just have to starve for the rest of the day since there wasn't a lunch on that itinerary."

She chuckled, perfect, white teeth flashing at me. "We can go for days without food as long as we have blood. They've no doubt forgotten that other races need actual food more often."

And yet I'd been existing on the vampire diet for days now.

Starving, I quickly wolfed down the food, which mainly consisted of bread-like pastries; *sartin,* their most common fruit with dark red skin and sweet centers; and *fragler sticks,* my favorite treat from last time. It tasted like dried sticks of syrup.

Len appeared a moment later at my side, a plate of food in his hands.

"No need," I said, waving him off as I finished the last sticks on my plate. "Hattie saved me some."

She stepped closer to the fae, her smile even more brilliant, if that was possible. "Figured it was the least I could do since Simone will be at a disadvantage today, no matter what."

Right, great. Thanks for reminding us all of that.

Len didn't return her smile, and even though his face was expressionless, I could tell he was unhappy. I'd forgotten his little rule about not eating food he hadn't checked, but it was Hattie. She didn't want to be in this selection either.

Done, I dropped the plate on the table, and we headed in the direction of the stairs so we could ascend to the second floor and the Stone of Katu.

"I'm hoping this obstacle course is super hard," I said as we walked. "I'm not allowed to throw this competition or they'll kill me, but if I'm honestly eliminated, no one could say anything. I'll be putting in my full effort and hoping I lose."

Hattie blinked at me. "You genuinely don't want to win?"

I snorted. "Genuinely and beyond. This is not my world, and I'm not a fan of arranged matings. If someone wants to be my mate, then I expect them to fight for me. Because I sure as fuck would fight for them."

The partial lie felt stale on my tongue because I'd already decided to walk away from the one supernatural who'd ever called to my shifter soul: Lucien. To be true to myself, I should be fighting for him, but it had to go both ways.

As I'd said, my mate had to fight for me too, otherwise it was not a real mate bond.

So my plan remained solid.

Hattie let out a deep sigh. "You're so right about the fighting part. We should do everything in our power to fight for our true mates and let the rest go."

Her words reminded me that she was in love with the vamp next door, and I sincerely hoped that she would find a way back to him with her family's blessing.

We reached the long hall and joined the long line of selecteds slowly making their way up to the stone. I really didn't want to touch it again; my skin felt clammy at the thought since the last time I'd had my throat ripped out.

No doubt I was about to get majorly triggered, but I couldn't refuse to play my part now. I would give them no reason to kill me.

As we got closer, I observed the master's platform. It appeared that all of them were in attendance today, and an eleventh chair had been added for Carter.

He was far from the center of power—Lucien and Donovan's chairs—but he was up there.

Claiming his throne. Silver House.

I'd be happy for him if this claiming wasn't seriously impacting my damn life.

Bastard better keep his promise of releasing me in the end.

As we stepped closer to the stone, I could feel Lucien's gaze on me. My body responded like it had been dropped into a pot of warm water. Everything heated inside, my legs grew wobbly, and even though I'd been telling myself not to stare, because a room full of vampires was no place to get hot and bothered, it was impossible not to look his way.

He wore no expression as he relaxed in his chair, long legs out in front, sexy man-spread going on. *Damn him.* His arms rested on the sides, shoulders filling out the entire back of his fancy-ass chair, with only a few crimson stones peeking out of the sides.

He looked powerful and commanding. Like a king observing his people.

Only he was just observing me.

Having all of his attention was almost too much to handle.

As discretely as possible, I wiped at my forehead, wondering if I was starting to sweat. I didn't miss the slight smirk playing around his lips.

Stop it! I mouthed at him, trying to breathe calmly.

His smirk grew.

How was it possible that Lucien had fucked me not even an hour ago and already my body was responding like it wanted more.

Needed more.

You have to walk away. You have to walk away.

Maybe if I repeated it enough, I'd fucking remember it.

"You've got someone's attention," Hattie said in a low voice near my ear.

"I know," I murmured, finally able to tear my gaze from Lucien. I glanced toward her, only to find she wasn't looking at Lucien. Her head was turned toward Carter, and sure enough, the other master, whom I'd barely noticed, had his eyes locked on us.

Unlike with Lucien, his position on his chair was rigid and uncomfortable, but there was no denying his focus was all on me.

It was one of my least favorite tropes in books, when the unassuming, plain heroine suddenly had the attention of every desirable male—and female—for absolutely no reason. It wasn't like I thought of myself as a nothing, or even particularly plain, but there was no good reason for both of these gorgeous, powerful, master vampires to be pursuing me like this.

There was more at play here. Was it simply that I'd broken the rules and touched the stone, triggering a power that'd called to Carter? And in return, Lucien had to feed me his blood, forming this bond between us?

Carter knew nothing about me and my life. Not one damn thing. Lucien, on the other hand, did know me. The real me. I'd let my walls down with him last time, and we'd spent more than a few sleep cycles talking about our lives.

He'd let little bits and pieces slip, mostly events from his time with Shadow and the merry band of assholes, but every now and then, the true heart of Lucien had shone through.

Those nights had been like a dream... the sort of connection I'd always craved.

Hence why I'd never been able to settle for less since.

Carter might not understand it, but no burst of power from a stone would convince me to mate someone. I would always want and demand more.

Always.

Chapter Thirty-Six

A s I neared the stone, my thoughts of mates and tropes dried up to be replaced with anxiety. What would happen this time when I touched the stone?

Lucien sat straighter as I approached, but he didn't give me any indication that I shouldn't touch it.

Not like I had any choice; this was part of the selection process.

Julietta, her platinum hair pulled back in a high bun, highlighting the stark beauty of her features, was the one in charge today. Her outfit was white, a power suit that left her boobs pushed up and all but spilling from the top button. Vampires never hid their sexuality, and I was on board with that trend.

"Hatilda of the Jade House, please step forward," she announced.

Hattie took a deep breath beside me and then strode toward the huge stone. I hadn't known she was from Donovan's enclave; her master's smile was broad as he watched her approach.

"Hatilda, do you honor our gods?" Julietta asked.

Hattie nodded as she lifted her right hand. "I do. Always." She murmured a few other words that were not in a language I understood, but it sounded ancient and powerful. Then she reached out and placed her hand on the stone, and the light grew infinitely brighter, just for a few seconds, before fading again.

It was almost as if the Stone of Katu was absorbing some of the vampire's power, growing a little stronger with each touch.

Hattie wore a serene smile, appearing right at home with her hand resting against the stone. "Thank you," the master said. "Your blessing has been accepted. You may join the selected to the left."

For the first time I noticed two red-faced females had moved to the right side of the room, away from the main group of blessed. This reminded me that I could fail out here. The tier one masters couldn't do anything if the stone rejected me.

They'd never go against their gods.

"Simone Lewison of the shifter pack in Torma, step forward."

I was the last, and all eyes were on me. With a sliver of hope in my heart, I approached the stone, hoping desperately that I wasn't triggered with some sort of panic attack or flashback when I touched it.

Fail. Fail. Fail. Fail.

One word chanted over and over in my head, even though I knew if I did, part of my heart and soul would stay in this world. At least it would only be part—if I remained in the selection any longer, it might be all.

"Simone, do you honor the gods?" Julietta asked me.

I tore my gaze away from the red, gold, and black sparkle of the stone and looked into her silvery eyes. "They're not my gods, but I will show them the respect they are due."

She nodded, her expression remaining neutral. "Touch and receive your blessing."

I was confident that I wasn't the only one holding their breath as I reached out and placed my right hand against the middle of the massive stone. Bracing myself for a burst of energy like last time, I was surprised when all I received was a warm blast of air across my body. The stone lit up in a spark of power before that power died off again just as quickly.

Julietta stepped forward, looking down at me from the edge of her platform. "It appears the blessing was accepted. Please make your way to the left side of the room."

My wolf howled in my chest, satisfied with our strength. From the start, she hadn't been on board with failing, a feeling that had only grown stronger since she'd started treating Lucien as our alpha.

I walked toward Hattie, who was smiling broadly at me, and I couldn't help but turn my head back. Both Carter and Lucien were on their feet, staring my way again.

Carter looked pleased, his lips curved and eyes lit up. But Lucien's expression was more closed off.

Either way, I hadn't failed out at the blessing, so that meant we were onto the next part.

The obstacle course.

THE SELECTED WERE quiet as we left the Master Chambers, heading into the maze of Crimson City. We took an exit that I hadn't been through before, and when I saw Galco guarding one of the gates, his bald head reflecting off the red sunlight, I waved and got an enthusiastic wave in return.

In the streets, the vampire's speed picked up, and I found myself unable to keep up.

Len took pity on me, wrapping an arm around my waist as he zipped off after the vamps, almost managing to stay with the group.

"Their speed has always pissed me off," Len grumbled as he reached for a stone in his jacket. Once he got his hand on the quarter-sized, opaque aqua stone, he picked up speed.

In no time we were in the outer area of Crimson City. It would have taken me hours to walk the distance, but we'd made it in minutes at vampire pace. "The course is set out in the Zone of

Osida," Julietta called. "Masters Carter and Lucien will be waiting at the end to see who makes it through and what condition they're in. This will help them decide on who they want to continue on in the competition."

"None of that sounds remotely ominous," I murmured, and Hattie, who was nearby, snorted.

"Don't worry; I'll stick with you," she told me.

My stomach roiled unexpectedly, and I pressed my hand against it, hoping to calm myself. It was just an obstacle course, and I wanted to lose anyway. I had no idea why my body was rebelling by trying to send me straight to the nearest bathroom.

As a shifter, I wasn't really struck down by stomach issues. Our system was quick to repel any bacterial invasion, so this had to be nerves. Nerves that would not take me down. If I could touch the Stone of Katu without freaking out, I could get through this obstacle course.

Or fail spectacularly trying.

Ignoring the gurgling of my gut, I followed the group as we moved clear of the city and into the countryside that surrounded it. I'd never been this far into Valdor and was curious what it was like out here under the perpetual red light of their sun.

In our immediate area, the ground was flat and covered in a short layer of yellowy grass. Reaching down to run my hand across it, I marveled at how soft it felt—almost like velvet. Moving through this grass, we appeared to be heading toward pockets of forest a few hundred yards away. Beyond this were more treelike structures and even some mountains. The weather remained in an eternal spring here, so there was no snow to be seen on top of the red mountains.

When we reached the forest, it was to find trees a hundred feet high and dozens of feet wide. The entire ecosystem looked ancient, filled with many foreign plant and animal species. I mean, foreign to me, anyway.

"All you have to do," said Julietta, the only master to accompany us, "is make it to the other side of this forest. Head for a large water crossing, which signals the end of the obstacle course. If you exit without finding a water source, you've gone the wrong way. At the request of one of the masters, we've also added a few blockers around the perimeter, which will somewhat limit speed and strength in vampires to make it fair for all contestants."

Many pissed off looks were shot my way, and I forced myself to remain calm, even as my stomach jumped once more. These bitches needed to realize that I was not here of my own free will and the full twenty-plus of them left just had to get their asses out there and win. Because I didn't want to. The master who'd requested the blockers had to be Carter because Lucien was on board with my plan to lose.

"Best of luck, selected," Julietta called. "Your time starts now."

There was a rush of noise as the females let out a war cry, and then they started running. I'd been at the back of the group, so I got to watch their vampire speed until they moved between the first trees, the blockers slowing them from there.

I got more glares then, but soon they were all gone from view.

"I'll wait for you at the end," Len said, nudging me forward. "Go before they decide you're throwing this section."

"Right, right," I said.

Hattie linked our arms together and dragged me along at her speed, sending my stomach into a roiling mess until we reached the trees. As the shadows engulfed us, her speed dropped right back to my normal pace.

We were finally in the first task, and I honestly wished I was anywhere else.

Chapter Thirty-Seven

Hattie didn't stop until we were well into the first lot of trees and the golden fields were completely gone from sight.

"Keep an eye out for traps," she said, her head swiveling as she took everything in.

"What sort of traps should I expect?" I asked, calling on my wolf for some focus. It wasn't dark in here, but it was certainly much duller with only slivers of red light filtering through the canopy.

"It could be anything, but I'd anticipate a few loose frodens—small, armored creatures that roll along the ground and can knock you down in a second."

In my head I imagined a bowling ball with vampires as the pins.

"Okay, are they dangerous and easy to spot?"

She shook her head. "Not really dangerous or easy to spot since they're only the size of your hand, but you can usually hear them coming. If you pay attention."

Vampire hearing might pick up on them, but I was shifter with fluctuating senses.

Hopefully, Lucien's blood would continue to improve my strength and senses because at the moment all I felt was a little queasy.

"Outside of frodens, what else should I expect?"

As I said that, a huge-ass birdlike creature zoomed out of a tree and over the top of us. If Hattie hadn't shoved me to the floor, its massive talons would have taken my head clean off.

"Tracker rens," she said in a rush. "I don't know what the equivalent is in your world, but if they get their claws into you, you're going into the nest to be eaten by the rest of them."

Back on our feet, we both looked around, but it seemed that the giant bird was once again hiding among the trees. "Okay, I think we should start moving and deal with shit as it shows up," I said, taking a step forward on shaky legs. "Standing here feels like we're just offering ourselves up to be eaten."

Hattie nodded, her face drawn. We ducked our heads low and headed in among the trees. It wasn't tightly packed, with almost no undergrowth outside of the same short, yellow grass from out in the open planes. All we had to do was dodge the tree bases, and we would be fine.

Neither of us spoke for many minutes, choosing to focus on possible ambushes. Without further incident, we reached the first obstacle: a rock wall, probably thirty feet high, and blocked on either side by thick tree trunks.

"Got to go over," Hattie told me.

She raced forward, and moving like a damn mountain goat, scaled up the side, finding handholds that I couldn't see from the ground. "Hurry," she called down to me when she reached the top.

"Yep, coming up," I called. Normally, I'd be able to get over this wall with almost no effort, but the gurgling of my stomach was getting worse and whatever strength I'd felt from Lucien's blood appeared to be fading into a cloudy mind and weak limbs.

Was this the next step in my hybrid nature? If so, I wasn't too impressed by it.

Moving toward the wall, I found a few hand and foot holes and started to pull myself up. At this point, Hattie was sitting on the edge at the top. "Great job," she called down. "Do you want me to wait and help?"

I shook my head, wedging my hands into the next set of crevices. "No, go on. I'm going to be a while." She didn't need to be hanging up there as a target for those tracker-vulture birds.

"Okay," she said quickly, and by the time I looked up again, she was gone.

Forcing myself to focus once more, my thoughts even more scattered than usual, I continued to climb slowly. So slowly it was almost painful. But I remained on the path I'd chosen, and within fifteen minutes, I'd finally reached the top.

Swinging my leg over, I gave myself a minute to catch my breath, wishing I hadn't eaten breakfast after all. Kind of felt like the lot was about to reappear.

Had my days without food affected my stomach or something?

I'd never experienced this before, and I had no idea if I'd make it out of this obstacle course without a bathroom break.

Moving my weight over the wall, I thankfully found some footholds and scaled down the other side. It was harder since I couldn't search out the best route, and when I was about halfway, I decided to just drop off and hope for the best.

It was only a fifteen-foot fall, which should be nothing.

Except I wasn't exactly in peak physical condition right now, and when I hit the ground, the force jarred every bone in my body. I remained on my feet as a small whimper escaped me. Brushing a hand across my forehead, I was surprised at how sweaty I already was. If this was the aftereffect of consuming vamp blood, I might need to reassess my future plans with Lucien.

Looking around for Hattie, I felt a bite of panic when I couldn't see her. "Hattie?" I called, peering through the trees.

There was no response.

My heartrate picked up. *Shit, shit, shit.*

Had she been attacked while I was climbing? Or had she taken my "go on" to mean for the rest of the course? If that was the case, I wasn't too worried, but I hated to think she'd been attacked while she was waiting for my slow, broken ass.

I tried to call up my wolf to shift, needing her strength and senses, but all I got was a sad whimper. I'd have been super concerned, except that had been par for the course lately, and with no other options, I just stumbled forward and pushed on with this stupid course.

If Hattie needed help, my best chance was to get to Lucien.

In the next part of the forest, my churning stomach was the only audible noise. Followed by a sharp cramp that almost sent me to my knees, and I coughed and dry-heaved as I tried desperately not to vomit.

Clawing my way back to standing, I fought against myself, advising all of my body parts that there was no bathroom here. Just as I got up, a low thud had me turning in time to see a dark grey ball careen across the floor and smash into my right leg, sending me flying sky high in a great tumble of shame.

When I crashed down, I landed on my back, and all the air expelled from my body as I gasped and clawed at the ground. No doubt this would have been hilarious to watch, but living it... not so much.

When I managed to breathe again, I turned to find the bowling ball was coming back for me again. A rumble of annoyance joined my rumbling gut, and as the creature raced toward me, I decided I was done with this shit.

Reaching out, I managed to snatch the ball—a froden, I assumed —up in my hand.

Holding the solid weight, I forced my aching stomach muscles to pull me to a sitting position as I looked down at what I held. At first, all I could see was a hard shell, but then it uncurled from its spherical shape to reveal what looked like a baby hedgehog. The hard shell relaxed, and spikes sprang free from where they'd been curved protectively around the little guy. Strangely enough, nothing stabbed into my skin, but I had the sense its shell could be used as a weapon. If needed.

It blinked big eyes up at me, and the urge to fling it across the world faded somewhat. "Dammit," I murmured. "You are too freaking cute to be such a pain in my ass."

It didn't try to escape, seeming curious about what I was, and I didn't let it go just yet. Getting to my feet, my stomach let out its loudest gurgle, and I had to pause to breathe through it. "Apologies if I vomit on you," I told the froden in my hand. "Apparently, I have the supernatural equivalent of food poiso..."

My words trailed off as a thought hit me. *Food poisoning.*

Hattie had given me a plate of food this morning. Hattie who was not here, having taken off the second she could. "That fucking bitch!"

The froden squeaked, and I realized I was holding it a touch too tight. Loosening my grip, I ran a thumb over the soft belly. "Sorry about that. I was just lamenting the fact that women should not be trying to destroy each other like this."

Being betrayed by a woman just hit differently.

Was it possible that Hattie had been playing me all along? From the first moment she inserted herself into my life in the hallway? But why? I'd told her from the damn start that I didn't want to be in the selection.

Did this have something to do with Donovan and House of Jade? That smile he'd shot her way now took on an entirely new meaning. Maybe this had all been one big plan originating from her tier one master.

Leaning over, I gently placed the froden on the ground. "Go free, little one," I said. "Hopefully you find less terrible friends than me."

I took off then, marching fast as anger fueled me. Part of me was still hoping I was wrong and this was all a big coincidence.

Maybe someone else had tampered with the food when it was sitting on the table before Hattie picked it up?

Or maybe I was making excuses for her shitty behavior.

Just had to get to the end, and I'd find out.

Chapter Thirty-Eight

Turned out getting to the end was easier said than done, especially after I started to vomit every few steps. The only bonus was the little froden hadn't left me yet, and its presence was somewhat comforting as it pressed against my foot every time I stopped.

Its presence also appeared to be deterring other bowling balls. I'd heard a few thuds, but the creatures never came too close to my new animal companion.

"Still not in a fucking fairy tale," I shouted to the sky. Fate had a wicked sense of humor, but I didn't hate my new companion.

We pushed on through the forest until we arrived at a small stream. It couldn't be the large waterway that had been described by Julietta, but maybe it was an offshoot of that, which would mean I was heading in the right direction, at least.

I didn't trust the water was clean enough to drink, but I did splash my face to refresh myself from the vomiting and to, hopefully, wake me up enough to reach the finish line. No doubt the other vamps were far ahead now, but I'd never been competing with any of them. My determination to finish was for one reason only: I was going to kick Hattie's ass.

The stream wasn't deep, so I thought nothing of splashing into it to cross to the other side. Should have known nothing would be that straight forward in this obstacle course. The moment my boots hit the sandy bottom of the creek's center, they sank to my ankles, and no matter what I did, I couldn't pull them free. The worst part was every time I wiggled, all I did was sink deeper.

The froden, who I'd nicknamed Bowley, short for bowling ball, sat on the side staring at me with those huge eyes, probably wondering what sort of moron drowned in three feet of water. Bending down, I tried not to jolt myself deeper as I worked the laces of my boots, hoping to slip my feet free. I got the right out easy enough, but by the time I had, the left was deep enough that my entire boot was covered. Gathering up my strength, right foot pushing off the remains of my boot, I yanked my left with all the strength I had.

I didn't think it was going to work, but at the last second before my energy gave out, there was a pop as I was thrown across to the other side, landing ungracefully on the bank.

Breathing heavily, I looked over to see Bowley curl up in a ball and scoot across the top of the water like it was skating over ice. It reached me in a second, and now I knew how to cross water here—swim without touching the bottom.

Pushing to stand, there was a moment where my legs didn't hold me, but somehow, I found the fortitude to stay upright. Moving forward, I tried to ignore the hot and cold flushes in my face and the faint taste of vomit in my mouth that made me want to heave. Not to mention the cramps that felt like they were going to kill me. But I didn't stop. No fucking way was I letting Hattie win. That backstabbing bitch was going down.

The next obstacle in my path turned out to be water again, only this time it was boiling. As I closed in on the massive hot springs, steam shot up from where they bubbled. Judging by the temperature of the air, I could only assume falling into this water would mean instant death.

There was only one path through the center, trees blocking both the right and left side. I took my time, moving very slowly, until I eventually reached the final stretch of hot spring. Of course, when I was two feet from freedom, the narrowest section of path crumbled under my feet.

A shriek escaped, just as my new friend, already proving more loyal than the last one, bowled into me from behind and sent me flying. I landed hard, my head slamming into a tree, and there was a brief moment where I lost consciousness.

The next thing I felt was a sharp nudge at my side. Forcing my eyes open, I found Bowley rolling into me, making small snuffling sounds. Thankful my little buddy hadn't been boiled, I turned to see what had it so riled up and gasped as a tracker ren loomed over the top of me.

Holy sins of the shadow beast.

This was it, the way I was going to go out... eaten by a damn bird and all of its family.

"Fuck you, Hattie," I screamed, and it was so sudden that the ren jumped back a foot from me.

Finding strength I didn't know I possessed, I lurched to my feet and dove toward it, claws springing to life as my wolf raged through the pain in our body.

Maybe this was what I'd needed all along to get my wolf moving.

Life and death. Fight or flight.

Base instinct.

I'd never know if it was the screaming, the claws, or my vomit-breath, but the tracker ren decided it wasn't interested in my particular brand of crazy today, taking off into the air. My adrenaline died off as quickly as it'd arrived, and I ended up in the fetal position, hugging my gut to ease the one big cramp that felt like it was taking me over completely.

"Save yourself, Bowley," I croaked as it rolled close to my face. "I'm done for."

Bowley was not the best listener, since it didn't move at all, not even when I started vomiting again, and all that came up this time was red liquid.

Whether the blood was Lucien's or my destroyed stomach lining, it was not a good sign, so I forced myself once more to stand. The vomiting episode had eased my cramps for a moment, so I started to run. This was it, my last chance to make it out of here before my body quit on me completely.

I'd done a lot of hard shit in my life, and this was just one more to add to the list.

Hattie thought I was weak and that she could take me out, but she had no idea the determination I'd been born with.

Not to mention if I died here today, I'd never have another moment with Lucien, and that was too terrible a thought to even consider.

I was already on a countdown clock, and I would not have that cut short.

Not by any fucking vampire.

Chapter Thirty-Nine

Bowley made a few chirping sounds as it continued to roll on next to me like we were the best of friends. At this point, maybe we were because I sure as hell wouldn't be trusting anyone else in this competition.

The forest started to thin out as we ended up in a field of house-sized boulders. I couldn't tell what the obstacle was until I got closer and saw the swampy land surrounding the large stones. It was hard to tell that it wasn't grass, but I saw the way it wobbled, indicating it wouldn't be safe to try and walk between the stones.

Heading toward the closest boulder, I managed to scramble up, losing some skin in the process. My healing was extra slow, but the scrapes weren't painful enough to stop my climb. At the top I looked around and let out a groan; I'd basically chosen the one boulder that didn't have any closely situated boulders to jump to. But at least I could map out the best route from here.

Once I'd sighted the path I wanted to take, I scrambled back down. "I've got to climb and jump across," I told Bowley. "Can you do your float thing and meet me on the other side?"

It let out a squeak and bumped against my bare foot, which I took as a yes. Leaning down, I brushed my hand across its little spikes. "Stay safe," I whispered, and then I moved to the boulder I needed to climb. My debris-covered feet gave me some traction on the surface, and when I finally got to the top, I was breathing heavily. The urge to vomit pressed in on me, but I refrained.

Taking off, I ran across the surface of the boulder, almost slipping on the smooth edge, before leaping across to the next one. I didn't stop there, moving in the same manner, jumping and almost dying so many times it was borderline a joke.

But I made it to the end.

Sliding to the ground, my breaths were labored as they wheezed noisily from my mouth, lungs aching with each pull. I'd never felt this bad in my entire life, and I wasn't sure where I was going to find the energy to keep going.

Who freaking knew how much longer the obstacle course even was? Or if there was any one left in here beside me. Except for Hattie-bitchbag, I hadn't seen one other selected since stepping foot in the forest. Knowing my luck, I was going the complete wrong direction... Or maybe they were all just fifty miles in front of me.

Either way, I had to keep moving.

After a few minutes of breathing, I realized that Bowley hadn't made it to my side yet, and I felt a tear escape at the thought I'd left him behind with no way to cross.

Not like I could have climbed and jumped with him in my condition, but that wasn't the point. You didn't leave friends behind. It was a basic-as-fuck rule.

Groaning, I forced myself up, determined to go back. As I got up to a sitting position, my stomach protested, and I had to roll over and vomit up more blood. Once I started, I just couldn't stop, heaving and clawing at the ground.

"Bee?"

At first I thought I was hallucinating, but then he called my name again.

Lucien had found me.

"Go away," I croaked, blindly waving one arm while the other one wobbled and barely managed to keep me up. "I don't want you to see me like this."

Cool hands brushed across my face, highlighting my fever. "Simone, what the hell happened?" he asked, voice tense.

I hadn't been able to lift my head and see his face yet. "Food poisoning," I gasped, black dots dancing in front of my vision as I swayed. My arm finally gave out, and I would have face-planted if Lucien hadn't scooped me up. He pulled me against his body, standing as he did.

My stomach lurched, and I gasped, heaving again. "Put me down," I begged, tears running down my heated face. "This is gross stuff I really don't want you to see."

He just growled, and I finally pried my eyes open to see his face wreathed in thunderous anger as he said, "You've eaten food here before, so this was deliberate." A statement, not a question. "Who did this to you?"

I held no loyalty to Hattie, but I needed to confirm my suspicions before I dropped her in the shit. "I will let you know once I've had a chance to interrogate my suspect."

Lucien muttered something not very nice as he turned and started to march away, not even pausing when I wiggled against his hold. "Put me down," I demanded again, wishing I didn't sound so weak.

"No!" he snapped back. "You will die if I don't get you medical help. Your blood smells like *tatan root*. It's a rare herb that we use to dilute blood. In small quantities, it's fine, but in large doses like this, it will boil you from the inside out."

Well, that explained the heat. "I have to finish this trial."

He finally slowed. "I thought you wanted to lose."

"I do," I shot back quickly. "You know that I do. But some asshole tried to take me out, and the best revenge is finishing."

With a shake of his head, Lucien started walking again. "I will drop you near the finish line so you can cross, and then we will deal with the betrayer."

That wasn't going to work for me because they'd still think I cheated.

"Can you do me a favor first?" I said in a rush, hoping to distract him.

He let out an exaggerated huff, but he did stop moving.

"I made a friend out here, a froden, but I had to leave it on the other side of the boulder swamp. Could you check if it's still there and bring it across for me?"

Lucien stared at me like I'd just grown two heads and started singing a different national anthem from each. "You made friends with a froden?"

"Yes," I said in a rush. "I thought it could cross the swamp, but it hasn't shown up. I can't just leave it."

"They control this area of the woods," he told me, eyebrows still tightly drawn together. "It's in no danger."

I mimicked the stare. "I don't leave friends behind, not even bowling-ball creatures of destruction."

Lucien started to mutter again, and I wondered if I'd finally driven him over the edge of sanity. "Fine, I will go and check, and you will wait right here. If you're in trouble, shout out; I'll hear you."

He set me down near a tree and took off as fast as he could within this area. Using the tree for leverage, I immediately headed off in the opposite direction. Finding Bowley and finishing this course on my own were my two goals, and with Lucien's help, I might achieve both.

I knew there was a reason I liked that vampire.

The stream appeared in front of me soon after I left the tree. As I approached the bank, I could see others gathering out in the vast open space beyond this forest and felt the slightest lift in my mood.

This end of the obstacle course.

And my chance to confront my saboteur.

Chapter Forty

Lucien hadn't made his way back to me yet. The poor guy was probably searching for Bowley, cursing me out as he did. He'd be pissed when he realized I wasn't where he'd left me, but hopefully, he'd forgive me soon enough. If the burning under my skin was any indication, I probably wouldn't be alive that long for him to be mad.

After taking a few seconds to check for any new dangers or creatures—nothing to be seen—I waded into the icy water. The jolt of cold helped me focus, and I made sure not to touch the bottom as I paddled the ten or so feet of calm water. When I crawled out on the other side, I heard an angry growl, and rolling over, I found Lucien standing on the far bank, his eyes black.

There was no sign of Bowley, which made my heart ache. "I had to finish," I said in a rasp.

Lucien appeared to be doing some deep breathing and counting to ten exercises, but he didn't approach me. Instead, I got a nod, and then he was gone.

I pulled my broken ass up and stumbled across the finish line, thankful that my last swim had washed off any remaining vomit and cooled me enough to feel fresh as a damn daisy when I collapsed at Carter's feet.

The master let out a huge roar before he reached down and roughly lifted me from the ground. "What happened here," he rumbled so loudly it felt like my eardrums were aching. "She smells like tatan root powder."

Lucien had said the same thing, so we could probably tick that one off as the source of my illness.

Now I just needed to find my betrayer.

Carter was too fired up to notice my reaction as he swung us around, shouting at the other vampires. "This much powder would kill a vampire, let alone a shifter."

"Ugh," I groaned, and finally, he slowed his spin and gently placed me on the ground. My legs wobbled but managed to hold me. With a singular focus, I scanned the crowd, looking for an angel-faced bitch.

And there she was, standing off to the side and blinking at me like she couldn't understand how I was here. Stumbling closer, I dragged my wolf's energy to the surface, pushing her through the sludge of the powder inside me.

"You're an evil piece of shit, Hattie," I said without inflection.

Almost instantly her confused expression was replaced with one of mocking. "I have no idea what you're talking about." She sounded like the superficial bitch I'd first met that day in the hall when she'd been checking out Len like he was the last piece of Faerie cock in the world. I should have known that version was the real Hattie and the rest was fake.

It had all been a con. From the moment she'd opened the door and assessed my plain clothes and lack of makeup, she'd known to come at me from the girl-next-door angle.

Feeling like a fucking moron, I forced myself to smile sweetly. "You'll never take me down this way. Both of the masters now know exactly what you're like, and they'll no doubt think twice about taking on a mate as conniving as you."

She lunged forward but didn't make it two feet before she was grabbed by Carter, who held her up off the ground. "This is the selected who poisoned you?"

I nodded. "Yep. In my breakfast this morning."

My stomach swirled at the memory of that food.

Carter's chest rumbled, his eyes darkening to navy as he threw her to the ground. "Hatilda of House of Jade is eliminated from the competition," he snapped.

Hattie's entire cocky demeanor vanished in the next second, and I almost laughed at how fucking confused she looked. "Eliminated? Do you know who my parents are? Master Donovan is my uncle." Bastard had probably hooked her up with all the inside information.

That entire family was trash and needed to be thrown out.

Another cramp hit me, and I curled forward as the heat grew inside once more. A strong arm wrapped around my body, and I realized Lucien had returned. He gently lifted me into Len's waiting arms.

"Where were you?" I murmured to the fae, disoriented but trying to piece it all together.

His silver smile was darker than usual. "When you didn't emerge with the other selected, Lucien and I went looking for you. He saw you crossing the finish line, so he doubled back to let me know you'd been found. Now he will deal with Hattie."

"You knew about her," I groaned. "I saw that look on your face this morning."

Len shook his head. "I didn't know, but I've learned to trust no one. I hoped that Hattie was as legitimate as she appeared to be. I'm sorry I was wrong."

"Me too," I sobbed, pressing my burning face against his cool jacket.

Lucien was there then, his hand on my face as he turned me toward him. "Drink this," he said, handing me a bottle of red liquid.

"I love you," I croaked, my hand shaking as I lifted the bottle to my lips.

Lucien didn't react to my declaration—I could have been talking to the blood bottle for all he knew. I wasn't, but again, he didn't know that.

I moaned at the first sip, a familiar cherry flavor coating my tongue. I tried not to cry or overthink the fact that he'd gone out of his way to ensure this was his blood. "Drink it all," he told me. "It'll give you enough strength to counter the powder until I can get you back home."

"If you didn't have a fresh source of Lucien's blood in your system already," Len told me, "you'd be dead by now."

Good to know. "Will this fix me?" I asked, drinking more from the bottle.

"No," Lucien said in a harsh breath. "But it will slow this final stage until I can get you home and bleed it from you."

I almost dropped the bottle.

Bleeding me now had an entirely different, very, *very* sexual connotation, and I started to wonder if Hattie had done me a favor. Hattie, who was still on the ground spluttering and crying, reddish tears tracking down her cheeks as she reminded them that her parents were important master vampires, her uncle was a tier one master, and she was their crowning glory.

"They'll take all of your heads for this," she shouted, but no one was paying attention to her. They were all waiting to see what Lucien did next.

He gave me another look, seeming to reassure himself that I was not going to drop dead in the next two minutes, and then he nodded to Len. What that nod meant, I had no idea, but I was no doubt about to find out.

As I drank the last of his blood, Lucien turned away and moved toward Hattie. When he reached her side, he stared down at her with the sort of expression I hoped he'd never send my way. Dark and electric, I could feel the particles in the air charge with his fury. His words were soft, though, without any inflection. "Why did you sabotage Simone?" His power followed that question, and I recognized it intimately.

Compulsion.

Hattie, who had been spouting off about how strong her family was, succumbed to his control in seconds. "I was told that she would be my greatest competition but also the easiest to eliminate." Her voice was robotic as she answered. "Carter called the selection for her, and you joined in for her. The rest of us are only here because Simone can't be with both of you, which left one master free." A brief pause. "I wanted to ensure she didn't steal either of our eligible masters."

Lucien's power ramped up a few notches, and she gasped.

"If she was a favorite," he murmured, "what made you think you'd get away with it? If your family is strong, then you must be aware that the penalty for pissing off a master is death."

Hattie snorted. "I expected she would die in the forest and no one would ever know how," she said. "How is she even alive? I triple dosed her—enough to kill a damn vampire."

Lucien's gaze left her for a moment, clashing with mine as we both remembered our little sex session this morning. A session that'd literally saved my life. Maybe Katu was on my side after all.

When Lucien turned back, he appeared done with this line of questioning as he lifted the sobbing vampire in his hands. Before she could make another sound, he ripped her head from her body and tossed it halfway across the damn field.

For a second, silence descended, and then the screams started. The other selected lost their minds, crying and shouting, hiding behind each other as if they would be next.

Julietta started to shout as well, while Carter stood there looking rather pleased, as if he'd been the one to destroy Hattie. Lucien didn't show any reaction except to drop her headless body at his feet.

"Take this as a warning," he said into the clearing. "A selection is won on individual strength, not on sabotage."

He then crossed to Len and me, and the fae didn't hesitate to hand me over.

We left the field at vampire speed, and somewhere along the way I finally passed out.

My first relief from the pain in hours.

Chapter Forty-One

W hen I came to, I was in a large bath surrounded by warm, red-tinged water, in what I could only assume was Lucien's home. Familiar, golden-skinned arms were wrapped around my middle, holding me against his body, and the scent of cherry and oak was everywhere.

A sense of safety surrounded me, and it was as intoxicating as his blood. "What happened?" I asked, my voice husky. "How long have I been unconscious?"

The pain was gone from my body, and for the first time since eating the food, I felt strong and healthy again. "You've been unconscious for half a sleep cycle," he said, and it was so nice to hear his voice. "I had to bleed you almost to death to get all the powder from your system. I'm sorry I couldn't ask for permission, but I figured that saving your life gave me a pass."

My laugh was dry and weak. "Yes, you get all the passes." Waving my hand across the bath, I asked, "This is my blood?"

"No," he tightened his hold, pulling me higher on his body. My curves sank into his hard strength once more. "It's my blood. Your skin can absorb my energy, and you need all the extra you can get to return your strength. On top of the blood you've drunk."

My mouth watered like a damn addict.

Lucien lifted me even higher, and I finally figured out what he'd been maneuvering me to do—flip my position so I was now straddling him.

I met his black-eyed gaze as he bared his teeth. "Feed," he ordered. "I can feel your hunger."

My wolf surged up before I could even call for her, this time shifting only our jaw and teeth. Lucien tilted his head to the side, and I bit him without thought. A low moan escaped as I took his life-force into mine, and a small part of me was starting to freak out about my current addiction.

I'd never had an addiction like this before—Oreos and licorice did not count. It scared me to think I'd have to wean off Lucien soon, but if I didn't, I might lose the will to ever resist.

If one day he was gone from my life, I couldn't crave him like this and not have an outlet to feed it. Tonight, though, I was in too deep to back out.

As more of his rich crimson filled my mouth and body, I started to rock against him, subconsciously moving to relieve the ache in my center. Lucien shifted our position, sliding me down onto his cock. The thick tip pushed slowly inside me, and he felt so damn good, the hard length like silky steel as it filled me completely.

Groaning and drinking, I cried out as Lucien thrust roughly, his hands on my hips as he lifted me for additional leverage. Blood bubbled from my mouth as I screamed, and the bathwater surged around us as Lucien fucked me like a vampire escaping his demons.

Water hit the tiles of the bathroom floor in time to the rhythm of our bodies crashing together. My body had been parched of life and health in that forest, and now it was drinking up everything Lucien offered.

The first orgasm hit me fast, but it lasted much longer than I'd expected when Lucien slowed his pace to draw out the pleasure. This vampire's consideration was going to be my undoing one day. I'd always wondered if it was true that females experienced more intensity during sex when emotions were involved, and I had to say, it felt like it was happening for me.

This was more than just sexual attraction and a shared mission. Lucien and I were bonding.

He cared about me, whether he wanted to admit it or not.

"Bee," he rumbled. "I need to taste you."

When I lifted my head, the bite wound I'd inflicted faded from his skin almost instantly. Leaning forward, I continued to ride him as he released his hold on my ass to wrap both hands around my tits.

His touch was firm over my hard nipples, and I cried out at his caress. I was so sensitive, and when he leaned forward and took my right nipple in his mouth, swirling around it with his tongue, I barely held onto a scream.

I came the moment he pierced the areola on either side, the sensation of him sucking both my blood and the hard peak into his mouth enough to destroy me then and there.

"Crimson, fuck," I panted, so grateful to have survived the obstacle course. "What are you doing?"

His chuckle was low, rumbly, delicious, and intense. All of my feelings were bursting from me, and I could barely stop the tears hovering on the edge of my burning eyes. "I never knew sex could be like this," I gasped, lacing my fingers into his hair to hold his mouth against my chest.

Lucien rumbled beneath me, his fangs retreating as he licked across my nipple. "As far as I'm concerned," he said darkly, "there's been no sex in your life until now. I will wipe all other touches from your memory. All other seeds from your body. I will claim every part of you until there's no memory but me."

Lucien was super possessive, and I was still super into it. "No man has ever made me come," I told him softly before I tilted my head back and cried as he thrust harder. "A female did once, but that's another story. I was all but a virgin when I met you."

He didn't seem satisfied by that, and I gasped when I found our positions reversed again, only this time I was on the bottom, my back against the side of the bath while Lucien slammed into me, his strength the only thing keeping me from sliding under the water and drowning.

The spiraling buildup of my next orgasm had my head spinning. I opened my legs as wide as I could, one of them ending up over the top of Lucien's right arm while the other was wrapped around his waist. His eyes were locked on mine, and I loved how dark they were. That was when his emotions were the strongest, sending my heart into pulses as strong as the ones in my pussy.

"Crimson," I whispered, desperate to tell him how I felt, but he changed angles then, hitting my G-spot, and all conscious thought vanished.

I screamed, raking my nails across him as my wolf rose up, claws cutting through his skin as cherry and oak filled the bathroom once more. Lucien rumbled my name, his strokes growing slower and stronger until I felt the swell of his cock. As he came, the spirals of pleasure inside me exploded, and I continued to pulsate around him.

When I finally managed to catch my breath, I asked, "Why did that feel like... more?"

Unsurprisingly, Lucien didn't answer, choosing instead to stand and lift me from the tub, taking us both into the nearby shower to wash off. I found myself sleepily falling against him as he turned on the water to near scalding and his hands made light work of soaping me up and cleaning me down.

I knew I should do the same for him, but I just couldn't find the energy. He didn't seem to mind, taking his time to caress every part of me. Eventually, I ended up in his bed, thick, warm covers pulled up to my chin. "Shouldn't I sleep in my room?" I asked, yawning as my eyes fluttered closed.

"Not a chance," he shot back. "I'm not letting you out of my damn sight until this selection is over."

That had my eyes opening briefly. "Wasn't I kicked out after the obstacle course?"

Lucien looked grim. "No. Carter decided that you were unfairly disadvantaged and should be able to continue on. The council agreed."

Of course they did. They'd been following Carter's bullshit from the start.

"You killed Hattie," I murmured sleepily.

There was a brief brush of his hand against my cheek, and I could have sworn he said, "Killing her once wasn't nearly enough," but I was already drifting off.

Chapter Forty-Two

A rhythmic thudding woke me, and when I surged upright in the bed, I was surprised to see red light filtering in through the windows, highlighting the otherwise empty room.

A quick glance at the bed made it clear that I was the only one in it, but before I could worry about that, another thud distracted me.

Slipping out of bed, I followed the sound to the bedroom door and, uncaring that I was naked, jerked it open to find a ball of energy spiraling into the room.

"Bowley!" I exclaimed, falling to my knees and holding my hands out so it could zoom right into them. "You found me." Bringing the froden close to my chest, I ignored the few little pricks from its spikes. "I'm so sorry I left you in the forest. I was not in the right frame of mind, and I sent Lucien back to search, but you were gone..." I kept rambling on, just so relieved to see the creature again. This incredible creature who must have tracked me all the miles from the forest.

It made quiet squeaking noises, and it appeared happy, those huge eyes staring up at me unblinking. Sitting on the bed, I cradled Bowley to my chest and, at some point, must have drifted off again.

Yelling woke me sometime later, and as my body attempted to jerk into a sitting position, I found my right arm and side held down by a heavy weight. It took a few more attempts to open my eyes, and when I did, all I could see was a huge nest of spikes, each of them large enough to impale and kill me if I leaned into them.

What in the shifter's hell was happening here?

"Lucien," I called.

"Bee!" the irate vampire snapped back. "Are you okay? There's a froden stopping me from getting to you?"

His possessive tone was familiar, but it was a touch of fear that bothered me the most. "It's Bowley?" I said softly. Lucien's words had helped me figure out what the large, spiked mass was. "And just to be clear, I'm not a princess in a fairytale!" My voice rose significantly. "This is my animal sidekick, but I repeat, *not a princess.*"

There was a microsecond of silence, probably while both of them tried to figure out if I'd lost my mind.

"Can you ask your animal sidekick to please reduce its size?" Lucien asked, and it definitely sounded like those words were forced out through a very clenched jaw.

"Bowley," I said again, patting its spikes. "Can you go smaller again, please."

It let out a loud chirp, and there was a blast of air that filled the room and ruffled my hair. In the next breath, the froden was once again palm sized, resting on my chest.

"You are so awesome!" I cried as I scooped it up and moved into a sitting position—taking the sheet with me so I wasn't flashing the world my goods. "How did I not know you could change your size?"

Another lie from Hattie the bitch. She'd all but told me they were harmless because of their size. It was really great news that she was dead.

"They're one of the top predators here," Lucien told me drily, eyes locked on Bowley like he wanted to reach out and yank it off my chest. "Back in the forest I'd thought it was the powder causing you to imagine a friend. I indulged you by searching because you were very upset about it, but it turns out you've got an affinity for dangerous creatures."

Len snorted at that, crossing his arms. "Who'd have guessed those were the ones she'd attract."

Bowley rolled over onto its legs, staring up at the vampire master. Len, ignoring them, strolled closer to me, but the moment he got near the bed, Bowley shifted his form into the size of a large dog, once again getting between me and everyone else in the room.

Len held his hands up and backed away. Reaching out, I brushed my hand along Bowley's spikes. "Bowley, these are my friends, okay? We don't attack friends."

It bristled under my touch but, thankfully, started to shrink again before it rolled up my arm and disappeared under my hair to rest near my shoulder. "Bowley?" Len asked me then.

I shrugged. "They remind me of a bowling ball, the way they smash us down like pins."

Len's smile was broad. "Guess it can be grateful that you didn't go with ballsy, right?"

With a snort, I shrugged. "I don't have a nickname for you yet, so it's best not to give me any ideas."

He just laughed, and we were both interrupted by Lucien. "Still waiting on how you tamed a froden." He looked like he was counting to ten again. Not that it appeared to be helping, if his black eyes were any indication.

I shook my head. "I don't know. It knocked me down, and the next time it came my way, I just reached out and scooped it up. We had a moment, and I couldn't resist its cute little face. It stayed by my side the whole way out." A strangled laugh escaped. "I had a feeling it was keeping other creatures away from me, but I really couldn't understand how when it's so adorable."

"They're literal wrecking balls," Lucien said, letting out a deep breath and seeming to finally relax. "I know ways to disarm them, but

I couldn't do anything when it was draped across you. Not without risking you in the process."

This powerful master had been scared for me, and I was just thankful that I'd woken up before anyone got hurt, including Bowley. I had no doubt Lucien could have taken the poor little guy out if he wanted.

"How long have I been asleep?" I asked, yawning and stretching. Bowley shifted on my shoulder with the movement but didn't fall off. "When is the next part of the selection due to start?"

Before Lucien could answer, Len lowered his tall frame to crouch beside the bed. Bowley made a chirping sound but didn't move from my shoulder.

"I need to head back to Faerie," the fae told me. "Just for a few days. There's been some problems in the Silver Lands that I have to take care of, but Lucien assures me that he's more than capable of handling Simone duty." He seemed privately amused by this. "I promise to be back before you're crowned the new Mrs. Lucien. I wouldn't miss that for anything."

Lucien snarled at him, but Len just winked and stood.

"Thanks for guarding me up to now," I told him. "I really appreciate the backup."

Len's mirth faded. "I didn't do the best job. You were hurt and almost died under my watch, but the limitation of not being with you at all hours of the day made the task more difficult than anticipated."

"No," I said with a decisive shake of my head. "It was my fault for eating that food before I checked it. Hattie knew exactly how to play and manipulate me. The poison was on me."

He ran a hand through his silvery hair, sending the shorter strands into attractive disarray. "What's *on you* is on all of us," he said. "You may not understand this yet, but you're part of the inner circle now. You've joined the ranks of the few beings I give a shit about. Mera, Angel, and you are the first new members in centuries."

Lucien shot him a look I couldn't decipher but didn't argue.

"I've never had a pack," I breathed. "Just Mera, so... thank you."

I couldn't find the words to really express what I was feeling in this moment, but Len appeared to understand, his smile gentle. Then he leaned over to kiss my cheek, which produced another small rumble from Lucien. "I'll see you both soon," the fae said. "Stay out of trouble."

Then he was gone, and I wasn't surprised to feel a pang at his absence already. Once a wolf found a pack, she wanted to be with them all the time.

"Is everything really okay with him?" I asked Lucien. "Like, back home in Faerie?"

He nodded. "Len didn't indicate this was anything more than a call back for some obligatory royal duties. He'll let us know if he needs assistance."

A sense of relief hit me. "Okay, great. Now back to the selection."

I'd been in bed for too long, so I turned to drop my legs off the edge and stand. My legs wobbled, but I didn't feel too bad. Still, Lucien must have been worried since he was at my side in a moment, reaching out to steady me. Bowley made a small squeak on my shoulder but didn't come out from under my hair.

The entire way to the bathroom, Lucien supported me, the burning print of his hand on my skin. I was completely naked, but it didn't feel uncomfortable. Probably due in part to the fact I was a shifter, but also due to Lucien and whatever this was between us.

"I'll let you shower," he said, "and then we can go over the selection itinerary for this awake cycle." He pointed toward a set of drawers near the huge bath we'd been in last night. "There're new toiletries in the drawer for you." His voice got a little harder then. "Your animal sidekick can wait outside, princess."

I glared as hard as I could without breaking my face. "Call me that again and I will straight up murder you."

Lucien's smile was slow and did things to me, but I could also tell that he wasn't going to budge about Bowley. Not wanting to fight, I slid my hand under my hair to find the froden. Lifting if off my shoulder, I placed it on the floor. "Off you go," I told it. "I'll be back soon."

It brushed against me and then rolled away into the bedroom. Lucien's smile grew, and I slammed the door in his face because that vampire was driving me crazy.

In all the ways.

Alone, I took a second to focus on the bathroom, since my last time in here I'd been very distracted. It was quite luxurious, with navy and white tiles, a huge tub spanning almost the length of one wall, and an equally oversized shower stall.

There was also a surprisingly modern toilet—Lucien had said more than once he enjoyed many aspects of Earth—and after I was done using it, I moved on to the shower and took a nice, hot rinse, allowing the water to beat over my sore muscles. That tatan root powder had really done a number on me, and even now, hours later and full of Lucien's blood, I was still feeling the effects.

I had no doubt it would have killed me if I'd ingested that as a regular shifter.

Hattie hadn't known I'd been feeding from a master vampire, and it had saved my life.

And cost hers.

Chapter Forty-Three

When I was done, I left the bathroom wrapped in a bath sheet, entering Lucien's room once more. On the bed was a pile of clothing, along with a selection of shoes and boots on the floor.

Sifting through the items, I recognized many from the wardrobe back in the Master Chambers. Had Lucien packed up all my things from there?

It was against the rules for me to stay in his house, but I really hoped he'd decided to say "fuck the rules," seeing as I'd almost died on the master's watch.

When I'd chosen an outfit for the day—black jeans, a red shirt, and a black jacket, all of which made my hair look darker and my skin more olive—I slipped into a pair of black biker boots that gave me another half inch of height. My hair fell straight down my back, and I felt as prepared as I ever would be to take on this day.

Moving the rest of the clothes in the pile, I noticed the edge of a cream-colored envelope, which must have been placed with the outfits. Pulling it free, I recognized the official itinerary for the day with the same fancy swirl as the last one.

There are twelve selected remaining in the competition.

Congratulations.

You are one of them.

Below is your agenda for today. Do not miss any of the items, or you will be disqualified.

First: Breakfast with the masters. Refuel and relax. One-on-one conversation with both Master Lucien and Master Carter.

Second: Hunting. Whoever claims the biggest prize will win a date with the master of their choice. Runner-up will date the other master.

Third: Stone of Katu blessing. You may have fallen from favor with the gods. Do not rest on previous blessings.

Fourth: Dinner for all selected.

Of all the things, it was the first line that knocked me the most. Only twelve selected remaining... How the heck was I one of them when I'd finished dead last in the obstacle course? Carter and his pull over the tier one masters was starting to be a real pain in the ass. They clearly looked after their own and would do anything to ensure that he brought this eleventh enclave to Crimson City.

All of which was great, except for the fact that he wanted me at his side when he did it.

Leaving the room, I heard a thud and leaned down to scoop up Bowley, allowing him to spin up my arm and onto my shoulder. His spikes gave him great traction—without tearing me to pieces, which was nice.

"Are we ready to take today on?" I asked my animal sidekick in a cheery voice. "And by that, I mean get ourselves eliminated for real."

Lucien, who appeared in the hall a moment later, must have heard my statement. Surprisingly, he didn't cheer me on. "I think at this point, it's best to get to the end of the selection, and I will choose you. I think the plan for elimination is over now since Carter is determined to push you all the way through."

Tilting my head to the side, I moved toward him; in usual fashion, something about Lucien drew me closer. "What if Carter chooses me too? Who decides then?"

Lucien leaned closer, and I swallowed hard at the way my body reacted to his energy and scent. "We fight for you," he said softly, near my cheek.

Holy shifter gods. Now *that* might be worth making it to the end for. If it wasn't for the small chance that Lucien would get hurt or worse, I'd have been wanting that every single day of the week.

"Let's just hope it doesn't come to a fight," I partially lied. "The stone will probably reject me this time anyway, and no one can counter that."

Lucien straightened, crossing his arms over his chest. He wore a simple black shirt, and I tried not to notice the way it did nothing to hide all those warrior muscles. "With the amount of my blood in your system," he said seriously, "the odds of a Katu rejection is almost zero. Can you even feel your wolf today?"

I stilled, searching deep to find just a whisper of her energy. I'd been so damn distracted with almost dying and Bowley's appearance, I'd forgotten to check on my wolf.

"I can barely feel her," I choked out, pain lashing at me. "What does that mean? Is she dying? Should I stop taking your blood?"

Lucien didn't appear to know the answer; he just stared at me, lips thinning. "I'm not sure what to do to help you now. When I drained the tatan root powder from your system, it was clear that the vampire blood from the first time I saved you has now infiltrated into your cells. No matter what happens, I cannot remove it completely. You are now and always will be part vampire. A vampire who will need blood to survive."

I shook my head like I could make his words untrue with that motion. "I mean, I know we discussed the possibility of me being a hybrid, but it's still hard to wrap my head around." And I'd kept shoving it into that box in my head, refusing to deal with it. "I mean, how is this even possible? You can't generally change other beings into vampires, right? That's just made-up human lore."

"Correct," Lucien said. "We cannot change most of the races, but apparently shifters are compatible in a way we never knew. You're the first of your kind, and we're feeling our way in the dark trying to figure out what's happening."

"Fucking great," I grumbled. "I never wanted to blaze trails. I told my parents the same thing when they dragged me to pack mixers, dressed me up like I was their doll, and made me be 'pretty and silent.' All in an attempt to gift me to an alpha...."

I trailed off as Lucien took a purposeful step forward, irises black. "Your parents tried to sell you off?"

Some of my fury faded under his. "Yeah," I shrugged, "that's a fairly close representation of their actions."

My face burned from the heat he was suddenly throwing off. "That will never happen again," he told me, voice rasping as his fangs extended. "Not while I'm alive and can kill anyone who tries to control or hurt you."

He'd already killed once for me, and now he was vowing to take out others as well.

It was kind of sweet. "You romance in the oddest way," I said, finding myself reaching out to touch him. I needed to touch him. "My parents can't hurt me anymore. Mera took care of them by stripping their wolves. They're out living shitty human lives."

He relaxed under the touch of my hand on his chest, but his eyes remained black.

"Thank you for Hattie yesterday," I went on. "No one has ever defended me in that way. Are you in any trouble over her death?"

He clasped his hand over the top of mine, pinning it to his chest.

Signature move apparently.

"Nothing I shouldn't be able to handle," he said in his low, rumbly tone. "Her family does have some power and connections, but few want to take on a tier one master. In Crimson City, we are judge, jury, and executioner."

I swallowed hard against my dry throat. "Right, well, I guess we should head to breakfast and hope this time I'm not poisoned." If we didn't move soon, I was going to drag him back into the bedroom and forget the selection.

Lucien didn't release me, and I wondered if he was feeling the same primal urge. "Crimson?" I rasped, resisting the impulse to clench my thighs against my rising need.

I was going to give Mera a run for her money in horniness if this kept up.

The heat around us grew, and before I could say his name again, he released my hand only to loop his arm around my waist and pull me into his body. "Leave," he growled, and I had no idea who he was talking to until Bowley squeaked and rolled from my body, landing on the ground, and took off down the hall.

Lucien lifted me higher, and on instinct, my legs wrapped around his waist. His mouth landed on my neck, and I tilted my head to give him all the access he needed. As his fangs sank into my skin, a jolt of pleasure slammed into my pussy, and I orgasmed in a freak sudden event. It was so damn strong that my body clenched with the sensation, and Lucien let out a deep rumble, which only sent the spirals of intensity higher.

He pulled back a second later. "Feed," he told me, eyes a hypnotic swirl of darkness. It was full-on when he was like this, but I liked it. More than I'd ever admit.

When his darker energy was in control, it turned my body into a needy, wanton, desperate beast that would do anything to feel its master's touch.

"Feed," he repeated, and I didn't even hesitate to bite him.

Except I'd forgotten to call on my wolf, which would usually mean I had blunt teeth that could not cut through vampire skin. And yet, somehow, I did, and his blood filled my mouth.

I moaned again and rocked against him as I fed. Lucien's hard length pressed into me with enough force that even through my jeans he was hitting all the right spots.

Rocking harder and faster, I chased my next orgasm, and I was so lost in the sensation of feeding and riding him that I didn't notice him spin us around until my back was against the wall. He used that structure to brace me so his hands could make short work of getting both of our pants unbuttoned and pushed down, and when his cock thrust inside me, I screamed and thrashed against the sensations. I came so hard that my mouth was jerked off his neck and I almost smashed my head into the wall.

Lucien caught me and, with a low laugh, slowed his next stroke to give me a chance to sort my shit out. I was going to embarrass myself if I kept this up. He started to thrust up in long, sure strokes, pulling all the way out before sliding deep into my pussy.

I lost sense of anything else in the world.

I forgot about the selection.

I forgot about my near death.

I even forgot about my wolf, and she was such a huge part of me that I couldn't understand how Lucien kept doing this to me.

But I never wanted him to stop.

The early pull I'd felt toward him had exploded into an obsession, and part of me knew that nothing would stop this now. Not until we crashed and burned. But I couldn't care about the inevitability. I would take whatever lay at the end of this path because Lucien made me feel so good, both physically and emotionally. This warrior vampire protected me, cared for me, and gave freely of his blood to me.

I'd never had that before, and I was greedy for more.

I wanted it all.

He leaned into me, tilting his head to the side again, and I was surprised to see that the healing skin held only a small bite wound.

Not quite the two pricks of a vampire bite, but certainly far less ravaged than my usual wolf teeth.

There was no time for me to truly comprehend what this meant because when Lucien filled my body like this, my brains turned to absolute mush.

Maybe in the near future I'd have a freak out over my new teeth, but for now, there was only one focus in my mind.

My next orgasm.

Chapter Forty-Four

When we were once again dressed, sated, and ready to take on the world, Lucien and I headed to breakfast, pausing only for me to find Bowley downstairs and situate him back on my shoulder.

We moved quickly, and for once we talked the entire way, as if we had a desperate need to delve deeper into each other. In more than the fucking sense.

"You'd never been to any places outside of Torma until you came to the library?" he asked. "Were you prisoners?"

"Yep. Alpha Victor was an asshole who controlled his shifters to the extent that we were prisoners within Torma. Shadow did us all a favor when he turned that guy into a ball of flames."

Lucien shook his head. "I don't know how your wolf handled that. I've fought so hard against being tied down, and there's not a world in the Solaris System I haven't explored a hundred times over."

He'd lived so many lives before I'd even been born. It made me feel weird. Or maybe the weird part was that he still didn't want to be tied down.

"Didn't you find all the new experiences were a touch... empty?" I asked as we passed a large group of vampires in the street, all of whom stopped and stared but didn't approach us. "Always on your own? Being mated doesn't mean you're in prison. It just means you have someone else to share this life with."

Lucien stared down at me like he wasn't quite sure what to make of my words. "I'm starting to wonder about the emptiness, you know?" he finally said. "The bee is essential, after all."

That knocked my breath from me, and I found myself unable to speak as we continued through the streets. If Lucien kept this shit up, there was no way I could walk away in the end. Did he feel the same? Or was this all just some elaborate game this vampire was playing because I "belonged" to him during this selection?

When we reached the guarded gates to the Master Chambers, Galco was stationed there again. "Simone!" he exclaimed, a brilliant smile lighting up his face. "I've been worried about you. So wonderful to see you healthy."

Clearly word had spread about the Hattie incident, and while my instincts on her had been wrong, I really hoped Galco was as genuine as he appeared. Bowley hadn't popped out on my shoulder and tried to kill him yet, so that had to be a good sign.

"I'm feeling great, thank you!" I said. "Appreciate you worrying about me."

Galco rubbed a hand across his bald head and smiled once more. "Aw, I've admired your resilience from the start. Couldn't have been easy knowing you were competing in a vampire world. But you never complained or asked for special consideration. You've shown a lot of grace under fire here, and I'm still hoping you win the heart of Master Lucien."

Lucien, who was at my side, didn't correct the guard. Instead, he moved closer to me, and there was no doubt Galco noticed. He shot me a wink as we started to walk through, and I couldn't stop his words from repeating in my head.

Win the heart of Master Lucien.

I'd started this day determined to be eliminated, but Lucien and now Galco had me wondering if I should be trying to win. Because the truth was, I wanted Lucien's heart. Not the fake alliance we'd been rocking to try and get through this, but the real deal. All of him and a mate bond.

I hadn't forgotten that the first time I was in Valdor he'd told me he would never settle, but he was so far from that cold and aloof vampire now that there had to be more going on than either of us could explain. Right?

When we got inside the master's building, Lucien led me to the breakfast room. "You head in first, and I will linger a few seconds behind. I'm supposed to arrive alone, but I need to ensure you make it in there safely first."

"Do you think they'll lose their shit at me today?" I asked, a touch concerned by what might have transpired among the masters and selected while I was unconscious at Lucien's.

"Not if they value their lives," Lucien said simply.

And there he went again, romancing me like a psychopath.

Guess I was one too since I liked it.

As I turned to leave, Lucien grabbed my left hand, holding it firmly in his. "Even though I'm keeping an eye on you, use whatever extra senses you've been afforded through my blood to stay safe. Hattie's family is powerful, and while they will hesitate to stand against me, they might realize that you're a weakness of mine."

Lucien had no idea how powerful that statement was, or at least how powerfully it hit me. I let out a feeble chuckle to try and offset my current shock. "If they do realize it, then they know hurting me is a surefire way to piss you off."

He didn't laugh with me, and I desperately wanted to reach up and smooth away the concerned lines between his brows. Lucien didn't usually carry tension in his face, being an eternal vampire and all that, but this selection was weighing on him.

"They're driven by grief," he reminded me, "and they won't care about the consequences of angering me. The only reason they haven't taken me on directly is because they know they'll lose. But if they can hurt me in another way, I'm afraid they will choose that path."

The shocks continued. "Hurting me would hurt you?"

Lucien didn't mince words. "It would break me. Now, go to breakfast and eat nothing until I get there."

Then he kissed me with a fierce intensity that made the first few wobbly steps into the dining area hard. Inside, I forced myself to focus and take some responsibility for my own safety.

Awareness was the key to that.

It was a quieter affair today, and what little noise had been in the area died off the moment I appeared. The selected were glaring hard at me, but none of them approached, and I was perfectly fine with that.

My only efforts had to be toward staying alive and not ending up as Carter's mate.

Speaking of Carter, he was the first to rise and approach me. Wearing a light tan, linen suit and with his hair slicked back today, he looked far less woodsman than he had the first few times I'd seen him.

Behind him I could see where the two tables were set up for the morning *conversation with a master* from the itinerary. All four seats were empty, as they no doubt were waiting for Lucien to arrive. I wondered what all of them would think if they knew he was late because he'd been destroying my body in the best possible way.

"Simone," Carter said, distracting me from all the delicious memories. His gaze ran across my face like he was memorizing it. "How are you feeling? I tried to see you after the obstacle course, but Lucien blocked all access, citing that you were healing and couldn't be disturbed."

Lucien, the guardian angel I'd never known I wanted and wasn't sure I deserved.

No wonder I was head over heels for the vampire.

"I'm feeling much better," I told Carter. "Lucien made sure I had the best healing behind me, and I've woken today with no trace of the tatan root still in my system."

"Good, good," Carter said, and then he reached out and took my arm. "I'd like you to be my first guest for breakfast, if that's okay with you?"

Okay then, seemed his interest in my almost death was done. Thankfully, before I could say anything about eating with Carter, Lucien strolled into the room. His appearance captured the other females attention, though their smiles faded when he made a direct path for Carter and me.

"Simone?" Carter snapped. "Will you join me to eat?"

"She's with me first," Lucien growled, wrapping an arm around my waist to lift me full-bodily away from the other master. Bowley squeaked on my shoulder, but thankfully, no one seemed to notice. "I need to verify her food is safe, and then she can take her turn with you."

My stomach growled at the thought of food I could trust, and even my poor wolf poked her head up. At least with Lucien vetting the safety of my food, I should be able to eat and enjoy it. Might even add some energy to my wolf.

Other parts of me were stronger from the vampire blood, like my eyesight and sense of smell. Not to mention my hearing, as I caught Carter's mutter about killing Lucien.

My next hope was for an increase in speed. Accessing the vampire's way of moving about Valdor would be a true benefit of blood sharing. Not that I would willingly sacrifice my wolf for any extra senses, but I still had high hopes that I would figure out how to build her back up within my new hybrid nature.

I needed to talk to Mera about it, but I wasn't sure what I'd do if she told me I'd have to lose my wolf, like she had, to evolve into my ultimate form.

No time to worry about that now, though, since Carter and

Lucien were done with their little battle and I was being led to the table on the right.

"Everyone grab food," Lucien told the room as we walked. "We will call you up one by one to converse. Don't wait for us to eat since it's best to get as much sustenance in as possible before the day's events."

When we reached his table, he pulled out the chair for me. "Sit, Bee," he said. "I'll feed you this morning."

I was halfway into my chair when he said that, and I felt those words deep in my gut. Maybe even deeper than that.

My body vibrated, stimulated by his words, and I saw Lucien's eyes darken.

No doubt he could scent my arousal.

The word *feed...* had so many meanings to it now.

All of which were set to destroy me.

Chapter Forty-Five

By the time I finished sinking into the chair, Lucien was already at the table of food set up under the window. He spent his time examining each option, and I spent my time examining him, trying desperately to squash all my feelings for him back into a box. It was just too hard now, the emotions too big—the tugging sensation in my center was his blood, and I was addicted to it. And him.

"I'm in trouble, Bowley," I murmured. It shuffled closer to my neck, making a small squeak before settling against me once more, hidden by my hair. Felt like it agreed with me, though, after having seen just how wrecked I was over this vampire.

Lucien returned then, placing a plate piled high with food in front of me. "I selected the best of each piece," he said, looking proud of himself, eyes so clear and green that I was afraid I'd fall into their depths and never leave. "All free from poisons and all designed to elevate your strength."

"Thank you," I said, pleased when my wolf lifted her head once more. Providing food to your mate was a huge part of shifter culture, so this impacted both of us.

Lucien didn't return to the buffet for food; he sat across from me, gaze locked on my face. "Eat," he said softly.

There he went with the commands again. As hungry as I was, I decided that today, I'd make him work for my compliance. "What are we supposed to discuss during this breakfast?" I asked, leaving my plate untouched. "What would you normally ask if you were looking for a mate?"

The only vampire close enough to hear us was Carter, and he appeared to be deep in conversation with a blonde vampire.

"Eat," Lucien repeated, with more bite. "You're still rebuilding your strength, and part of your shifter's weakness might be from not balancing the blood with food. You're feeding only one side of your being now."

Bastard had straight up ignored my question. Narrowing my eyes, I crossed my arms, and instead of scowling, Lucien shot me a wicked grin. Which should have told me I was in trouble.

Moving at super speed, he wrapped his hands around the side of my chair and dragged me around so I was beside him, situated between his spread legs.

We were drawing attention now, but Lucien didn't appear to care. "You will feed, Bee. Or I will force you."

His scent wrapped around me, and I had to literally grip the table to stop from moving forward and biting him. The word *feed* tapped into my base instincts.

I opened my mouth to finally comply, but he must have thought I was going to argue since he lifted a pastry and pushed it against my lips before I could speak.

When I bit into the pastry, a burst of sugary goodness exploded across my tongue. Between that and Lucien feeding me by hand—a shifter mate move—my equilibrium was completely out of order. The vampire, looking far too pleased with himself, offered up another piece of food, fruit very similar to a green apple. "Bite," he murmured, and dammit, I was going to obey.

Leaning forward, I sunk my teeth into the skin, managing to nip his finger with it. I didn't draw blood, unfortunately. "If you eat," Lucien told me, words edged with tension—sexual or other, I couldn't tell, "then I will talk."

I nodded as I took another bite and chewed the piece of tart fruit.

"You asked me what I'd talk about if I was truly looking for a mate," he said. "And the truth is, I would tell them that I'm a broken, damaged being. That I don't know if I can be a great mate, but that if I found the one who called to my blood, I'd destroy worlds to keep them safe."

I stopped chewing, completely mesmerized by his words.

He dropped the apple and picked up some spiced meat, adding a dose of protein to my breakfast. "There is nothing I wouldn't do for my mate," he continued as I took a piece from his hand. "And that is a dangerous path. My parents had no logic when it came to each other, and I've inherited that."

This was a continuation of the conversation we'd started earlier.

I swallowed another bite. "I do understand that, but I stand by my previous statement. No one is designed to walk this world alone. We need our mates."

He chose another piece of food, and I didn't even look at it before taking a bite. A rich cocoa flavor filled my mouth, and I almost sighed. My favorite treat here.

"I'm a warrior," Lucien continued, his emotions hidden away again beneath a blank expression. "There's no room for loneliness. I'm also a master of Crimson House. We're a strong clan because I haven't been distracted over the centuries. My logic is not weakened by emotions."

Reaching out I captured his hand before he could pick up another piece of food. "Love is not weakness," I told him, as serious as I'd ever felt. "If you've been missing half of your soul, then you've been missing half of your strength. You need to consider if maybe, in the end, your parents' weakness had nothing to do with their devotion to each other and everything to do with their personalities.

"I spent years making excuses for my parents, saying how busy they were with important jobs. But the truth was, they were just selfish assholes. In acknowledging that, I choose not to be the same. My children will never come second to duty." I paused and cleared my throat. "I mean, if I have children, of course. I've never believed that we are simply on this world to repopulate it. However, if I find myself on a path that includes children, I will embrace the gift of being their mother with every part of my being. Logic doesn't have to fade under love. I promise."

I'd seen many devoted couples who could extend their circle of love to their children. I knew it was possible. And I truly believed I could do that too.

Lucien could also have both logic and passion.

He was silent, hand still under mine, burning into me as his energy swirled. "How old are you, Bee?" he finally asked. "You speak as if you've lived many lives."

I shrugged, feeling Bowley shift under my hair with the movement. "I feel as if I have."

Before we could talk more, we were interrupted by Carter. "Your time with Simone is up," he called out. "Don't break the rules, master."

It was a threat, but Lucien didn't bite back. He already knew he was winning, and that gave him the upper hand. "Have you had enough to eat?" he asked without even looking at or acknowledging Carter.

I nodded, feeling full and sated—not just in my stomach but also in my heart and energy. Lucien hadn't dismissed my words, and he'd seen to my needs.

Progress.

He leaned in and pressed a kiss to my cheek. Or at least that's where I thought he was aiming until he shifted at the last second and hit the corner of my lips. Energy spiked down to my gut as butterflies took flight, giving me all the good endorphins.

If this was what love felt like, then it didn't surprise me that humans and supernaturals fought and killed for it daily. And I stood by my belief that this was the sort of love that could expand to include as many members of your family as you needed. Infinite love.

"Thanks for breakfast," Lucien murmured as he pulled away. "I look forward to continuing our conversation."

Pushing myself to stand on wobbly legs, I nodded, well aware that Carter and many others had their eyes on us. "Thank you, Master Lucien."

Fire blazed in his eyes as I used his title.

The spark within his gaze was stronger. Speaking of something more than just his possessive nature and our sexual chemistry. With that came hope, and we all knew that if love was the most dangerous emotion in the worlds, hope was a close second.

Both, if broken, would be my ultimate destruction.

Forever this time.

L eaving Lucien's table was harder than I'd anticipated, and I was happy to see that he immediately moved the chair back across from him so the next female to have his attention was nowhere near him.

That allowed me to relax and pay some attention to Carter. "Good morning," I said brightly, and no joke, he looked floored by my cheeriness. "I'm excited to learn more about you." Fake and a liar. Maybe I had learned something from Hattie after all.

Carter took an extended moment without answering, and I didn't let the smile fall from my face. My wolf perked her head up again, her energy already feeling stronger with the untainted food in my system. Lucien had been right, as per usual.

"I'd rather get to know you," Carter finally said, leaning back in his chair and crossing his hands over his stomach. "Who were you, Simone, before you came to Valdor?"

"I'm a shifter from the Torma pack in California." I didn't hesitate to answer, since my life was somewhat boring. "An only child, I grew up with enforcer parents who were important in the pack, working directly for the alpha. I spent most of my life alone or with my best friend Mera, who was the pack outcast but clearly had a much larger destiny than to stay in that craphole."

I continued on with my love of dance and reading. "I own my own bookstore," I said, feeling a longing for it come over me, "and I couldn't imagine running any other business. I mean, I match shifters with books and make lives better. I look at reading as food or medicine for the soul."

"Medicine for the soul," Carter purred. "I like that."

I nodded, my passion for this subject rearing up. "Yes! It's so important, and did you know, when I looked into the human world to find authors, I read all about how their funding for arts programs is continually cut." A rumble filled my chest, and I was so happy to feel my wolf rising that I almost cried. "Cutting from the arts, which is also the first place people turn for entertainment. Authors, actors, painters. All of this is soul food, and without it, there would be a massive increase in depression and other mental health issues. We need to start nurturing our artists."

Carter's smile was filled with genuine amusement. "As I noted the first time we met, I enjoy the fire in your soul, Simone. I believe we would be well matched."

Some of my happiness and passion died away. I'd momentarily forgotten the reason I was here with Carter. "Tell me about your first mate. What was she like?"

That sobered him up too, and I felt like a bitch. But if I had been truly considering a mate-bond with this vampire, I would want to know about that relationship and what I might be up against.

At first I thought Carter was going to ignore my question, but then he said, "Katra was my fire." His voice broke, but he continued. "My soul food. She made me a better vampire, and my greatest regret is that she was gone before we made the decision to create another life."

My chest grew tight at his genuine grief. "I'm so sorry for your loss, Carter. I really am. But do you honestly believe that anyone else could ever be your fire again? I know you told me that you are different now. Reborn. But I can tell that a part of you will always belong to her."

Some of the pain in his face eased as he leaned closer to me. "That's not as big an issue as you might imagine. I'll explain why tomorrow when we have the house viewing."

Confusion bloomed in my chest, followed by unease.

I'd never thought of Carter as unhinged—in general he conducted himself maturely, no matter how often I rebuffed his affections. This day, though, there was a hint of darkness in his gaze. "I'm sure there's nothing you could show that would convince me I could replace your soul fire," I said as I stood. "Don't forget to honor my choice in the end."

Carter nodded, standing as well. "I won't forget, Simone. You have my word."

"Thank you."

After that, I got to sit by myself and relax. Lucien delivered a glass of water to me halfway through the breakfast, and as I smiled my thanks, I had to ask, "Found a favorite yet?"

I was only half joking. He didn't laugh.

"There's only ever been one in this competition for me, Simone Lewison. You know that." He didn't call me by my full name often, but when he did, it tightened many parts of my body which had been previously relaxed.

"You've got someone waiting on you," I managed to say, needing him to walk away before I combusted.

Lucien didn't even glance at the stunning brunette vampire, who had her piercing blue eyes locked on us. "I'll be relieved to be done with this duty," he muttered before he let out a sigh and returned to his table.

It was like a slap of cold water in the face because even if he had been referring to the brunette in this instance, she wasn't his only duty.

He was only here in this situation to help me.

Was he ready to be done with that as well?

Chapter Forty-Seven

A fter the breakfast, four selected were eliminated by Lucien and Carter. The masters were weeding them out fast now as we headed toward the final rounds. The four who were asked to leave snarled and sneered at me like it was my fault, and I made a mental note not to invite them over for a girls' night any time soon.

Those of us remaining were led out of the chambers and into a small storage room built off the side of the main building. A tier one master met us there, and it was one of the males I hadn't really seen or heard from much so far.

He looked annoyed as hell to be here, scowling as he stared around at the remaining selected. He was beautiful, as most vamps were, with brown skin, blood-red hair, and eyes that were only a shade lighter than his hair.

It was a striking combination, but his personality left a lot to be desired as he let out an exaggerated sigh. "Hunting is next," he said slowly, his voice a warm, rich drawl, which once again, didn't go with his expression. "Select armor and a weapon. You might be required to fight a multitude of different creatures, and whoever brings us the largest or most kills will get a date with the master of her choice."

This entire part of the competition didn't sit right with me because, as a shifter, I didn't kill for fun or competition. I killed for food and protection.

The other selected didn't appear to have an issue with it, though, heading into the room to grab weapons, while I remained back near Lucien and Carter.

"Your vampire nature will once again be suppressed during the period of this hunt," the arrogant master added. "Don't rely on your speed, strength, or senses. This is going to require skill. Something many of you have neglected to hone."

"You definitely neglected social skills," I muttered. Bowley squeaked and shifted on my shoulder before it burrowed back under my hair.

Carter snorted, but apparently the master in charge didn't appreciate my little statement. "You!" he snapped, pointing at me. "Come here."

I crossed my arms. "I don't think so."

He blinked before his gaze narrowed. "Did you just disobey an order from me?"

I mean, knowing Lucien stood at my back gave me a little extra confidence, but in truth, I didn't fear these vampires any longer. I'd been told many times now that shifters and vampires were not that different. We were compatible, and while I might have forgotten my own strengths the last time I was in Valdor, I never would again.

"You don't rule or control me, and I don't have to obey you. I'm here for the selection."

The vampire took a step toward me.

Just one step.

I prepared myself for what might happen next, but before I could even summon up a sliver of shifter energy, Lucien and Carter stepped in front of me.

"Nope," I said, pushing between them. "This is my fight, and I'm happy to take a stand against an arrogant assface who rocked up today with a woeful attitude."

Assface's snarl grew more pronounced as his gaze wandered between Lucien and Carter, making it clear that no matter what I said, he considered those two the muscle in the room.

"Can we just get to the hunt," I snapped, having no patience for their dick measuring. "Some of us don't have all fucking day to stand around and eyeball each other."

My wolf howled in my chest, and my eyes burned with emotion as I felt her strength. This was it. This was the moment I found my balance with vampire and wolf, when both were fed and strong. This was how we would get through this competition.

There were eight of us left, and I had a feeling tomorrow would be the final day of the selection.

Thankfully, Assface decided he couldn't be bothered with this fight any longer and waved me off, telling me to pick a weapon. The others already held their choices, so I stepped forward to see what was left.

Torma wolves were trained to use a wide variety of weapons, and even though I hadn't kept up with most of it over the years, I still knew what my best was: archery.

I'd been exceptionally good with arrows, which had given my parents some hope that I might end up as an enforcer too. As if I'd ever protect the alpha who'd tormented my best friend and killed her father. I'd been practicing to put a fucking arrow in his heart.

When I was suited up with breast and arm shields, I grabbed a recurve bow that looked about the size I favored and a quiver of arrows that strapped across my body in conjunction with the breast shield.

Normally, I'd pull my hair back, but with Bowley under there, I left it free.

"If you use your weapons against another selected," Assface drawled as I stepped out to join the others, "you will be eliminated and punished. This is about showcasing skills that might influence the masters' choices in a mate and bearer of offspring."

Could I roll my eyes any harder and not see my brain? Doubtful.

Why the hell didn't these masters just go on dates like normal people? I mean, at the end of the day, they still chose the one they wanted, like some sort of blood-filled bachelorette show, but there was very little normal dating going on.

This selection had already resulted in one death since competition drove the sanest beings to extremes. Even I was feeling somewhat competitive, which might in part have to do with the very real feelings I was developing for Lucien.

It felt like years ago we'd agreed to this show of "dating" so that he could choose me in the end if I wasn't eliminated. At no point had it felt like a show, that was for sure.

Assface led us from chamber grounds and into a street I'd never entered. There were so many entries and exits to this maze that I could live here for a hundred years and not explore them all. After about thirty minutes of moderately paced walking—moderate for vampires, anyway—we ended up in an area that had no houses or shops. I'd never seen anything like this in Crimson City before. It looked like an entire street of abandoned warehouses.

"This is where the most dangerous creatures from the outer regions are kept," Assface said without inflection. "We don't go out searching for them, but a few get our scent and refuse to return to the wilds. It's death or this."

Staring at the huge razor-wire fences, complete lack of trees or greenery, and derelict buildings, I wasn't sure if death might not be the better choice.

"What do they even eat here?" I asked. "Or do they eat each other?"

The master shrugged. "No idea. Not my problem."

How mad would Lucien be if I shot this guy with an arrow? I mean, I could say it slipped, right? One of the selected piped up then, before I could further plan out Assface's death. "I believe locals in this area feed them and bring fresh water. Around the other side there's more shelter."

Well, that was something at least.

"You need to head in and bring your kills back," Assface snapped, seemingly pissed off by existence. His and ours.

He stepped forward and opened the gates, careful where he put his hands so they didn't get torn up by all the razor wire. "The siren will sound when your time is up."

As the selected stepped forward, I turned to Lucien. "I don't want to kill animals," I whispered. "As a wolf I've eaten the occasional bunny that crossed my path, but I don't kill for no reason."

His expression didn't give much away. "I don't expect you to kill anything. Just make sure you survive—some of those creatures are not to be underestimated."

I reached up and patted my shoulder. "I've got my little security guard."

Bowley made a snuffling sound, and his spikes scraped across my skin without drawing blood as he shifted position.

Lucien brushed his hand along my cheek, pushing a few strands of hair back. "That creature is the only reason I'm allowing this to go on," he murmured, near my face. "I doubt the others will have much luck taking on the beasts inside. It's going to be a lot of running and hiding."

Carter snarled beside us, his glare on Lucien's hand, which was still on my face. "Enough, she needs to get in there."

Grabbing my arm, he pulled me away from Lucien with more force than was necessary. Spinning, I smacked his arm away, even as Bowley let out a growl near my ear. "Touch me again without my permission," I spat out, "and I will remove your fucking hand."

He reached for me again, his face creased into angry lines, and I jumped back far enough to whip out an arrow and nock it. Carter looked like he was about to plow right into the lethal tip, when Lucien moved in from the side and punched him so hard the other master flew across the space and smashed into the razor fence.

Silence descended over the industrial area, and I was mostly surprised and excited that I could still get my arrow nocked so quickly. Like riding a bike, apparently it was a skill I'd never lose.

Just a shame I hadn't gotten to shoot it.

Relaxing my stance, I let the bow fall as I walked to where Carter was picking himself up from the ground. Bleeding cuts sprinkled his skin and some clothing was torn as well, but at least he no longer looked like a hulked-out vampire about to do something stupid.

"Shit, sorry," he rasped when he saw me standing a few feet away. "Lucien touched you, and my instinct took over."

His expression pleaded with me to understand, but I didn't. "I think your true nature took over," I shot back, "the one that believes your mate belongs to you and you can control her with violence."

I didn't mind possessiveness, especially the way Lucien did it. He told me what he wanted and used his sexiness to get it, but he never inflicted violence on me.

Not like Carter just had. His face had told me very real pain had been coming my way if he'd gotten his hands on me the second time.

"Remember your promise," I said as I walked away. "I'm holding you to it."

Carter's expression fell, as if he was finally understanding that I would never choose him.

He'd had a small hope before that he could charm me, but he knew now it was over.

Now to wait and see if he'd refuse to accept it.

Only time would tell.

Chapter Forty-Eight

With the drama done, those who hadn't already started to move, headed into the fenced area to get this part of the selection over with. "Bring your kills back," Assface shouted as he ushered us inside. "Drop them off so we can count them."

As I stepped inside, my wolf stirred, rising at the feel of predators around us. There were none visible in the large open space before the first building, but I knew they were out there.

I could feel eyes on me like ants crawling over my skin, and if I'd been wearing my fur, it would be bristling. Nothing weak or prey-like had survived in this prison, and I would hazard a guess that what remained in here was the strongest of their kind. Of course, vampires would be the larger threat, so none of them were concerned. But I wasn't a full vampire.

"Bee!"

I turned to see Lucien near the fence. "You get your ass right back here if it gets too much in there. Do not risk yourself, do you hear me?"

Unlike Carter, he didn't inflict his will to stop me going. The order was because he cared, and that was where the other master had a lesson to learn.

"I hear you," I called, and with a deep breath, I readied my bow and walked slowly into the grounds.

There were no other selected in my line of sight, all of them having taken off the moment the hunt started. My wolf howled inside, and I knew she wanted me to let her free. *If it gets bad, we'll shift,* I told her.

When we reached the first building, I peeked inside and immediately backed away. It was pitch black, and even with advanced senses, I could only pick up a vague shadow. Stepping into another creature's territory when you were blind was suicide.

There had to be another path around, or least another path to get me out of the sight of the masters so it looked like I was giving this my full effort. If I failed out for lack of kills, that was okay, but I couldn't fail out for not trying.

Rounding the side of the building, I found myself in an empty lane. It was dirty, filled with some old bones and what looked like half-chewed tree stumps. The ground was a heavy gravel and the side of the warehouse grey-brown, conveying no happiness or joy.

It was almost as if this entire place was devoid of color, with the red sun unable to lighten the dark. There were no creatures though, or at least that was what I thought until I was about halfway along that path.

A scuffling sound had me grinding to a halt. Bowley popped its head out, and I felt my wolf push against her cage again. Trusting those two, with stronger instincts than mine, I lifted my bow and waited for the inevitable. Not like I could really get through this entire thing and not see a creature.

"Bowley, watch my back."

I felt my hair shift as it moved into a better position to keep an eye out, and I stepped slowly forward, arrow nocked in place. This bow, as unfamiliar as it was, felt comfortable in my hold. And while I wasn't planning on killing anything, I would shoot to scare or maim it if needed.

The first creature emerged from the shadows a moment later, and I paused, examining it while it examined me. It reminded me of a brown bear, but its structure and shape implied that it remained on all four legs permanently. It also had a bulky and hairy body, large snout and jaw, and ears that stuck up high in narrow points. The face was more catlike with two elongated eyes above its snout.

As it lifted its head and scented the air, I forced myself not to panic. Keeping my heartrate steady, I made no provoking movements, even going so far as to lower the weapon. No matter what happened, I would not be bringing back a kill count. Winning Lucien's heart would have to be done another way.

Bear-cat sniffed and moved forward, and I continued to hold the line.

And hold. And hold.

Right up to the point it was all but sniffing at my face, the cat eyes examining me like it had no idea what I was. My wolf continued to linger just under my skin, but she wasn't aggressive, and I wondered if I might have an advantage here after all—two predators recognizing each other.

"I don't want to hurt you," I said softly, having no idea if it could understand me. "I'm just here to stay alive. If you walk away, I'll do the same."

Bowley moved again, sliding across my shoulder and racing down my bow arm.

I elevated my hand slightly so it wouldn't just fall off.

Bear-cat reared up before landing heavily on all fours again. I expected it to attack, but instead it nudged the froden on my hand with its snout. Then the two remained locked in eye contact for a long time. I had no idea if they were communicating, but since no one was attacking, I didn't move.

As the three of us lingered in this weird standoff, more creatures started to appear. They crept out of the shadows, and I had to blink at the many different shapes and sizes. Some were large and horse-like, others smaller and standing upright on strong hind legs like a hare. Nothing was the same as an Earth creature, but I could find enough similarities to liken them to familiar animals.

The more surrounded I was, the scarier it felt, but still... nothing attacked. "Should we be running, Bowley?" I asked it, looking around as they closed in on me. "I'm not sure even you can take this many on."

It made some squeaking noises, which gave me no real answer.

"If you want me to run, return to my shoulder and hold on," I said in a low murmur. "If it's safest for us to stay, just remain where you are."

Bowley quivered, rolling into a little ball, and my muscles tensed in ready for it to return to my shoulder.

Only it didn't.

It curled up where it was and... relaxed. A second later the bear-cat rubbed its head against my hand.

Now, I'd never had a pet, but I'd seen enough shows to know that was a very catlike move of affection. It wanted to be petted. Using my arm not holding the bow, I reached out and brushed my hand over the head of the creature. Its fur was coarser than my wolf's, but still soft under my touch.

"They said you were all feral and dangerous," I murmured, as it started to purr.

Fucking purr.

None of the other animals moved closer, remaining where they were in a circle surrounding me. An idea of what I was going to do now came to me, and it was crazy as hell. But, seriously, what part of my time here hadn't been weird?

Keeping one hand on the bear, I continued to pat it as I slowly turned to retreat out of this alley and back to the open section before the fence. All of the animals followed my movements, almost like I was the sun and they were orbiting in my gravitational pull.

As I started to walk forward, the bear-cat fell in at my side, my hand on its head. Bowley returned to my shoulder, and I let the bow fall to the ground, it and the nocked arrow clattering as they landed. Next was the useless quiver. These creatures didn't need weapons—they needed someone to give a shit about them.

I made my way back toward the barbed fence; a quick glance around told me that there were dozens of animals with me. As we got closer, Carter and Lucien came into sight, right behind the closed gate. There were more tier one masters here now, along with many other vampires. All waiting to see who would win.

Looked like I was about to demand change with a big audience in tow.

Or as some might call it, an army.

Chapter Forty-Nine

The crowd was dead silent as they observed me and my animal contingency. "These creatures are not dangerous," I said without preamble, ignoring gasps and shocked looks. "Killing them as part of a selection is disgraceful. I demand you release them right now."

Donovan stepped forward, and I really hadn't missed seeing his face. "Excuse me? Who are you to demand anything from us?"

I let my wolf break the surface, my face shifting so canines and fangs appeared together. "I'm a hybrid shifter-vampire, and I will not stand by and allow you to harm creatures for your own damn amusement."

Before Donovan could respond, a battle cry rang out from behind me, and I turned to see a selected female charging for the animals near the back of my pack. She held her sword high and clearly thought she'd hit pay dirt with this many creatures standing harmlessly in a group. When would these fuckers learn that there was no victory in hurting those weaker than you?

With a snarl, I swung around, and Bowley rolled off my arm. It zipped through the creatures, turning much larger when it had a clear run to crash into that dumb bitch. Her sword went flying as she landed hard.

She got back to her feet in a flash, and I stepped forward, snarls ripping from my chest. "Don't even think about it," I got out. "Bowley will kill you, and it will be your own fault." I waved my hands toward all the creatures. "They're under my protection."

Her eyes were black as she shot me the darkest look I'd ever seen from another selected, but she took my warning seriously, grabbing her sword and returning to the building.

Spinning back to face the masters, I waited for Bowley to zip over, lowering my arm so it could spin up it. When it was safely situated, I took a step forward. Behind me, all of the creatures followed, and at no point did I worry that they were all at my exposed back.

My wolf and I were treating them like pack members.

"These creatures cannot leave this area alive," Donovan said, crossing his arms over his chest and stretching his blue jacket out to give the appearance of more muscles than he actually had. "They always return to Crimson City."

"Let's trial them leaving this time," I said firmly, not wanting to antagonize him and risk the chance of freeing the animals.

"How in vampire gods is she controlling the creatures?" someone shouted from back in the crowd. "Is she magic?"

"Has to be the Shadow Beast," someone else said as chatter exploded.

Ignoring them, I turned toward Lucien, grateful to see that Carter was no longer near him. Lucien crooked one finger at me, and I found myself stepping forward, my army behind me. Most of the vamps near the fence gasped and jumped back, but Lucien didn't even blink an eye, looking far too pleased with himself as he drew me forward.

"What are you trying to prove here, Baby Bee?" he drawled. "Just how far you can push the masters before they crack?"

I smirked in return. "I'm not starting a war, you know that, but it seems I might be starting a revolution."

He leaned in closer, and I didn't like how near his face was to the spikes. "War and revolution are often the same thing."

I shrugged. "Maybe, but I like the sound of a revolution better."

He chuckled, and I felt my spirits lift. "Open the gates and let her out," he called to the masters, eyes remaining on me. "We can take the creatures on if needed, and why not give Simone a chance. I'd prefer a mate who chooses to use discretion in killing. Makes me less inclined to sleep with one eye open after pissing her off."

Some laughter finally filled the area, dispelling a fraction of the tension. Master Donovan looked like he wanted to argue, but I had the feeling that he also wouldn't. It might make him appear afraid of the creatures. And fear was weakness.

"If this goes wrong, it's on you," he snapped at Lucien, before waving his hands toward the gates.

They opened immediately, and I waited until they stopped moving before I stepped forward. The crowds pushed away from the opening, leaving us a very clear exit path.

Moving slowly, since the vamps were on edge, I exited the warehouse structure. No one approached us and none of the creatures left my path, following with so much trust that the strong sense of having a pack threatened to pull me under.

Somehow, I'd fallen into this role of champion of Valdor's animals, first with Bowley and now this random array of creatures. Could it be my hybrid nature that called to them? I wanted to discuss it with Lucien, but for now he was keeping his distance, moving ahead of me as I left the warehouse. "I'll lead you out of the city," he told me.

I nodded, and our pace picked up as we moved away from the vampires and into the streets. There, Lucien paused and waited for me to reach him, and then he took my hand. "Ready to go fast?" he said.

I looked back at my creatures, coming near face to face with the bear-cat. "Can they keep up?"

He nodded. "Oh yeah. Everything in this world has super speed."

Lucien took off, and I expected him to scoop me up and take me along, but before he could, I found myself keeping pace with him. *What in the worlds?*

"Bee," he rumbled, head turned toward me as we moved. "You're moving like a vampire."

"I know," I gasped. "It's your blood."

The exchange of blood was doing its job, turning me into a true hybrid.

Lucien picked up his pace, then, until I couldn't quite keep up, but it was still the closest I'd ever come to vampire speed. And since my wolf felt strong too, there was no sense of loss like I was sacrificing one side to have the other.

Thank the gods for that.

Lots of vampires in the streets gasped and jumped out of the way as we raced by, no doubt freaked by the creatures on our tail, but none of the denizens of Crimson attacked.

When we arrived in the outskirts of the city, with its golden plains and forests off in the distance, Lucien slowed. "They can find territory from here," he said. "This is their test to see if they take this freedom or head back into the city. I've long reasoned that it's the vampires calling them back, either to feed or for sport. Let's see if this time, without their influence, the creatures return."

My gut was telling me they wouldn't.

Shaking out my limbs from the tingling sensation of moving so fast, I turned to face the creatures. "There're so many," I gasped as even more arrived. "I didn't have this many behind me back in the industrial area."

"You did," Lucien said, surprising me. "While you were talking to the masters, they were still sliding out of the shadows. I would estimate that by the end, you had every single imprisoned creature with you."

The relief of that almost knocked me down. I'd been worrying about those left behind and in the hands of those selected females. Bitches be vicious when some vamp cock was up for grabs.

"You need to go," I called to the gathered beasts. "Take your freedom and don't come back to the city. The vampires will destroy you if you do."

A lot of growls and roars and howls rose from the group, and I realized it was the first time they'd made any significant noise.

I loved it.

Tilting my head back, I howled with them, the spirit of my beast rising inside of me and performing a partial shift to better facilitate the sound. Lucien watched from nearby, and when my howl died off, his eyes blazed. "You burn brighter than any star I've ever seen. One day I'd like to kill your parents for ever making you believe that you were less. There's nothing less about you, Simone Lewison. Not now and not before."

Somehow, I didn't fall down in a heap of tears at his words.

Lucien wasn't the sort of being to give false flattery, so what he'd just said meant more than any other compliment I'd ever been given. Words were usually used as weapons against me, not as gifts.

Especially since, unlike with my parents, Lucien's words were backed up with actions.

Actions that showed he cared for me and considered my feelings.

If he kept this up, there was no way I could walk away from him.

The gods would have to destroy me first.

Chapter Fifty

The creatures moved slowly at first, but soon they were sprinting across the golden fields. It was quite a moment, watching them race toward freedom, and even as part of me mourned the loss of my short-lived pack, a larger part rejoiced at their new lives awaiting. The happiness and safety of your pack should be the number one priority of an alpha, something Victor never understood.

"Did the masters ever truly try and free them?" I asked Lucien as we stared across the field. "Because they don't look like they want to return to Crimson City."

"I was never here during any of the alleged freeings," he finally said, and he sounded upset about that. "We got told about their imprisonment, and I didn't care enough to investigate."

"They're important," I reminded him. "Equally as important as spoiled-ass vampires whose greatest worry is where their next bottle of blood is from." Lucien didn't argue, and I hoped from here on, he would give consideration to all the living beings in this world.

In the end, Bowley and the bear-cat were the only two creatures remaining with me. "Time to go free," I said to the purring beast. "I hope we meet again."

For a beat, it didn't appear that it was going to leave, but with one final rumble, it loped away to a far-off pocket of forest.

"What about you, Bowley" I whispered, feeling bereft. Wild creatures deserved to be wild, but that didn't mean I wouldn't miss this little guy. "You are absolutely welcome to stay with me forever, but if you want to return to your home or family, I will visit."

Bowley squeaked and rolled down my arm to land on the ground. It uncurled in front of me, and I bent down to brush my fingers over its smooth belly. "Thank you for everything," I said, understanding its decision. "You saved me, and I'm really going to miss you."

Bowley curled up into a ball again and zoomed onto my hand for one last cuddle. Then, with a final sigh, it was gone, zipping across the short grasses, heading back to its home.

I tried to push my sadness down. For all my talk of not being a princess with an animal sidekick, I would miss Bowley so damn much. But it was pure selfishness to keep the froden with me when it was wild.

Even if, for a short time, I'd felt like I had a real pack.

"You're not alone."

Lucien's words sliced into my already aching chest, hitting me right in the heart. The heat building behind my eyes was painful as I tried to breathe through the need to break down. The fact that he understood what I was feeling and sought to comfort me was almost my undoing.

"I know," I managed to say. "And now it's time to end this bullshit. I'm done with the selection—you both need to choose tonight so life can go back to normal."

Lucien wrapped an arm around me, and goddamn, this guy was wrecking me.

"You're right. I will announce my decision tonight, and Carter can either get on board or bow out. He never should have sought a second mate when his first still owns his heart."

The mention of Carter's first mate reminded me of his vague words of explaining why his feelings for her weren't an issue. Words that still sent a slither of unease along my spine. "Carter seemed kind of unhinged today," I noted. "Do you think the stress of this selection is getting to him? How truly powerful is he? Like, what would happen if he lost himself completely and tried to take the masters on?"

A lot of questions, but they needed to be asked. Never walk into battle and not know what you were up against.

"Carter is much older than me," Lucien said. "Ancient and untested, to be honest. We've left him alone for years, and I doubt many alive have seen his true strength."

Untested wasn't great. "He promised me that he would honor my decision in the end," I told Lucien. "But after today, I have my doubts."

Lucien's expression hardened. "That's why I wanted to give you my blood in the first place. I don't trust him at all. He has no issues with manipulating your kindness in the hopes of taking advantage. We already know he was trying to use compulsion on you. He would have expected that, being so new to this world, you wouldn't under-stand the subtle underhandedness of vampires."

I snorted. "Dude, there has literally been not one subtle thing about you since I returned to Valdor and this stupid selection. I keep waiting for you to brand your name on my skin and drag me off to your sex cave."

Lucien didn't laugh as I'd expected; instead, he appeared to consider that suggestion. "I've spent a lot of years around Shadow," he said with a shrug. "His animalistic nature has rubbed off on me, and team it with my natural possessiveness..."

"I didn't say I was complaining," I told him, a little breathless. "I'm still a shifter, born and bred, so deep down, I'll always crave a primal sort of love. Blow the worlds up and all that jazz."

He stilled, and I could have kicked myself. The word "love" had slipped out then, and now, I'd no doubt freaked him out. As I went to make a joke to dispel the tension, there was a shout from behind us, and we both turned to find Galco, our security guard friend, hurrying over.

"Master Lucien," he called again, waving his arm before he picked up speed and reached us in another second. "You need to get back to the chambers. That selected who was killed, her family is there declaring that justice must be served."

"Hattie's family?" I asked.

Galco looked at me and nodded. "Yeah, they're asking for a death sentence for Simone. And for Lucien to have his tier one status stripped."

"For fuck's sake," I muttered. "Every time I step into this godsforsaken world, I get a death sentence handed out to me. You guys are a little kill happy."

I was half-joking, but Lucien held no amusement. "They won't touch you," he rumbled, voice dropping into the octave of a pissed off vampire. "I'll deal with this. Galco, can you take Simone back to my house? The gate will open for her."

He turned to leave, but I grabbed onto his arm before he could. "You're not going without me," I snapped. "Hattie's family is not the only shit we need to deal with. We need the selection over."

His eyes shone as he met my gaze. "You have literally no pull at all with the masters. Storming in there and demanding anything is a surefire way to get yourself killed. We need to approach this politically—"

As soon as he mentioned *politically,* I had an idea. "We have to bring Shadow in," I burst out. "I know he said he can't get too involved, but he still owns part of my being, and that part he has sovereign right over."

No one owned me, of course, but if I could use my creator against the vamps, I sure as shit was going to do it.

Lucien's chest rumbled. "He has no right over you," he bit out.

266

"We don't need him to defend you; I have my own power here. Trust me to defuse the current situation, and then we can deal with the selected."

My instincts screamed at me that this was a pivotal moment with Lucien. A moment where our relationship could go either way. And if I didn't trust him...

"Okay," I finally said. "One day, though, we will face these battles together. I'm not a queen to cower behind her king. I stand at your side, or I don't stand with you at all."

That declaration might have been even stronger than the *love* one, but I was past hiding my feelings. If he wasn't all in like me, then it was time to get all out.

I couldn't do the half-fake bullshit any longer.

Lucien moved in a blur, kissing me hard and fast until my head spun and legs were weak. "Stay safe, Queen Bee," he murmured, and then he was gone.

Queen Bee. Holy shit, he'd taken my king and queen analogy and run with it.

Maybe I wasn't the only one trying to win a heart these days.

Chapter Fifty-One

There was less pep in my step as I followed Galco through the streets to Lucien's compound. Lost in thought and worry, I never even noticed he was picking up the pace, until he let out a booming laugh. "You're a vampire!" he exclaimed. "I was going almost full speed, and you stayed with me."

We reached Lucien's gates as he said this. "It's one of my favorite changes with this hybrid nature," I said, feeling a touch happier.

Galco patted my shoulder. "Glad to have you in the family. Do you need any help getting inside?"

I eyed the gate that Lucien had said would open for me, even though it never had before. Stepping forward, I pressed my hand to the mechanism spanning the center of the steel frame. As soon as I touched it, there was a click as the locks disengaged and the gates opened.

Well... okay then.

"Never thought I'd see the day," Galco said with a shake of his head.

I turned to him; one eyebrow raised. "What do you mean?"

"Master Lucien doesn't allow anyone to have unmonitored access to his inner sanctuary. You are special, Simone."

My cheeks grew hotter, and I pressed a hand to one, wondering why I was burning up. It was as if his blood inside me enjoyed these moments too. "It's probably only temporary," I said with a sigh. "Don't think too much on it, Galco."

The security guard just smiled, flashing fang and amusement my way. "Whatever you say, shifter-vamp."

I shook my head and walked inside, the gates closing behind me. Galco stayed until the gates were secured, and then he waved me off, presumably heading back to his job. Meanwhile, I went inside and stewed over the events of the day.

It was so frustrating that Hattie had tried to murder me, and now her family was here acting like she was the victim. While I'd have appreciated a touch more support from my parents growing up, I never could get behind parents who refused to acknowledge their children's misdeeds.

Yes, defend and love them, but it was equally as important to teach them responsibility and consequences for actions. If your kid tries to kill someone without provocation and, in the process, gets themselves killed... well, you might just let that one go.

Since there was nothing to do until Lucien returned, I decided to take a shower and unwind, best as I could, anyways. Once I was up the stairs, I took a moment to decide which bathroom to use.

With no idea if my spare clothes were still piled on his bed or had been moved to my room, I headed for Lucien's suite. Stepping inside, I breathed in the scent that lingered, even with the self-cleaning house. It seemed it couldn't quite remove that hint of spice, cherry, and sex. Our combined scent, along with the rays of sunlight lighting up the floor, allowed some clarity to return to my frazzled mind.

There were no clothes on the bed, so I continued snooping—because why not—heading into the wardrobe. Inside, there were walls of Lucien's clothing, ranging from expensive suits in multiple colors and styles to more casual army pants and shit-kicking boots.

Walking deeper into the room, I ground to a halt near the farthest wall.

It was filled with my clothing.

Not just the few that had been on the bed, but everything from the Master Chambers, including all the shoes. Opening a few drawers, I found underwear, socks, and scarves. Lucien had placed all my clothes into his wardrobe when he could have put them in the room down the hall.

He'd wanted me in this room.

He wanted me in his fucking room!

Today might be one of my favorite days ever, from Lucien's care and attention while I was sick to the creatures being freed and his response to my statements of love.

And now this... evidence that I was more than just some casual fling to him.

It might be time to ask him again his stance on mate bonds and a forever sort of relationship because his actions these days didn't match his previous words.

Feeling lighter, despite my continued worry that the vampire who owned my heart was being attacked at the chambers, I strolled out of the wardrobe and into the bathroom.

Stripping off my clothes, I kicked my boots free and entered the shower. The water was almost too hot, but I embraced it as I leaned against the wall and let the streams hit me. The only way this shower could be better was if Lucien were back here with me and Hattie's parents were in a different city. Or world.

Just as I was reaching for the body wash to clean myself, the bathroom door slammed open, and I almost killed myself slipping into the wall. Wiping away the steam on the glass, a familiar person came into view, and I let out an excited scream.

My best friend, with a baby strapped to her chest, was marching across the tiled area.

"Mera!" I shouted, flinging the door open. "What are you doing here?"

Her smile beamed as she stopped just outside the water pooling on the floor. "Shadow said that Lucien was in trouble, so he hustled our asses here. He dropped me off over the gates and then left for the chambers to assist his brother."

I snorted. "This was all Shadow's idea? Let me guess, you've been just calm back at the library while I've been in Valdor, right? Haven't tried to coerce Shadow into coming here even once?"

A chuckle escaped before she pressed her lips together. "His life has been hell," she choked out as more laughter burst from her. "I swear he's thought about killing me twenty times in the past week."

I laughed, too, before turning off the shower and stepping out to grab a towel. Once I was dry, I moved forward to hug my sister and our new baby. "How's she doing?" I asked as I gently wrapped my arms around them both. "Zapped you to any fun places?"

Mera squeezed me tightly, and the little girl didn't even stir, continuing to sleep soundly against her mom's chest. She was strapped in with a series of intricately wound scarves, and it looked super comfortable. "Nope, she's been on her best behavior since daddy had a talk with her about boundaries and powers."

I pulled back. "She understood him?"

Mera shrugged. "Look, I can't discount anything, but since the chat, she's been a pretty typical baby. I mean, when she's not occasionally heading off to see her new bestie, Damon."

"How is Angel's sweet boy doing?" I asked.

"Amazing," Mera said, looking just as in love with him as her own girl.

I really couldn't blame either of them. "Has there been a naming ceremony yet?"

Mera's eyebrows drew together as she scowled at me. "What sort of bestie do you think I am? I wouldn't have her ceremony without you. Don't worry, she knows her name, and soon we can all use it. We just have to sort out this bullshit in Valdor so you can return to the library."

"And Torma," I said, even though a part of me was secretly hoping that I might have more reasons to leave Earth in the future. Like... going on some dates with a certain vampire master.

A stubborn expression crossed Mera's face, one I was more than familiar with. "Nope. I made Shadow promise to build a section of the library for you to live in. I'm done being away from you. We need our family around us, our pack, and now that we have babies, it's more important than ever."

The joy I felt at the thought of having a home in the library was incalculable. "I'm going to hug you again," I said, tears sprinkling my eyes once more. No way I could stop them this time.

Mera cried too as she pulled me into her arms. We stayed like that for a long time, until the baby started to fuss, and Mera ended up on the bed, unwrapping her child to feed her. I went into the wardrobe to get dressed, leaving the door open.

"Has the baby taken to Angel now?" I called as I dropped the towel and riffled through the underwear drawer. Pulling on a matching set in plain black, I went for comfort over sexiness. Lucien was just going to strip them off me anyway.

"They're besties," Mera said as I wiggled into jeans and a black sweater. "I have no idea why she never moved for her in the womb, but it must have just been a small power struggle. Which they've now sorted."

When I walked out, I smiled at the peaceful picture Mera and her baby presented.

My friend had always been a bright spark dimmed by Torma. Now, she blazed like a galaxy, every part of her vibrant and brimming with energy.

"Does Shadow let Angel hold the baby?" I asked as I popped into the bathroom to quickly brush and braid my hair. A pang at Bowley's absence hit me, but at least he was out running free.

"Not exactly," Mera called. "But he lets her get within two feet.

It's progress, and little Au—" She cut herself off, grimacing as she shook her head. "Baby girl is always holding her arms out for Aunty Angel."

I'd returned at this point and hadn't missed that we had an *au* name. It didn't surprise me that my secret-hating bestie was struggling to keep the name to herself for so long, and I really couldn't wait for the naming ceremony.

"I hope she loves Aunty Simone as much," I whispered, crawling in closer so I could rest near them. "'Cause Aunty Simone loves her, even if she also scares the crap out of me."

Mera laughed, holding her arms steady as she did to not shake the baby. "She's going to adore you."

I hoped that was true.

We remained in a peaceful silence for a few minutes, before I just had to update Mera on everything that had been happening. "So, you know how Lucien used his blood to save me last time and we thought it was still inside, changing me?"

Mera nodded.

"Yeah, well, it's gone much further than that. I'm a full hybrid of a shifter and vampire now. Like, no take backs."

She stilled beside me. "Girl, I am going to need you to tell me everything. Right the fuck now."

The broadest smile creased my face, and I was so grateful for Mera in that moment that it took me a beat to find my voice. But when I did, I told her everything the compulsion allowed, focusing mostly on the frustrating, confusing, absolutely breathtaking new relationship in my life.

I didn't hold back, not about the blood or sex or my newly discovered kinks, knowing Mera would never judge me.

"This is amazing!" she shrieked, before lowering her voice when the baby stirred. "You're my sister and sister-in-law now since Lucien and Shadow are brothers." Her voice grew higher again as she hurried to say, "And don't even think about the logistics of that; no one is blood related."

I had to laugh at her obsession with reiterating that she was in no way blood related to Shadow. "Sister-in-law might be a bit much," I said as I sobered. "Lucien hasn't made it clear that he's in this for anything long term. Maybe I've misread it all, and in the end he'll go back to his old life."

Every part of me hoped that wasn't the case, but I'd been hurt by Lucien before, so it felt like self-preservation to consider the possibility that this could still all end when the selection did.

Mera pursed her lips and shook her head. "Not a hope in hell. I've known that vampire for years now, and never has he shown possessiveness over anything. Not food or people or items. He's so cool, calm, and collected. Just cruising through life without a care in the world. What you've described sounds more like Shadow and Reece with me and Angel. When these guys fall, they fall hard, and there's no middle ground for them."

She looked down at the feeding child. "I hope you like kids because these dudes knock you up fast too. Overachievers have freaking virile sperm."

More laughter escaped me, and I felt like a weight lifted from my shoulders just from being around Mera. "No kids for us, but I sure like to practice making them, if you know what I mean."

Heat literally burned across her skin as her energy soared. "Dude, I *more than know* what you mean. Shadow has this new thing where he uses his energy along with his enormous dick, and there are moments I think I'm going to die. And I'd take death if I could just have that pleasure over and over."

She went on, and I was in hysterics by the time Shadow and Lucien walked into the room, both looking unruffled and unconcerned about whatever had happened up at the Master Chambers.

The moment I saw Lucien, the mass of worry I'd been carrying eased. He was back and safe, and now we could determine the plan going forward.

Chapter Fifty-Two

S hadow went straight for his mate and child, scooping them up to place Mera in his lap as she fed the baby. He wrapped his arms around them both, and Mera tilted her head back to accept his kiss like she had no doubt it was coming.

Lucien approached my side of the bed, and I almost died when he and lifted me as well, settling me in his lap. We'd never sat like this before, so it was a bit weird and uncomfortable at first. Then his hand wrapped around mine, pulling me back against him. At that point I relaxed into his crimson scent, wondering how the hell this was my life.

The four of us sat like that for a long time in comfortable silence, letting the baby feed in peace. Lucien stroked his hand softly across my arm, and with his scent around me and heat seeping into me, it was a struggle to keep my eyes open.

This was a dream moment, and I didn't want to miss a second, so I forced myself to stay awake and enjoy the sensations of being surrounded by pack.

Mera and Shadow acted like this was totally normal, despite the fact that Lucien had never done this in their presence before. Their acceptance was huge, and now more than ever, I felt like I was part of their family.

It was enough to bring a girl to tears for the thirtieth time today.

Eventually though, our bubble had to burst—it was time to know what'd happened at the chambers with Hattie's parents and the masters.

"Tell us everything," I said, my voice seeming louder than usual after the calm silence. "How did you deal with the masters and Hattie's family?"

Lucien wrapped his arms tighter around me, and I prepared myself for what he might say. "The masters agreed to end the selection tonight." His voice sent goosebumps across my skin. "They scrapped the hunt's date prize since no one returned with any kills. Therefore, it's down to the stone's blessing, and Carter insisted that the selected still spend time in our homes."

My wolf reared up then, a growl rocking my chest.

Mera snorted. "You might be part vampire now, but that there was all shifter possessiveness."

She wasn't wrong, though I had it on good authority that vamps were equally as possessive. "I don't want the selected in this house," I told Lucien, attempting to sit upright. His strong arms kept me secure against him, though, as he let out a low chuckle.

"I've already told them that I've made my choice and don't need dates."

"Did Carter do the same?"

"No." A short, annoyed statement. "He wants the dates to go ahead, and I can't veto that since they already cut the selection short on my command."

At least I could remain calm knowing that Lucien was not bringing other selected into his compound. "Thank the gods it will be over tonight." I sighed as I let myself relax against him.

This time when his arms tightened around me, I could feel the hard length of him growing under my ass. He'd been hard since he placed me into his lap, but this was extra.

"I like your jealousy," he murmured near my ear, and I tried not to fidget against the unfurling tension between my legs.

"What about Hattie's parents?" I rasped out, needing a subject change. "Are they still calling for my death and your punishment?"

It was Shadow's turn to laugh, but as always, his was a rumble filled with dark intentions. "I reminded them that their daughter tried to destroy one of my shifters. Lucien reminded them that their daughter tried to destroy the selected he intends to call as his mate. They appeared to get the message that they might be outpowered in their vengeance quest and, next time, they should return with an army of thousands."

Mera smacked Shadow's arm. "You know they probably will, right? You long-lived bastards don't get over grudges; you just hold onto them until you discover a powerful stone or infiltrate a land of dead gods."

Shadow shrugged, unconcerned as usual. It must be nice at the top of the food chain. "Let them come. Our family only grows in power and strength. We have new babies, and Simone is our first shifter-vampire hybrid, proving that when I created shifters, I truly did take from all worlds and races."

Shadow claiming me as family would literally never get old.

"Shouldn't you already have known that your creation was pulled from multiple worlds and races?" Lucien asked drily.

"Drunken bet, remember?" Mera piped up. "This moron has no idea what he mixed up in his magic potion. Lucky for him, it worked out okay."

Suddenly, she jumped a foot and barely managed to stifle a moan... meaning Shadow must have sent a shock of his power into her. He caught her and the baby on the way down, and the bastard actually laughed. It was so disconcerting when he did that.

Instead of sitting back down, though, the power couple got to their feet indicating the end of our cozy bedroom scene and return to the real world.

"I'm not leaving until this is over," Mera warned Shadow.

He shook his head. "The masters do not want me to stay. They're worried about my interference, and to keep the peace for Lucien, we should let them finish the selection. Simone will return to the library tomorrow. I've got her room all set up as requested."

Lucien froze, his big body half in front of mine, blocking me from view. "What do you mean about Simone's room?" To my surprise, he sounded upset.

Did he not want me living closer by? From the library, he could visit daily if he wanted, with almost no effort.

"Mera wants Simone to live with us," Shadow said, "in her own wing off the library. I've been sprinkling some creation dust around and managed to form an area that Simone can claim."

"It makes even more sense now," Mera added, sounding happy. I couldn't see her to confirm this, though, since Lucien was still blocking me from view.

"What makes more sense now?" I called, unsure what was driving Lucien's behavior.

"Now that you're a vampire-shifter hybrid, you'll probably live a lot longer and will need blood. The packs can't provide for your needs, but the library can."

I'd learned long ago that the library could pull food from any of the worlds, which meant that everyone was able to get what they needed from its dining hall. Even those who were now kinda into crimson beverages.

"Living in the library will be almost as good as owning a bookstore," I decided. "Do you think I can bring some of my favorite books from Earth and fill my room?"

Shadow answered. "I've set up a sitting room with a fireplace and shelves. At Sunshine's request. You will have everything you need."

Lucien made a rumbling sound so deep I would have thought it was Shadow if I hadn't felt it pulse through the vampire's body. Shadow's response was to laugh again, but I'd had enough at this point. "What's your problem," I demanded, poking Lucien in the back and hurting my finger. "Why would you be so mad about me living in the library. I'll be closer."

He spun and I took a step back at the look on his face. He followed me, backing me up until he had me against the wall.

"This looks familiar," Mera said with clear sarcasm. I couldn't see her, but I knew the eye-rolling expression she would be wearing. "Merry band of assholes... all cut from the same cloth."

I wanted to focus on what she was saying, but a vamped-out Lucien had my full attention. Those black eyes bored into mine, holding me completely captive. "It's not close enough," he said, voice a hypnotic rumble. "You'll stay here, in my house. After the end of the selection, you will be my mate, and my mate stays with me."

The ability to swallow... or breathe... or think was completely gone. I just stared and stared, mouth half open as my brain short-circuited. Of course, Mera stepped in again to save the day, completely unafraid of a crazy vamp as she reached his side and poked him just like I had done. "Are you claiming her truly as a mate or just this same fake mate shit to get through the selection?"

Without taking his eyes from me, he let out a low snarl that was directed at Mera, and of course, that was when Shadow's beast came out to play. The fiery Anubis flickered across the giant's form, but Lucien didn't give a fuck. He didn't back down, and thankfully Mera got the hint and moved away a few steps to give him breathing room.

"His vampire is in control when it comes to Simone," Shadow said, sounding somewhat relaxed. "Don't expect anything rational until he sorts himself out."

Lucien leaned down and pressed his mouth to my throat, and as his fangs slowly extended, I moaned against the sensation. The knowledge that Mera and Shadow were in the room faded away, and I almost missed the beast dragging her out with a "They need a minute alone, Sunshine."

She complained, but her mate won, and then Lucien and I were alone.

Lucien lifted me so I could wrap myself around him, rocking into him to ease the slow drip of need in my center. The pull of his mouth against my throat almost destroyed me in the best possible way, and as I cried out, needing to feel more of his skin, my hands scraped at his clothing.

Lucien stripped us both bare, placing me back down to pull my jeans and panties off and drop to his knees. His mouth slid across my pussy as his tongue lapped at the need dripping from me. He ate me like I was his last fucking meal, and when my clit was so engorged that a simple touch of it would have sent me into orgasm, he sucked it into his mouth, fangs piercing the blood-filled bundle.

My scream made me near hoarse as I held onto Lucien's head. That and the wall behind me were the only things keeping me standing. The vampire, who continued to feed in a frenzy, sent one orgasm after another crashing through my body until I actually passed out for a moment, darkness taking me down into Lucien's arms.

When I came to, he was holding me tight against him, leaning over to kiss me. I could taste myself on his tongue, blood and pleasure mingling, and my exhausted vagina spasmed again to remind me that we apparently had infinite ability to orgasm.

First, though, I wanted to be the one to feed and bring pleasure.

Chapter Fifty-Three

Our kissing picked up the pace, and I briefly forgot my plan. But then he said against my lips, in a voice filled with sex and pain, "*Feed.*"

That was the opening I needed, and as I started to kiss along his jaw, I took my time to taste his skin, which held the faint scents of cherry, sweat, and spice. Lucien tasted like life, and considering I'd always thought of vampires as the "undead," it was quite ironic.

As I kissed down his neck, fine stubble made texture under my lips and tongue. He continued to hold onto my hips like they were his anchor to the world, and I'd never felt so wanted. So safe. So at home in my existence.

As terribly weak as it sounded, part of me would be lost forever if Lucien walked away.

Still, he'd called me his mate, and that had to mean something. Even if his vampire was in charge, Lucien was too old and strong to say what he didn't mean.

My wolf rose as I kissed and tasted my way along his body, my jaw shifting to incorporate my new fangs and canine setup.

Lucien's chest rumbled. "Feed, Bee. I can feel your hunger, and I need it sated. Right. Now."

I chuckled. "Patience, Crimson."

He growled again, and now he sounded like a shifter. Maybe my blood was affecting him, just as his affected me. I doubted vampires had fed off shifters before; we weren't big on sharing our blood with creatures of darkness. This was the unknown for both of us, but so far, I couldn't complain.

When I continued along the lines of his abs and down to the sexiest fucking V in the world, Lucien's muscles tensed under my touch. My fangs grazed him, small trickles of blood filling my mouth, and my mind went a little cloudy at this point.

Part of me wanted to frenzy feed like Lucien had done, but I'd had an aim with this path down his body, so I forced myself to focus. His cock was hard, the tip shiny as precum beaded the slit, and it drew me closer as I wondered how it would taste and how much I could take.

I'd never done this before, my movements pure instinct at this point.

Darting my tongue out, I swiped it across the head, enjoying the low groan from the vampire above. His hands moved to my hair, sliding into the long lengths, and as he tightened his hold, parts of my body tightened with it.

The urge to touch myself while pleasuring him grew.

Opening my mouth wider, I swirled my tongue across the silky steel before I swallowed as much of his cock as I could. I had to be careful not to cut him with my sharper teeth, which meant I could only take about one tenth of his actual length. It didn't appear to matter to Lucien, who groaned, his hold so firm I wondered if he planned on keeping me here forever.

Fine by me.

My hand working his shaft, I sucked and licked across the head of his cock, tasting a spicy cherry, very much like his blood. Unable to help myself, my fang pierced the side of the slit on his knob.

"Fuck," Lucien rumbled. "Whatever you're doing, don't fucking stop, Bee."

At this point, I drank his blood and worked his cock with one hand, while my other hand was on my pussy, stroking the wetness pooling there. This was literally too much stimulation for me, and I knew I wouldn't be able to maintain this pace for long. I needed to climb my vampire and screw him until we were both breathless.

Or dead.

Whatever.

I'd take death at this point just to keep feeling all of this.

When I'd had enough blood, I allowed my fangs and canines to recede to really give this dick sucking a thorough attempt. Lost in the moment, I almost bit a chunk from him when Lucien's hands shot under my arms and lifted me. It was so fast that he popped from my mouth with a loud sound.

He was inside me in the next second, and to no one's surprise, I came almost instantly.

The orgasm was fast and intense, but I rode it straight into another one. Lucien came with me, groaning my name as he thrust a few more times, both of us breathing heavy enough to wake the damn dead.

"Fuck," he repeated and didn't say another word.

No other words were really needed.

When we managed to catch our breath, he strode toward the shower with me in his arms, cock buried and pulsing inside me. In the stall, he finally released me as our bodies separated, and I wasn't okay with that, to be honest.

We didn't linger under the water, since Shadow and Mera were somewhere in the house, probably laughing at how damn loudly we'd been fucking. Also, I was ready for this selection to be done, which meant getting back to the chambers and ending it.

Lucien took a moment to wash me gently; he never used a cloth, preferring his hands on my skin. "Why didn't you answer Mera's question about claiming me truly as a mate?"

The question slipped out before I could stop it. We weren't even really together, and I was already acting like a damn clingy girlfriend, but...

You know what, fuck that noise.

There was nothing clingy or wrong about asking for clarification from the dude you were sleeping with. If he had my body and my blood, then I deserved to know where this was going. From this day forward, I would be stronger than I ever had before.

I was done being the poor, unlovable shifter.

The damage from my parents might be real, but it didn't have to last forever. I had the choice now to try and grow past it, and I was determined that eventually I would.

"My vampire was in charge, and we could think of nothing except claiming you," Lucien said. "The library is not your damn home," Lucien repeated his words from before, "because your home is here. With me."

Butterflies took flight in my stomach, but I needed more clarification. "With you. As in forever? As in, you want me as a mate? You said you would never take a true mate, so...?"

Lucien stepped into me, backing me against the wall, his big body completely covering mine as his cock slid against my pussy. He was hard again, and I needed to feel all of him, but not until he answered.

"I know what I said," he murmured, low voice sending tingles across my skin, his lips pressing to my throat. "I've been fighting against the pull between us for too long, but since we started feeding... I haven't needed blood."

Despite his lips on my throat and dick between my legs, I managed a coherent sentence. "You've drunk my blood."

Lucien's laugh was low and husky. "Exactly. I've been filled with energy from your blood alone. Which shouldn't be possible except with a—"

"Blood call bond," I whispered, finally understanding what he'd been trying to tell me.

His fangs scraped against my skin. "Your blood tastes like life," he murmured. "It tastes like energy. I can't let you go now, Bee. If you don't feel the same, then you're going to have a fucking vampire following you everywhere to ensure your safety while he tries to convince you to take a chance on love. You're part of me now." He leaned back far enough to clamp a hand over his chest. "You're in here. In my blood and energy. In my cells. There'd be no point to life without you. So, yes, I am claiming you as a real mate."

Holy shit. We were doing this. We were really fucking doing this, and I was so overwhelmed that my fuzzy head felt like it was about to float away.

Get it together, Simone.

This was an important conversation, and I needed all of my brain cells.

"Your blood tastes like life to me too," I told him, my voice wavering. At the truth of this, tears slipped down my cheeks to mingle with the shower water. "Not just life, but home. I've never had that before. My parents' house was not a home. The closest I ever had to feeling like I was part of a family or a pack was with Mera. And I still feel that, but she has her own little pack now, which has left me on the outside."

"Not with me," Lucien said fiercely, his hands cupping my cheeks. He then leaned in and kissed me softly, his tongue tracing against mine and then across my cheeks to catch my tears. "You're never on the outside. You're everything."

"You chose me," I choked out. "Even when you didn't have to." Blood-call bonds might be fated, but Lucien had never been the type to follow a path unless he wanted to.

He nodded, those brilliant green eyes boring into me with not a sliver of darkness. "Long before I knew the taste of your blood, you consumed my mind and thoughts. My vampire had already claimed you; the rest of my stubborn ass just had to catch up."

My throat closed over, and I was crying so hard that my chest shook. I didn't try and stop it this time, allowing the cleansing nature of tears to wash through me and wash away past pains and hurts.

Lucien didn't say anything, he just held me.

When I pulled away, it was to find peace on his beautiful, perfect face, and I couldn't believe I got to look at him for the rest of my life.

We just had to end this selection first.

Chapter Fifty-Four

When we finally made it out of the bathroom, dressed and ready to leave, we found Mera and Shadow downstairs. Shadowshine Jr. was on her belly on the rug, waving her arms and legs and making sounds that were almost words. Because the kid was all of a week old and that made sense.

In this world, it probably did make sense.

Mera jumped to her feet, and the moment she saw my face she shrieked. She knew something big had happened because she knew me that well.

"Ahhhh," she shrieked again, uncaring that she'd scared the shit out of her baby, who was now wearing cry-face. "Finally. You two have *finally* sorted your shit out and realize that you're perfect for each other."

She hurried forward and threw her arms around us, her godlike strength squishing us all together. Shadow let out a low laugh as he lifted his daughter into his arms and patted her back a few times, settling her with ease. "I approve of this mating," he said as he stepped forward. "Our pack and family were destined to join. I'm starting to understand the reason I bonded with my brothers, and now I believe that Mera's friends are the catalysts for the other mates."

Mera's eyes went super wide, and she pressed a hand against her throat as she turned to Shadow. "You've never told me that! How long have you been thinking that this is all part of a larger design?"

He shrugged, still patting the baby gently on the back. "For some time. I've been following the tapestry woven from all our energies, and your friend Sam is connected as well. I just haven't figured out how or why."

Mera's face fell. "Sam isn't much of a friend these days. She never talks to me. I just wish I could help her, but I've had to learn that at the end of the day, if people want my help, they'll ask for it. Forcing them is not always the answer."

Mera was a steamroller when she wanted to help someone, so that had been a painful lesson for her to learn.

"I haven't really spoken with Sam either," I said. "I mean, I talk to her occasionally, but she always cuts it off after about five sentences."

I'd been worried because I could tell she was unhappy, but I also always heard the resolve in her tone. She was in for the long haul, ready to do her duty for her pack. I just wished she'd trust us enough to help her.

"We should try again," I decided. "One last time. I know what it's like to feel hopeless and stuck in a shitty situation." My eyes caught Lucien's. "But I also know what it's like to find your path. Sam deserves a chance to have that as well."

"Yes!" Mera fist-pumped, and when I laughed, she shrugged. "What? Just because I've learned to step back doesn't mean I've stopped worrying."

I patted her shoulder. "That's what makes you an amazing friend."

"But before we deal with Sam, we need to get Simone through this selection," Lucien said. "The Stone of Katu blessing is soon, and then I'm hoping she can refuse her time at Carter's home on the grounds that she's already taken. Either way, it will end tonight."

"Let's get to the Master Chambers," I said, bouncing on the spot in an attempt to pep myself up. "I probably owe Carter a nice gift since his stupid selection gave me a literal true mate."

Lucien wrapped his arms around me and pulled me back against his chest. "You owe that vampire nothing. He's just lucky I don't rip his fucking head off like I did Hattie's. That's the only gift he's got coming."

I snorted but didn't argue, more than a little content to be hugged against his body like this while he plotted more deaths.

Mera was grinning hard, and I loved to see happiness spreading through the pack. "We should go now," Lucien finally said.

"Mera and I will wait here," Shadow told him. "I don't want to interfere and start a war. But my"—his gaze flicked across to Mera— "gorgeous mate is refusing to leave Valdor until Simone is free from her selection duties."

Mera nodded. "Yep, no leaving until we're all safe in the library. We can ensure there's room for Lucien in Simone's new digs."

Lucien didn't react except to tighten his hold on me. Tilting my head back, I looked up and smiled. "We can have two homes. Valdor feels like it only has half your heart and energy anyway."

When he kissed me, I lost all train of thought for a beat, but no one could miss Mera's loud and happy sigh. "I'll get my carpenter on the expansion as soon as we get back," she choked out.

Shadow growled something about being *a fucking god and not a carpenter,* but no one bothered to comment.

I hugged Mera goodbye, patted Shadow and the baby on their shoulders, since neither of them were big on personal contact from anyone other than Mera, and left with Lucien to enter the maze of Crimson City. We didn't speak as we walked, and I kept up with his vampire speed easily.

For the first time, I was walking into the Master Chambers prepared to claim my mate and move on with my life. There were no more doubts. No more worries that this would all be torn away from me in a heartbeat. Finally, my wolves were in a row, and I could start dreaming of a true future and pack.

As we made it through the security, I looked around for Galco, but he wasn't there. Taking a second look, I didn't recognize any of the guards, which was odd since the rotation was usually pretty solid.

Lucien didn't say anything as he also took in all the faces staring at us. No one stopped or approached us, opening gates and doors before we even got to them.

Lucien pulled me closer as we stepped inside, and I wondered if maybe we should have brought Shadow and Mera with us after all. War or not, they were both gods and could probably snap their damn fingers and dissolve a vampire into goo.

Maybe Lucien could do that too... I'd never thought to ask.

Hopefully, all of these worries were just last-minute nerves and once I touched the stone that'd started this all and rejected Carter, all would be okay.

The chambers were quiet, and I held my breath almost all the way up the stairs until we entered the long hall. When we arrived, there were only a few masters lingering around, and it seemed that for once, I was early to a selection event.

"Lucien," a female called. "Take your seat while we wait for the others to arrive. She waved her hand to his usual spot, and there continued to be no reason for suspicion or apprehension... and yet I felt both. My wolf stirred, pushing forward with the swirling vampire blood.

Deciding to ignore the worry, I embraced the other parts of myself. This day I felt strong and confident, and the fact that Lucien hadn't left my side for his chair, our hands still firmly entwined, only added to this feeling.

No matter what bullshit they might have planned, we were strong enough to overcome it. Together.

Chapter Fifty-Five

The five other masters in the room talked amongst themselves, and no one asked Lucien to take a seat again. Donovan wasn't here yet, or Assface or Julietta; it was mostly masters I'd had nothing to do with in the selection.

The conversation died off when Carter appeared, back to wearing his woodsman-hunter outfit from the first time I'd met him. His expression was closed off, and it didn't change when his eyes lowered to see Lucien's hand wrapped around mine. "Made your choice, I see." There was no anger in his tone... If anything, he sounded resigned.

I hated to hurt him, but I had zero regrets about how this had ended up. "I'm sorry, Carter," I said with a sad smile. "Lucien has been the one for a long time now. We both tried to fight it, believing we were from different races and could never form a true bond. But this selection has only shown us that there's no fighting a blood call bond. At least we know now that shifters and vampires are compatible. We're born of the same energy, and I'm excited to see where we can go together."

Carter didn't say anything for a long moment, his attention focused on me like Lucien wasn't even there. "I understand," he finally said. "The selection wasn't the best plan, in hindsight. I should have gone with my initial idea. Next time I'll trust my instincts."

His smile wasn't nice, stretching his lips; fangs appeared as his eyes darkened.

Lucien had had enough at that point, sidling in front of me and blocking Carter's view. "Walk away now," he warned the other master. "You're dangerously close to pissing me off, and as a newly mated vampire who hasn't finished the bonding process yet, you really don't want to do that."

His body hulked out before me, and I placed my hand on his back, hoping to calm him. Carter might be annoying, but we had to remember that he'd lost. We could afford to ignore his digs.

Carter just laughed. "You skirted the edge of the rules of the selection," he told Lucien. "You didn't win with honor since you never gave me a fair shot. For that, you will pay, but let's see what the stone says first."

Lucien's body was vibrating under my touch, but he didn't move. We both knew Carter was baiting him, and while I totally understood Lucien's need to punch that arrogant fuck in the face, I hoped he didn't waste the energy.

"See you soon, Simone," he called, and I heard his footsteps as he headed for his throne on the master's stage.

Why did his *See you soon* sound like a not-so-vague threat?

"Do not move out of my line of sight," Lucien warned as he turned to face me.

Other masters were arriving now, including Donovan. The four other remaining selected were also there, which meant this party was about to get started.

"I'm not going anywhere, mate." I would literally never get tired of saying *mate* to Lucien. "Let's get this shit over with."

He brushed a hand across my cheek and leaned in to press his lips to my forehead. It was a long, lingering touch, and I wasn't the only one who let out a hushed breath at the gesture. Silence followed the movement, and as he walked to his crimson throne, I stared after him, stunned.

Lucien had claimed me in front of them all in a gesture that could not be missed or misinterpreted. The silence told me that none of them had ever seen him act like this with another female, which had my wolf and his blood roaring inside. The feeling of home settled within me, even as the rest of me soared.

Whether it was fate or not, he chose to be with me when he'd never wanted a mate.

He chose me.

As Lucien sank into his chair, he locked his gaze on me, and I thanked the gods for this life. It took every bit of strength I possessed not to cross to him, lean between his muscled thighs, and...

The heat rose, and I had to cut off all sexy thoughts, or we'd soon be making a scene.

A smirk creased the corners of Lucien's lips, and I didn't even have to guess at what he was thinking. We were on the same train of thought today.

I wondered how long we'd be consumed by this fiery passion—hopefully forever.

Donovan stood and cleared his throat, the first to make a sound since Lucien kissed my forehead. "Thank you all for gathering one last time," he said. "We are down to the final five selected, and Masters Lucien and Carter have decided that they'll make their decisions after the blessing from the stone and a brief visit to Carter's compound."

He called up the first selected then: Lucil. She was not a vampire I'd seen or paid attention to before today, but now that there were only five of us left, I noticed a pattern. The others were all blonde. Not just blonde, but the same long, straight, white-blonde hair. They were all tall with olive skin, too, and could have been sisters in how similar they looked. Was this Carter's normal type?

When Lucil touched the stone, there was a brief burst of light before she was approved and moved to the right. Donovan called on the others one by one: Jelna, Yal, and Merin. All of them passed their blessing, and it seemed that the glow of the stone was extra bright when I stepped up. Last as usual.

Wiping my hands on my jeans, I tried to ignore my nerves. They were stronger than usual today because I didn't want to fail. I wanted to claim my master, and if that required a blessing from Katu, then I hoped it wasn't my day for rejection.

I mean, Lucien was a master and could do whatever he wanted, but if Katu rejected me, it would make it so much harder to establish our relationship as an official one. It might even weaken his enclave, and I couldn't have that.

Still, I held onto the truth that we had a blood call bond. A true bond.

Katu couldn't reject that, right?

Reaching out, I noted that there was a white dot to indicate where we should touch. I placed my hand there without another thought. The moment my hand touched, a small prick of pain hit my palm, and there was a huge burst of light. Lucien sat straighter in his chair, and just as I was about to pull my eyes from him to see what had cut my skin, warmth bloomed under my palm on the stone.

Glancing at my hand, I noticed that there was a long trail of blood spurting from underneath. *What?*

With a gasp, I tried to jerk my hand free, but it wouldn't move.

The heat surged, reacting against the swirling energy inside of me.

Two opposite forces crashing together.

As I opened my mouth to call for help, I felt the world shift under my feet, like fate was reevaluating my path. The heat pulsed unbearably, and as Lucien raced toward me, the light grew too strong. Too bright.

He couldn't fight against it, and I had the sense that this might be the last time I saw him. "I love y—" spilled from my lips, cut off when the heat reached its pinnacle.

The force of the explosion tore me to pieces, and everything went dark.

LUCIEN

Whenever the darkest recesses of my vampire soul took control, I saw only in shades of grey, with no bright colors penetrating the darkness. Before I'd met Simone, it had happened maybe a dozen times over the centuries, but since she'd come into my life, there'd been no control.

She released the primal beast in my soul, and the oddest part was that when I vamped out around her, she was always in color.

A crimson red highlighted her eyes and lips, with her hair an even deeper shade of red.

If I hadn't had centuries of dealing with my baser urges, I wouldn't have been able to stop myself from capturing her and stealing her away the very first moment I saw her.

The first moment I scented her blood.

But she'd been an innocent—a shifter who knew nothing of the vampire world. And it was safer for everyone to keep her away. So, I'd left and avoided her, done everything I could to keep her alive. And then she'd ended up in Valdor anyway.

Leaving her in my compound had done nothing to dull her pull. Every damn time I closed my eyes, she was there. If I breathed deeply enough, I could smell her flower and aniseed scent in every part of the city.

She was in my blood long before I'd tasted hers.

My determination to remain without the burden of a true mate bond had almost cost me the ultimate peace. The ultimate pleasure. The ultimate joy.

Simone was too good for me, her kindness and empathy beyond my understanding, since I'd long stopped giving a shit about anything other than my brothers and my enclave. But somehow, she made me a better vampire.

A stronger one.

One willing to fight for a chance at true happiness.

A chance to give her the life she deserved.

As she touched the Stone of Katu for the final time, I was mesmerized by the pink in her cheeks shining brightly. It was the sort of pink I liked to see when my mouth was on her body. My fangs inside her.

I'd spent centuries refusing to let another feed from me, but I'd been compelled to give her my life force that night in the chambers when she'd been near death.

I refused to let her die, and now I knew why.

True mate. She was my blood call mate, and I intended to complete the ritual as soon as we were done with the stone's blessing today.

The light grew stronger around her as the stone accepted her touch, and it was only when the scent of her blood hit me that I realized something was wrong. She pulled her wide eyes from mine, glancing toward her hand, and I was already on my feet moving forward.

In that moment, the light turned blinding as heat filled the room.

My vision darkened as I growled at Carter, knowing what that bastard had done. As soon as I saved my mate, he was fucking dead.

Only a few masters knew that the Stone of Katu was more than just a gift for blessings—it had a double purpose. The core was infused with a swirling well of energy that could be turned into a weapon if needed. The triggers to initiate it were not complicated, but since it required the blood of an ancient tier one master, it also wasn't easy.

Carter knew Simone was feeding from me, and he'd used my blood inside her to trigger the heat-filled center. He must have had one of the other selected add some sort of point to break Simone's skin when she touched the side.

Screams filled the hall as the other masters sensed the danger, and I was sure they were taking off, but I couldn't see a damn thing through the blinding light. As I fought against it, it burned my skin in an attempt to hold me away.

I pushed forward to get my mate.

I had to be there to protect her. To stand between her and the blast.

"Simone!" I bellowed, rage growing inside of me fueled by pure fear.

My Bee wasn't a full vampire—she would not survive a direct blast of the stone's energy.

Through the light, I caught a glimpse of her terrified face. She opened her mouth, and even though I couldn't hear her, I read her lips. "I love y—"

The explosion ripped through the space a second later, and I roared, throwing up shields. I was grateful to be powerful enough not to be taken down, because I had to save Simone.

The fire raged on, burning me, while my energy repaired the damage just as quickly. I had to hope that my blood was doing the same for Simone—keeping her alive until I could get to her through the light and chaos.

No part of me would accept that Simone was gone.

My bloodline was the most powerful in Valdor, and it would give Simone a fighting chance.

When I finally reached the stone, I searched for her body, only to find a trail of blood where she had been. Whoever had taken her had come from the far end of the room, away from the blast radius.

The Stone of Katu was still mostly standing, with only a small exit wound where the energy had emerged. Punching out, I smashed my fist into the stone, sending it crashing to the floor and shattering into a million pieces. This blessed and sacred stone had taken my mate from me, and I felt nothing of its destruction.

Pocketing some pieces in case they came in handy later, I zipped around the room and checked who was still here. Carter was the only one missing, which all but confirmed my suspicion that he'd planned the entire thing.

He'd had help, though, and I would kill everyone who'd assisted him.

Shadow came into my vision, his energy raging. Behind him was Mera, her fear tingling across my tongue. "Lucien," Shadow roared in his beast form. "Where is Simone?"

"Carter took her," I rasped, voice filled with sharp edges and broken pieces. This was what I'd feared about having a mate, but I still wouldn't change my decision for anything in the worlds. I would get her back and destroy every fuck who'd touched her.

"I need to find and kill him," I continued. "Him and anyone who helped him with this."

Shadow nodded before turning to Mera.

"Is Simone alive?" she shouted, and whether she was talking to me or Shadow, he was the one that answered.

"She's gone from my vision," he said softly. "But there's always a chance to save her. We just have to find her first."

Gone from my vision.

Shadow was her creator, and he could feel all his shifters.

Even with the vampire blood, that shouldn't have taken away his ability to track her. "She's alive," I bit out. "She has to be."

If she wasn't, I would walk into the fucking underworld to get her back.

Without my mate, the world was darkness, and I would be as well.

"We have to search for her," Shadow said to Mera. "While we do, can you go back to the library and rally the others? We might need all of them."

Mera made a raging sound as flames burst from her, grey in my vision. "Find her, Shadow. I don't care what you have to do or how many worlds you rip apart."

My fangs lengthened, and as Donovan came up to me, shouting about the stone, my hand shot out and closed around his throat. "You're the reason Simone was here in the first place," I rumbled. "You took Carter's side and then you took Hattie's. You've almost been the cause of my mate's death twice now."

Before he could say a word, I flexed my fingers and sent out a burst of energy, severing his head in a way that not even a vampire could recover from. Uncaring, I dropped Donovan at my feet, stepping over him like he was mere debris from the blast.

Mera hugged her child to her chest as she shot me a twisted smile. "Now take that level of brutal and unleash it on this fucking world until you find my sister."

"I'm finding my mate," I rumbled. "Any that stand in my way will die."

There was no mercy in my soul. No give or understanding.

And that was if Simone was alive.

If she wasn't, the world would end today.

Chapter Fifty-Seven

As the daughter of a pack enforcer, I wasn't a stranger to pain. My father had been a big believer in tough love, especially when he was trying to teach me a lesson. After all, no good enforcer would flinch in the face of torture, right?

And what was the best way to ensure I wouldn't flinch? Years of staggered torture.

You get used to things, he'd say to me. Pain and fear could be overcome with strict training.

Mom had stopped him from ever going too far, but I'd still been on the receiving end of his "training" many times. This training was how I knew after the blast of the stone that my body was broken, burned, and shattered.

Mera had always wondered why I'd been a "sucker for punishment" as she put it, sticking around as the best friend of the pack's punching bag. I'd never told her the truth because she had so much going on already, but I was never afraid of school bullies. There was a much worse one in my house.

As I went in and out of consciousness, knowing that the stone had torn me to pieces, I was aware that someone was gathering up the parts of me that were no longer attached. Gathering them and stitching me back together.

This pain was beyond all torture, as I was burned and pierced and cut with no relief in sight. I welcomed it when the pain got too hard to handle and the darkness found me.

I should be dead. There was no doubt in my mind. And even as my body was rearranged and placed into a huge bath of liquid, I had no idea how I was alive. Not just *how* but also *who* had done this? Who held me now?

It wasn't Lucien; the blood in the bath was foreign, and while it might be healing me, it also made me want to vomit all over my broken self.

Eventually, the healing reached a point where I could crawl out of the pain-filled space in my head and force my eyelids to lift. It was hard. It felt like a million tons of bricks sat on my face, but I worked my way through it.

The room came into view slowly, and as the shadowy area grew clearer, my blinks slowed over gritty eyeballs. There was nothing familiar around me; I'd never been here before, but from what I could see, the room wasn't much bigger than my apartment back home. The walls were dark grey stone, and the equally grey metal bath I floated in was much wider and longer than my body.

I couldn't move my limbs or even really lift my head, but I could see just enough down my body to note that half my right leg was gone and my internal organs were floating on the outside.

Nausea rose in my throat at the sight, so I lifted my gaze to the ceiling, breathing through the moment. Needing another focus, I wondered again who was to blame for this. Was it Carter's doing? Or had it been Hattie's parents?

Or was there another enemy out there I was unaware of?

Only one way to find out. "Hello?"

I always hated in horror movies when the person about to die stupidly alerted the killer to their location by repeating "hello" over and over. In this instance, though, it wasn't like I was hiding. Someone had put me in this bath. Someone was out there watching me. Someone had better let me know what the fuck they wanted from me.

"Show your fucking face," I called, voice sounding perfectly fine even though the rest of me looked like a damn woodchipper had done me over. "Face me like a man."

In the back of my head, I blamed Carter for this. And I might have been wrong, but I couldn't shake the feeling.

A deep, echoing sound suddenly filled the stone room, like someone had beat one of those large brass gongs. It was eerie, seeming to build in strength the longer it went on. The room vibrated, and as the water around me shook, I wanted to scream and cover my ears, but I still couldn't move.

Closing my eyes again, I moved my focus inward, hoping that I might be able to push the healing of my body along. Inside, the pain was almost stronger than outside, and I found my wolf in agony, taking so much of it into herself to protect me. *No,* I whispered. *We face it together. Release the pain and rise.*

Her howl was broken, and it broke me too. I'd have taken the torn skin, burns, and severed muscles any day if it meant *she* didn't ever have to feel this pain again.

It took more coaxing, but eventually she released the bubble of energy she'd been using to shield me, and I screamed as new and more vicious agony raged through me. My scream went on so long that I felt like I'd suffered permanent damage to my hearing and voice by the time I could stop.

Pain was odd in that, if the initial shock didn't kill you, your body adjusted. Your pain threshold grew so you could handle more than you ever thought possible. Once the first burst of pain registered, I was able to compartmentalize it so I could go back to figuring out who was in the room with me.

My wolf wrapped around me and offered her sight to help me

see. Not that there was anything other than stone walls, ceiling, and a metal bath visible.

The gong continued on, and I prayed for the ability to lift my hands and cover my ears. Until it suddenly stopped, and a voice rumbled around me.

"That's what you pray for, child?"

It was deep and dark, like a dream and nightmare collided. It came from nowhere and everywhere, and I sensed that I was about to find out exactly who had dropped my body parts into a bath of blood.

LUCIEN

Bodies lay at my feet. So many that I could no longer tell one from the other. The only one still standing was Shadow, his beast form in place as we cleansed the vampire world of the disease. Turned out there was more than one vampire who'd contributed to the events at the blessing. Carter was top of my list, but that bastard was in the wind with Simone. No matter how many internal organs I'd ripped from fucking chests, the only thing his accomplices knew was that he'd taken her somewhere to heal.

Everyone who'd helped him was dead now.

The two selected who had prepped the stone. Almost all of the upper echelons of Jade House—with their tier one master already destroyed, they'd crumbled fast. And a few of the security guards.

"Donovan planned this all along to help Carter," Shadow rumbled. "But why? Why was this so important to Carter?"

That part I still hadn't figured out, but I was going to when I found my mate. She was still out there; the faint trickle of blood that we shared continued to pulse within me, and it was the one factor preventing me from becoming a mindless monster.

Well, more of a monster—my kill count was close to twenty today. But so far I'd managed to spare the innocent.

"Where do we go now?" Shadow asked. "Mera still hasn't returned, so I should check on her and see why she hasn't been able to track down our brothers."

I nodded. "Yes, do that, and I will continue my interrogations."

Shadow's heavy hand landed on my shoulder. "We're going to find her, even if we have to search the damn underworld to do it. Don't give up hope."

"She's barely here," I rasped. "Just a thin thread that feels like it could be cut with a light breeze. Her life force can go either way."

His hold tightened on my shoulder, and the pain was nothing to the fire raging inside me. "We will find her," he repeated. "I'll be back with reinforcements."

I didn't need help dealing with vampires, but I always felt better when my brothers were around me. *My pack,* as Simone would put it. Vampires might normally be solitary creatures, but I hadn't been a normal vampire for centuries.

My blood was part wolf now, too, and I couldn't live without my pack.

Without my mate.

"I'll see you soon," I told Shadow. "I have one more lead to track."

His hand lifted. "I'll follow your energy when I return to Valdor."

Then he was gone.

Walking to the sink, I washed my hands, removing blood and debris. The killing itself gave me no pleasure; my emotions were shut down tight so I could remain focused on finding my mate. I'd been through all the master's chambers, including Carter's, and there was no sign of Simone.

After I'd cleaned up, I rolled up the sleeves on my jacket to hide the blood stains and exited the estate of a tier two jade master. In the streets, I followed a path I hadn't taken in decades. The vampire I was going to see was an old friend of my father's. I'd never liked or trusted this vampire, but he had his finger on the pulse of this city.

As one of the oldest vampires I knew, there was very little that went on without Emanuel's knowledge. He lived in a small, nondescript home that blended into the shops on either side. He was one of my last hopes for information, and I didn't hesitate to slam my fist into his door.

I'd give him one minute to answer before I busted inside.

At fifty seconds, the door opened, and the vampire stepped into view. Emanuel looked the same: burly and snarling with an unruly beard and black hair. He was almost as big as me, just as my dad had been.

"I've been waiting for you," he snapped, pulling the door wider. "Get the fuck inside."

I entered, unbothered that he had fewer than zero social skills. I wasn't here for tea and catching up. I wanted answers.

He led me inside, and although I'd never been here before, it looked as I expected: a small, dark rat's maze. Emanuel had always enjoyed the way Crimson City was set up, and since he'd had a hand in the original design, it wasn't a surprise to see his home's layout was similar.

"Where is my mate," I snapped. "Just give me one place to look."

We were in a skinny hall, and he couldn't easily turn back to look at me since our shoulders were almost touching the walls. He could speak, though, but chose not to as he led me into a sitting area with shelves of books and a few couches.

"Where. Is. My. Mate?" I growled between gritted teeth. My fangs were permanently extended at this point, but it wasn't to feed. I'd never feed from any but my mate.

I might have ripped out a few throats today, but none of that blood touched my lips.

"I don't know where your mate is," Emanuel growled back. "But I do have one piece of information that might help in your search."

If he didn't tell me what that information was in the next five seconds, he would be dead.

"There's a series of ancient tunnels that run under Crimson City," he continued. "Not just this city but across much of Valdor. It was a network used eons ago to infiltrate other cities, back when we were a little more war loving. They were closed off long ago, but Carter is aware of them. Only a few of us ancients remember them now."

"Carter might be using them to get around," I said. "To take Simone out of the city and make it harder to track her."

Emanuel took his life into his hands when he clasped my shoulder in the same spot Shadow had.

"Let your vampire free," he said as I shook him off. "You will track her blood that way. You're holding yourself back by trying to stay rational. Trust me, your vampire will not let you down."

Embracing the fire burning through me, I stepped forward, and he was smart enough to retreat. "Where is an entrance?"

"I have one here," he said, stepping back again.

Whatever expression I was wearing had him wary, and that pleased the simmering darkness in my chest. When I moved toward him again, Emanuel turned and raced away.

In my heightened state, I easily followed him through the winding path of his home. It had clearly been designed to confuse, but Emanuel didn't miss a turn as he led me to a nondescript opening next to a set of stairs.

Dust covered me the moment I stepped inside the stone-lined walls, and it was clear no one had been down here for centuries. "If Shadow comes looking for me," I said to Emanuel, sending one last glance his way, "send him down here as well or he will kill you."

The vampire just nodded. "Good luck, Master Lucien. Fight for your mate."

I was already down the stairs and didn't bother to reply. Simone was literally the only reason Valdor and everything in it still stood.

If she wasn't in one of these tunnels, those who had betrayed her would find out soon enough... Their time was coming to an end.

Chapter Fifty-Nine

My heart pounded hard in my broken body as my anticipation grew for discovering the owner of the voice. This gave me a slight reprieve from the pain; it was still there, of course, but it wasn't all I could think about.

The voice had asked what I prayed for and called me a child. And it didn't sound anything like Carter or the other masters, so who the hell was in here with me?

"Who are you?" I asked, my breaths shallow. "What do you want from me?"

A pause and then... "I want you to make a choice."

Great, another fucking cryptic wizard. "A choice about what?"

The pain grew until I wanted to pass out again, but I couldn't until I knew the choice.

"You can choose to go back or forward, Simone of the Torma shifters." The voice surrounded me on all sides. "Right now, you exist in limbo. Limbo is painful because you're torn between two worlds. If you pass forward into the light, the pain will end and you'll be free of any further hurt and suffering. If you return to the darkness, you will need to claw your way through it to find the light and there's a great risk of future pain."

The words were registering but it took a few moments to process them. "Limbo? Are you saying I'm not alive right now?"

"You are." No hesitation. "Or at least you're lingering on the edge of life and death, hence the choice."

"I want to go back to Lucien," I said without a second thought. "Back to my pack and family. Pain is not forever, and I can heal."

Especially with my mate.

"It won't be as simple as that."

That made me want to rage and throw myself out of the bath, but of course, I couldn't move. "Why?"

"It started when the Shadow Beast created life."

Uh, okay then. Not the start I'd expected, but I was completely invested now.

"He was young and without knowledge of what he was doing," the voice continued. "He is a god, as am I, but I'm an original from the birth of creation. I'm known in many forms throughout many cultures, and in this world, I guard the souls which are due to be reborn. Without knowing or understanding what he was doing, Shadow pulled his shifters from the rebirth pool. All of you have ancient souls, many of which were connected to other worlds and races. You, Simone, have a soul that originated in Valdor. Originated as the true mate of Carter."

If he'd told me my soul had belonged to a frog in my previous life, I'd have been less shocked.

"But... I was born," I whispered. "From parents. I wasn't one of the originally created ones."

The voice rumbled around me. "Shadow Beast pulled from that pool, so all of your souls are from that pool. He opened the pathway between it and shifters. There are no new souls in the Earth shifters, which is how you possess a soul that was once in Carter's mate."

"That's why my energy called to him," I groaned. "Why it awoke his need."

The next rumble felt like an agreement.

"Does he hold my body back in Valdor?"

Another rumble, and I felt weirded out to know my physical form was most likely unconscious in Carter's lair. "Why did I decide to be reborn?" I asked the nameless god. "Because clearly there's a choice since many go on to live a pain-free life in the next existence."

"You weren't done with this existence yet," the god replied.

The implication was there that my need to return was for Carter, but I knew better.

Lucien was the one who owned my soul.

"I don't care what pain I have to work through or how many Carters I need to kill. This soul might be recycled, but in this life, I've made my choice. Male, female, shifter, or supernatural, Lucien is the only one to call to my soul. To my blood. Carter was mistaken about his mate being a true one because this soul belongs to Lucien."

Another rumble. "Okay, child. I am a god who believes in free will. I believe in choices. In truth, I tried to pull your soul through from the moment your body was destroyed, but it was too strong. You held on and refused to leave. I'm proud of your strength."

No one had ever told me they were proud of me. Especially not my parents. I mean, I'd never really done anything to warrant a proud moment, but it would still have been nice to hear.

The gong from before started up again, and it was louder than ever, the vibrations picking up tempo as the volume increased. It went on and on, filling the space and shaking the walls until the crumble of rock turned into large boulders. They landed all around me, but nothing hit the water or my broken body. Instead, it was as if the fabric of reality was being destroyed.

I could only hope it was breaking to be rebuilt.

As the noise grew louder, it filled my mind and body until my eyes shut, and I desperately scrambled to hold on to my sanity. There was no anchor in this place, so I clung to my wolf, needing her strength once more.

Together we rode out the shattering of limbo, and as her energy swelled within me, I let her go, pushing the change so I could feel whole once more. Whatever weakness I'd felt from her over the last year was gone as the final cohesion between vampire and shifter occurred.

She was whole. Brilliant and strong. Smart and lethal.

A true predator that all should fear.

Especially Carter.

Chapter Sixty

LUCIEN

The tunnels seemed never ending, but once I lost myself to my vampire energy, I was able to follow the pull of Simone's blood. The connection was faint. So weak that I knew she would not be in this world much longer without my blood. It tore apart the sliver of rationality I'd managed to hold on to, and as I raged through the darkness, I was nothing more than need and instinct.

Need to save my mate and instinct to destroy whoever held her.

I ended up well past Crimson City, under what I'd estimate was the edge of the dry lands. This area had once been a vast waterway filled with the purest plasma. Vampires didn't always have to drink from another for sustenance. Our world had been perfectly suited to our survival, but the early ones had taken too much. Been too greedy. They'd destroyed the plasma lakes with overconsumption and war.

Ever since then, we'd been reliant on others to sustain the energy within our cells.

All of our gifts and blessings came with a curse, a need for energy from another, unless you could find your true mate. A truth I now understood all too well.

Following the pull in my chest, I found a doorway hidden in the rocks. There was no obvious sign of an entry, but I could see an indent. I smashed my fist into it, discovering that it was a thick layer of stone. My next punch destroyed the first few layers, but more remained. Undeterred, I continued to smash against the door until, finally, my fist went right through.

It was going to take too fucking long to create a hole big enough for me to get through, but I would not give up until I did. Drawing up my strength, ancient power flooding my veins, I took a short run and threw my body against the stone.

The wall shook, debris raining on me as I did it again and again; the jagged rocks tore at my skin, which only spurred me on harder.

In a few minutes, I'd smashed my way through the wall, landing in a stone room.

Moving further inside, I spotted a huge silver tub in the center. Even in the darkness, I could see Simone's body floating in it, her thick, dark hair spread out behind her, while the rest of her was naked and perfect.

There was not one tear or rip in her skin nor any visible sign that she'd been hurt.

Up until this moment, her energy had been a weak wisp, like the smallest breeze would blow her lifeforce out. But now, as I moved toward the bath, she was blazing.

Strong and powerful.

Almost as if she'd just come back to life.

As I moved closer, Carter stepped from the shadows, where he'd clearly been watching my mate, off to the side of the bath. With a scowl, he dragged Simone up into his arms. "Move and she dies," he snarled at me.

Everything went dark in my vision, and as I debated my next move, the bastard slit his wrist and placed it against my mate's mouth. Feeding her.

Healing her with his energy.

The darkness reared up, and I embraced it.

Carter would be praying for death when I was done with him.

Chapter Sixty-One

The trip back from limbo was a rough one, and in reality, I didn't expect anything less. This was a rebirth, and I'd heard the stories from Mera and Angel.

There was no birth without pain.

Eventually my shaking eased, and I rejoiced at the lack of pain. Strength infused my limbs, bones, and muscles as my wolf howled in my chest, feeling stronger too. Vampire blood infused her shifter soul in a true hybridization.

Opening my eyes, I felt Lucien's presence, just as someone jerked me out of the bath. I knew it wasn't my mate, even before Carter snarled some bullshit and slit his wrist to force blood down my throat.

Hunger rose in me, but stronger than that was disgust. Only a trickle of blood made it into my mouth, and I spit that out as my mate's roar rocked the foundation of this stone room. Lucien had shown up for me, and that was amazing, but what was even more amazing... I could show up for myself.

Drawing on my own power, I shifted in an instant, and Carter howled as my wolf swiped claws across his face, tearing from his right eyeball down to his lips. Five slashes marred his features, and I was out of his arms in a heartbeat.

It wasn't until I was crouched outside the tub, preparing to attack, that I saw the way Lucien and Carter had both frozen. Staring at me.

It was so hard for me to tear my gaze from Lucien, his golden face wreathed in darkness, eyes blacker than night as his body heaved with fury, but I managed to look down long enough to see that my hybrid wolf form had changed.

I was bipedal. My limbs were covered in hair, arms and legs longer and more muscled than in my humanoid form. Five lethal claws tipped the end of each hand; hence why I'd been able to leave those marks on Carter's face.

Speaking of, the male grabbed me once more, hulked up as blood spurted from his face. "You belong to me," he roared.

His power wrapped around me, and I recognized the use of compulsion, having had it forced on me too many times. Lucien's rage was palpable as Carter tried to roll me. "You belong to me," he repeated, more of his power smashing me in the face.

Panic hit me at the thought of losing my will again, but even as Carter poured everything he had into me, all I felt was a brush across my mind. There was no control or the cloudiness that usually followed. Not only that, but the compulsion band that had been in my mind whenever I'd tried to speak of what happened last time in Valdor was gone too.

Holy shit.

I had truly been reborn, and now, I was too strong for compulsion.

As a smile sprang across my face, I grabbed Carter's throat and tore it out. The master's shout was garbled as his blood bubbled from the wound, and I was glad when he reactively threw me across the space.

Lucien's scent wrapped around me as he caught and held me

close. His face buried in my neck—my hairy-as-fuck neck, yo!—and he breathed me in.

A howl escaped me, and I was happy to still sound like my wolf.

I still felt like her too, and in some ways, more complete.

This was my ultimate form, which, from what I could see, was like a lycanthrope—a beast I'd thought was just a human myth.

Carter, his throat healing quicker than I would have liked, lunged toward us. Prepared to take him on, I was a little disappointed when Lucien slid me behind him and crashed against the other master. They hit with the force of two semitrucks colliding, the crash so loud that it reminded me of the gong I'd heard in limbo.

Lucien immediately got the upper hand and sent Carter crashing against the side of the bath. The liquid spilled over, and I tried not to lose my mind at the splashes of Carter's blood in the water. The fact that he'd used his blood to save me—after almost killing me, of course—didn't mean I was his.

Not in any way, shape, or form, and when he was dead, we'd all feel a lot better.

Another howl spilled from my lips, and I was the one to leap across the space now, jumping about three times the distance I could usually make.

Which meant I overshot Carter and ended up behind him.

"Simone!" Lucien bellowed. "Bee, please get your ass over here, or my vampire energy is going to turn this place to dust."

"No," I rumbled back, and *holy fucking fuck...* I could talk.

I mean, it wasn't super clear, sounding exactly how I'd imagined a wolf would if it had the vocal cords to talk, but it was definitely speech. "This is my kill," I got out.

Lucien released a long sigh, but didn't argue, instead choosing to take a step back and give me a chance. I started to circle Carter, who was pulling himself slowly to his feet. "What have you done to my mate?" he snarled. "You corrupted her pure soul by sharing blood with Lucien?"

"Your mate is gone," I rasped in my wolf speech. "My soul was reborn, and it belongs to Lucien. It has always belonged to Lucien. You stole and claimed it in a previous life when it wasn't yours to claim." Sure, I had no evidence of this, outside of the way I felt for Lucien. But instinct told me I was right.

Lucien's face blazed in my sight, and unlike the normal monochromatic nature of wolf vision, this hybrid beast could see all the colors. More than my usual color spectrum, actually. Lucien's eyes were so green, and I could see the multitude of pigments that formed his unique color.

"Mine," Lucien said, a soft promise that made me want to shift back to human and climb him.

At this point, Carter truly lost his mind, grabbing the sides of the metal bathtub, and hefting it at me in one solid thrust. I had no idea how heavy it was, but as I braced myself, I caught it with ease. Not just caught it but threw it back so fast that I even took the vampires by surprise.

It crashed into Carter and slid him along the floor to pin him against the wall.

He was able to push away in seconds, but seconds were too slow.

Lucien and I got there at the same time, but he didn't fight me for this kill, understanding that I had to end whatever ties I had to Carter. Once and for all.

Like a true mate, Lucien protected my back and gave me all the support I needed to finish this.

Carter's wide eyes were the last thing I saw before I swiped out, my clawed hand filled with all the energy and power inside me. This time I wouldn't stop with just tearing his throat out... nope. This time he had to die.

White noise filled my head as the wolfish instinct took over, and I howled as I cut through his neck, completely severing his head in one brutal swipe. It hit the floor with a thump, and I felt a slightly queasy pull in my stomach—first kill and all that—but my wolf shielded me from stronger human emotions.

We were more bonded like this, able to move between animalistic and rational with ease.

Lucien's hand landed on my shoulder, and I wasn't sure what that gesture meant until he remained there, offering comfort as I pulled myself together. With a long exhale, I released my wolf and all but collapsed into his arms.

I'd been strong, and now I got to be needy, fully embracing the multifaceted nature of my personality.

"You are spectacular," Lucien murmured against my lips as he lifted my naked ass higher. "I don't know how I missed your soul through the centuries, but I'm so fucking glad I found this version of you."

He'd apparently figured out the reason behind Carter's obsession.

His kiss stole the air from my lungs, but I didn't give a shit.

A second later, when it was just starting to get good, there was a huge gust of energy from the far side of the room. Lucien spun around to block me from view as Shadow, Reece, Galleli, and Len burst into the space. Lucien dropped me to my feet, ensuring that he kept me completely shielded as he faced his brothers.

"Luce," Len exclaimed. "Is Simone okay?"

"She's fine," he said, and I pressed in closer, needing to touch him.

"Carter's dead?" Shadow raged, and I guessed he had noticed the headless master. "Well, fuck. That was my kill."

I snorted. "Actually, it was my kill, and I'm pretty impressed with it."

Peering around Lucien, I noticed how they all stared at the motionless lump of Carter's head. It lay on its side, the neck visible and showing signs of having been severed and jerked from the body. We all knew that a regular shifter didn't have the strength to do that, and no doubt many questions filled their intelligent minds.

Shadow walked toward us, sniffing the air as he followed the scent of my new energy. "What happened to you?" he asked.

When he was two feet from us, Lucien's hand shot out and

landed on his friend's chest. "Too close, brother," he bit out. "She almost died and now she's naked and I'm feeling a little possessive. I don't want to fight any of you, so back up a touch."

Shadow didn't appear remotely upset by Lucien's push as he nodded and stepped away. There was no way my mate was going to let me move while still naked, so I decided it was easiest to shift. It would cover me up and answer Shadow's question.

Two wolves with one stone.

Chapter Sixty-Two

Lucien relaxed as my body grew larger behind him, the hybrid energy unmistakable in the air. When I stepped into the open, there was an extended moment of silence as they all stared. "Gonna make a girl feel insecure here," I rasped in my wolfish voice, and Len dropped the crystal he had been shifting through his fingers. It comedically clanked on the stone floor, rolling across to almost land at my furred foot.

A snort of laughter escaped Lucien, and that appeared to break the tension. "Simone has evolved into a true hybrid, and she's fucking spectacular."

His tone, once again, had me wanting to ditch the fur and drag him out of here.

Maybe I was the Neanderthal after all.

Shadow approached me, and this time Lucien allowed it. "This is like Mera's new shape," he said, shaking his head. "I wish I'd thought to make wolves as strong and perfect as Simone is right now."

Wow! Was the all-powerful beast admitting that maybe he could have done it better?

Speaking of...

"I found out some information about your shifters," I rumbled. "Turns out, when you were intoxicated and making a bet, you kind of drew on power you weren't supposed to. Apparently, you're the prime example of *just because you can, doesn't mean you should.*"

He stopped examining my new form. "Explain," he said shortly.

"When the stone of Katu detonated, I died," I told them. I felt Lucien vamp out and grow larger, and his arms banded around me as he yanked me back against his chest.

"What?" he raged. "You died?"

He wasn't the only one; the others reacted violently with growls and furious expressions. It made me feel as if Lucien and Mera wouldn't have been the only ones to mourn my loss. This whole "having a family" thing was going to be my undoing. In the best way.

"The blast tore almost all of my soul from this world, and I ended up in limbo. Apparently, my desire to stay with Lucien was strong enough to keep a small sliver grounded. Being in limbo meant that I could choose—to go on into the afterlife or return to Earth."

"What was limbo like?" Len asked, his eyes glowing near silver as he watched me closely.

I swallowed roughly; even in my wolf form, my chest tightened at the memories. "Painful. Really fucking painful. It was like I had to heal the broken and burned parts of my body while I was making my decision. But there was a voice; he said he was one of the original gods known by many faces and names. He told me he's in charge of the pool of souls that have made the decision to be reborn. It was from this pool that Shadow pulled all the souls of his shifters when he created them. It means, even when we're born from other shifters, our souls are all from that pool."

Shadow's face turned as shadowy as his name, and I could see the tension in his rigid jaw.

"All of the shifters are recycled souls from the many worlds. And my soul was originally a vampire." I paused, not wanting to say it but needing to. "And it was originally in Carter's mate."

A burst of flame escaped Shadow, and I whipped around to find that Carter's head and body were on fire. When I returned my gaze to Shadow, there was a slight smirk on his lips. "Whoops," he said, and I couldn't stop the weird wolf-laughter from shaking my body, even as Lucien continued to hold me.

"I think you've been spending too much time with Mera," I choked out.

Lucien rumbled. "Should have been me destroying him. That bastard never deserved your soul, in this life or previous ones. Hopefully, this time, he stays fucking dead."

I nodded. "My hope too, but at least now we know why I always felt so at home in Valdor, and why you're my blood call mate. Your blood and soul call to mine, and I think it always would have." I let out low breath. "Shadow bringing my soul back into this world righted a wrong. Carter should never have been my mate. Never."

Lucien's hold tightened, and I could sense he was nearing the end of his patience.

I'd just dropped a lot of information on him, including the fact that I'd almost died, and I didn't even have to ask to know he was ready to cement our bond. I wasn't sure how that happened, exactly, and I didn't care. Whatever it took, it would be worth it for a true blood call bond.

"I'm shifting back now," I warned them, and to their credit, they turned their backs and gave me a moment. Not that I cared about nudity, but the possessive, growling vamp I was in love with cared an awful lot.

When the wolf faded from my skin, my body was shorter and less muscled again. Lucien pulled off his shirt and draped it gently over my head. It ended up mid-thigh on me since he was such a giant, but he was satisfied by this.

"She's covered," he told his friends. "Now, I need to take my mate and finish our bonding process."

The guys stepped forward one by one and slapped a hand on his shoulder before dropping a kiss on my cheek. "I'm so fucking happy for you," Len said, the last to hug me. "Seeing my brother so complete... There's hope for all of us."

I nodded. "Yes, there's so much hope, Len. I feel it. And now that we know shifter souls have been pulled from all the different races, maybe your mate is on Earth. Remember that call you felt..."

He blinked at me like that thought hadn't remotely occurred to him until this second, but I'd never forgotten Shadow's words about seeing our paths intertwining. We had to start paying attention to the clues the universe was giving us. "I will consider your words," Len said to me with a nod. "Thank you."

"Thank you for showing up," Lucien told all the guys as they moved to exit the stone room. "We'll see you in the library soon."

Shadow turned back. "When you're ready, meet us there for the naming ceremony. My baby girl deserves to be honored with an official name."

"We wouldn't miss it," I said, choking up a little. "I can't wait to learn her name."

They left then, and it was only Lucien and me in the cave room. I didn't care much about the place Carter had brought me to, my focus all on my mate as he lifted me into his arms. "I know you're strong and fast enough to keep up with me," he murmured, mouth pressing against my throat like he was tasting the pulse of blood there. "You couldn't have killed an ancient master like Carter if you were anything less than master level yourself. But I need to hold you."

I wrapped my arms around his neck and my legs around his waist, feeling the ache in my center as I pressed against him. "Run, Crimson. Run as fast as your powerful thighs can go because I *need* y —" He kissed me before I could finish, and then we were moving, zipping along a very long tunnel.

"These tunnels run all throughout Valdor," he managed to say between kisses. "I never knew of their existence, but some of the oldest vampires remembered. Carter was using that to his advantage, thinking I'd never find you with all this stone blocking your blood. Little did he know I would find you any-fucking-where in the multiple worlds."

"I never doubted it," I whispered, pressing my face into his neck and breathing him in. "I never doubted my choice to return to Valdor. To return to you."

My fangs and canines elongated as I drank in the scent of his life-force, and Lucien's pace picked up. "If you feed now," he rasped, "we won't make it to a bed."

"Fine by me," I murmured. I sank my hybrid fangs into his throat, moaning at the first hit of his blood. Still like a damn drug, and I still gave zero fucks that I was hooked for life. This was how it was meant to be, and fighting it had done nothing except make us both miserable.

Lucien slowed before grinding to a halt, holding me as I fed. When I lifted my head and licked along the small marks, it was his turn. "There's no trace of Carter in my blood," I told him. "I burned through it in my rebirth and spat out the extra drops he tried to taint me with. It's only me and you."

Lucien's fangs sank into my throat, and as he did, he thrust inside me. My nakedness under the shirt gave him all the access he needed. Somehow his cock was free, too, and filling me completely. Even as wet as I was, there was some resistance, but soon, I was feeding and fucking him so hard that all I could hear was the slapping sounds of my wetness, which only increased as I orgasmed, once and then again, and he didn't stop, lost in the moment and the blood and the healing.

We were alive. We were together.

It was a future that I'd only ever dreamed of, and now it was a reality.

Chapter Sixty-Three

We eventually made it back to Crimson City via an odd house of a bushy-bearded, angry-faced vampire. Lucien somewhat reluctantly thanked *Emanuel,* but he didn't stay for any sort of catch-up, whisking me off into the streets and back home. It was the middle of the sleep cycle, so Crimson City was empty, and I wondered what had happened to the other masters and selected in the wake of my disappearance.

I asked Lucien as we entered his gated compound, but he just rumbled that he'd tell me later. That was fine by me; my body still needed more from my mate.

I needed the final bond to be completed.

Lucien set me on my feet as we made our way upstairs, linking his fingers with mine so we could walk together. "I have to shower," I told him. "I know Carter's blood vanished in my shifts between human and wolf-girl, but I want to be clean."

Lucien didn't argue, just followed me into the stall and hit the buttons to send out multiple streams of water. I sank down to the floor, happy to curl up under the cleansing water for some time. Lucien followed, facing me with our legs tangled together.

"Tell me everything about your life," he said, watching me so closely. "This life and every other one you remember."

My chest was hurting like a bitch, but it was the good kind of hurt. Choking on a few sobs, I reached out and took his hand, which was resting on his raised knee. His naked body was certainly a distraction, thick cock against his thigh as he faced me, but somehow, I managed not to lean over and take it into my mouth.

He'd asked me a question, and there was no rush for the rest. We could be here for days... months... years...

There was no end in sight for us, which allowed me some perspective.

This moment was for bonding in the wake of almost losing everything.

"I'm twenty-eight years old," I started. "I was born and raised in Torma and, basically, never left until Mera took off on her journey and I found myself in this new, magical world. To say I was sheltered would be an understatement—"

I continued to give him a play-by-play of my life, and even though he knew a lot of it already, I went a little deeper. "I've lived in fantasy worlds via my books for the past half a dozen years," I said. "Some days I would just read all day and night and escape from reality. It kept me sane, you know, but it never completely fulfilled me. Always felt like something was missing. I contemplated writing my own books to find the right blend of story, but now that I've found this with you, I know that what I was craving was to *live* my own fantasy story. Reading it just wasn't enough."

Lucien pulled me toward him, and as my legs slipped under his, which were slightly bent at the knees, we were so much closer. "You are the only one I want in my fantasy world, Bee," he murmured. "You won't ever have to escape into books again. Any adventure you desire, we'll find it."

I lifted myself so I could kiss him, tasting his life and energy with one swipe of my tongue. We were breathing a little heavier when we pulled apart, but I wanted to take a bit more time before I lost myself to the frenzy of sex and feeding.

"Tell me about your life," I murmured. "Tell me of the adventures you've already taken."

He shot me a slow smile that had my body clenching in all the right places. "The only important ones happened recently. Before that it was politics and vampires and a few wars I'd rather not remember. I'm long-lived, but everything was in shades of grey before I met you. After some time, my emotions just evened out and there were no more highs or lows. No pain but also... no joy. Everything feels like *more* now. I honestly don't know what the fuck to do with all the energy buzzing inside of me."

A chuckle escaped me. "I completely understand. Funnily enough, as a shifter we see in shades of grey in our wolf form, but in my new form... everything is brighter than ever. My hybrid form appears to see in shades of color beyond my regular sight. It's incredible."

He kissed me again, pulling my body against his, and this time I had to lift myself so I could slide onto his lap. I rocked against his hard length, which wasn't inside me yet, but the heat of his shaft throbbed against my clit and pussy, sending pulses of pleasure into me. "Simone," Lucien murmured. "Bee. Will you join with me in a true mate bond?"

"Yes," I choked out without hesitation. "Yes. Yesterday, today, and every fucking day."

This time when he kissed me, his fangs sank into my lip, my blood filling both our mouths. Then I tasted his spice mingling with my own, which told me he'd busted his lip as well, mingling our bloods. He lifted my body, hands firm and strong on my ass as he lined me up and thrust up into me. I couldn't groan, my mouth too filled with our energy, so I just kept kissing him and holding on for life as he slowly moved inside me.

With each thrust of his cock, the curl of pleasure grew in my stomach, and as it reached the pinnacle, my orgasm was unable to be denied any longer.

The cry burst from me, and Lucien's pace increased. He started to whisper against my lips. *"Katu of blood. Katu of pain. Katu of pleasure. Katu of power. Join us under your holy glow. Join our souls in a soul call bond. A forever bond."*

This wasn't all he said, but the next words were in a language I didn't understand.

But I felt them in my ancient soul.

Repeating the blessing, Lucien reached out of the shower and grabbed the pants he'd ditched earlier. I couldn't see much of what he was doing, my focus on the heat rushing through my body. It wasn't just the heat of Lucien's blood or the orgasms or my hybrid nature... it was a deeper, more intense fire that felt like the bonds of our souls knitting together.

When Lucien pulled his arm back into the stall, I didn't see the sliver of stone until he pressed it between our chests. I glanced down at it, still moving against him. "The Stone of Katu," I breathed, recognizing the bluish hue. "What happened to it?"

"I smashed it," Lucien said shortly. "This is enough to bless our bond. To seal it."

"It's the least it could do for us," I whispered, feeling the essence of the stone seeping into my being.

"My love," Lucien murmured. "In this life and the next, your soul belongs to mine."

"You soul belongs to mine," I whispered back.

Lucien, still buried inside me, moved faster, and both of us were breathing heavily as we headed toward orgasm, the final catalyst to seal this bond.

As I fell into the detonation of spiraling ecstasy, the stone lit up my chest, like a brand, but there was so much pleasure inside me that I barely felt the pain. Lucien was right there with me, groaning as his movements slowed to complete the bond.

The pain faded then, and when I glanced down, the shard of

stone was completely gone. But where it had sat between our joined chests, I could feel warmth under my skin.

Lucien stroked a hand over the spot, and the warmth increased. "You'll always feel me here," he said, leaning over to press his lips against it. "You can always find me by following the pull of our bond. Being apart will be hard until we get used to the pull to return to each other."

Throwing my arms around him, I drew us tightly together, wanting no space between us. "Let's never get used to it. No need for us to be apart for at least a few hundred years."

He laughed, sending more pulses of pleasure through me. "You're stuck with me, Bee. As I said, in this life and the next, we are soul-bonded."

The spot in my chest warmed, and even though I had no experience with this blood call bond, I was sure I felt his power and energy. "I'll know when you're hurt or angry, won't I?"

Lucien nodded. "Yes, and it will only grow stronger with time."

That felt right to me. I'd been taking Lucien's blood into my body for a long time now, and I felt no unease that another part of us was connected.

It was his blood that had bonded to my wolf soul, and I was so thankful to not have lost her.

My father might have prepared me for torture, but no one had prepared me for this sort of love. Love that I was excited to experience and grow into over the years.

I would never take any moment for granted.

Chapter Sixty-Four

Later that day I was in bed, Lucien holding me against his chest as he slept. We were both exhausted, having done our best to break the record for hours having sex after almost dying. Mera probably had a decent stronghold on that number, but Lucien and I were giving her and Shadow a run for their money.

I didn't want to wake him, so I just lay there in his arms, wondering how I got so damn lucky. "Why is your favorite color crimson?" he murmured against my back, and I laughed, realizing he wasn't as asleep as I'd thought. "Has it always been crimson?"

"Yes," I whispered. "When I was a little girl, there was this field of red flowers behind our house. They didn't grow anywhere else in Torma, so I always thought of them as mine. You know. My house and my flowers. The color is still one I've never seen anywhere again until you brought me to Valdor. Your sky and the stone of your house... they're the exact color of my flowers."

The last time I was here, I'd tried not to think of all the ways I felt tied to Lucien and this world, because it hurt to know it was all temporary. But now that it was forever, I could really embrace the connections we'd shared for most of my life.

My father had destroyed the flowers when I was twelve to punish me into doing what he wanted. If I hadn't hated him before that, I'd certainly hated him after it.

"What do the flowers look like?" Lucien asked, and there was a weird tone in his voice. "What's the petal structure and length of the stem?"

Shifting over to see his face, I tried to read his expression, but it gave nothing away. "They're small," I said. "And they grow about four or five flowers per stem, so they're close together, looking almost look like a car—"

"Carpet of flowers," he finished for me, and I paused before nodding.

"Yes. How did you know?"

"They grow here," he told me, and holy shit, was I awake now.

"Show me!" I demanded, trying to leap from the bed, but his firm hold remained on me.

"You said they only grew behind your house?"

I nodded again. "Yes. Nowhere else in all of Torma, and I could never find out any information, like their name or anything, in a normal plant database."

"Did you ever do anything out in that area before the flowers grew?"

That gave me a moment's pause as I combed back through my memories. "I don't think so... Wait. I mean, I got hurt out there once. Fairly sure I bled through the knee of my pants because my dad was an asshole about it afterwards. But could it be plausible? I mean, that wasn't the only time I bled somewhere, so maybe it was something else."

Lucien sat, bringing me with him. "Who knows, maybe at that point you were calling out for something more and your blood found its connection to Valdor. Or maybe it was a coincidence. Either way, I will always believe it was your blood calling you to this world. To me."

"Show me the flowers," I demanded again, and this time we both hopped out of the bed and had a quick shower together. It spoke of how many orgasms I'd had in the past dozen or so hours that I managed not to attack my mate while he was naked under the shower, looking like a wet dream.

He didn't seem quite as exhausted, reaching for me with that sexy hooded expression, but sadly, I had to shift out of his reach. "Plenty of time for that later," I said in a rush. "We've got some flowers to find."

To see them again was another dream come true. To know they'd been created from my own connection to Valdor in a previous life made it even more surreal. Had I created Crimson Heart on Earth, too, somehow? Or were Valdorian items just drawn to Torma because there were vampire souls there?

In reality, most of these questions would probably never be answered, but it was cool to wonder all the same.

We got dressed in a hurry, and this time when we escaped his house, the streets were filled with vampires. Crimson House vampires. "Master Lucien! Master Lucien," they called.

A short vampire with thick black curls and dark skin pushed in closer. "Is it true that half the masters are dead and new ones will be brought forward to fill the spots?" he asked, eyes wide and confused.

I paused, turning toward my mate. We'd discussed a lot of things since sealing our bond, but somehow, he'd failed to mention that half the masters were dead—a somewhat relevant fact, considering the circumstances.

Lucien shot me a slow smile like he was reading my thoughts, or maybe he was sensing my emotions through our bond. A bond that must be visible because before he could answer the dark-haired vampire, someone else shouted, "He's bonded! Our master has a blood call bond."

That set them all off, and if it wasn't for Lucien's chest rumble and fuck-off expression whenever one of them stepped too close to me, I would have been hauled up in a pile of vampire hugs for sure. Luckily, they read the room and stayed a few paces back from the newly mated and possessive master.

"Yes, there has been some upheaval in the masters' ranks," Lucien said as he projected his voice to those gathering. "They conspired to have my mate taken by Carter. I handled that the way any true mate would, and now there will be changes in Crimson City. Unfortunately, I can't guarantee no fallout from this, but we are prepared, correct?"

There were shouts and cheers.

"I will be here to smooth the way," he said, "but I think they will heed my previous warnings and stay clear of our enclave for some time."

None of his vampires appeared worried, and it spoke to the way he let them govern themselves, for the most part, that gave them that streak of independence. There was no overreach of leadership in Crimson House.

Lucien spoke to them for a few more minutes, and when we eventually walked away, it was to congratulations and cheers. "You killed the masters?" I asked when we were out of earshot. "Who else did you kill?"

He shrugged. "Hattie's family. And the masters' families that were in cahoots or tried to interfere. I left the children and innocents."

I blinked, a little sad I'd missed him raging like that, to be honest.

"They hurt and stole my mate." Lucien's voice grew deeper, like the memories were sending him to the darkness again. "It was the least they deserved. I sent word to the rest of the council that I won't hesitate to raze this fucking city to rubble if they pursue this further."

"I love you." The words burst from me, feeling right. "Thank you for fighting for me."

He stopped and swept his arms around me, pulling me up into the tightest hug. "There's no reason for living without you, Simone," he murmured. "My love for you is beyond anything I've ever felt. It's beyond any words I can give you, but I promise my actions will always speak of my utter devotion toward you. You'll never want for anything again, emotional or material."

I coughed through my tears. "This probably makes me a psychopath, but I find the fact that you killed a bunch of vampires for me super romantic."

He laughed and just held me tighter. "We're a perfect match. Now let's find your flowers."

We made it through the rest of the city without issue. Only a few dark looks were thrown Lucien's way, and it seemed that for the most part, the other vampires were wary enough to not approach him. He even got some cheers in other enclaves, where vampires were clearly excited to be rid of their previous masters.

"Many of them had ruled with violence and fear for too long," Lucien told me. "I should have stepped in decades ago, but I was complacent. My emotions had shut down, and I forgot how to give a shit."

That wasn't the case any longer, and hopefully, now Crimson City could rebuild.

If any of them decided to come back at Lucien for this, then they'd have to take on our entire family. We were growing stronger with every new member, and that gave me a sense of relief. No one could take this from us. Not if we stood together.

Chapter Sixty-Five

As we walked, Lucien told me that the red flowers had no official name but were referred to as *crimson life*. "They used to be everywhere when this world was filled with plasma lakes," he said. "They would span the banks of the waters, acting as a red beacon so we knew where to look for sustenance. But when the lakes dried up, the flowers died off."

"The lakes dried up? You used to have lakes filled with plasma?"

He nodded. "Yep, this world provided everything vampire cells need for survival, the same way your world provides water. But previous generations were greedy and took too much. Everyone was trying to hoard it, but if they'd just consumed what was needed and allowed natural regeneration, no one would have missed out."

"There was a river in that obstacle course," I reminded him. "Two actually."

"Yes, but they're just water—no plasma remains now. We create our own lakes as a poor imitation of what we used to have, importing water from other worlds including Earth."

It broke my heart to know I'd never see those ancient bodies of plasma, and I wondered how any red flowers were left if the plasma was gone. Lucien must know of a secret stash somewhere.

We ended up sprinting across the golden field, running for what was probably a hundred miles at least—it was hard to tell when we were going so fast. Lucien finally brought us to a stop on the edge of a forest.

"Wow," I said, tilting my head back to follow the height of the trees. "I thought the ones in the obstacle course were huge, but these are... wow."

They had to be near twice the height and width of the trees in the other forest, the tops almost too high for me to see. Stepping into their shade, there was an ancient feel to the energy, and the spot in my chest that was bonded to Lucien heated as he also reacted to their energy.

"This is the last of the early lands," he told me, voice hushed. "It's been forgotten by most, as they stay in the cities, but this is where I come when I need to escape. It's the only place I've seen the flowers still bloom, in sections of the trees."

It took some time before I witnessed what that meant. There was a huge trunk, about six feet wide and bulbous, looking like you could carve a house from its base. Right there, growing out of the side of the wood, was a perfect circle of the flowers.

My flowers.

"That's them," I whispered, pressing my hand to my mouth as overwhelming emotions crushed me. "My exact flowers."

I ran my hand over them, gently brushing the velvety carpet, as a hundred memories assaulted me. I'd gone to the flowers any time my father hurt me or my mother ignored me. I'd curled up on their red blooms and let them comfort me.

"The fact that they grow from the trees here," I said softly, also feeling the need to talk in hushed tones, "means that plasma runs in the trees, right?"

Lucien nodded. "Yes. I believe it does, but I've never mentioned it to the masters or enclaves. We don't need to steal the land's plasma any longer, and if it resides in plants and under the ground, then it can stay there."

Turning toward him, I held out the hand not stroking my flowers —which sounded dirtier than it was. As he grasped on, I pulled him to my side. "Thank you for bringing me here, and I totally agree, no one can know the truth of what treasures are held in this ancient pocket."

We stayed like that for a long time, standing in silence with the flowers of my childhood. In my old life, I'd never truly understood what peace felt like... but I was sure I knew it now. My entire body was still and calm... and content.

Eventually it was time to return to Crimson City.

"I need to stop in at the Master Chambers," Lucien told me as we walked out, hand in hand. "Then we can head over to the Library of Knowledge."

I nodded, more than ready to be with our pack and celebrate our new babies.

It was hard to believe I was finally free to do both.

When we returned to the city, we reached the chamber's security gates quickly.

All of the original guards were back in place.

"Galco!" I called, hurrying forward with the intention of hugging him, only to have my mate cut me off with a low growl. Oh, right... No touching other males yet.

I should have known because the thought of another female being anywhere near him had my possessive wolf sharpening her claws.

"Master Simone," Galco said with a wink. "I'm so sorry to hear of what happened to you. I should have known something was up when they asked all of the regular guards to take some time off during the final selection blessing."

My heart fluttered at his use of *master* with my name, but I didn't draw attention to it. "It wasn't your fault," I told him, ignoring my rumbling mate with a pat to his shoulder. "They had it all planned out with multiple masters and powerful families. It was best you weren't here to get hurt."

His smile was broad. "From what I heard, the one to worry about was Lucien. Your mate tore through the corruption without mercy."

"Should have dragged their deaths out longer," Lucien grumbled. "Bastards got off easy because I was in a rush to find Bee."

We all laughed like the straight-up psychopaths we were, celebrating some murders. "We'll see you again soon," I told Galco, waving as we passed through the gates. "Hopefully in happier circumstances."

"It's nice to see a true blood call bond after so many years of drought," he called after us.

As I waved my final goodbye, his words brought up a previous thought. "I wonder if more vampires could find their blood call bond with shifters."

Lucien didn't look surprised by my musing thought, which meant he'd been thinking it as well. "I believe there's a decent chance that they could. We'll explore that avenue later."

There would be plenty of laters, and that was the most important part.

When we stepped into the Master Chambers, it was quiet. The selection was done, and the master's ranks had been decimated. It was time to see what had grown from Lucien's destruction.

At the end of the long hall near their thrones we found a path of blueish stones, embedded into the ground, and leading to where a dozen or so vampires gathered. "The Stone of Katu," Lucien noted, and I figured out then that this new path was made from the shattered stone of their god.

Leading the way for continued vampire blessings.

Warmth from the power of the stones filled my body as we walked toward the masters, aided by Lucien keeping me firmly against his side with a strong arm around my shoulders.

"I'm here for the meeting," he said into the silence. "Let's hear your complaints now and deal with them accordingly."

One of the females, from a house with a dark purple stone, stepped forward. She looked a bit like Mera: beautiful, with golden-red hair and curves for days. She wore tight black pants, black boots, and a killer red jacket that I'd really like to have in my wardrobe.

"Master Lucien," she said, and there was no malice in her voice. "There's nothing to discuss. Someone attacked your blood called mate, and you were within your rights to demand justice. We will not seek any vengeance for this, and new masters have already been appointed to the enclaves."

She waved a hand, and six master vampires stepped forward, two females and four males. "We have pledged our loyalty to you, Master Lucien," she continued. "You're now the grandmaster, as the most powerful with a true mate bond on which to build your strength."

Lucien sighed. "You know I've never wanted to be grandmaster. I have turned it down every time it was offered."

Ah, now I understood why Donovan had been spokes-vamp so often. He must have been the previous grandmaster, taking point in major events.

The redheaded vampire shot him a broad smile, while her eyes told him *too fucking bad, buddy.* "You will be fine," she said. "You don't have to be in Crimson City all the time. You can come and go as you have, and we'll ensure you're given plenty of notice before any meetings and events."

Lucien looked like he wanted to refuse again, but her expression must have registered with him as well. She was determined he take on the role, whether he wanted it or not. "Fine, but I want my mate added as a tier one master, since she's as strong as we are."

She nodded, her expression falling a touch before she recovered. "Done. It's time for change."

Yeah, a hybrid master might be a little too much *change* on top of everything else, but it seemed for now, they were determined to back Lucien all the way. Maybe that was due to the fear of what he'd done to the others, or maybe they truly did want a different future for Crimson City. Only time would tell.

"Now that it's settled, we'll be gone from Valdor for a while," Lucien told them. "So, have your shit sorted out by the time we return. All new masters need to get their enclaves in line, and if I hear of corruption going this deep again, it will be dealt with the same way."

They all nodded, no one arguing. I did catch sight of a few glares from new and old masters, but even stronger than their annoyance was their resignation. They would not fight him today.

Maybe over time their anger would build and they'd come after us, but we'd deal with that when it happened. For now, they all appeared to agree to this new world order, which gave us the time we needed with each other and our pack.

Chapter Sixty-Six

"**S**imone!"

Mera's scream rang out through the library the moment we stepped through the Valdor door. She had felt me with her godlike powers, and just the sound of her voice was enough to have my chest tight and eyes burning.

So much had changed in my life that I barely recognized myself or my wolf these days, but one thing that would never change was my love for Mera. My OG family and pack.

She barreled toward me, not stopping until we were hugging so tight that I couldn't breathe, and I didn't care. Her strength didn't crush me the way it had last time, and that was a good indication I was so much stronger.

I'd stepped into her world, and finally, I felt like I belonged there.

"I can't believe you're back here. Alive. Safe. Beautiful and perfect." She was rambling, her words spilling over each other as she held me and rocked back and forth like I was a baby to comfort. "When Shadow told me all the shit that happened, I was ready to raze Valdor to the fucking ground. How dare they hurt my best friend! How. Fucking. Dare. They!"

Shadow chuckled as he appeared behind her, baby in his arms. "There was no need, Sunshine. Lucien tore through them like wet paper. He cleaned house for his mate, and Simone ripped the head off her kidnapper. It worked out exactly as it should have."

He shifted the baby, and I noticed she was already holding herself up in his arms and looking around. It really didn't surprise me at this point—all the beings in this room defied nature, so who was I to question one extra-special child.

"My duty," Mera shot back, still holding onto me like I might disappear if she let go. When Lucien stepped up closer to my back, she growled at him, and I felt the heat rising around her. She was not in the most stable of moods, but at least Lucien didn't view her as a threat, because he stopped moving, keeping a few feet between us until Mera calmed down.

Eventually Shadow had to pry her off me, and I discreetly wiggled my body to get the blood flowing again. Mera, finally in a rational frame of mine, examined me closer. "Holy fucking shifters." She shook her head. "You look amazing. I mean, you're always gorgeous, but the glow, my friend. Your power is calling to me."

My lips twitched as I nodded. "Yeah, I've officially stepped into the reborn club. This is the new vampire-shifter hybrid form, and I have to say, I quite like it."

Lucien pulled me against him like he couldn't wait another second. "As do I, mate."

Mera, with her million-moods-a-second, sighed as tears filled her eyes. "This is the best fucking day. Naming ceremony, Angel and Reece are here with Damon, Len has finished with his fae business, Galleli agreed to officially bless our child, and my best friend is a badass eternal like the rest of us."

Her head whipped around toward Shadow. "She is, right? She's not gonna die in the next few hundred years from old age?"

"Right," he told her in what could even be considered a gentle tone, for a beast like Shadow.

Mera's smile could have lit this room up all on its own. "As I said, best fucking day. There's just one more thing we need to decide before our baby girl gets her name blessing."

No one said a word, waiting for her to continue.

When her gaze met mine, I recognized that mischievous expression.

"What is Simone and Lucien's couple name?"

Lucien groaned in my ear, but I was excited to hear her options.

"Shadow and mine is Shadowshine. Angel and Reece's is Desert-Angel, though I would have been just as happy with Angel and the Asshole."

"I heard that," Reece bellowed, appearing in the distance. He had Damon in his arms, who was also up and watching everything. The desert god stopped right next to Shadow, two huge-ass warriors cradling tiny babies. It should have been comical, but I was fairly certain my ovaries hurt just looking at them.

"Annnddd I'm pregnant," Mera muttered, fanning her face.

Shadow rumbled at her, but then his baby girl patted his chest, and he calmed down.

So. Fucking. Weird.

Angel appeared a moment later, as stunning and ethereal as always. Her wings were away, and she wore a simple, white shift dress that perfectly complimented her lithe frame. With her golden-brown hair back in a braid, she wore an expression of complete serenity. Mera often wore that expression too, and now I finally got it.

In my mate's arms, our bond pulsing between us, I felt part of this magical world.

No longer on the fringe, but dead in the middle of it.

We were getting a couple name.

"Come on," Mera said. "We should eat and discuss this."

"After the naming ceremony," Shadow told her, and she pouted but didn't argue.

"Yes, okay."

Len and Galleli appeared from the shadows of wherever they'd been, somehow knowing it was time for us to gather. "Everyone get your Sunday best on," Mera called. "We're blessing this baby girl in style."

I looked down at my jeans, sneakers, and plain white shirt. I was not dressed in any best, let alone Sunday's. Mera must have seen my panic.

"Your room is set up for you," she reminded me. "Wardrobe fully stocked. I took the liberty of laying out a dress for you already, so you don't even have to think about what to wear."

With a chuckle I shook my head. "Still a pain in my ass, best friend."

Mera smiled broadly. "That will never change; now go and get dressed while I ponder your couple name. Sucien does not work at all. Just saying."

Laughter filled the library, followed by more calls of other variations on Lucien and Simone that just didn't work. "They're never going to find a couple name for us," I said with a chuckle when we started in the direction Mera had pointed for our room.

"We don't need a couple name," he murmured, wrapping his hand around mine and making me again feel like I'd won the fucking lotto. "We have a blood call bond. Our blood and souls call to each other, and even more than that, we have love we chose. There's nothing else."

Boom. Pregnant.

Truth be told, I wasn't sure if we would ever have children. It wasn't a discussion we'd had yet, and I didn't feel strongly on it either way. I was still young in this world and happy to explore it with my mate for many more decades before thinking about children.

Unless the sexy talk got me.

"I'm starting to understand what Mera meant by *you won't miss the room*," Lucien said, distracting me from my baby thoughts. I focused to see that my door, near the dining hall's entrance, was crimson. Of course it was. Outside of Lucien, Mera was the only one who knew the why of my favorite color. Knowing how smart she was, she'd probably put it together now with my love of Crimson City and a certain Crimson House master.

"My bestie is better than your bestie," I told Lucien, over-whelmed with emotion. "She found our shade of crimson."

"Your besties are my besties," he reminded me. "And we are lucky to have this family."

I hugged him tightly, just needing to feel him close for a moment. "So lucky I can barely believe it."

He lifted me off the ground, and I wrapped my legs around his waist, the full-body hug the best thing I'd ever felt.

Well, almost the best.

It had already been too long since my mate was inside me.

Too damn long.

Chapter Sixty-Seven

B ehind the red door was the most beautiful set of rooms. The first one we walked into was a sitting area and library with dark timber shelves lining the walls. My lips quivered at the sight of all my favorite stories already filling the shelves. Not to mention thousands of new titles that I hadn't had a chance to read yet.

Almost all of them were romance and fantasy, with just two other shelves of what I could only assume were Lucien's favorites because western, action, and thriller didn't do it for me. No judgement, though, because a man reading was sexy. End of story.

There was a roaring fireplace in our library, a stone and timber hearth surrounding it. Arranged nicely nearby were three green-tartan couches and a thick, white wool rug that I was dying to curl up on and read... among other things.

"I love this room," I said, spinning on the spot and closing my eyes like I could drink it all in. "It's perfect."

"It is," Lucien said, but he wasn't staring at the room. He was watching me, hunger in his gaze, and I stopped spinning.

"We need to get dressed," I reminded him. "We'll christen this place later."

With a resigned sigh, he nodded and took my hand so we could continue on.

The next room off the hall was a dining room and kitchen with a white and crimson theme. Everything was open and light. Huge wooden beams lined the ceiling, and red cabinets tied the entire space into the library and the front door.

It was so beautiful, perfect, and unexpected, that I felt speechless for the first few minutes of staring.

"With the dining hall next door, I thought we'd just eat there," Lucien said, looking around.

"Mera knows I've dreamed of a big, amazing kitchen," I murmured, taking in everything from the huge freestanding oven with its fancy clawed feet to the built-in fridge and dishwasher— appliances exactly like the ones I used to circle in catalogs when I fantasized about building my own house.

"Can you cook?" Lucien asked me.

Tilting my head toward him, I smiled. "Actually, I can. My mom is quite a few generations removed from a Japanese pack, but she took a lot of the handed-down recipes and passed them on to me. One of the few bonding experiences we shared. I haven't had many chances in the last few years to cook, but this kitchen has everything I need to start again."

Mera was ensuring the last of my childhood dreams came true, and I could never repay her for that. Between Lucien and Mera, I was probably going to have a heart attack from the joy pounding in my chest.

"Come, let's see what clothing Mera picked out for you," Lucien said softly, pulling me along with a gentle tug on my hand.

The next rooms were a bedroom and bathroom that rivaled the beauty and size of Lucien's back in Valdor. Everything in here was neutral, with light walls and rugs to complement the massive four-poster bed in the center of the room. The wispy white curtains that hung on either side were tied back in a way that reminded me of images I'd seen of hotels in the Caribbean or other beachy paradises.

The bathroom was just as beautiful, with a giant claw-foot tub and shower in the corner, a double sink and mirrors, and thick crimson-and-white striped towels already waiting in the shelves. Opening the drawers, I confirmed what I'd expected: They were fully stocked with makeup, toiletries, and hair accessories.

Mera appeared in the doorway behind me, as if she couldn't wait a moment longer to see my reaction. As I turned away from the vanity toward her, I just burst into tears. The emotion had been building since I'd stepped into my dream home, and I couldn't seem to stop as hot trails spilled down my cheeks.

Mera laughed and hurried forward to hug me once more. "I knew you'd love it. I've been throwing myself into getting this ready while I panicked about what was happening in Valdor. I wanted you to return to all my love for you."

"I love you too." I sobbed harder. "Holy fuck. I think between you and Lucien, you guys broke me."

She patted my back. "You deserve nothing less. Now go and put that stunning-as-fuck dress on. It's black, sexy, and your man is going to want to ravish you." Her voice got harder. "Don't do it, Lucien. My baby needs her name so I can stop almost accidentally saying it before she's been blessed. You will wait until after the naming ceremony to love on my girl. You hear me?"

Lucien, thankfully, didn't lose his alpha shit over that order. "I hear you, Mera Callahan. Now get the hell out so I can dress my mate."

Mera also didn't take offense, stepping back and clapping her hands in delight. "Mate. I will never grow tired of hearing that."

"Me either," I whispered, still overwhelmed but no longer bawling like a baby.

Not that any of the current babies in our lives appeared to bawl. They were too mature for that.

Mera left us as soon as she was satisfied I was heading into the wardrobe; a room as large as my old apartment in Torma. The walls were lined with shelves and hanging space, and all of it was filled with clothing—along with a full-length shelf of shoes. And it wasn't only clothing for me; there was a decent section of male items as well.

Mera had thought of everything.

Hanging on a round rack in the center was the dress she'd chosen for me. It was black and corseted, with a shorter front and longer tail behind. The skirt was tulle and sleekly layered. "Holy shit," I gasped, circling it. "I am not wearing the right underwear for this."

Lucien's eyes darkened as his gaze flicked between me and the dress. "Put it on," he commanded in a low, rough voice, "without underwear."

Fuck. Fucking fuck.

Deciding to call him on the promise in his voice, I walked toward the hanging rack, losing pieces of clothing with each step until I was completely naked. Feeling powerful and sexy for once, I let my hips sway a touch more than normal.

Up close, the dress was dazzling, with sparkling threads woven through the black material. Pulling it from the hanger, I found that it didn't have a zipper at the back; instead, there were laces that would loosen or tighten the corset top.

Turning, I found the black-eyed demon of my dreams two feet away. He hadn't touched me yet, watching me "obey" his command in the way only an alpha could enjoy.

Or a master, in his case.

Same-same, really.

The dress was surprisingly heavy as it slid smoothly down my body. I'd never had curves like Mera, but I claimed C-cup boobs. And this dress, with the corseted waist, pushed them up like I had a perfect set of fakes attached.

Lucien growled, moving toward me, but I held my hand up to stop him. "You can only touch me to lace the back, okay?"

His chest rumbled louder, his eyes the blackest of blacks, but when he stepped around me to lace the back, he was careful not to brush any bare skin. He pulled the corset in firmly, and I groaned, the tightening against my skin corresponding to the tightening of other parts of my body. He'd asked for no underwear, and now my thighs were slick with need, nothing there to slow its path down my legs.

When I was laced in, Lucien found a pair of black boots to go with it, and it was the exact pair I would have chosen myself. I followed him toward the full-length mirror near the shoe shelf, and he knelt before me. "Permission to touch," he murmured, staring up at me like a golden god of destruction.

My destruction.

Clearing my throat, I nodded. "Permission granted."

He wrapped his long fingers around my left ankle, lifting that foot so he could slip the boot on. His touch scraped across my skin, and I fought back a moan as the scent of my arousal grew stronger. Lucien repeated the motion with my right foot, and by the time I was standing with an extra four inches of height, my legs were shaking with need.

Lucien's firm touch traced up the sides of my legs until he was gripping my bare thighs.

"I can smell your arousal," he rumbled as my trembling worsened.

His hold on me tightened, and he leaned in, breathing deeply.

"Crimson," I moaned, desperate. "Touch me, dammit."

With a low chuckle, he pushed forward, his mouth finding my pussy. I cried out, clutching his blond hair to keep myself standing. In the mirror I could see everything as he lifted my dress and his tongue swiped across my slick folds, taking all of me in until I was screaming his name and coming so hard I saw stars. He didn't stop there, his tongue circling my clit as he drew out the jagged sparks of pleasure hitting me.

Lucien ate me until I was completely fucked, not stopping until he'd cleaned up all the evidence of my orgasms. When he stood, there was no masking the hard length straining against his pants, and I reached for him, but he shook his head. "No, baby. There's no time for me, but I will always ensure my mate's needs are satisfied."

"My mate's needs must be too," I growled, my wolf raising her head.

Lucien captured my hand and pressed a lingering kiss to my palm. "You satisfy me just with your existence. I can wait for later. Shadowshine Jr. needs her name."

Knowing he was right, I still pouted for a moment before resigning myself to letting this one go. There would be all the time later.

Taking another look in the mirror, now that my body wasn't being destroyed by a vampire with a darkly magical tongue, I decided I loved Mera's choice of outfit. The dress fit like it had been custom tailored. The dark length brought out the blue-black highlights in my hair, and I decided I needed some makeup to give my face the same dramatic look.

While Lucien was dressing, I entered the bathroom. Probably safer to get out of the room while he was naked anyway, or we'd never leave.

My legs were still a little wobbly, but I managed to prop myself up at the sink and spend the next few minutes applying eyeliner, mascara, some smoky eyeshadow, and a nude lip gloss that accentuated the fullness of my lips.

By the time I was done, Lucien was perched in the doorway looking fucking delicious in a black suit. He'd opted for no tie again, going with an open white dress shirt topped off by a fitted jacket that accentuated his broad shoulders and tapered waist.

"Fuck," I groaned. "You're not playing fair."

He strode over to me, only a head taller now that I wore heels. "I play to win."

I swallowed hard. "I really need to put underwear on. Otherwise, I'm going to slip on my own fucking arousal."

Lucien's lips twitched, and then he was laughing.

I really liked making him laugh.

"I'll catch you, don't worry," he told me.

Bastard.

Since, apparently, I wasn't going to have underwear on any time soon, I just did my best to think unsexy thoughts. Of course, that meant never looking at my mate, but for Mera and our soon-to-be-named baby girl, I could manage it.

For a few hours anyway.

Chapter Sixty-Eight

The naming ceremony and blessing took place in Shadow's private library. Since the only time I'd been in here had been at the birth of Shadowshine Jr., I hadn't had a chance to explore, so I paid close attention as we moved through the vast, dark timber shelves and rooms that appeared to move about at will.

We ended up in an area that looked like an observation deck from a space station. It reminded me of images I'd seen of human astronauts seeing Earth from above, but instead of Earth, we were staring into a galaxy outside the wall of windows.

"This is where the power lies for the Solaris System," Shadow told us as he stood with Mera. Inky and Midnight floated above them, hovering near their bonded ones.

Mera held the baby against her chest. My bestie was in a bright red dress, floor-length, with the same corseted top and tulle skirt as me. She looked stunning, wild and powerful, her red hair left out in loose curls, and I was glad I'd decided to put a few curls into mine as well. Shadow wore a black suit like Lucien's—all of the males were dressed similarly. And they looked amazing. I would hazard a guess that there was no better-looking group of eternals anywhere. Especially my mate.

Angel stood near Reece, looking angelic of course, in a corseted white dress. I was seeing a pattern here in the outfits Mera had chosen for us, and I loved it.

Were you really besties if you hadn't matchy-matched for special occasions?

Galleli stepped forward, and Lucien grasped my hand. I'd heard the transcendent speak in my head a few times, and it wasn't the most comfortable feeling... I appreciated Lucien's support.

We are assembled here today to bless a child born of true mates and a powerful bond, he started. His voice always sounded like the gathering of a powerful storm, and it sent a tingle through me that was far different than the one Lucien usually created.

A name is honored in the Shadow Realm. This child will be honored in our family for all of our days, along with Damon, another new family member. Our warrior babies. Our next generation of power.

He turned to Mera and Shadow. *Name your child. Bring their power and honor to light. Honor their heritage in the Shadow Realm.*

He started to hum then... out loud. It was the first time I'd heard him make a noise, and I was mesmerized by the haunting beauty of the sound. The words that went along with the humming only happened in our minds, and it wasn't in a language I understood, but it sent goosebumps across my skin.

Mera and Shadow turned toward the windows showcasing the power outside, their hands joined to hold their daughter higher. "We honor you," Mera said, choked up. "Our perfect blessing, born of love and power and a true bond. You will never want for love while we exist. You will never want for a home. You will be part of this magical, incredible family forever, which includes your aunties: Simone and Angel, and your uncles: Reece, Lucien, Len, Galleli, and Alistair, who is watching you from the next life."

There was a moment of silence as everyone remembered their fallen brother, and I held onto Lucien's hand even tighter, knowing that it would forever hurt him to not see Alistair in this world. No matter your faith, the knowledge that your loved one's life is beyond your reach is a hard one to live with.

"We honor you, child," Shadow continued, sounding emotional for the beast. His eyes were blazing with gold and red, and even though he looked calm, there was a wild energy sliding across his skin. "We love you. We will destroy worlds for your safety, and none will stand against us."

A different sentiment than Mera but, in the end, they were saying the same thing. This child had been born into an amazing family who would love her more than anything and also destroy worlds for her.

What more could a child want from life.

Galleli's humming and blessing song grew louder as Shadow lifted the baby toward the stars. "Welcome to the world, Aurora," he called. "You are the epitome of Sunshine and Shadow meeting at the dawn of each day, and you are our perfect creation."

"And already got daddy wrapped around your damn finger," Mera choked out, laughing and crying. "My Aurora."

Galleli's song in my head faded as he added the final blessing, and then there was silence. Until... a single cry from Aurora stole our attention as she floated above her father's hands, soaring up to the highest pane of glass to press her hands against it. No one moved or said a word; we just watched that extraordinary child do whatever she was doing. Midnight and Inky hovered close, weaving around her, but they were not the ones holding her in the air. She did that herself.

"Is she bringing the stars closer?" Mera gasped, stepping toward the windows too. "Look, they're moving."

They were, growing brighter and larger in our vision.

"Just like her daddy," Shadow said, puffed up and proud of his offspring. "Come here, Aurora." He held out his hands, and she drifted down immediately.

I think we were all grateful to know that, as powerful as Aurora was and would grow to be, she had equally powerful parents to teach her how to use her gifts for the greater good. Well, maybe the greater good wasn't exactly Shadow's forte, but he'd at least keep her in line.

"We need to celebrate now," Mera called. "I convinced Shadow to bring the food in here so we could stay in our family group without interference. Gaster wanted to be the one to set it up for us, but he knows he's invited to dine and bring joy as well."

The goblin who ran the Library of Knowledge was big on duty. Gaster would have wanted to make this dinner perfect for Mera, Shadow, and Aurora, and he was no doubt setting up something amazing as we stood here at the ceremony.

"Goblins don't do naming ceremonies," Len added, looking taller and more mysterious in his dark suit, which contrasted beautifully with his silvery hair and eyes. "But they definitely do celebratory feasts. Food is a massive part of their culture."

"Mine too!" Mera declared. "And I'm freaking starving."

There were cheers and calls from the others, all of us ready to celebrate.

Lucien and I had so much to be thankful for, and I couldn't wait to see what tomorrow would bring. For once, the future was so damn bright it was blinding.

Gaster had set up the table near a large fireplace.

It was a solid timber table, large enough to seat twenty, and was set for all of us and Gaster, by the look of the numbers of plates. There were also two white, cane bassinets for the babies if they grew tired. Not that I'd seen Aurora or Damon out of their parents' arms for extended periods of time yet, but maybe they'd put them down eventually.

Or maybe not.

I wasn't a mother and didn't understand the bond, especially when I'd never had it with my parents. I imagined that it would be hard to let your child go... those perfect pieces of your soul.

Lucien and I sat side by side, my hand in his, the touch helping to keep our bond calm and content. Food came out soon after on magical trays, floating by the power of the Shadow Beast. To my surprise, blood-filled goblets were placed before Lucien and me. "We don't need these," Lucien said softly, eyes on me. "My mate sustains me in all ways."

Mera let out another sigh, and it was so dramatically happy that I couldn't help but chuckle. I totally understood the feeling that one sound had conveyed.

As the food settled onto the table, I was excited to see a variety from the different worlds, including Earth and Valdor. Lucien and I hadn't eaten for a long time, so we enjoyed not just the nourishment but also the friendship, laughter, and joking taunts that were a natural part of this group.

"Did you two think on your couple name?" Mera called from where she sat at the head of the table. She'd insisted it was her spot, and Shadow had indulged her with a look on his face that said he'd enjoy finishing the argument later. Naked.

"Did *you* think on it?" I asked her with a laugh. "Or are we stuck with Sucien?"

Mera screwed up her face. "Not a chance. There has to be something just perfect for you two blooded-up vampire mates."

"Simone is *Bee* to me," Lucien said. "Not just because of her blood type, and the fact that the bee is absolute essential to Earth's survival, as my mate is to mine. But now we have a blood call bond as well. Another *B* word that encapsulates everything important in my world."

The smooth-talking side of Lucien was just as potent and deadly as the growling alpha side. Both had me wishing I was wearing underwear. Or nothing.

Mera nodded as her smile grew. "It seems that we need a couple name that incorporates Bee."

"CrimsonBee," I said in a whisper, my throat too tight for louder words. "Crimson is Lucien, and it also represents the parts of my past that were tied to my future. My forever."

Lucien's next words took my breath away. "You're what I've been waiting centuries for: The perfect mate and life I believed was not for me. But now... I would not exist without you. CrimsonBee is our past, present, and future. It's the full circle of our journey."

There was a moment's silence.

"That's it," Len said, clearly as invested as Mera. "CrimsonBee is your couple name for sure."

Brilliant green eyes met mine.

"Holy shit," I whispered. "We have a couple name."

Lucien's laughter lit up his face. "Also a complete soul bond, but the couple name is what cements it for you." Before I could say anything, his mouth captured mine and the rest of the world faded away.

I had no idea what I'd done in my previous lives, but it must have been something good to end up with this mate.

No matter what happened, I'd never take any of it for granted.

CrimsonBee forever.

NOT READY TO LET THIS world go yet? Make sure to check out my group www.facebook.com/groups/jayminevenerdherd for updates on the next spinoff, *Glamoured: Shadow Beast Shifters Book 6*.

Len and Sam's story.

AFTERWORD

Thank you so much for sticking with me through this Shadow Beast journey. I can't imagine ever leaving this world now, even as I know the stories are coming to an end. Ugh. Let's not go there today.

Can I just say, Simone and Lucien were so much fun to write about. They have a slightly different vibe to the other couples, being more of an allies to friends to lovers to mates. Less of the enemies and more of the love for a change. I've honestly fallen head over heels for my vampire/shifter duo.

Big thanks to my PA, Jane Catherine, for all the amazing teasers, support, and help with keeping my world functioning. Thank you to my small team of readers checking for final errors and giving such wonderful feedback. Thank you to my editor, Jax, who weeds out the Australianisms and makes my words shine. And my cover artist, Tamara, is a literal magician. No one can convince me otherwise with her stunning cover art.

Finally, thank you to all the readers who continue to show up and support these stories. Without you, I wouldn't be here.

I'm the most grateful to you.

xx

ALSO BY JAYMIN EVE

Demon Pack (PNR/Urban Fantasy 18+)

Book One: Demon Pack

Shadow Beast Shifters (PNR/Urban Fantasy 18+)

Book One: Rejected

Book Two: Reclaimed

Book Three: Reborn

Book Four: Deserted

Book Five: Compelled

Book Six: Glamoured (Release 2022)

Supernatural Prison Trilogy (Complete UF series 17+)

Book One: Dragon Marked

Book Two: Dragon Mystics

Book Three: Dragon Mated

Book Four: Broken Compass

Book Five: Magical Compass

Book Six: Louis

Book Seven: Elemental Compass

Supernatural Academy (Complete Urban Fantasy/PNR 18+)

Year One

Year Two

Year Three

Royals of Arbon Academy (Dark, complete Contemporary Romance 18+)

Book One: Princess Ballot

Book Two: Playboy Princes

Book Three: Poison Throne

Titan's Saga (PNR/UF. Sexy and humorous 18+)

Book One: Releasing the Gods

Book Two: Wrath of the Gods

Book Three: Revenge of the Gods

Dark Legacy (Complete Dark Contemporary high school romance 18+)

Book One: Broken Wings

Book Two: Broken Trust

Book Three: Broken Legacy

Secret Keepers Series (Complete PNR/Urban Fantasy)

Book One: House of Darken

Book Two: House of Imperial

Book Three: House of Lights

Book Four: House of Royale

Storm Princess Saga (Complete High Fantasy)

Book One: The Princess Must Die

Book Two: The Princess Must Strike

Book Three: The Princess Must Reign

Curse of the Gods Series (Complete Reverse Harem Fantasy 18+)

Book One: Trickery

Book Two: Persuasion

Book Three: Seduction

Book Four: Strength

Novella: Neutral

Book Five: Pain

NYC Mecca Series (Complete - UF series)

Book One: Queen Heir

Book Two: Queen Alpha

Book Three: Queen Fae

Book Four: Queen Mecca

A Walker Saga (Complete - YA Fantasy)

Book One: First World

Book Two: Spurn

Book Three: Crais

Book Four: Regali

Book Five: Nephilius

Book Six: Dronish

Book Seven: Earth

Hive Trilogy (Complete UF/PNR series)

Book One: Ash

Book Two: Anarchy

Book Three: Annihilate

Sinclair Stories (Standalone Contemporary Romance)

Songbird